Alma picked up the stem of the broken wineglass, then hurried back to the phone and said, "I'm going to drive down to my uncle's house. Send the police."

The line disconnected.

Alma grabbed her car keys and backed toward the door, keeping her eyes on the staircase. A swishing sound came from upstairs and she held still. She opened the door slowly and stepped outside. As she jumped from the porch into the side yard, she realized the swishing sound was a window opening. She whirled around and looked at the roof just as a dark figure descended on top of her.

She and the attacker sprawled to the ground. Alma lost her keys but held tightly to the broken wineglass stem, which she jabbed into the torso on top of her. The man cried out and grabbed at his ribs. Alma twisted sideways and ran.

Now there was only one direction she could go. Up into the mountains . . .

Please turn to the back of the book for an interview with Tess Collins.

By Tess Collins
Published by Ivy Books:

THE LAW OF REVENGE
THE LAW OF THE DEAD

THE LAW
OF
THE DEAD

Tess Collins

IVY BOOKS • NEW YORK

For Joseph Sherman Collins
and
Charlcie Brock Collins

And very special thanks to my writing mentor, James N. Frey, Waimea Williams, Miriam Goderich, and Judy Jones for encouragement and a sharp eye; and to my agent, Jane Dystel, and editor, Susan Randol, for their unique and supportive abilities to polish coal and find a diamond.

An Ivy Book
Published by The Ballantine Publishing Group
Copyright © 1999 by Theresa Collins

www.randomhouse.com/BB/

Library of Congress Catalog Card Number: 99-90042

ISBN 0-8041-1795-0

Manufactured in the United States of America

First Edition: May 1999

10   9   8   7   6   5   4   3   2   1

1

The gibbous moon, fuzzy behind a watery layer of clouds, still cast enough light to give a shimmery gilt to the limbs of the willow tree. Kitty Sloat blew out a long stream of smoke and held on to a bough of leaves that nearly touched the ground. She passed through the curtained branches, letting them caress her face. At the edge of Silver Lake she flicked the half-smoked cigarette on the mossy bank.

Anxiously, she watched her lover kneeling on a rock that jutted out over the lake, his face buried in his hands. Was he praying, she wondered, or crying? Finally she broke the silence. "I'll do whatever you say I ought to." He looked up, stared over the lake's surface, but said nothing.

In the near distance a motorcycle's roar droned to a stop. She turned and looked in the direction of the sound. Probably kids going to their regular make-out spot, she figured. She'd been at too many of those places, as a teenager, a young woman—and now, here she stood, a few years shy of forty and still secretly meeting men at a high school lover's lane.

Kitty walked back to his car, opened a powder compact in the beam of the headlights, and combed out her waist-length blond ponytail, teasing the bangs to hide the black roots. Her gray eyes were streaked with starbursts of dark blue, immediately noticeable, her best feature. Only one other person in the family had eyes like hers, a cousin she hadn't seen in over a decade. Not likely to see 'em anytime soon, she thought. Her cousin was a big shot in Crimson County, a few mountain ranges to the west.

She looked at her lover and wondered for a moment if she should have the baby. If she did, he'd have to pay child support. In the long run that would be worth a lot of money. That's what she'd done with Danny. His father kept the child support coming and she never revealed his identity. Unruly, unkempt Danny who now ran the streets at night as if he had no home. It wasn't her fault. He was a boy. A lot like his father. In two years Danny would be eighteen and the money would stop. What would she do then?

"Kitty?" her lover said.

"Please, God," she murmured to herself, quickly applying a layer of pink lipstick. "Please, God. Let me do this right."

Mist traveled across the face of the lake, and depending on the angle, sometimes the white path of the moon streaked across the water. There were times when this lake spooked her. She'd always heard it was haunted. But tonight not even the spirits of the dead could dissuade her from what she needed to do. He raised his head slightly, looking out over the smooth black marble surface. The sound of water gently lapping on the shore was mesmerizing. He tilted his head toward her and his light blue eyes were startling in the darkness. She steeled herself, ready for recriminations.

"Your face pains me," she said, taking a step closer to him. "I can't stand that this hurts you. I'll do the right thing. I'll get it taken care of, but I'll need money—for the procedure, and for, you know, pain and suffering.''

He looked back out over the water and shook his head, eyes closed. Glancing up once at the dark sky, then again at the ground, he panted short, quick breaths like an exhausted animal. All at once he stood and raised his arms toward the lake. With a low moan, like a chant, he inhaled all that his lungs seemed able to hold, and his entire body shivered as if invoking some ancient lake spirit.

For the first time Kitty began to tremble inside. She wondered what to do if he denied being the father. "Best I go out of state," she said, to keep things moving her way. "You need to protect yourself from enemies. That's why we need to go to the people I know. They can keep a secret for a price. Ten thousand dollars ain't that much. Not for a man like you."

Shame welled up in her chest and a gasp of air caught in her throat. She stared at the ground, wanting to bore into it. Her eyes watered and spilled over. She told herself to remain clearheaded. What was wrong with her? Had she simply done this too many times? She no longer knew how much was her act and how much she really felt. Feelings had to be dispensed with at times like this, she'd always told herself. This was business. "Yes, ten thousand," she said again, squeezing her hands behind her back to ward off any sign of timidity.

He touched her cheek and gently lifted her chin. With his other hand he wiped her tears. "Kitty," he said, "I will not desert you."

A well of emotions sliced through her body, a kind of longing she'd experienced the first time she'd been in love. But she hadn't felt this powerful a feeling for years—part yearning for a love just beyond her fingertips and part indulgence in the memory of deep passion. "I'm so sorry," she whispered.

"I know. I know." Gently he pulled her into his arms. "My poor, sweet Kitty," he murmured as he stroked the back of her hair.

Oh, God, she thought, I should never have done this, never should've gone and got myself pregnant. Not by him. Not by him.

"I won't be any trouble to you," she said softly.

"No, no, no." He ran his fingers through her ponytail and pulled several strands loose. He cupped her face in his hands. "With me, there will be no more pain and judgment in your life."

She drew back and regarded him from a slight distance. What, she asked herself, was he saying? He smiled kindly, as if to banish the puzzlement on her face.

"Are you saying what I think?" she asked in amazement. She dropped to her knees, hoping the cold earth would shake her to reality. He bent over her and kissed her forehead. "It'd be better if I got rid of it," she said. "There'd be no trouble."

"You will bear my child, and be my child." He raised her up and held her by the waist so she wouldn't fall again. "Life is a cherished gift. I will not take it. I will not ask you to take it."

Kitty lay her head on his shoulder. She could hear his heart beating. His arms squeezed her tighter, and they stood together in a gentle sway. She had thought there would be yelling, accusations, that she'd have to bluff, and if necessary, threaten. Her chest throbbed as if it were splitting open. Some bygone ache she'd held on to her entire life broke and poured from her as he cradled her in his arms. She sobbed out all the pain in her soul.

After a while she pulled away from him and stepped

onto the rock where he'd knelt. In a hoarse voice she said, "I should just throw myself off of here for what I've done." She sucked in air, trying to calm herself. "You're so good to me." She turned toward him and drank in his appearance—tall, silvery, almost like he was made of stardust. "You're a good, good man."

"Want me to drive you home?"

"My truck's up around the bend where nobody'll see it." She smiled and suppressed the wave of emotion that his kindness evoked. "I want to sit here for a while. By myself."

He stared at her for several seconds then smiled. "You'll hear from me soon." As he turned to leave, he touched his fingers to his lips and sent a kiss through the air.

She watched as the lights of his car disappeared then encircled herself with an armful of willow limbs as she looked out at the lake and rocked back and forth. How could she have been so wrong? She'd have the child. It'd be his baby, and he'd love it, and her, too. She wrapped both arms around her stomach and breathed in the wintergreen scent of the leaves. Her body pulsed with life. What could she have been thinking? Tomorrow would bring a whole new world to her. Maybe he'd even marry her. Maybe, in time, she'd be as respectable as her cousin. Maybe they'd even go out to a fancy restaurant and have lunch. She was filled with more happiness than she had ever known.

The crunch of a foot against gravel startled her. She whipped around and asked, "Have you come back?" No one replied. She peered into the darkness. "Honey?"

"Kitty," a voice whispered.

"Is that you?"

"Kitty, Kitty." Louder but still a whisper.

"Who are you?"

Again, there was no answer. The tone of the voice was unfamiliar, or maybe faintly and weirdly familiar. A low crackle of laughter mixed with the crinkling sound of the willow limbs as she untangled her arms from them.

Kitty walked toward the road, feeling uneasy. The footsteps followed her. She looked over her shoulder. No one. A chill spread up her arms. Despite an involuntary tremble, her hands felt heavy, as if pulling her to the earth. "I'm leaving now," she said firmly. "I don't want no trouble, and neither do you."

"Kitty, Kitty, Kitty," the voice said louder, like calling a pet.

"What do you want?" She breathed in erratic gasps as panic invaded her muscles. She sprinted up the path. Oh, God, she thought, if I can just get to the truck.

2

Jeers and taunts filled the morning air like the sudden release of a thousand balloons. "Scum! Union busters! Stone the scabs!" Those who weren't yelling at the Highland Toy Factory marched in front of it carrying signs with equally inflammatory slogans—GIVE US BACK OUR JOBS. I GOT CHILDREN TO FEED. PEOPLE NOT PROFITS.

People in Kentucky didn't often demonstrate in public. Citizens of Contrary, a midsize mountain town, were more reserved than most unless issues offended their sense of fairness or threatened their home security. Then they could and would stand up for their own with the ferocity of a mountain lion. When a mountain craft, the Yellow Jacket Stinger, became a nationwide sensation, the factory owners sensed a killing in the market. What parts of the stuffed animal weren't farmed out to third world countries were now being manufactured by nonunion workers in the same building where unionized Contrary folk had manufactured the toy for nearly twenty years. That was when the Mirror of Our Soul Congregation helped organize the ongoing protest.

Across the street from the factory, Commonwealth Attorney Alma Bashears stood with Mayor Buddy Hudson and Police Chief Arch Coyle. "You're the prosecutor," Hudson yelled to her above the ruckus. "What do we do?"

Alma cupped a hand next to her mouth so she'd be heard and leaned down to the mayor, who was an inch shorter than her five-foot-six frame. "If you're asking me have they broken any laws, they haven't. If you're asking me to make this all go away, you're asking the wrong question. I can't."

"Then why the hell did I support you in the last election?" Hudson huffed, his portly figure gyrating with each word.

Alma took a breath before responding. "Mayor, you might take the initiative and encourage the factory owners to offer a settlement."

"That's right!" Hudson spit out the words in his high-pitched whine. "Turn it back on me. People out here committing crimes and you try and dump it in my lap. Your predecessor would have taken charge."

"Then the former commonwealth attorney would have been overstepping his authority," Alma said with a growl in her voice.

Sam Merkle, the factory owner, appeared in the front window of the office and caused a frenzy of hooting and catcalling from the protesters. The hefty man stood like a statue, arms crossed around his protruding stomach, a sour frown stretching into his loose jowls.

"I could round 'em all up for disturbing the peace," Chief Coyle volunteered as he rocked on the heels of his snakeskin cowboy boots.

"I wouldn't recommend that," Alma said. "Violating their freedom of speech and assembly is exactly what they want the city to do. It'll bring more attention to them, their cause, and the Mirror of Our Soul Church."

The mayor paced, his hands clasped behind him. He stared at the ground and shook his head, loosening a lock of gray hair onto his forehead. "Sam Merkle was my largest contributor last year."

"Not to mention the free building he donated for the city day-care center," Coyle added with a sideways glance toward Alma.

She knew they expected a solution from her. Hudson was a good-ole-boy politician accustomed to getting what he wanted. Though he worked for the city and she for the state, it would be foolish for her not to court the local power base. She surveyed the protesters. Many were hard-working hollow people who were simply trying to hold on to their jobs. In many ways she sympathized with them. "If you can get Merkle to agree to a meeting," she said, "I'll ask the workers to stop the protest, pending the results of the talks."

"They won't do nothing you say," Coyle said. "They follow that snake-preacher, Harlan Fuller. He's the only one with any control on them."

"Harlan Fuller." The mayor lit a cigarette. "His congregation controls nearly twenty percent of the vote in this town. You know what that means?" His face scrunched up as he exhaled a quick puff. "If a vote goes fifty-fifty, he's gonna be the one to decide the election." Hudson flicked the cigarette into the gutter. "I don't need this," he said, "especially now."

"Let's concentrate on the situation here, not the next election," Alma suggested.

"Why are you two coddling these lowlifes?" the chief asked, straightening his back to shadow his six-foot frame over both the mayor and Alma. "Haul 'em off to jail for a night. Then they'll start appreciating the value of earning an honest living." He swizzled the last liquid from a soda can and crushed it with one hand.

"It's not exactly like they expected their employer of twenty years to turn them out," Alma said.

This wasn't the first sparring among the three of them, and it probably wouldn't be the last. In the year since Alma was elected commonwealth attorney for Crimson County, she had come to realize that the small town politics of Contrary were as devious as any she'd dealt with in the city.

Her hometown of Contrary lay half in Kentucky, half in Tennessee. The population of 15,281 was educated and ignorant, religious and atheist, rich and poor—instilled with the pioneer ruggedness of its English, Scottish, Irish, and German ancestors. The Choctaw and Cherokee bloodlines of many others were evident in their strong-boned brows and high cheekbones. The town anchored the southernmost edge of Midnight Valley. The Appalachian Mountains draped around it like the curves of a snake on a tree limb.

Sam Merkle's toy factory topped one of the dozen small hills that lined the western edge of town. From here, other buildings spread out with the laziness of a cat stretching in the sun. A long strip of retail stores was focused on the northern end of Contrary where city hall, the police station, and the courthouse formed a triangular base. The commonwealth attorney's offices were housed on the fourth floor of the courthouse. Neighborhoods spread out from one main avenue to hilly sections that formed hollows at the southern end.

Alma always liked looking at the town from this distance. Encircled by the Appalachian Mountains, it reminded her of a sleeping woman all wrapped up in a warm winter blanket. How she wished for that level of calm now.

The protesters chanted "Give back our jobs!" They formed a human chain in front of the factory door, wide enough to allow entry but so intimidating that no one dared go in or out.

"Mayor, we got to act," Chief Coyle said. "I'm worried about them no-gooders. That's Lonnie Hicks and there's Cash McGee. I arrested both last year for misdemeanor graffiti, disturbing the peace, and public drunkenness. With them two here, I guarantee there's gonna be trouble."

McGee and Hicks sat on the back of a white Toyota truck and took turns drinking from a bottle wrapped in a brown paper bag. Coyle eyed them with a frown.

"Uh-oh," Alma said as the heavyset Sam Merkle charged through his door toward the protesters. He swung a baseball bat, missing a group of people by a wide margin. Protesters scattered but just as quickly sprang forward and looped around him. They waved their signs above his head, hovering like a flock of vultures descending on a wounded animal. The heckling further enraged the factory owner and he swung the bat backward.

A handful of photographers snapped pictures of the scene. The mayor ran a hand through his gray hair and said, "I leave this in your hands, Miss Bashears." He winked at her, his blue eyes pierced with the perception that it was time for him to exit before the press approached him.

"Send in your men," Alma yelled to the chief. "Now!"

Coyle laughed out loud. "Why?" he asked with a sneer. "It's just getting interesting." Alma glared at him as he slowly waved an arm over his head, and police swarmed in from all directions.

Protesters screamed and the crowd surged as the mayhem expanded into the street. The demonstrators defended themselves, using their signs as weapons. Officers doused them with pepper spray, and Merkle swung the baseball bat in a wide circle. Alma crossed the street to help a woman who'd fallen on the curb. People began running in all directions, bumping her as they struggled to escape.

She turned around and collided with Jefferson Bingham. He grabbed her arm and pulled her out of the way of a woman fleeing with a baby in one arm and carrying a sign that read MY CHILD IS HUNGRY. "Get inside!" he yelled.

A loud bang sent a shock through the crowd, and for a few seconds, there was silence. Alma pulled from Jefferson's grasp as Sam Merkle yelled, "I'm shot! I'm shot!" Cash McGee jumped onto the flatbed of his truck and scrambled into the cab through the missing back window. He started up and screeched away with two police cars in pursuit.

Two gray-suited men from the factory rushed outside to help Merkle. He held his shoulder as a scarlet circle of blood spread through his white shirt. The police had a dozen people handcuffed and other protesters stood far enough away to be confused with spectators. Alma shouted at the chief, "I meant grab Merkle, not attack the demonstrators!"

The press cameras clicked away, especially after spotting Alma in the middle of the scene. "Miss Bashears," one reporter called out, "are you here in support of management?"

"You're damn right she is," one of the cuffed protesters cried out before she could answer. "We saw who you were standing alongside. She's as much a Benedict Arnold as Sam Merkle!"

Alma recognized the man as someone she'd known in grade school. "No," she started to say in her defense, but the others joined in with him as a show of solidarity against the factory and against Alma.

"Get a little schoolin'," a woman jeered, "get a little money, and you think you're better than the rest of us."

"I tried to set up a meeting . . . " Alma began, but the groans from the crowd overshadowed her voice.

"You're one of them, Alma Bashears!"

"Either you stand with us or lie with liars, and it looks to us like you're lying, Alma! What'd you do, forget yer from the hollows?"

"Reverend Fuller stood up for us, why won't you?"

Police officers loaded the arrested protesters into vans. They continued hurling insults at her as if she represented the factory owner. Alma knew if she walked away, they'd believe she'd turned her back on them. Hurtful as the verbal assaults were, she faced them so these people would realize she was as much from the hollows as any of them.

"They don't look so downtrodden from this side of the fence, now do they?" Chief Coyle whispered behind her.

Alma ignored him and walked in the opposite direction as the last police cruiser pulled away. Jefferson Bingham was waiting at her car. His I-told-you-so expression sent a stab of resentment through her.

"You look like you're going to cry," he said, the wind whipping his blond bangs onto his forehead.

"Not today," she responded and leaned on the car's front panel to take some deep breaths. The firmness of resolve she held five minutes earlier began to crack and she looked to Jefferson for sympathy. "Did you hear what they said to me?"

He crossed his arms over his chest. "Can you blame them?"

"I was trying to help, even though this has nothing to do with me."

"What would you do if someone as rich as Merkle came at you with a baseball bat?"

"Jefferson, not now!" His support of the shooting rankled her more than his lack of defense for her. She waited several seconds before looking at him. He didn't seem any more sympathetic, and his green eyes studied her with the intensity of a geographer drawing a map.

"Why'd you let this get so out of control? The bullet nicked Merkle's shoulder, about here." Jefferson pointed to a spot above his own collarbone. "Another inch lower, and he'd be dead."

"Imagine that," she huffed. "Then there'd be no toy factory, no strike, and no Stinging Yellow Jacket—Yellow Jacket Stinger," she corrected herself.

"Now you'll be the one prosecuting a man from the hollows for protecting himself."

The comment stung Alma. Not only was it true, but Jefferson knew damn well that her hands were tied. She represented the state and had to prosecute the shooter. "I'll consider the charge carefully."

"Seems like since you left private practice with me to be the commonwealth attorney, about all you do is consider."

"Perhaps we better continue this at my office."

Jefferson opened the car door for her and stepped aside. "It'd be best," he said, "if we spoke in front of a judge."

"A judge . . . " she repeated, understanding that he was regarding her as a legal opponent, not a friend.

"Yeah, I'm going to defend him—that is, unless *your* police chief catches him first, then there'll be no need for a trial. We both know what'll happen to that man before he even sees the inside of the jail."

The threat of tears burned Alma's eyes. Why, she wondered, did he always have to side against her?

His arm came around her and held the car door. She got in without saying good-bye and stared ahead. "He's not *my* chief, he's Contrary's chief, and if you don't like it, you're as much a citizen of this town as I am."

She slammed the door and drove away, watching Jefferson's reflection in the rearview mirror. He looked after her, his hands in his pockets, with as hurt an expression on his face as she felt on her own.

Law partners do not make a good choice for lovers, and lovers can make dangerous opponents. She remembered her words when she'd told Jefferson of her decision to break up their partnership and run for commonwealth attorney. He hadn't responded, just touched her cheek and walked away. He had been so in love with her, he couldn't concentrate on work. She'd known it was best for them to cease being law partners. After successfully defending her brother on a false charge of murder, deciding to stay in Contrary and abandoning a job, home, and relationship in California, she hadn't been as ready as Jefferson to dive into a new romance. Part of her wished that he'd simply given her a little more time, but part of her feared he wasn't the right man.

Maybe I'll find a message from him at my office, she thought. Yes, he'll call and apologize. As the car angled through town she checked her makeup in the rearview mirror and combed a hand through her shoulder-length black hair. Her high cheekbones revealed a Cherokee heritage, and she pressed on them, wishing her face showed less age.

She'd turned thirty-three in November, though it seemed only yesterday she had been a girl whose only thoughts were how to escape Contrary, Kentucky. Looking into her own eyes now, she no longer saw that girl. At times she saw versions of ancestors who'd come before her, but mostly she saw the features of her father—a man who disappeared twenty-three years ago. He was the only man that Alma wished could see what she'd made of herself, but their relationship was frozen in time—a little girl who adored her father.

When Alma arrived at her office only one message awaited her. To her disappointment, it was not from Jefferson. Reverend Harlan Fuller had called to invite her to Sunday's church services.

3

"Are you gonna marry Mr. Jefferson?" Alma's four-year-old nephew, Eddie, asked from the backseat of her car. "Do you think he'll buy me a Yellow Jacket Stinger?"

"His name is Mr. Bingham," Larry Joe corrected from the front seat with all the surety of his six years. "And that toy is sold out. Everybody knows that."

Alma chuckled uncomfortably, checking Eddie in the rearview mirror. His almond-shaped blue eyes blinked and he smiled, showing evenly spaced baby teeth, when he saw that she was watching him. The boy's mention of her and Jefferson meant that the family had been discussing them, and obviously, they had hopes. "If I got married, I wouldn't be able to baby-sit my favorite pirates."

"Then don't do it," Larry Joe said, shaking his head. " 'Cause when people get married they don't eat as much ice cream."

"How do you explain that?" Alma asked.

"Well," Larry Joe pondered. "Momma's married to Daddy and she don't let us eat ice cream after six o'clock."

"Yellow Jackets go buzzzzzz," Eddie said to no one.

Alma quickly glanced at her watch—a few minutes after six. "I think before I take you boys home, we can raid the ice cream parlor."

"Just like pirates!" Larry Joe squealed and rubbed his hands through his buzz-cut auburn hair.

"Aunt Alma, what's an old maid?" Eddie asked. "Buzzzzzzz."

At the red light she pressed the brake harder than intended. Larry Joe put his hands against the dashboard to brace himself. He looked up at her curiously then back at his brother as if to shut him up. "Don't worry, Aunt Alma," he said and patted her arm. "My seat belt's fastened."

After ordering three ice cream cones, Alma dropped her nephews at home without going in to speak to her sister. She waved from the car and toasted with the last of the cone before popping it into her mouth. The tight grimace on Sue's face told Alma she'd gotten some sisterly retaliation for the "old maid" remark.

There was only one more unpleasant task left for the day. She had to convince Jefferson not to represent Cash McGee. After reviewing photos and videotape of the protest, she intended to ask the grand jury for a charge of attempted murder. Though she figured they'd return an assault charge, at least going for the more serious crime would pacify political concerns. She didn't relish the idea of opposing Jefferson, especially with things so tense between them.

Alma parked then spent the next ten minutes pacing in front of Jefferson's four-story apartment building. She finally circled the block hoping to calm her nervousness. Several houses were decorated with signs reading SUPPORT HIGHLAND'S WORKERS and COME NOVEMBER, WE'LL REMEMBER. A rustle in the hedge caused her to glance around. She saw nothing and the noise ceased. Another block down she thought someone was following her. She waited at the corner. A man passed but took no notice of her. Look at what this is doing to you, she chastised herself.

She came again to Jefferson's building, paused beside a rhododendron bush, and tore off a leaf, folding it into tiny pieces as she shifted from one foot to the other.

"I have a date at eight," a voice above her said. "So if you're coming in, it might as well be now."

She looked up. Jefferson leaned out his third-floor window, resting on his elbows and sipping from a coffee cup. Realizing he'd probably been watching and enjoying her angst, she entered the building more irked than nervous.

Inside his apartment, the humidity of a recent shower filled the living room and misted over a shelf of family photos. Jefferson handed her a cup on a tray with cream and a bowl of sugar. "You always know when I need a caffeine fix," she said, adjusting her position on the corduroy sofa.

Jefferson poured coffee for himself and started to sit on the sofa as well, reconsidered, and chose the chair across from her. He sipped his beverage, and she sipped hers. She commented that it seemed he'd filled another shelf with books, and he slid some law journals under the chair with his foot. The small talk finally wound down to Alma asking about his date. "Anyone I know?"

"Why would you care who I'm going out with?" His tone was both defensive and cold.

"I don't. I mean I do—just not in a nosy way." She had an urge to reach out and touch his arm but stopped herself. If I touch him, it'll only encourage him, she thought. I can't hurt him again.

"A woman from Liberty," he said, rubbing his hands against his jeans just above the knee. "We see each other occasionally."

"Have a good time." Alma smiled. "I do want you to be happy, Jefferson."

His expression hardened as if the comment had ruined his prospects for a pleasant date. The thought made her feel even guiltier. She forced herself to speak about the case. "I hope you'll reconsider taking on Cash McGee as a client."

"It might be a good idea for him to be captured and charged before you start arranging my work schedule." Jefferson put down his coffee cup with a thud. His lantern-shaped jaw was set so firm it seemed locked. "The shooting was an accident. I've seen the videotape."

"I'm asking for attempted murder."

"Attempted murder? You're covering your butt with city hall."

"I do represent law and order."

"In this case," he said flatly, "you're representing yourself."

Alma squirmed in her seat. "I'm giving you fair warning of my intentions . . . "

"Don't you dare say 'as a courtesy.' " Jefferson pressed his lips together and stared hard at her. "I'm also representing the strikers."

"Jefferson, be careful," Alma said. "I know you're not representing the workers' union, so that leaves . . . "

"Harlan Fuller is a small part of the protest organization." He stood up and paced to the window. "The union turned its back on those people. They were locked out despite their contract."

"But Fuller will use you. He'll make this a political agenda for his church activities."

"I've been dealing with these types long before you came to town," he said, turning toward her.

"This guy is smart," Alma remarked. "He even had the audacity to call my office and invite me to church."

Jefferson refilled her cup. "Are you going to accept?"

She stared steadily at him, unsure how to take the question. "Get your soul saved?" he asked, a little more ironically.

"I'm wary of people who offer salvation—it tends to lead to ethnic cleansing."

He laughed, but his amusement turned into a serious expression. "Stay away from Fuller, Alma. He can be more persuasive than you think."

"I'm hardly the type to be recruited."

"I realize I'm giving you back your own advice," he said, softer and with more empathy, "but I'm more accustomed to dealing with these people. Fuller's sincerity is closer to Elmer Gantry than Billy Graham." He picked up the tray and returned it to the kitchen.

A heat of annoyance rushed through Alma and she clenched her teeth. There he goes again, she thought, telling me what I should do. She realized Jefferson resented that she had managed to do what he could not. The year before she'd returned to Contrary, he had made an unsuccessful bid for the job against the entrenched incumbent Walter Gentry. Jefferson's resounding defeat had kept him clear of politics ever since.

He came out of the kitchen with his hands in his pockets, reminding her of the way he'd watched her drive away that morning. "I'd better go," she said, standing up. "I just thought we should have this talk in private rather than in the parking lot where half the county's reporters will be taking notes."

A clatter of dishes from the kitchen interrupted them. She looked over sharply, then asked, "Is someone in there?"

"No." He moved back and blocked the door.

"Someone's listening to us, and you didn't tell me!" She stepped forward.

Jefferson took hold of her shoulders. "He's not there to hear this conversation."

Alma tried brushing his hands aside but he held her tighter. She seethed and struggled to escape his grasp. "Jefferson Bingham, I want you to know I consider this the ultimate disregard for professional ethics!"

"It's not what you think." He hung on to her.

From around the kitchen door stepped a lanky, six-foot figure. His black hair, crooked smile, and gray eyes that resembled her own were unmistakable. "Howdy, Alma," her brother said.

"Vernon," she growled.

"W-we were playing checkers," Jefferson stammered, his cheeks flushing bright cherry.

"And talking about you," Vernon added.

"Oh, great!" Jefferson gave him a stern look and released Alma.

"I've been having a fine old time listening to you talk about going to church and all. You know, Momma used to go hear Reverend Fuller preach." Vernon stepped into the light of the living room, squinting from having been in the dark kitchen. His black hair was buzz cut nearly to the scalp, emphasizing his round face. He wore army fatigues and a red T-shirt inscribed I LOVE OLDER WOMEN.

Alma scolded Jefferson, "How could you let me go on talking while someone, especially him, was listening?"

"I'm kin," Vernon argued. "I won't tell." He batted his dark eyelashes and flattened his grin, feigning hurt feelings.

"Oh, yeah," Alma said, doing all she could to keep from smacking him. "This checkers crap is you two gossiping like old hens about me!"

Jefferson rolled his eyes. "We were talking about you, but you entirely overestimate your charms."

"We were just saying how much you've changed since becoming commonwealth attorney." Vernon's grin widened.

Alma despised the way her brother stirred up trouble. "I

have a responsibility to this town and to the law. I take my responsibility to heart."

"Your intentions are not what's in question, Alma." Jefferson moved in front of Vernon to block her view of him.

She stepped back and looked Jefferson up and down. "Are you saying my abilities are in question?"

"Well, look, Sis." Vernon peered around Jefferson. "All you did your whole career in California was the kind of law that let millionaires cheat the IRS. When you came back here, Jefferson had to carry your butt because . . . "

Alma clenched her teeth. "As I recall, I came back because your butt was in a sling, and I had to get it out!"

"Just what I mean." Vernon spread his arms wide as if to indicate she might be on the way to understanding. "You got me off that murder charge 'cause you played dirty with Walter Gentry." He paused a moment to watch her response. "It ain't that I ain't grateful. If it hadn't been for you, I might be doing life."

"What Vernon is saying, Alma, is . . . lately . . . you seem to regard yourself as the town's only weather vane."

"What Jefferson is saying is that if Walter Gentry was commonwealth attorney he'd have that Cash McGee in the pokey already and would have reined in ole-grand-holy-chief-of-police a long time ago. You're losing your edge, girl."

"It's a way of knowing, Alma," Jefferson said. "You turn a blind eye, thinking people play by the rules while everybody else in town knows what's going on."

Alma slowly turned away, keeping her back to both of them. She could hardly believe what she'd heard. "Fuller is hiding McGee," she said as she moved toward the window that looked out over the western end of town. "That's what you're telling me." Neither of them answered, and she knew she was right. "Then why won't Coyle go there and arrest him?"

Their silence could have implied many things, she thought. The police chief might be setting up a media arrest to enhance his own tarnished image; he might be manipulating a way to embarrass her; he might be afraid of Fuller. Whatever the reason, his inaction would eventually compromise her, especially if it looked as if she had known.

Lights from distant houses twinkled like stars, each far apart, a solitary pattern that reminded her of children longing to link hands. She wondered if the rest of the town felt the same as Jefferson and Vernon. She'd won the election by a narrow margin and would have to prove herself again in three years.

"All I'm saying," Jefferson said in a conciliatory tone, "is Contrary will follow its own path and play its own cards in its own way. You have to adapt to them. Don't expect to change it overnight."

"Your manner of thinking ain't always caught up with the rest of the town." Vernon scratched the side of his head, mimicking an illiterate hillbilly. "That's why us plowboys are so popular on Saturday nights—our forward way of thinking."

"The only thing you think with is your—"

"And I think I'll go get some relief for it," Vernon said. "I believe Jefferson was on his way to do the same. Reckon you'll sit home in front of the TV tonight, huh, Alma?" He pulled Jefferson by his sleeve, opened the door, and turned the inside lock. "There's some videos you can borrow. Don't take the ones on the bottom shelf, you're not old enough. Door locks on your way out."

Jefferson made a slight protest but Vernon dragged him away willingly. Her brother's high-pitched laughter echoed down the hall. "Go to church, Alma. You need saving!"

Sometimes I wish I'd left him in jail, she thought. She rushed to the window and shouted, "Don't leave the state of Kentucky! You're still on probation!" At least, she chuckled to herself, I got in the last word. Her younger brother was one of the few people in the world who could work her into a frenzy. And he enjoyed doing it on a regular basis.

Watching videos was the last thing she intended to do tonight. Fuller had to be dealt with. She said grimly to the empty room, "Maybe what I do need is my soul saved." She picked up the phone and dialed her mother's number.

"Hellloo," a soft, sexy voice answered.

"Momma," Alma said.

"Oh, it's you."

"Well, I'm sorry."

"I was expecting J.D. to call. He's coming over."

"Seems everyone has a date tonight," Alma murmured to herself.

"Don't blame me, missy. I offered to fix you up with Bobby Harmon."

"Momma, that's not what I want to talk about. Did you ever go to the Mirror of Our Soul Church?"

Her mother squelched a congested laugh. "Back when I dated Junior Johnson. He got religious in a silly way, so we broke up."

"How would you like to go to church tomorrow?"

"I do my duty Christmas, Easter, and Remembrance Day, and this Sunday ain't one of those."

"Momma, I have to see what goes on in that church." Alma heard the click of another caller trying to get through.

"That's J.D.," her mother said. "I've got to go."

"Tomorrow, okay?"

"Jesus, Alma Mae, church!" Another click. "Oh, all right. Might as well go see how ole Junior's aged."

After her mother hung up, Alma wondered what went on at the services. She hoped they were nothing like the holy rollers she'd seen once on a PBS documentary.

Next door she heard a party getting started. I'll probably end up watching TV after all, she decided. Loneliness crept through her. She shook it off and told herself, "Work . . . work and you won't feel bad." If Harlan Fuller was hiding Cash McGee, she'd sniff it out. She figured Chief Coyle was satisfied to wait him out and not upset the political balance of the town. If he caught McGee with Fuller, he'd have to play by the rules. If he caught him somewhere else, he might just exert his own violent brand of justice.

"Okay, Reverend Fuller," she said again and stood up to go. "You want me in church. I'm sure you're expecting a wolf, but I'll come quiet as a little lamb."

4

"You don't take a Bible to the Mirror of Our Soul Congregation." Merl Bashears knocked the book off Alma's lap.

"Well, Momma," Alma said, biting back her irritation, "what do you take to this church?" As she steered the car she leaned over to switch on the air-conditioning. Her mother's manner of explaining had a way of confounding her into a mild perspiration.

"Not a Bible." Merl rolled her eyes as if weary of the fact that her daughter never seemed to listen. "And they call themselves a congregation, not a church. They're nondenominational. They live by sayings—you know, like from the Bible, the Koran, the cabala, Confucius, speeches of the pope, Chinese fortune cookies, for all I know."

"Don't some of those philosophies contradict each other?"

"Well." Merl hesitated, obviously not well-read in any of them. "I guess, but by the time Reverend Fuller is done with them, contradiction is as minor as a single flea on a big dog."

"I see," Alma said.

"No, you don't." Merl waved a wand of mascara in front

of her while trying to balance a compact on the dashboard. "Drive a little slower, Alma. I've got my other eye to do."

Alma turned left through a gate of mountain laurel. "I've heard that none of the other local ministries have ever recognized Fuller's church."

"Congregation, not church."

Alma shook her head. The more her mother explained, the more perplexed she felt. After the Merkle shooting yesterday she had spent the night scouring newspaper files for articles on the Mirror of our Soul Congregation. Fuller was a former TV weatherman from Indiana and his wife a librarian turned New Age guru with a specialty in tarot cards. Alma had talked to many people in her office. Most saw them as harmless kooks, but a few described them as cultish and weird. Alma could hardly wait to get her first look at the church. "I hear he tells fortunes."

"He reads the potential of the stars." Merl snapped the compact shut after a final inspection of her teased blond bouffant hairdo and mascara-rimmed eyes. "Local folks resented him at the start. All that was about ten years ago. His different ways brought more followers, so I reckon the regular churches figured if they let him be, he'd go away. I can't figure how he knows what's in those prayer requests without opening them, but I tell you, Alma, I've seen him hold a sealed envelope to his forehead and answer it."

"I think I saw that once in Las Vegas," Alma said flatly and pulled behind a line of cars driving into a blacktop lot painted with bright yellow parking spaces. "What about the snake handling?"

"That's only during revivals."

"He's so eager to manipulate that he'd risk his life?"

"Well, he has to prove his faith, honey."

About a hundred yards away stood a two-story house as long as a basketball court where Fuller lived with his wife and daughter. The facade was English Tudor, a design seldom seen in the mountains except in the wealthiest neighborhoods. A stone archway marked the entrance and clusters of daffodils, irises, and lilies grew throughout the yard. Alma concluded that the ministry was obviously supported by a well-to-do flock. "If Fuller gives the interpretation of the teachings, doesn't that make him a David Koresh–type character?"

"Oh, Alma," her mother interjected, "we don't have people like that here—not in Crimson County."

Alma shut off the ignition and studied the parking lot crowd heading toward the building. She recognized Davy Case, manager of the local steak house restaurant; Julie Kelly, who owned several beauty shops; and Constantine Ebersole, the real estate agent. About a dozen other people strolling toward the house looked more blue-collar. Near a side entrance stood a group Alma recognized as from the hollows. She had to admit she was impressed by Fuller's ability to bring together such a wide range of people in the same congregation. Usually the two communities were as juxtaposed in faith as they were separated by where they chose to live. Everyone was dressed casually. Alma gave her gray Evan Picone suit an uncertain glance.

Her mother noticed and said critically, "I told you to wear that nice blue pantsuit Sue made you last Christmas."

"Momma. I explained to you I can't wear polyester."

"You always were so fussy about the kind of clothes you wore, even as a little girl." Merl sprayed perfume in the air around her and waved a hand to bring the mist toward her.

"I tried to tell both of you it'd just be best if you let me buy my own clothes. It's not a style issue, it's a preference—" Alma cut herself off abruptly, thinking that a senseless argument was not what she needed. "I'm surprised to see so many people casually dressed for a congregation meeting."

"A lot of them," Merl responded without skipping a beat, "go to regular church, too. That's why classes are Sunday afternoons. Reverend Fuller welcomes diversity. Something I'd think you would appreciate."

"You almost sound like a convert," Alma teased.

"Fix your hair, honey. You might even meet a man today." Merl jumped out of the car.

"Meet a man?" she repeated under her breath. She shook her head, paused, tossed the Bible into the backseat, and got out. After a few paces, she returned to adjust the side car mirror and smooth her hands over her hair.

As Alma and her mother strolled up the walk, they joined others headed toward the building. Merl was all smiles, saying proudly, "You know my daughter, the commonwealth attorney—the one who beat Walter Gentry in the last election." Alma tugged at her mother's sleeve and smiled as humbly as she could.

She paused and stepped toward the group of hollow folks who were standing in a semicircle around a tree stump. "Hello," she said. None of them spoke. A woman holding a snuff can spit onto the ground beside her. Alma knew it was an insult toward her. "Nice to see you," she said and turned away.

Behind her, she overheard someone say, "Looking for votes?" and a volley of laughter followed. Alma made her way back to her mother who stood on the porch. Her face stung.

"Now, honey," Merl said as they came to a mammoth wooden door, "try to stay open-minded."

"I promise, Momma," Alma replied, hoping it would shut her up.

The door opened and they were met by a girl of about

fourteen with a long straw-colored braid down her back. Her milky-white skin made her look as homegrown as the farm girls in produce advertisements. She gave them a wide smile before saying, "Good afternoon."

"This is Cassidy Fuller," Merl said, "the reverend's daughter."

Alma held out a hand. The girl shook it with a firm grasp and held on, staring into Alma's eyes as if they were long parted friends. Alma cleared her throat in discomfort and gently pulled her hand away.

Cassidy smiled wider and steered her to a table. She held out a handful of envelopes and a cup of pencils. "In case you'd like to make a prayer request?"

Alma took an envelope and noted it had two sides, one for the request and the other for a donation.

The hallway was sparsely furnished with tables and numerous coatracks, all empty because of the warm June weather. Extending off to each side were large areas with couches and chairs. A billiard table anchored one end of the room to the left, and a large-screen television was the focus of the room on the right. Homemade crafts filled each room—crocheted doilies on the chairs and tables, crayon drawings by children lined the walls. This was obviously a private living area. A tray in front of the TV held a plate of half-eaten food and a soda. Behind the six-foot television screen was a door. There was barely enough room to move between the two. An odd place for a door, Alma thought.

"Perhaps you could tell me a bit about what the congregation believes?" she asked Cassidy.

For a second there seemed to be a bored edge to the girl's Stepford-like expression. Her smile flipped back into place and she batted blond lashes over her whitish-blue eyes. "People learn about us best by joining in. Father's about to begin the afternoon lecture in the Living Room, Mother Fuller is conducting a tarot class in the Den of Zen, as she calls it, and some of the upstairs rooms have individual study classes. Feel free to wander. You won't interrupt."

"But I'd like to hear it from you," she said. "You must have a unique perspective."

Cassidy stood still for several seconds appearing not to know what Alma meant. She clasped her hands in a flustered gesture of one afraid they might appear clumsy. "I have been trying to shoulder some of the responsibilities of our congregation," she said. "My father works so hard. I know you'll like him."

She's tight as a tray of ice, Alma thought.

Outside a loud motor spewed sound like a rain of hail, and Cassidy sped to the window. Over the girl's shoulder Alma saw a motorcycle doing wheelies in the parking lot. Cassidy started for the front entrance, then stopped and looked back at Alma watching her. The innocent smile that had seemed so confident was now insecure and strained.

"We'll find our way," Alma said, releasing her from any obligation.

Cassidy walked demurely to the entrance, opened the door, and closed it behind her. Once outside she raced like an Olympic sprinter toward the motorcycle.

"Every Christian to their own set of sins," her mother said and nodded to Alma.

"Let's go in here." Alma pulled her mother into the room to the left. "I want to see where that door leads."

"Alma, this is their private living quarters. Nobody's allowed in here."

Alma turned on the television so no one would hear them.

"You act like you're looking for a stash of bootleg money."

"In a way, I am." Alma glanced at the foyer. "It's called Cash—Cash McGee. Stand guard."

"You brought me here to ride shotgun against a preacher?" Her mother pursed her lips and sighed. She threw up her hands then looked down both hallways outside the main room. "I swear to God, Alma, the older you get, the more you get like me."

Alma pushed the television a few inches. She squeezed her body behind the frame and reached for the door. It opened into a narrow closet. On the right wall was a smaller door with a hatch lock. She unhooked it and stepped into a two-foot-wide hall. The faint sound of a voice vibrated, but she could not make out the words. Using her hands, she guided herself along the wall until a bluish light illuminated the distance.

She squinted as she drew near. The glow came from a large square cut in the wall that was about a yard high. She turned toward it, then jumped back when a man stared directly at her. She let out an erratic gasp and covered her mouth with a hand, hoping she hadn't been heard. Slowly she peered at the square again. It was a one-way mirror.

Inside the room, three rows of people intently watched a man pacing in the center of their half-moon circle. The man, Alma realized, was the same person who'd stared directly at her a second before. Undoubtedly the Reverend Harlan J. Fuller.

To the left of him, a huge fireplace, constructed with shiny black coal, was framed with a shellacked piece of oak with words burnt into the wood: THE LIVING ROOM. On each side of the unlit hearth stood two large oak chairs upholstered in purple velvet. Fuller enthroned himself on the one nearest her. He was as handsome as she'd heard, at least in profile. Even from the side she could see the startling whitish-blue of his eyes—the color more solid than on his daughter—impenetrable, almost as if it had been painted. Alma moved closer to get a better look.

The audience sat on a hodgepodge of recliners, overstuffed futons, orthopedic, and a few straight-backed chairs. Several people enjoyed afternoon snacks on trays. The walls were filled with snapshots of congregation members—casual photos, taken at both church and individual family events.

Fuller rose and stepped away from where she stood. Alma shifted to follow his movements. She bumped against a shelf and he turned toward the window again. She held her breath. His eyes narrowed as he stared into his own reflection. *He knows someone's back here,* she realized, and prayed there was no immediate way for him to reveal her presence.

As he turned again to his audience, Alma sank down onto a stool. On the shelf she saw a headset, mike, and a basket filled with prayer requests. A speaker hung just to the right of the mirror. Alma shook her head, amused by her discovery. This was how the mighty and prophetic Reverend Fuller knew what was in the prayer requests. After the envelopes were gathered, they were passed to someone in this passageway who read them and transmitted the contents to Fuller. He probably had a second basket from which he pulled empty envelopes and pretended to "read the potential of the stars."

She turned a knob on the speaker and a rich baritone voice filled the corridor like a well-trained Shakespearean actor. "Split apart, we are broken. We yearn, all our days, for completion." Fuller paced in front of the group but never failed to check himself in the mirror. The muscles of his face tightened as if he struggled with the thought. "It is not that one of us leads and the other follows, but rather that man and woman have an organic following."

He came back into her range of sight. His lips were heart-shaped, and his prematurely gray hair was brushed back from his head in a flowing wave. His mane was shades of silver, mixing dark pewter with frosty ash. He appeared to be about forty, but his blue jeans and maroon rugby sweater suggested a younger man. Not your typical charismatic, Alma decided. Across the back of the room was a hand-drawn sign with the word REVIVAL. She immediately thought of the snakes and shuddered, becoming nervous in the dark. What if the snakes were stored in this passageway? She realized the foolhardiness of entering without a flashlight.

"Socrates depicted man and woman as a whole," Fuller announced. "Now, in our naive minds this image might seem like a funny movie monster—two heads, two legs, two arms—two . . . Well, two, but different . . ." The comment drew mild laughter. "This concept represents union. Man and woman as one." He clasped his hands in front of him and made a dramatic full circle. "And in this union we were complete—whole."

Alma choked inwardly at his slickness but noticed how people around the room who had been sitting back comfortably in their seats were now leaning forward. Some had their hands folded as if in prayer and rested their chins on the tips of their fingers. Their eyes followed Fuller as he walked among them, their fascinated gaze leaving him only to take notes on something he'd said. The audience's trance kept Alma so preoccupied she hardly heard his message.

Fuller's body language didn't have the gloss of a television minister or the passion of a fire-and-brimstone preacher—what his fluid motions and roundness of gesture gave him was the sensuality of dance. Alma felt her eyes half close as she watched him. Listening to the richness of his voice she found herself lost in his words.

"Is it not this union that we all long for?" Fuller asked. "Deep down, ask yourself this question—don't we all want someone to chase us down? To take us by the shoulders and say, you . . . you, Sara Colby. You, Jason Jones. You, April Dunlap, you belong to me." He clenched one fist and thrust it into the air. "You are my completion!"

Alma stifled a laugh and said in a low voice, "Sounds like stalking to me."

The sound of his voice had lost its mesmerizing effect on her. She had heard enough. Time to confront him about Cash McGee. When she retraced her footsteps and came to the end of the passageway, she pushed on the wall and found herself standing behind her mother. "Boo," she said.

"Jesus, Alma Mae, it's you!" Merl exclaimed.

"Of course," Alma joked.

"No. There, on television." Her mother pointed at the large screen.

A video played of the strikers, and the camera shot had tightened on her. "They've been showing that all day," Alma said. "Help me move this console. I want to see if there are other hiding places." Merl didn't move. She stood pointing at the television, her face pale as porcelain. "Mother?" Alma asked.

"Again," the news anchor said. "A woman's body has been found at Silver Lake and unidentified sources have said it is Crimson County's commonwealth attorney, Alma Bashears." The anchor paused a few seconds. "It is widely speculated that the same man who shot Sam Merkle may be responsible for this death since Miss Bashears seems to be involved with the strike at the Highland Toy Factory. We'll have more on this story on the evening news."

Alma and her mother stared at each other. "I'm dead?" Alma croaked.

"Mamaw," her mother said, raising a hand to cover her heart. Instantly Alma understood her mother's concern. The older woman's health was fragile and might shatter if she heard the news unprepared.

Alma grabbed her mother's arm and hurried her to the door. "You've got to get to Mamaw," she said. "Call the rest of the relatives from there."

Merl let herself be hustled outside then asked with a look of alarm, "Where are you going, Alma?"

"Silver Lake," she replied and ran from the building.

5

Silver Lake reflected like a mirror shattered into a thousand pieces. Alma shaded her eyes as she looked at the basin that fed the water supply of Contrary, Quinntown, and Liberty. Pear-shaped with clusters of marshy coves, it had been created in the 1970s by blocking up a hollow and diverting a series of streams. Alma vaguely remembered some press coverage about the people who'd lived in the hollow being forced to give up their homes, but the memory was too unclear to complete the thought.

She slid down the gravel path from the paved road to the lake shore, grabbing on to swamp rose shrubs to steady her descent. Midway, she removed her high heels until she landed at the bottom of the slope. Her heart raced as she wiped a film of sweat from her upper lip. Yellow police tape blocked the dirt road leading to the water where a few detectives were examining tire prints. She motioned to a state trooper to walk her into the crime scene.

Chief Coyle stood on a stratum of rock with his back toward her, looking out at the lake as she approached. Alma figured he was the source of the rumors of her demise. "Is this a joke?" she said from behind him.

"Damn," he muttered under his breath.

"Do you know the upset you've caused my family?"

Alma stepped onto the rock, and as she looked up at him she fought the urge to knock off his cowboy hat.

"Nice of you to drive up," he said, turning toward her and putting on a pair of mirrored sunglasses. "You're a pinch overdressed."

"I thought you, the mayor, and I agreed that statements to the press would come through the city's information officer." She pushed back her hair after the breeze blew it into her face. Coyle took a toothpick from his shirt pocket and chewed on the end as he listened. "It's the best way not to jeopardize a case by someone speaking prematurely."

"I didn't tell a soul you were dead." Coyle shoved both hands deep into his pants pockets.

"No," said a voice from behind her. "What he did say was he wished you were dead."

Alma turned to see Nathan Deever, the Crimson County coroner. He knelt at the head of the body covered with white plastic and half-hidden underneath a hillside of Black-haw shrubs. The blood-spattered white flowers seemed surreal. As she stepped closer, the metallic smell of blood gagged her. She waited as he covered the torso securely then helped himself up with the aid of a hand-carved cane. They stepped toward each other at the same time and shook hands after he snapped off a latex glove. "Good to see you," she said. "Very soon, we have to make it somewhere other than a courtroom or a crime scene."

Deever smiled, showing straight white teeth that flattered his maple-toned skin and matched his snow-colored hair. Behind him the body of the deceased gave a sober reality to their pleasantries. A gentle breeze from the lake lifted the end of the plastic covering and revealed frosted, medium-cropped hair. Alma looked back at Coyle who'd followed her over. "Blond?" she asked. "That didn't give you a clue it wasn't me?" Coyle shifted uncomfortably but stayed silent.

"Alma," Nathan said, handing her a set of gloves, "you need to see this. The chief is correct in one aspect."

"But wrong in the most important one." She glanced back at Coyle.

"You better take a look," Nathan said and took her by the arm. Alma knelt, snapping on the gloves. "But first," he added quickly, "let me warn you to be prepared."

Alma whipped back the covering and stared into a misshapen version of her own face. "My God!" She fell backward, catching herself on the palms of her hands. Purplish-brown intestines were wrapped around the woman's neck like a scarf and draped on her arms as if she'd been dressed with a shawl.

Blood rushed from Alma's head and the scenery in front of her seemed to disappear. Nathan offered his cane. The intense need to touch a live human being filled her and instead she reached for his arm. She held on to him for several seconds then stepped away, needing the movement of her body to keep focused. Hesitantly, she looked back at the body.

A deep cut through the woman's larynx went almost to the spine. Her face had been neatly sliced as if the killer had outlined her eyes, nose, and mouth with a marker, the skin ripped away, then sloppily mashed back in place. Alma pulled off the gloves and dropped them. Except for some splashes of red on the surrounding foliage, most of the blood had seeped into the ground. The dry earth had sponged it up as if thirsty for nourishment.

She walked into the swaying leaves of a willow tree and held on to a vinelike limb. After a moment she motioned for Coyle. "Her name is Kitty Sloat," she told him. "She's my cousin." Alma took a deep breath and coughed it out to prevent a wave of nausea from overtaking her.

"We may never figure out her story," he said, "but I bet it's them strikers behind this."

"You damn well better find out who did this to her."

Coyle wrote Kitty's name on his pad and slipped it into his shirt pocket. "You pissed off them ole boys. Bet it's a case of mistaken identity."

Alma looked directly into Coyle's dark brown eyes. "Are you saying that because you believe it, or are you trying to make me feel guilty?"

"At a time like this?" he asked softly. "I got feelings, too, Alma." He leaned closer to her. "Sometimes I wish you'd let me show you."

Alma's insides felt like they'd been wrung out until nothing was left. She turned toward the lake and wished she could dive in. "Did anyone see anything?"

Coyle straightened up, pulling his frame to its full six feet and stood beside her staring out at the water. "The kids that found her had come down to go swimming. I got my men talking to the teens that go parking in this area. We usually get their names when we clean it out every week or so."

"Are you saying this is a lover's lane?"

"That don't mean nothing." He started to turn away then stopped. "She could have been brought here."

Those were the first sincerely kind words Alma had heard from Coyle. As much as they surprised her, she knew better than to acknowledge his admission that being in the area didn't mean that a murder victim was a slut. He'd read more into her appreciation than she meant. "I've got to go tell my mother." Alma stepped away to leave.

"You want me to drive you?"

"I'll take her," Nathan said, coming up behind them. "My assistant can finish from here."

Alma nodded in agreement. As she watched Chief Coyle brief the detectives, she wished that she had the strength to stay longer. He wasn't a rocket scientist when it came to police work. He was barely trained in law enforcement, but right now, all she could think of was getting home to her family.

Nathan waited patiently by her side as if sensing she needed to speak. "I never made an effort to see Kitty . . . only talked to her twice, maybe three times," she said. "I don't even know who she was anymore. And for her to end up like this." She let her hands rise and smack down against her sides. "When we were about twelve Kitty gave me her new navy-colored dress to wear for a Labor Day speech that I was to give at school assembly. The next year she put up signs all over school urging kids to vote for me for class president, then when I lost to a downtown kid, she toilet-papered his locker. I—I . . . I should have . . . " Her voice broke.

Nathan touched her shoulder and squeezed it. With his other hand he brought a feathery willow branch toward them and held it in front of Alma. "You ever notice how the weeping willow doesn't look like any other in the forest?" He pointed at the tree-lined mountains that surrounded the lake. "Look at them. Their leaves are shaped different, they grow different heights, some have flowers, some cones. But they're all alike in that they reach for the sky. The willow is the only one that turns its fruit back to the earth."

Alma felt tears welling in her eyes and breathed in deeply to hold them back.

He let go of her and stroked the willow branch as if it were a pet. "My grandmother used to say the willow watched the injustices of the world. It saw the Cherokee walking on their Trail of Tears, saw my ancestors enslaved, saw coal miners shot down as they fought for a decent wage, and even saw our Lord as he died on the cross. I asked her how a tree could know about things so far away and long ago. She told me that the roots of the tree descended into the earth and heard of all injustice, even the ones the world will never know of, the troubles of those who are sick at heart and those who no longer have a voice to speak. It witnessed, and in its sorrow, the branches soon draped down like tears and fell back to the earth. The Witness Tree, she called it." He broke off a leaf and pressed it into Alma's hand. "I never forgot that story."

Alma smoothed the leaf between her fingers, thinking how much the sickle shape looked like a long tear that had drifted down someone's cheek. But this tree can't tell me who killed Kitty." She brought the leaf to her lips and held it there, wishing that some transference of cell memory could infuse her with its knowledge. "My mother and her sister had almost no family. Aunt Sarah died about ten years ago. Kitty didn't have anybody."

"She didn't die alone, Alma. This tree was here, and as long as it was here, then God was here. Think of it that way. She's returned to souls who love her."

Alma let him lead her to his car and allowed him to make arrangements for one of the policemen to drive her car back to Contrary. She watched the willow tree as a breeze lifted the branches in a soft sway. She wished it could take away her hurt, for now she was truly sick at heart.

6

"Who will I live with if my momma and daddy die?" Eddie pulled on Alma's pant leg as she switched the phone to her other ear.

"How could you lose him?" she whispered to Chief Coyle and cast a glance toward her grandmother's kitchen, hoping that the family in there couldn't hear her. "He's a sixteen-year-old boy—"

"A teenage delinquent." Coyle's voice cut into hers. "He head-butted one of my detectives and slit the tires of my cruiser before taking off on a beat-up motorcycle."

"And thanks to you Danny is out there all alone." She reached down and petted the top of Eddie's head as he waited patiently, looking up at her with puppy-dog eyes.

"We shot at him so he knows we mean business."

"No wonder he ran away from you." Alma could hardly stand hearing of Coyle's incompetence from his own lips. "Did you ever consider shooting at Cash McGee, or is it only people related to me that you want in your sights?"

"Alma, that's not fair. I'm doing the best I can."

"Then why hasn't Harlan Fuller been brought in for questioning? Better yet, why haven't you even searched his church? I'd bet a month's salary that's where you'll find Cash McGee."

Coyle was quiet. Whether from anger or grudging agreement, Alma couldn't tell. He coughed once then cleared his throat. "There's something you're not considering," he said. "This kid could be a suspect."

"Oh, please." Alma picked up Eddie and balanced him on her knee. "There is nothing at the crime scene to indicate that. Nothing in the Sloat house, and none of the friends or neighbors said there was any kind of problem between them."

"Sometimes this kind of stuff runs in families," Coyle said with a slice of vindictiveness.

Alma knew he was referring to the fact that her brother had once been charged with murder. "You find Cash McGee," she ordered through clenched teeth.

"You have a conflict of interest, Miss Commonwealth Attorney." His words ended with a sharp huff.

"Enough!" she said loudly, sending Eddie sliding off her lap in fear. She reached out for him, but he ran to the kitchen only to return with his great-grandmother. Mamaw maneuvered her wheelchair into the room with Eddie on her lap and Larry Joe riding on the rear. Alma turned her head toward the wall and ended the conversation. "I'll be at the station in twenty minutes. I want an update on Cash McGee, and by that time, hopefully, you will have located my homeless, motherless cousin—unless you find the assignment too difficult, in which case any hunter from one of the hollows can easily track a teenager." She clipped the phone down and turned toward her grandmother and the kids.

"Answer me," Eddie insisted. "Who would I live with if Momma died?"

"Sweetie, nothing's going to happen to your mother," Alma said and cupped his cheek in her hand.

"But what if it did?" He looked directly into her eyes

with such worry that Alma stroked his back. He slid off Mamaw's lap and balanced his tiny hand on Alma's knee.

"Who is Cousin Danny gonna live with?" Larry Joe asked as he joined his brother in front of her.

Sensing Alma's discomfort, Mamaw pulled both great-grandsons to her. "I have some strawberries in the refrigerator that are just waiting for two little boys to gobble them up, and they can use their fingers." Larry Joe took Eddie's hand and they slunk off to the kitchen, seeming to know their questions would not be answered.

Mamaw stared out the window at the police cruiser that had been assigned to escort Alma around until Cash McGee's capture. At the side of the porch Uncle George and Uncle Ames were cleaning the rabbits from their morning hunt. She rolled her chair closer to Alma and said, "Can't say I ain't wondering, too."

"I know Danny Sloat's not your blood kin, Mamaw," Alma said. "It's something me, Sue, Vernon, and Momma will have to work out."

"Now, Alma," she said. "You know that's not how I meant it." She pulled at the end of the long gray braid draped around her shoulder. Her eyes stared steadily at her knotted arthritic knuckles. One hand rose to stroke the area of her heart as she spoke slowly, choosing her words with the skill of a diplomat. "Him and his momma lived in Quinntown, and his doings was known all the way over here. You sure it's something you need to take on?"

Alma stood up and paced toward a two-toned tan oil stove that was used as a flower and picture stand throughout the summer months. Out the window she could see a pile of gray rabbits over which Uncle Ames sharpened a hunter's knife. George turned on a hose to wash down the blood. "I don't know that we have a choice. Danny's sixteen and he doesn't have anybody else." She looked at a picture of her family taken the previous Christmas—herself along with Mamaw, Sue and her boys, Vernon, their mother, Aunt Joyce, Uncle George, and Uncle Ames. How happy they all were. Kitty and Danny had probably been alone that holiday. Why hadn't she invited them over? Why hadn't she visited? She couldn't recall if she'd even sent a card.

"Him and a bunch of boys was accused of burning down those deserted houses last Halloween," Mamaw said.

"I think I heard something about that," Alma remarked, her guilt increasing. Inwardly, she hated admitting that perhaps Kitty's problems were part of the reason she'd never stayed in touch. The clean smell of the recently washed curtain prompted Alma to move closer to the window. This house was so safe for her. This family was so safe. Poor Kitty had never had that comfort. And she deserved it, Alma thought to herself.

"Alma, I don't mean to speak ill of the dead." Mamaw raised herself out of the wheelchair and took short steps to a floral-patterned couch, settling in on her favorite side that was indented with her frail shape. "But more than one married woman would've stomped Kitty into the ground if they'd had the chance."

Alma stared out the window as Ames placed a butcher knife at the joint of a rabbit's paw and snapped it off. She turned away when he placed the blade at the neck. In Kitty's defense she said quietly, "She was the one cousin who knew how to talk to me during some of the most difficult times in my life."

"What do you mean?" Mamaw asked.

Alma bit her tongue at her mistake of speaking before thinking. There was much about her youth she never wanted her grandmother to know. Mamaw was a protective matriarch and Alma feared she would blame herself if she discovered what had happened to her granddaughter. "Things like Daddy's disappearance," she said hesitatingly. "Everybody telling me he was dead. Never knowing what really happened to him. It about drove me crazy. Kitty knew how to be kind. She knew how to simply be there and make me feel better. Whatever kind of woman she became doesn't erase what I feel I owe her."

Mamaw was quiet as she stared up at a row of pictures of her family. One from each generation. She settled on the picture of Alma's father. Round of face, half-moon eyes, jet black hair, and wide straight-toothed smile, he could have been Vernon's double. "Ever thought of locating Danny's father?"

"I don't know if Kitty even knew who the father was." Alma spoke gently and felt embarrassed. She faced the window again to hide her feelings. Uncle Ames had slid the knife into the back of a headless rabbit and slit it down the back. She watched as he stripped the fur off the pinkish flesh.

"She was a wild girl." Mamaw pulled Alma's arm and turned her around. "It's one of the reasons your momma moved in with me instead of her sister after your daddy died." She gestured toward her son's picture on the wall. It amazed Alma that her grandmother always referred to him as dead even though no one knew Esau Bashears's fate. One holiday season he left for Detroit to earn Christmas money and never returned. The money he'd saved was never found and the family believed he'd been killed for it. "Think carefully before you make this boy your responsibility," she said. "I don't mean to sound mean-spirited, but there're people in the world that can't be taught, helped . . . or controlled." She leaned back on the couch, her lined face drawn with concern and fear for her granddaughter. Again, she glanced at the police car and the two patrolmen who sat on the porch drinking sodas. "No use locking the front door when the Devil has the key to the back."

Alma touched her grandmother's shoulder then walked out the door. Outside she stepped through a pack of hunting beagles gathered around her uncles for the spoils of the hunt. She motioned to the two policemen that she was leaving. Three skinned rabbits, headless, pawless, and quartered, lay on a slab of concrete, ready for the freezer. Uncle George slit the stomach of a skinned rabbit and reached inside it with two fingers, pulling out all the innards with a strong jerk. The pack of dogs lapped at his feet as he threw the lump to the ground. Alma couldn't shake the thought of her cousin, lying on that lake shore— dying as her blood seeped into the ground. She'd seen plenty of animals skinned and cleaned while growing up, but somehow, this time the sight spooked her. She could barely manage a wave at her uncles, who simply nodded in reply rather than take their bloody hands from the task of preparing their meat. As far as she was concerned, who- ever had killed Kitty was the Devil. Could it have been this boy? Could Kitty's own son have killed her?

7

Alma opened the door to the police station and a blue uniformed officer flew past her, landing in a heap amid a clutter of trash cans. The clank and bang of metal mixed with a commotion of angry grunts, yelling, and swearing. Carefully she peered inside.

"Lit ve guu," a bearded, longhaired man spat out as he struggled with three officers. He was cuffed and shackled but still managed to shove backward and push them against an occupied desk. The clerk jumped behind a set of file cabinets to escape.

"Whack the bastard!" one policeman yelled.

Off to one side another man and a young blond woman shouted while Chief Coyle and two more officers held back the couple with batons. The woman strained against the men's outstretched arms, looking ready to join the fray at any moment. "We'll sue you for this!" she screamed, her face streaked with tears and smeared mascara.

The man with her remained motionless—a poise so intense Alma could sense a vibration of energy from him. Black haired and brown eyed, with a three-day growth of beard and a ponytail, he stood about six feet tall, his worn black leather vest giving solidity to his stance. His well-developed biceps and rippled chest suggested he could have taken on any of the officers and won. "Kevin! Stop fighting," he shouted at the struggling man and glared at the police. His words had an effect that no one else had been able to produce despite a great show of force. Kevin reluctantly gave in and lay facedown on the desk.

Alma stepped in closer to the scene. Almost in slow motion, the man beside Chief Coyle turned to look at her. His auburn-brown eyes had a piercing quality that flashed through her with a sense of recognition. His gaze followed her as she walked over to the chief. One officer raised his baton to strike the handcuffed man, turned to his boss for approval, and found himself looking at Alma. His smile died. He glanced at Chief Coyle, back at Alma, and the baton lowered a millimeter.

"I think you've successfully subdued him," Alma said. Four policemen forced Kevin off down the hallway to the holding cells. All the while he yelled in a language she didn't recognize but felt most surely was cursing.

"Thank you," the dark-haired man said, staring deeply into her eyes.

She nodded and noticed his accent—perhaps English or Australian. To Chief Coyle she said, "I came to get copies of the reports." She hesitated for the slightest moment to gather her thoughts. "Nice to see you've been busy."

"Motorcycle trash," Coyle said. "You just witnessed the arrest of the man who killed Kitty Sloat."

"He didn't kill anybody!" the blond woman shouted.

The heat of irritation filled Alma's chest as she began to suspect that the chief had allowed the situation to get out of control. "Will you explain?"

"We've never been to that lake," the young woman insisted.

Alma noticed that her accent was American, with a northeastern flavor. "Miss," Alma said firmly, "the police will have to conduct their investigation, and from what

I've seen of your friend's way of cooperating, he doesn't have a lot going for him."

"He rides a motorcycle. Tracks are all over the lake area," Coyle said. "They'll match his bike, all right."

"We're a student group from Whitehall University in Scotland," the dark-haired man said. "We're spending the semester seeing America—on motorcycles—and when we return home *The Celt*, the Scottish equivalent of your *Time*, will publish an article about all we've experienced."

The chief glanced at Alma as if he'd noticed the irritation on her face. "Now, just 'cause he says that, don't mean it's true."

"How many tire castings did you take at the scene?" Alma asked.

"It's June, for godsake." Coyle looked like a fox with a trapped paw. "We could only get the ones left in the shore area."

"And?"

He hesitated. "They were cars," he whispered in a low growl, "but I got detectives out there now looking for more."

"Smart thing for a killer to do, don't you think?" the man said. "Leave tire prints in the mud."

Alma took a deep breath. "I trust you'll have no problem answering one of our detective's questions about your visit to our region," she said to the man.

"Yeah, like we're not gonna talk to a lawyer first," the blond woman blurted.

"There is, however, the issue of assaulting an officer," Alma said coolly.

"I understand," the dark-haired man interrupted, his full lips spread slightly in a smile of acknowledgment as to how the game was to be played. "We'll answer whatever questions you have."

"You also won't mind showing us your passports?" Alma asked, just to give herself the assurance that his co-operation was genuine.

"Look, we're camping out a few days until we can make some repairs on our bikes. We don't have time for trouble. Question Kevin and the rest of us. We'll be here till the week's end."

Alma looked at Chief Coyle. He stared at the floor, his lower lip pushed into his upper. "Chief?" she asked.

One foot scuffed against the floor. He turned and yelled in the direction of the holding cells. "Let him go!" With a final glare at Alma he charged down the hall, and a few seconds later, the slam of his office door shook the walls.

"Thank you again," the man said, his voice softer. He held out a hand.

Alma shook it, but as she pulled back he held on. His grasp was firm and enclosed her entire hand. The warmth of his skin shot through her and an involuntary smile escaped her lips. "Chief Coyle doesn't like being wrong," she said quietly. She stepped closer. "I wouldn't stay any longer than the end of the week, if I were you."

He smiled widely and nodded. Releasing her hand, his eyes quickly took in the rest of her body. "I will heed your advice."

"A detective will be with you shortly. I assume Kevin will behave?"

The man nodded and winked as if to indicate his complete trust that the situation was being handled to everyone's satisfaction. Alma turned to follow Chief Coyle, but at the doorway she couldn't resist a backward glance. The man was watching her and smiling that same smile, which by now had become more than friendly: it was flirtatious. She felt the heat of it enter her, and was a bit sorry he'd be leaving so soon.

* * *

After picking up copies of Coyle's investigation files on Cash McGee, Harlan Fuller, and her cousin's murder, Alma hastily retreated to her office for some peace and quiet. By the end of the day she'd gone through them twice without a break. Swallowing the last of a cup of bitter coffee, she returned for a third read.

As she finished each page she slapped it down in frustration. It wasn't simply that she couldn't link Harlan Fuller and Cash McGee, but even Cash's possible involvement in her cousin's murder seemed farfetched. He'd taken a potshot at Sam Merkle but that didn't mean he was a sick killer who cut off a victim's face. What if this stranger were involved? What if it were someone in Kitty's life they didn't know about? What if it was Danny? She hated thinking the thought but knew it was a possibility. Worse yet, what if she herself had been the intended target?

The breeze from an open window brought in a scent of honeysuckle from vines that grew along the facade of the building. The aroma invoked a memory of her father stringing them together to make necklaces for her and Sue. For a moment she daydreamed. How safe he'd made her feel when she was a little girl. And yet now in this same quiet town where she'd been born, even with two policemen outside her door, she didn't feel completely secure.

She tossed the file marked MIRROR OF OUR SOUL into a basket and stood up to stretch. The empty office suddenly seemed lonely. Alma liked working into the evenings, but tonight she wished she could wrap herself in someone's arms and hold him until she slept. It had been a long time since a man had held her, or even touched her.

At the window she looked out at the empty street. Darkness had fallen and the street lamps cast eerie shadows over the triangle between the courthouse, police station, and city hall. She often enjoyed sitting in the office after dark and looking out over the courtyard. And yet something seemed strange. Perhaps it was just reality sinking in: a woman whose blood was joined to hers had died—ceased to exist in this world. The grasp of death was never so saddening as when life was taken unfairly by murder. No one understands until it cuts you, she thought. She knew she'd never view a homicide quite the same way again. She longed for the security of her home and family and scooped up her belongings to leave.

On her way out the door, Alma paused at the window and looked out at the courtyard again. A breeze caused a shift in the shadow patterns of the full-leafed oak and maple trees. She still sensed an element out of place. With a loud gurgle, the park fountain turned itself off for the night. She concentrated on the scene as if it were a picture she'd studied many times. Her eye caught the imbalance. A shadow that didn't move in the breeze. Underneath the nearest tree a person stood as still as a coiled snake. She started to call out for the police guard but stopped. The elongated shadow stretched out in the light from the street lamp and moved forward.

Alma squinted and shifted position. She caught sight of a raincoat and the top part of a man's bald head. The stride was familiar as he walked toward her window, looking up at her. No, she thought. No. That's impossible. Why would Walter Gentry be watching me?

8

———————

"Why did you bring me here?" Alma asked. She swallowed hard so her voice wouldn't tremble. The hospital corridor was dim and the overhead fluorescent lights flickered, casting an eerie shade of green on the walls. At the end of the hall, Walter Gentry stared out a window.

"I know I told you that if you'd come with me, you wouldn't regret it," he looked into his own reflection. "And that many things would become clear to you, but . . . you are the only person who can give meaning to what is about to happen."

Alma walked three steps in Walter's direction but was not compelled to go any closer. "Why did you bring me here?" she asked again.

Walter shifted so his profile entered a shaft of light. His shaggy beard nearly touched his chest, and the redness around his nose and rims of his eyes suggested illness. Alma knew better. In her lifetime she'd looked too often into her own eyes swollen from tears that she couldn't control. Too much of that sorrow had been caused by Walter Gentry. As teenagers their paths had crossed in the worst of ways—he'd been responsible for her rape. Now, seeing him suffering a grief he could barely control, she almost felt glad.

He inhaled deeply, then coughed out the breath as if to

steady himself. "She asked for you," he said and pointed to a room marked INTENSIVE CARE. A handwritten sign had been taped below it—PRIVATE SUITE.

Alma closed her eyes. The antiseptic aroma of the hospital merged into the smell of death. "I can't go in there." She crossed her arms over her stomach. "Even if you don't believe me, Walter, I am sorry for you. But you must know this is a mistake."

"It is the last thing she'll ever ask of me." His voice quivered and he sniffed, wiping his mouth and nose with the back of his hand. "You will see her? Please?"

Alma peered though the vertical window on the right side of the door. A bank of medical panels lit the room in an array of red, green, and yellow lights. The bed was pushed against the window. Outside was a view of the Appalachian Mountains as beautiful as a detailed oil painting. A long, thin lump, barely lifting the bedcovers, was all she could make out of Walter Gentry's mother.

Every instinct told Alma to turn around and walk away. She glanced back at Walter. His face was buried in the palms of his hands and his shoulders shook slightly as he sucked in deep breaths to hold his composure. Alma looked away from him, less to give him privacy than to distance herself from his emotions. If there was any family in Contrary, Kentucky, from which she withheld pity, it was the Gentrys. Most of her life, the Gentrys had run the town—to the benefit of those who chose to live by their rules.

When Alma reluctantly returned to Contrary as a successful California attorney, she had expected to leave within one week. But she had stayed . . . and in staying she had been forced to confront the Gentrys. They went after her and her family with vengeance worthy of an enraged deity. To save her brother from a murder charge, Alma had destroyed Walter Gentry's political career, costing him his job as commonwealth attorney. But even these events were far from her first encounter with the almighty Gentrys.

A strand of shoulder-length black hair fell from the barrette that held it high on her head. She curled it behind her ear then pressed her fingers to her lips as if the gesture could help her think. Could she find enough compassion in her soul to forgive the woman she'd hated nearly all her life? The answer her heart gave was not comforting. She wasn't sure. She just wasn't sure.

Hesitantly and very slowly she reached for the door handle.

"Alma Bashears." The sound of Walter's voice stopped her cold. She did not turn toward him, but from the slight echo in the hall she could tell he wasn't facing her. "There's not much rage left in me," he said flatly, "but if you say or do anything that hastens her death by one minute . . . there's enough . . . there's enough . . . "

When the door clicked shut behind Alma, she saw Charlotte Gentry's reflection in the window. The old woman opened her eyes and stared into the glass where the room was traced on the dark surface. Alma held her breath and willed herself to stay silent, but her thoughts would not. This woman's poison had wound through every aspect of her life. How she had hated the self-appointed guardian of the town's morals. Because of Charlotte, Alma had learned a brutal lesson about the influence of money when she was just seventeen.

She remembered the humiliation of twenty-five thousand dollars fluttering around her—more money than she'd ever seen in her life, but to Mrs. Gentry it represented an inexpensive way of doing business. If Alma left town the Gentry name would remain unstained. How stupid Charlotte had been. The horror of being held down by Walter while his friends raped her was a secret the teenage Alma would have taken to her grave.

One bony hand rose from the bed and pointed at Alma's reflection. "You think you've won." The words seemed to crack as they spilled from her lips.

Alma didn't move. Charlotte's sheet was pulled high on her chest and her legs shifted slightly underneath. Her white hair, combed straight back from her face, made her head appear small and shrunken. A deep cough shook her but she kept pointing at Alma's reflection.

When the spell of congestion passed, she spoke again. "You're just like your father." The trembling hand slowly lowered to rest on the old woman's chest. "He died a horrible death—far away from his family and everything he knew. And you, you think you've come back to live the life he missed. Well, let me tell you—you don't know as much as you think." She frowned, her mouth forming an inverted U, and she raised her skeletal head from the pillow. "Let me just tell you . . . "

The flatness of the window did not mask the old woman's eyes as they shot a pointed glare at Alma's reflection. She stared a minute longer then finally lay her head back down and looked away. "Allafair Adair is the one responsible for everything that happened." A congested chortle passed through her lips. "And to think you've wasted your life hating *me*." The last two words cackled out of her throat and ended in another coughing spasm. "For you to learn about your squalid stock—I just might have my revenge after all."

Alma waited. The old woman didn't focus attention on her reflection again. Finally Alma bit. "Who is Allafair Adair?"

"I've got a present for you," Charlotte said, ignoring her

question. "You have to promise me that you'll keep it all your days." She turned her head sideways but didn't engage Alma directly. The hollowed-out eye sockets reminded Alma of a horror movie, sending a shiver through her. "Promise me, little girl. Promise an old, bitter, dying woman." She pointed to a gold-colored gift box on the table. "Go on, open it."

Alma hesitated and studied her. Charlotte's slight smile was as spooky and untrustworthy as a crouching cat, but Alma's wariness was exceeded only by her curiosity. She pulled off the top of the box, reached inside, and drew out a snow globe, the flakes gently falling on the pink-cheeked porcelain face of a child's doll. The porcelain was clearly old, and the cracks around the edges looked as if the face had been broken. The eyes were missing, but the cherry-colored lips and delicately fashioned nose made the object as beautiful as a theatrical mask. The globe was fitted into a base of shiny black coal. The underside had been shaved until it was smooth enough to sit flat. "And this is supposed to mean?" she asked in confusion and turned toward Charlotte.

"By the time you know, I'll be long in my grave." The old woman tried to sit up but the weight of her frail body was too much. "And you know what pleases me the most?" she asked, not waiting for a response. "That's when you'll be the most sorry, Alma Mae Bashears. That's when you'll wish with all that's in you that I was here and you could talk to me—but I'll be nothing but a rotting corpse, and you'll hate me with all that's in you. You'll hate me for dying. You'll wish with your whole soul that I was alive."

The sharp tone of the heart monitor made a lonely, solitary beep. Mrs. Gentry chuckled to herself. Alma bit the inside of her mouth. She held the snow globe tightly in her hands and left the room. She knew that it wouldn't be long until whatever Charlotte Gentry had to say to her would no longer matter. All she was to Alma now was a dying, vengeful woman unable to let go of her vendetta.

9

There were fifteen families named Adair in Crimson County, another twenty in the three surrounding counties, and thirty-two in adjacent Tennessee and Virginia. Alma tossed the Middlesboro phone book on top of the stack she'd already gone through. Except for a number where she got an answering machine, she'd finished with Kentucky. No one there would admit kinship to Allafair Adair. Tomorrow she'd tackle Tennessee. The snow globe sat upright in her law bag and she'd looked at it many times during the day, wondering what kind of trap Charlotte Gentry had set for her.

"Val, has that pizza arrived yet?" she asked her secretary through the intercom.

"Not yet, but I'll send it in the second it gets here."

Alma checked the clock. Way past quitting time, she thought. Maybe the Liberty Adairs are home now. She dialed the number and got the answering machine again. At the same instant she heard a knock on the door.

"Pizza delivery," a voice said.

She stood, digging through her desk for money. "Come on in." She held out a twenty-dollar bill. In the doorway stood the dark-haired stranger from the previous day. He'd shaved and gotten a haircut and was dressed in what looked to be the most expensive navy-blue three-piece suit in town. All Alma could manage to say was "Oh, my."

He held the pizza box up to his nose. "Smells like bacon and . . . something fruity?"

"Pineapple," Alma said. "It's a Hawaiian. My mother likes them. I'm on my way to see her."

"Ahh, mother. Then I guess it's too late to invite myself for a bite to eat."

His Scottish accent had a way of distracting Alma's attention away from his actual words. "I'm sorry," she said, losing her train of thought. "I know who you are, but . . . I don't know your name."

"Ian Corey," he said. "I'm an assistant professor at Whitehall University and did my master thesis on Southern American literature. I have Ph.D.s in literature from Edinburgh University and in rhetoric from Harvard. I stopped by to thank you properly for all your help." He placed the pizza on the desk. "I asked around about you and was sent here."

"Yes." Alma felt her cheeks flush. "If you're looking for me, this is where they'll send you." She realized how foolish she sounded and squeezed her hands behind her back. "Oh, here's money for the pizza." She stepped toward him, holding out the twenty dollars.

"It's done," he said. "The least I can do is buy your dinner. That's why I washed up." He opened his arms to indicate his suit. "Every week or so, we rent a few hotel rooms and have a decent night's sleep—though this suit will probably find its way to a local charity. Not much use for it camped out under the stars."

"That's very kind of you," she said, returning the money to her desk.

"My group has been officially cleared of being the Contrary stalker."

Alma didn't speak.

"I apologize. I must have seemed flippant." His full lips pressed a comforting half-smile into his left cheek. "Were you close to the deceased?"

"She was my cousin," Alma said. "I hadn't seen her in several years."

Ian's face colored and he bowed his head. "You feel a mite guilty and I feel a lot ignorant."

"I bet you have another degree in psychology?" She smiled.

"Nosiness," he shot back. "Actually, empathy," he added with somewhat more distance, and even a trace of sadness in his voice. "I lost my mother at an early age, and with no father, I always felt guilty that I wasn't as good a son as I should have been." He stared out the window behind her, as if he couldn't articulate his thoughts, then glanced over to the shelf full of law books and, finally, to the floor. "But one thing I remember from those times was how helpful it was to keep my mind distracted and my time occupied— hence too much education." He looked up at her. The silence in the room seemed to drain all the oxygen. "May I join you for dinner?"

Alma found herself holding her breath and returning his easy smile. She stepped toward him and took his hand, knowing that her flirtatious behavior was inappropriate for her position and the situation but somehow unable to stop herself. Exhaling, she said, "Well, my family and I have a funeral to plan."

"Perhaps afterward for dessert?"

"I don't know," she said, his insistence throwing her. "I'm meeting them in Quinntown and really should leave now before the pizza gets too cold." She followed his gaze to the stack of phone books on her desk. Smoothly she pulled her hand back. "I'm trying to locate someone." She touched a finger to her forehead. "You must think I have very little to do around here."

"Far from the truth," he said. "I've checked up on you, Alma Bashears. The library has a thick file on you, and I'm grateful you convinced the police chief not to charge us. I'd fear going up against you."

"Actually, there'd be a long way to go before I got involved."

"I'll make sure I don't commit murder in your town."

"We appreciate that." She laughed.

He paused then said, "Kidnapping, possibly."

She chuckled. "I could think of worse things than being forced into dessert."

"Would you care to come out to where we're camped— Jesus Falls?"

"No" Alma said too quickly. She hesitated and looked out the window. "Not there."

"It's a beautiful setting." Ian spread his hands out in an expansive gesture. "The moon comes up over the water-fall and you forget about the rest of the world."

"Not there," she repeated. Her chest constricted and breath didn't come easy. "It's a place I don't visit unless I have to."

"I sense a history." His eyes narrowed and he studied her. "Very well," he said. His lips pressed into a slight smile as he waited.

"My house," Alma said. "Bring ice cream."

"Strawberry, I'll bet."

"Do you read minds, too?"

"No, I'm just a good guesser."

"Well, guesser," she said, "you don't have to guess

about this." She reached for a writing pad and wrote down directions to her house, not certain why she was letting this stranger into her life but feeling eager to take a chance on a man who might finally prove to be her equal.

10

"When the Devil smiles at you, make sure you grin back." Harlan Fuller's deep voice resonated from Alma's car radio. "For those of you in our listening audience, I hold in my hand a ten-foot-long smirkin' copperhead and I'm smiling. Is that not right?" he called out to his viewing audience. They responded with hearty yells of acclamation. "I'm smiling because the Devil's in my hand. He does not control me. Whether it be my weight, my love life, my finances, my health—I control my demons. And if you, too, wish to learn how to be in charge of your life, join us next Sunday." He drew out the vowels of the word *Sunday*, dipping low toward the end in a stiff imitation of a hypnotic charismatic. "If you're unable to visit us in Contrary, remember we have satellite meeting rooms in Liberty, Middlesboro, Quinntown, and Corbin. Soon to have satellite offices in Pineville, Harrogate, and Tazewell. Join us, won't you? Just join us."

Alma shut him off with a hard twist of the knob. Two thoughts kept pounding in her brain: Fuller was hiding Cash McGee, and McGee might have killed her cousin. If that turned out to be the case then Fuller was an accessory and as soon as she could prove her suspicions, she'd go after him like an eagle on a field mouse. No, a rat, she thought.

She came to a split in the road. One side led to Quinn-town, a small mining community with a reputation as rough as the people who lived there; the other went toward Liberty, almost an offshoot of Quinntown but its opposite in temperament. Kingsley University had been founded there and served as a guardian for preserving Appalachian culture.

She idled the car and stared at the giant Falcon Rock formation that overlooked Quinntown. The tip of the head rose above a sea of giant oak trees, and the rock eye seemed to peer in all directions. The two-lane road was smooth as a ribbon through the mountains and Alma chastised herself for not driving it more often. It wasn't that far to Kitty's house. Why hadn't she visited her? She took the fork toward Quinntown and just prior to entering the city limits turned into a cul-de-sac of trailers surrounded by a thick forest of pine trees. Alma found her mother's and sister's cars outside the Sloat lot and pulled in behind them.

Parked on the roadway was Jefferson's black Mazda. Suspicion itched at her. "What is he doing here?" she murmured aloud.

Quickly Alma got out, taking time only to wave back at the police car that had followed her at a discreet distance. From the uneven concrete porch she could hear voices but couldn't tell if the conversation was intense or casual. She opened the door, hoping to take them by surprise, but no one—her mother, Sue, Vernon—paid any special attention. She dropped her law bag on the couch and set the pizza on a center table where Vernon immediately attacked it. Jefferson stiffened the slightest bit at her presence and that was where Alma focused. "Afternoon," she said to everyone then asked Jefferson, "Did you come for pizza or pity?"

"Alma, do you have to be so rude at a time like this?"

Sue complained. She held up a maroon dress and a blue suit in front of their mother.

"Neither one of these work," Merl said, feeling the material of the blue suit. "Kitty was more naughty. She wouldn't want to be laid to rest in something her grandmother wore." She pushed aside a box in which Sue had begun to pack up some photo albums. Slowly she picked up a stuffed unicorn and wiped away a tear. "Let's see what's in the other closet." Merl touched Alma's shoulder as Sue led the way to the bedroom.

A piece of torn police tape was draped across a lumpy couch covered with a pink bed blanket. The detectives who'd searched the rooms had been careful not to leave the usual ransacked mess, knowing that Kitty was related to Alma. She tossed the tape into a wastebasket and picked up a picture of Kitty and Danny. Her cousin's features were similar to hers, though more lined across the forehead and fuller through the cheeks. Kitty had dyed her hair an ashy blond with whitish highlights around the face. It was waist-length in this picture, full and thick, drawing Alma to the memory of Kitty lying dead on the lake shore. Her hair had been short when Alma viewed her corpse, and the blond had been caked with dried blood. Must have recently cut it, she decided.

As she replaced the photo, even at an angle Kitty's eyes seemed to follow her. They frightened Alma with their familiarity—gray with a pattern shooting out from the iris like exploding fireworks. Danny's eyes were a lighter shade of gray and his hair was blond, prompting Alma to wonder how much the boy favored his father.

She turned toward her brother, who stood awkwardly in the corner wolfing down the pizza, and Jefferson, who lifted a few pieces of paper from the desk and looked through them. "You didn't tell me why you were here," she said to Jefferson. "And don't look to Sue to rescue you this time."

"He gave me a ride over," Vernon said, as if to diffuse the tension of her attack, and bit into his second piece of pizza.

Alma rolled her eyes. "As long as I've known you, Jefferson, you've never had any trouble speaking for yourself."

"I was Kitty's lawyer." Jefferson looked directly into Alma's eyes, an edge of defensiveness coloring his words.

Alma hoped she didn't look surprised and softened her voice. "I never saw a file for her when we worked together."

"There are some files I keep at home."

"To hide them from me?" His uncomfortable silence told Alma there was more at issue than he was saying. The expression on her face must have shown her hurt because he reached out and touched her arm. Instinctively, she pulled away. "I don't need friends who lie to me."

He walked to the door and opened it just as Merl and Sue exited from the bedroom with another load of dresses and began sorting them according to color. "Ladies," he said and nodded as he left the house.

Sue and Merl were too absorbed in their task to take much notice, but Vernon's stern expression spoke his irritation with Alma. Alma stepped around a box full of sports equipment, picked up a baseball, and tossed it at him to break the tension. Smoothly he caught the ball and set it aside. "Pizza needs microwaving," he complained and started on another piece.

"It seems our cousin Danny's athletic abilities have significantly aided him in avoiding the police," she said. "I think that means he should live with Vernon." Alma waited to see if anyone would respond.

"He'll live with me," Merl said matter-of-factly. "I just

wish we could find him, or that he'd call." She held up a pumpkin-colored silky dress and nodded that she liked it. "I don't want to have the funeral until Danny's with us."

"I've already talked to Miss Millie at the funeral home," Sue said. "She suggested we do this sooner rather than later."

"No," Merl said. "Not until Danny is with us."

"But Momma—" Sue said.

"I said no!" Merl wiped the back of her neck and sighed. "It's so hot in here."

"I don't think the coroner can release the body until Tuesday, Wednesday at the latest," Alma said softly, hoping to ease some of the tension.

Alma hesitated then decided against telling them that Chief Coyle regarded Danny as a suspect in his mother's murder. " Danny had a bit of a tussle with the police when they came here," Alma said and pointed to a broken mirror with glass still lying on the floor.

"I don't want to hear excuses," Merl said. "You know as well as I do, anybody from the hollows or Quinntown runs when they see a policeman."

"Much of that has changed, Momma," Alma said, even though it irked her to defend a department that included Chief Coyle.

"Alma, the reformer," Sue replied, a hint of sarcasm in her voice.

"He probably misunderstood, thought they were after him, and ran. Poor kid is going to find out about his mother in the worst possible way—the street."

"I'll get out and shake the bushes," Vernon said. "I bet him and me use the same hiding places."

Merl inhaled a deep breath. "This is so bizarre." She sat on the couch next to Alma's law bag and rested her arm on top of it. "Who could have done this to her?"

Alma knew she needed to change the subject quickly. If details of her cousin's death seeped into the conversation, speculation of the killer's identity would follow, and she'd rather them not know that Danny might be a suspect. "Speaking of bizarre," Alma said, "and a little off the subject—does this mean anything to any of you?" She pulled her law bag from under her mother's arm and opened the top flaps. Reaching inside, she brought out the snow globe containing the porcelain doll's face that Charlotte Gentry had given her. "It might be connected to a woman named Allafair Adair. Ring any bells?" They all had blank expressions, said nothing, and stared as if the globe were a trinket from a tourist stand. "Okay," Alma said, dropping it into the bag. "Subject closed."

"Poor little Kitty." Merl sniffed and covered her face with both hands before breaking into tears. The sudden upset took her daughters by surprise. Alma went to her side and Sue sat on the other to comfort their mother. A tear streaked down Sue's face as she held Merl's hand.

"Come on," Vernon said in a jovial voice. "I'm a man. I can't cry. This ain't fair. There you three sit like an oreo—two little black-haired girls and a big white-haired momma in the middle."

For a second, Merl laughed, acknowledging Vernon's intention. "Marilyn Monroe–blond, I'll have you know." She wept through her laughter and wiped her cheeks.

Alma pulled out a brochure from her law bag. "I was thinking of the chapel at Rose Hill Cemetery in Liberty Park."

"Don't you think first we ought to find out if she was a member of a church or something?" Sue said.

"Her mother was a Pentecostal," Merl said.

"Pentecostal?" Sue asked.

"Snake handlers!" Vernon said simultaneously.

"Not all of them," Merl replied, a coat of defensiveness in her tone. "In our day it was the only one within walking distance, and church was the place to meet boys. Well . . . till the Midnight Market opened down at the Route Ninety-nine turnoff."

"Okay, I'll look for a Pentecostal minister," Alma said. "Not the snake-handling variety."

The sharp crack of shattering glass came in the same instant that the shards sprayed them. Alma saw the flash of a body run past the broken window. "Everybody down," she screamed. "He might have a gun!"

Vernon covered Sue and Merl's bodies with his own. Alma crouched down behind the oak door and waited until she heard the voice of the policeman from the patrol car. She opened the door and pointed in the direction of the fleeing attacker. Watching him disappear around the trailer, then turning to see her family covered with glass, anger surged through her. She rushed outside to give chase.

She saw the back of a black motorcycle jacket as a six-foot man jumped a chain-link fence into the neighboring yard. The policeman struggled to heave his body over the fence and ended up landing on his backside. Alma looked ahead to see that the attacker was trying to make it to the mountain. He appeared to be alone. She ran back to the front of the trailer and to the end of the cul-de-sac, intending to cut him off. In her mind, the name Cash McGee repeated itself.

A dog tied up in a yard barked, and Alma knew she was ahead of the suspect. She cut between two trailers, slipping in mud and jumping over an open drainage pipe. Round the corner of a trailer she slammed into the man. The force of the collision sent her sprawling. She twisted around and froze. Above her, a blond-haired boy held an iron pipe. His face was twisted with rage. "You get out of my house," he yelled.

"Danny?" she asked.

"You get out of my house and let my mother out of jail!"

"Danny, I'm your mother's cousin." Alma managed to rise to her knees.

The boy swung back the iron pipe and Alma put her hands up in front of her face. "She don't have nothing to do with Blackburn," he said. "Let her out of jail or you'll all be sorry!"

"Look at me!" Alma shouted. "Look at my face. I'm your cousin."

The boy squinted. The mistrust in his eye didn't lessen, but her features clearly startled him. He lowered the pipe an inch and stepped toward her cautiously.

"Danny, we have to talk," Alma said softly. She stood to her full height, every movement slow and careful.

"Yonder he is!" The policeman ran up behind Alma. She turned to stop him and saw his drawn gun. Danny's pipe sailed past her and struck the officer on the shoulder. The policeman aimed.

"No!" Alma yelled and brought both arms up underneath the service revolver. The weapon discharged in the air as she shoved the officer backward. Alma turned again. The boy was gone.

After a cursory search of the woods, the policeman returned to tell Alma he hadn't found Danny. She could tell by his defensive attitude that he held her responsible for losing him. Frankly, she didn't care. The police locating her cousin was the worst thing that could happen, considering their trigger-happy disposition toward the boy. She took Vernon aside, described the events of the last quarter hour, then asked, "Do you think you can find him?"

"I'd better," Vernon said. "Look . . . " He bit his bottom lip and twisted his body to one side. "I'm not supposed to tell you this, but . . . " He hesitated, looking up at the ceiling.

"Give." Alma squeezed his arm.

"Jefferson thinks Danny might be mixed up with some ole boys that run a meth lab here in Quinntown. Thing is, the top dog is brother-in-law to Chief Coyle."

"By the name of Blackburn?" Alma asked.

Vernon nodded and spoke in a whisper as he glanced at the policeman. "Yeah, Jimmy Blackburn. They want Danny more than we do. They want him bad . . . 'cause they don't know what he's gonna say to you. They didn't know Kitty was related to you until she died . . . all the publicity."

"Oh, God." Alma let loose a wave of fear she'd been trying to suppress. "I'm not only responsible for Kitty's death, I've also put Danny in danger." She held tightly to her brother's arm. "You have to find him, Vernon. We have to get to him before the police or Coyle's relatives— this Blackburn person."

"Alma, don't take this on yourself. Jefferson don't think the strikers have anything to do with Kitty's death." Vernon lowered his head to make sure Merl and Sue couldn't hear him. "It could be the drug dealers. No telling what kind of trouble the boy got hisself into. Kitty's death could have been a warning to him."

"That boy is in way over his head." Alma moved away and stepped out onto the front porch. "They're not protecting me," she said, looking at the police cruiser, "they're watching me." She called to the policeman, "I don't need you any longer," and waved him off. "Go on, now. I'll okay it with Chief Coyle." She watched as the officer reluctantly got into his car and immediately began to call over his radio. Coyle was probably getting a full report. No wonder he's delaying so much on the investigation, she thought. He's trying his damnedest to get a patsy and probably doesn't care if it's the strikers or Danny, as long as his brother-in-law is protected.

"A modern-day moonshiner," Alma said under her breath. Unfortunately, she lived in a part of the country that the DEA didn't pay a lot of attention to. It was a problem she couldn't even safely attack. The drug dealers in Applachia had left as many bodies littering the mountains as the moonshiners had once left revenue agents. She had to find Danny and take him out of the state. That was the only way to ensure his safety. His words echoed in her head, *Let my mother out of jail.* The poor boy didn't even know his mother was dead.

11

The wheels of the 1998 Harley spit rocks and dirt over the edge of the cliff. Alma buried her head against Ian Corey's back as he steered dangerously close to a twenty-foot drop. Through squinted eyes, she saw the railroad track at the bottom of the cliff, looking like it might rise up to meet her at any moment. She squeezed her eyes shut rather than look again. Her arms tightened around his waist as the steady vibration of the bike became inconsistent lurches.

She lifted her head and looked over his shoulder. They'd left the road and were swerving along the bank of a gully above her house. Ian let out a whoop as he killed the motor. The bike coasted to a stop beside her toolshed. He swiped the kickstand, leaped off, turned, bowed, and offered his arm to her.

"I said a short ride down the hill," she managed to croak.

He smiled, as if some part of him enjoyed making her uncomfortable. "On a Harley, there's no such thing as a brief ride."

"I could sue you for this." She grabbed his arm to steady herself and led him toward her house. "But right now I want to dig into that Häagen-Dazs ice cream."

The sky faded to evening twilight and her windows

caught the last glimpses of the sinking sun. At the top of the mountain her house seemed like a jewel set into the side of the rocky wall. Shortly after she'd decided to stay in Contrary, Mamaw deeded her the property on the northern slope of the mountain. It was a good quarter of a mile away from the other Bashearses' houses in the hollow, and Alma liked it that way.

She'd begun plans for the house the previous spring: two stories, with a view of the town. When the roof deck was finished, she'd be able to stand on it and see the entire Midnight Valley. But what she looked forward to most was sitting outside on summer nights and staring up at a pageant of stars and constellations. She'd done that so often as a little girl, many times holding her father's hand as they climbed to the top of the mountain on summer nights and lit a campfire to roast marshmallows. Now, she had that same beautiful sight again.

As Alma held the door open for Ian to enter, she glanced at Venus peeking through the dusky summer sky, soon to be brilliant. Inside they plopped down on a tan leather couch that faced a western window forming the entire wall and looking down on the valley and the setting sun. Alma dipped out half the softened strawberry ice cream into two bowls and centered them on a glass coffee table.

"Bet the ride took your thoughts off your day," he said.

"When fearing for my life, I do find it difficult to dwell on strikers, stalkers, and Yellow Jacket Stingers." The *Contrary Gazette* was spread on the floor, the front page halved into sections about the strikers at the Highland Toy Factory and the murder at Silver Lake.

"We can do it again," he said, wide-eyed and expectant, grabbing her hand.

"Eat," she teased and pushed a spoonful of ice cream into his mouth. She sucked over the strawberry flavor and let the taste fill her senses. Resting back into the couch, releasing the tension in her muscles, she said, "I've been so close to death these past few days—seeing what it does, how it frightens, how it controls—it's made me appreciate some of the simpler pleasures."

"These people who are blaming you," Ian said, glancing at the article that suggested that Kitty was killed by strikers believing she might have been Alma, "they don't realize they inflict as much pain as the original transgression."

"The workers think I've betrayed them," Alma said. "And if it turns out that one of them is responsible for this—then I *am* partially responsible." She swallowed more ice cream to keep from choking on her words. "But there's a lot to be found out before we know what really happened."

"Meaning?"

"There are other suspects."

"Sometimes, you never find out why things happen." Ian scraped the bottom of his bowl and scooped out more ice cream. "My mother killed herself when I was fifteen, and I spent a lifetime trying to figure out what I'd done."

"Ian," Alma said, putting down her bowl, "you are intelligent enough to know the difference between what a child believes and what an adult knows is a human's free choice."

"I steeled myself to death after that." He said the words as if they were a line of poetry he was reading from a book.

Alma repositioned herself, pulling her legs up underneath her. The heaviness of his muscular body on the leather couch caused her to lean in his direction. "Losing a mother to suicide must be one of the worst things a child could go through, especially at fifteen. I lost my father at ten, and in so many ways I find I've never gotten over it." She fought down an involuntary shiver.

"What the dead leave behind can be scarring."

"His absence made me realize that death makes love such a tormenting emotion."

"I took responsibility for my younger brother after my mother's death. We lived in the streets mostly and for a while off the land. I never adjusted well to social services. Guess I was a bit of a rascal."

"I've always heard welfare's much better in Europe," she said, surprise in her voice.

"Maybe it was me." He shrugged his shoulders. "You know, it only takes one person to frame a kid's perspective on what is good and bad."

His view caused Alma to reflect. She could see from his inwardly focused expression that there was more of a story here than he was willing to share. "Amazing you turned out so well."

His face colored slightly in embarrassment, and he looked away. "My brother is still a wildcat, but a harmless one." He leaned past her to spoon out another scoop of ice cream. "For me, the turning point was late one night on the shores of Stonehaven, staring out at a sky full of lightning and wind raging with thunder, sitting there in the rain, scaling a fish and eating it raw because I was so hungry." He bit into the ice cream, his eyes seeming to focus on the distant memory. "I realized the rest of my life was going to be this cold, hungry, soulless world unless I did something . . . anything."

"And you did . . . what?"

"I went to school." He laughed as if the simple answer he gave were the punch line of a joke. "I walked up to the schoolyard and told the school mistress that I wanted to learn." He set his bowl on the floor and pointed to a wall full of books. "If I wanted to be superior then I had to know more than everybody else. And several scholarships, fellowships, and loans later, here I am."

Alma studied his angular face, rough and shadowed with an end-of-day beard. His black ponytail was tied with a golden-colored crocheted band at the nape of his neck. He seemed like both an intellectual and a curious child looking for the next adventure. "You've come a long way from that abandoned boy," she said, picking up the ice cream container to share the last of it. "You hide him well."

"We all hide things." Ian reached out and touched the tip of her nose. "The first time I saw you, I thought to myself, 'Now there's a woman with a few secrets to her.' " He leaned back, bending one arm behind his head so that the muscle flexed into a bulge that looked as hard as stone. "It was a face whose secrets I couldn't help wondering about." He hesitated. "Like why you won't come to Jesus Falls."

Alma felt her skin warm up despite the frosty ice cream. As the creamy taste swirled around in her mouth, she watched him, reflecting how much his hurts were parallel to her own and recognizing how those wounds defined them as adults—formed them to become driven people for whom relaxation always seemed to come as a surprise. Right now, his company made the outside world seem not to exist. She used it as an escape, knowing that the happiness he was giving her was temporary. "I'm going to show you something I bet you've never seen before." She pulled the ice cream spoon out of Ian's mouth and dropped it on the table.

"Will I need clothes?" he asked with a grin.

She tapped him on the top of the head, grabbed his hands, and pulled him up. "You keep your clothes on, buster." She held open the screen door, and they stepped into the backyard.

He turned away to look at the view of the valley. The nearly full moon was directly overhead, stars dotted the heavens, and the air was still warm from the day. "I conduct a university tour somewhere in the world about every two years," he said, "and in all my travels, I don't think I've seen a more perfect view. I always tell my students that to understand a country, they must study its landscape, its perfections and its flaws, and therein they'll find the soul of its people." Below them, fireflies beamed off and on among the trees and thousands of crickets chirped like the warm-up of an orchestra. "Now, let's see you top this."

"It's up the hill, just a little ways." Alma unhooked and lit a kerosene lantern hanging on the porch, then pocketed some matches and candles from a storage shed. As she walked up the dirt path, Ian came up behind her and took her other hand. "No one else in the world knows about this place," she said. "And I'm only showing you because you're leaving at the end of the week."

"There aren't any spiders up here, are there? I fear spiders." His voice contained a sense of adventure, and she felt his strength in the warmth of his hand. In his company, she felt safe.

Fireflies dotted the woods, making the pathway seem like a magical tour of a world inhabited by fairies. The ragged bark of birch trees cast silvery reflections; green moss-covered rocks and the occasional red reflection of a rabbit's eyes in the glow of the lantern were accompanied by the delicate scent of honeysuckle that breezed past them like the whiff of an elegant perfume counter.

"Here," she said and pulled back a layer of kudzu vines. "Fire up a candle, and I'll lead the way." She hung the lantern on a rusted nail driven into the rock, lit a candle, and stepped into the round entrance to a cave then turned to hold the foliage. "This used to be my secret hiding place when I was a kid." The temperature dropped as they stood inside the entrance. He rubbed her arms up and down to warm them.

"Will I find Elvis here?" he joked as he lit his own candle. "Memphis is scheduled on our tour."

"I'll hum 'Love Me Tender.' " Alma led Ian through a narrow passage that opened into a round space ten feet in diameter with knee-high boulders circling a pond fed by dripping water from stalactites above. The cold temperature began to sink in and she shivered. She lifted the candle so that the purplish roof sparkled with reflected light as if diamond dust had been thrown upward and attached to the rock.

"Beautiful," he said, bringing his own candle down to rebound on the dark surface of the pond. "That you would trust me enough to bring me here . . . " He stopped and reached out. With one finger he traced her lips then let his hand caress her cheek.

She took his hand in hers and kissed the tips of his fingers.

"I don't want to be presumptuous," he said.

"No," she said softly, hesitating the slightest moment and hating herself for it. "I know what I can do and what I can't. You are leaving at the end of the week."

He nodded and smiled gently at her, the candle flame reflecting in his dark amber-colored eyes. Then he took both candles and fastened them onto the head of a stalagmite.

"If you listen carefully," she told him, "the drips of water from the ceiling make a little song." Quietly, they listened and she hummed the tune.

He drew her into his arms. They stood close and slowly

danced to the music of the cave. "I think I hear Elvis," he whispered in her ear.

She smiled to herself with delight. After a few moments they broke apart, and looking into his eyes, Alma wished that she could lift her face to kiss him. But something held her back—not a fear of loving him, but a fear of losing him. In her heart, she knew it would hurt too much. "I have something else to show you," she said, breaking the intensity of their shared feeling.

"I don't know what could be more excellent than this," he said, somewhat dazed.

Alma pulled Ian over to a pile of rocks and held the candle up high. "No spiders. I promise." Stacked into the stones was an antique rifle. It was cocked open and held in place with an arrangement of small sticks. "It's an 1853 Springfield rifle. If you look at an angle, you can see it's loaded." She pulled back the trap on the rifle for him to look inside.

He peered at it closely but seemed to know better than to touch. "This is a great historical find, Alma."

"I know," she said, closing the metal trap to protect the cartridge. "I could easily get some professors from Kingsley University over here and put this into a museum, except, the only thing is—"

"They'd have to find out about your secret hiding place." He laughed. "I knew the answer to that."

"Selfish of me, I guess."

"Not really," he said "I am beginning to understand the secrets behind that face." He stroked her cheek. "And I am sorry to be leaving, but you've created one diary entry that will be in my memory for a lifetime."

As Alma headed toward bed that night, she couldn't help letting her imagination wander—wouldn't it be nice if Ian got a job teaching at Kingsley University? The time they could spend talking, exploring the depths of each other's minds, learning about the other's experiences and how each had formed their view of the world. Though Alma didn't regret returning to Contrary, living away for most of her adult life had formed a cosmopolitan outlook. The unique mountain community remained a legacy she felt honor bound to protect, but in taking that challenge, she cut herself off from the opportunities that not only might have fulfilled her career potential but also her emotional needs. In this last year she had come to realize that romance might be a casualty of her decision to come home.

She picked up her law bag and set it in the hallway before starting up to the bedroom. The moon positioned in the skylight at the top of the stairs was a few slices from full. The near fullness of it reminded her of the snow globe, and she returned to her bag to get it.

Flipping open the flaps, she dug through several compartments. She didn't find it and went out to search her car. Not there either. She inspected the law bag again, finally emptying it. The snow globe was gone. Certain that she'd returned it after showing it to her family that afternoon, she retraced her steps in her mind. No one else had been close enough to get into her bag without her noticing, except for the short amount of time when she'd run from the house to chase Danny.

Someone in her family had to have taken it. Alma reviewed the possible motives but came up with no answers. She hadn't even told them that Charlotte Gentry had given it to her. Why had they taken it unless they recognized the snow globe or the name Allafair Adair? And why did they hide this knowledge from her? Someone in her family had a secret. A secret they didn't want her to know.

12

Mayor Hudson smashed a Wedgwood vase against the wall, causing a bevy of secretaries to run into his office to see if everything was all right. "Get the hell out of here!" he yelled at them. He stormed from one side of the room to the other, rounding a seated Alma and passing Chief Coyle, who leaned against the wall. "Did you just say to me," he demanded and shook his finger at Alma, "that this damn investigation is none of my damn business?"

"I believe I used more diplomatic language," she answered, deliberately lowering her voice to counter his ranting.

"Everything that goes on in this town is my business," he said hotly. "You might work for the state, but this is my town, Miss Bashears." Hudson plopped down in his leather chair, air hissing from the springs. "Until somebody takes my job, it's best you not forget it."

"You instructed Chief Coyle to divert men from the homicide division to burglary?" Her voice rose the slightest degree, but she kept it controlled enough to let him know she would not be bullied. "Don't you think at a time like this the three priorities are to find Cash McGee, determine his involvement in the Sloat murder, and to locate Danny?"

The mayor leaned back in his chair, his face filled with a

politician's smile. "You make it sound like we're a big city crime force. We have four detectives. There's three on burglary because of all the trouble at the Highland Toy Factory—most of which you caused. Kitty Sloat is only the second murder this year." He leaned forward on his desk and spread open his arms in a conciliatory gesture. "I understand your personal involvement, but let this town take care of itself."

"What about my cousin's son?" Alma asked, her voice edged with anger. "If his mother's killer is still free, he could be in danger."

"There's no evidence of that," the mayor said.

"There's no evidence that I was the intended victim either. In fact, since I've ditched my Contrary bodyguards, not a soul has tried to harm me. What do you think that says?"

There was silence in the room as the mayor rubbed his forehead. "I think it best if we tried to locate the boy using more low-key methods. You know, no sense scaring him out of the area."

Alma started to speak up, but she sensed a plausibility gap and wondered why the mayor was suddenly more passive. "Why are you determining how the police department investigates its case?" Again there was silence. She looked back at Coyle, who chewed on a toothpick and stared at the floor. He still hadn't said a word—intentionally, she realized. A misdirection in order to protect somebody— but who? "I'd like to talk to the Quinntown police," she said, watching Coyle with a sideways glance. The foot he had jacked up on the windowsill came down. He grimaced at the mayor. "Who knows, they might know something about the way Kitty and Danny lived that could shed some light on things. Don't you think?" She looked back and forth between the two of them.

The mayor bit his bottom lip and jiggled the keys in his pocket. "My ulcer's bothering me," he said and slapped the intercom button to summon his secretary. "This damn Highland Toy strike. I wish I'd never heard of a Yellow Jacket Stinger."

Alma waited as he drank liquid straight from a cobalt-blue bottle. She suspected he changed the subject to avoid a discussion of Quinntown's drug trade, which raised her suspicions of how much Contrary's police force must be involved.

A drop of milky white substance dripped from the side of the mayor's mouth and he wiped it off as he centered the bottle on his desk. His hand rubbed his stomach, then he pulled a pack of cigarettes from his top desk drawer. She started to speak, but the mayor stood up and said, "I've got an appointment. I can't talk about this anymore." He turned to the window and stared at the building far across the courtyard where her office was located. "That damn strike committee and Highland's management are going to meet here—at my urging, of course." He held his hands behind his back. "Now, take my advice and give us some time to work things out."

Alma crossed her arms. She didn't mind that he was taking credit for her idea, but she was worried that he'd manipulate a settlement in favor of Highland's management. Mayor Hudson walked toward her, lit a cigarette, and blew downward. She waved a hand through the whitish smoke. "My mother is refusing to even schedule a funeral until Danny is found," she said, standing to avoid another stream of smoke. "If by the end of the week Cash McGee is not in custody, and Kitty's son not delivered safely into my hands . . . " She paused to look directly at Coyle. "Rest assured I will call the State Police and get them involved and in charge of this case." She opened the door and stepped into the outer office. "By the way, I heard about your little petitions circulating to have the state attorney general remove me from office." The mayor's face reddened. "Send one over to my building. I'll post it on the bulletin board." She closed the door but purposely left it ajar. Alma took a few steps then surveyed the area. No one around. She returned to the mayor's office and leaned into the crack of the opening.

"I leave this in your hands," she heard the mayor say. He could only have been speaking to one person. Chief Coyle.

"Is eavesdropping part of the job for the commonwealth attorney these days?" a voice behind her asked.

Alma jerked around so quickly that the mayor's door nearly flew open. She grabbed Jefferson by an arm, pulled him out of the reception area and into an alcove with candy machines and a manned coffee vendor. "I know about Quinntown," she said. "Coyle's so nervous, he's about to jump out of those snakeskin boots."

"There are a lot of issues involved here, Alma." Jefferson's voice warmed and she recognized the man she knew so well. "Don't get involved in that side of things. It's too dangerous."

She reached up, hugged his neck, and whispered in his ear, "They might have killed Kitty. I must protect Danny."

"I wish I could say more," he told her. "Right now, we can only hope for the best."

"Jefferson, you're still hiding things from me." She pushed herself away from him. "All the hurtful words that have passed between us are just like twelve-year-olds getting out their last bit of adolescence. Is there any reason to be this way with me?"

"Then buy me some coffee as a peace offering. I have ten minutes before I see the mayor."

They stood in line for the coffee vendor. "Hudson just told me he'd set up a meeting. I'm glad he did that, but I'm afraid it doesn't help my reputation with the strikers."

"When the facts come out, people will know whose side you're on."

"Now tell me what you know about the Quinntown drug dealers, especially Blackburn." She ordered two coffees and handed a five-dollar bill to the vendor.

The man looked at the money then up at her. "We sell union coffee here," he said and spit on her hand.

Alma stepped back at the same time that Jefferson pulled her aside. He reached across the counter and knocked over the entire pot, causing the man to curse. Both of them brushed through a scattering of people to get away.

They parted outside the mayor's office. "Are you okay?" Jefferson asked.

She nodded even though her stomach lurched. She frowned. "I'll get the Feds involved if you can give me enough information on Blackburn to whet their interest."

He shook his head. "Alma, for now, you'll just have to trust me." He touched her shoulder to calm her.

Alma peered in after Jefferson as he entered the mayor's office and saw that Hudson was alone. She continued down the hall, but her thoughts kept coming back to the oddness of a meeting between only Jefferson and the mayor. Why wouldn't the strike committee or Highland's management be there? She chose to walk down four flights of steps instead of using the elevator to give her some recovery time from the coffee vendor's ugly insult.

She looked up at the sound of someone hurrying down on the staircase above her. The person suddenly stopped. She continued down another flight and the steps behind her began again.

She halted and the footsteps stopped. "Is someone

there?" she asked. No answer. Her heartbeat pounded, and she realized she was holding her breath. Again she continued down and the footsteps behind her started. They were heavy, but she couldn't tell if it was a man or a woman. She waited at the turn of the staircase, but so did the person behind her. "Hello?" A few seconds passed. "I know you're there." No response. A jolt of adrenaline outpaced any alertness that caffeine could have put in her system. She exited the stairwell and raced to the lobby.

Once in the safety of a crowd she waited at a pay phone to see if anyone came from the stairwell. The only person she saw was Chief Coyle, marching from the elevator with the quick strides of an angry man.

13

As Alma pulled into her mother's driveway her stomach felt as if it were full of tadpoles metamorphosing into frogs. Why would a member of her family steal the snow globe? Perhaps someone knew the secret behind it. Ever since the globe had disappeared, she'd expected someone to come to her. The story behind that doll's face involved a secret to be hidden at all costs, she thought. There were far too many of those in her life.

She turned off the ignition and sighed. Pulling information out of Sue and Vernon would be like extracting teeth. Her mother, on the other hand, could never keep her mouth shut.

Merl lived in a middle-class residential area populated by "retirees and divorcees," as she described it. The red-brick house was a one bedroom with a large basement below ground. The basement had been transformed into one of the largest bedrooms Alma had ever seen. All the usual basement items—water heater, washer, dryer—had been shoved into other parts of the house.

Two days' worth of newspapers lay on the porch. Alma fought a spear of apprehension as she knocked on the door. After several seconds she knocked again, harder. No one answered.

Down the block she saw Sue's blue Buick parked about

fifty feet away. She would have preferred to talk to her mother alone. Until she knew the meaning of Charlotte's gift and figured out who'd taken it, limiting her family's involvement would avoid trouble with the Gentrys. For reasons Alma never clearly understood, Merl had a way of twisting Mrs. Gentry's arm. The flare of a memory— Charlotte shouting at a teenage Alma, demanding that she had to leave town and throwing a handful of cash in her face. Merl had stood up to the town's matriarch, forcing her to triple the bribe. Alma never knew how her mother managed this and the shame of taking the money caused her never to ask.

Alma walked to the side of the house and peered down the walkway. Her mother's red-and-white Plymouth sat in the backyard. The shades were drawn on the upstairs bedroom window and the basement. A sense of alarm began to replace Alma's nervous anticipation.

"Momma!" she yelled. No answer. She returned to the porch, jiggled the door handle, and kicked over the newspapers still leaning against the stoop. When she peered in a front window she saw the evening news on the television.

After banging on the door again, Alma tried the rear entrance. It was locked, too. Through the window she saw her sister's coat and purse on the kitchen table. "Okay," she said, "Sue got in somehow." A window over the kitchen sink was half open, but she wasn't sure she could get through it. She pulled a lawn chair across the yard, stood on it, and slid her head and torso inside the house.

"Sue! Momma!" she shouted. No reply. A spigot pressed into her chest as she grabbed the edge of the sink and pulled herself in. One elbow caught on the faucet handle, and cold water sprayed her in the face. "Damn it!" She struggled to turn the water off and landed sideways on the kitchen floor.

Indistinct voices rose and then faded into a pool of white noise. She thought perhaps she'd heard the television. In the living room she switched it off and listened. The voices were underneath her—in the basement.

On the kitchen table she noticed an unusual clutter of family pictures and yellowed newspaper articles. She picked up a photo of her mother and father. They were young enough to be teenagers. Her mother's hair was a light ash blond and her father's as black as coal. Both of them stared into the camera, unsmiling and intense. Her father's arm encircled Merl's shoulders. Other pictures included her, Sue, and Vernon as children. Several had been taken on the Thanksgiving her father left, including one of the entire family beside the packed-up car.

Alma put down the family photo, shaking off the pain it conjured up inside her. The newspaper articles reviewed her father's disappearance. LOCAL MAN FEARED DEAD IN DETROIT. ESAU BASHEARS: STILL MISSING AFTER 3 MONTHS. THE MYSTERY OF ESAU BASHEARS. A wave of hurt shuddered through her body as the memories of those years surfaced. She took several deep breaths. "Okay," she said, "let's find out what's going on."

As she headed for the entrance to the basement, the sound of voices ceased. She knocked loudly and called out, "Is anybody there?" With a jerk she pulled open the door and stepped down the spiral wooden staircase. She met Sue halfway.

"Would you stop that banging!" Sue's face was crinkled like a squeezed sponge. "There's something serious going on."

"How did you get into the house?" Alma asked.

"I used my key."

"You have a key?" Sisterly jealousy welled up in Alma's chest. Sue smirked. "Where's Momma?"

Sue pulled her up the stairs, back to the utility room. "Locked herself in the basement. Alma, I can't get her to come out."

"When did this happen?"

"I don't know. I came over because she hasn't answered the phone and her boyfriend called me to find out if she'd dumped him."

"Has she?"

"I don't think she's been out of that basement all day."

"Or maybe it's the other way around. He is a little young for her."

"Well, it's not like there's a wealth of men in this town. You ought to know that."

Alma rolled her eyes. "Are you telling me we're dealing with unrequited love?"

"I don't know what we're dealing with, but I can't get her out of bed. She's lying there crying, holding on to a stack of papers for dear life. I half believe they're love letters. And I'll tell you, Alma, if they are, I don't think I want to know about it."

"I thought she was a little too emotional the other day." Alma turned around and went back down. "Wait upstairs. I'll see what I can do."

At the bottom of the stairs Alma faced another door; it looked as if Sue had forced the lock. Splintered wood in the frame revealed the reddish tan of the underlying raw lumber. Alma pushed the door open and stepped into darkness, holding on to the wall until her vision adjusted. The room had the dusty smell of being closed up. She flicked on a lamp.

Her mother lay on a frilly canopy bed. The palpable misery in the room was incompatible with the pale pink walls and gold-speckled furniture. Merl's body was curled in a fetal position with her back toward Alma. A rose embroidered bedspread covered her.

In the corner a stereo played "Precious and Few" by Climax. Alma turned it off. "Momma, we're all upset about Kitty."

"Go away." Her mother's voice was hoarse.

"Momma." Alma sat on the bed. "Life is passing you by. You've never been one to like that very much."

"I don't know what you're talking about. I just want to be by myself."

"Momma, what's wrong?" Alma took her arm and tried to pull her up, but Merl wrestled free and tightened her body back into its curled position. A round object peeked through the folds of the covers. Alma pulled the blanket taut and the snow globe rolled toward her, the white flakes swirling around the miniature doll face. She picked it up. "You took this?"

"What are you talking about?" Merl turned to her with a completely puzzled look then saw that Alma held the globe.

"Tell me what this means."

Her mother sat up, leaning against the headboard. She had made the room as dark as possible by pulling all the curtains across the basement's series of high windows that ended just above ground level. "Don't you remember? Don't you remember anything about it?" Merl clutched a pack of letters tied with a pink ribbon. When she noticed Alma looking at them, her eyes filled with tears and she rocked back and forth squeezing the packet.

"Remember what?" Alma asked, a deep-toned ache constricting her throat.

"You were the prettiest little girl." Her mother's gaze drifted toward the ceiling as if her reality were focused on another time. She reached out and touched Alma's cheek.

Alma got up and opened the curtains, letting in the full force of the last sunlight and causing Merl to cover her eyes. When she removed her hand, Alma hid her shock at her mother's appearance. She'd seldom seen Merl without full makeup. Her face was saggy and the skin tone a pasty pink. Her eyes, swollen from crying, had heavy bags underneath them, and her plain lips were flat against her face.

Alma dragged a chair over next to the bed. "Is there someone you can talk to? Aunt Joyce? Mamaw? I'll go get anybody you want." Merl looked away then pulled out an old Polaroid from the folds of her robe. Alma's hands trembled as she reached for the picture. A voice screamed inside her, *No, don't look, don't look.*

The photo was of Alma as a little girl. She and Sue stood beside their father, and Vernon, still a toddler, balanced on his hip. Alma clutched a doll. A doll with straight black hair and starburst gray eyes that matched her own. The porcelain face was colored with pink cheeks and cherry red lips.

"Your daddy got it for you, honey. For your birthday, just before he left."

Alma grabbed the globe and held it next to the picture. The Polaroid was over twenty years old. The porcelain doll's face in the snow globe, still cracked around the edges, could have come from any mass marketed–doll of the 1970s. Because they looked similar didn't necessarily mean they were the same, she rationalized. She has to be wrong, Alma told herself. How would Charlotte have gotten hold of a doll given to me by my father? And why would she preserve it like this and give it to me now?

Merl heaved several breaths in and out. "You wanted so bad to go with him to Detroit and cried 'cause I wouldn't let you." One of her legs dropped over the side of the bed with a sense of wistfulness.

"I hid the doll in his car," Alma said, her voice rising in pitch and the upset inside of her beginning to match her mother's. "I thought if he had it, it would be just like me going with him. It can't be the same doll."

"Look at the corner of the left eye." Merl pointed to the porcelain mask in the snow globe. "Don't you recall . . . you were so unhappy that you drew a teardrop from the baby doll's eye."

Alma held the snow globe up to the light, streaming through the window like a flood. Faded ink around the doll's eye matched what her mother said . . . and now matched her own memory of drawing the tear she'd been told not to shed on the day her father left. "Oh, my God." Thoughts raced through her mind like a waking nightmare. "How the hell did Charlotte Gentry end up with this?"

Her mother didn't answer.

In the light from the window, Alma could see a return address on one of the letters that Merl clutched. *Bashears, 646 Sandusky Road, Detroit, Michigan.* "Momma, those letters are from Daddy." Her voice softened, curiosity overtaking her. Merl tightened her grip on the packet, her focus still far away. Alma reached out and took hold of the letters.

"No!" Her mother twisted away, holding the letters tight.

Alma crawled across the bed after her, even as Merl kicked out a foot to stop her. "They're mine. I don't want anyone else to see them."

Alma snatched at a letter that had come free. The small cursive writing spelled out her mother's name. The envelope was postmarked January 1975. The sight of her father's handwriting flooded Alma with memories; then shock hit her. He had been reported missing on December 20, 1974.

She peeled open the letter and looked at the heading, the month January, the year 1975. "Momma, this letter—the date . . ."

Her mother's face seemed to break into a million pieces. Alma fought her own fears that rose up like an Old Testament demon. She grabbed her mother's arm. "Please, tell me." Merl jerked away, holding the remaining letters to her chest. "How many of them?" Alma demanded. "How many of them do you have?"

"I never wanted you to know."

Alma grabbed the entire pack of letters and looked at the first few. January 1975, January 1975, February 1975. The last one was April 1975. "What does this mean?" she asked slowly, leaning forward on the bed. She shook the letters in Merl's face. "What does this mean, Momma?"

Merl sobbed into her hands. "I never wanted you to know. I never wanted any of you children to know."

Alma pulled Merl's hands away from her face. "Tell me what this means, Mother! Tell me now! Is my father alive?"

14

Alma's house felt vacant. She collapsed into a kitchen chair and dumped the stack of letters on the table in front of her. Her father's tiny cursive writing was like rips in the paper. How can this be? she asked herself. Was he alive somewhere out there in the world? How could he have abandoned them? Did he have another family? Another daughter?

Her mother's hysteria had provided no answers and Alma had been too upset to discuss the matter with Sue. Now, alone in her own house, she touched the pieces of paper as if they were flesh and blood.

Holding a letter sent a chill through her even though the evening was warm and a film of sweat coated her skin. If the past was a tangled web of deceit, she knew that those lies would corrode the memory of her father and poison the future with her mother. She hesitated, then snapped loose remnants of old yellowed glue on an envelope that looked to have been opened and closed many times through the years. She pulled out a letter.

December 4, 1974
Dear Merlie-belle,
Double shifts again this week, not much sleep. It'll be worth it though to be able to get Vernon that bicycle

with the training wheels. I felt so sorry for him not being able to learn on Alma's big bike. The boy just needs a little confidence in hisself. Make sure you go down to JC Penneys and put two pretty Sunday dresses on lay-away for the girls but I reckon they'd rather have that tie-dyed stuff that's the fashion. I can just see Alma strutting down the road in that military way of hers— you can see her coming a mile off. She's gonna be one to cut paths, Merl, so don't you be too hard on her.

Alma dropped the letter and sobbed into her hands.

When she looked up later that evening her sight was so blurred she could hardly make out 8:15 on the stove clock. She wiped her eyes and inhaled deeply. Every joint in her body ached, and the cinnamon smell of her kitchen no longer offered the warm comfort she cherished. As much as she had to have answers, she hated thinking of what that knowledge might do to her—might do to her entire family. For a moment she wondered if any of them knew. It wouldn't be the first time her relatives had kept secrets, believing unpleasantness was best buried in the past. The past always finds a way to speak, she thought, shuffling the letters but unable to read another.

The shrill ring of the doorbell jarred her. "Oh, no," she said aloud. The bell sounded twice more, an insistent and almost urgent tone.

As she walked to the front of the house, she saw Ian through a glass atrium built off the living room. He moved to a side deck and looked down on Midnight Valley. The sun had set minutes before and the last of the light sent streaks of red, purple, and pink shooting up from the distant mountaintops. The glow of Contrary, cushioned into the mountains, looked like a long diamond-strewn path leading to a holy shrine.

Alma stopped at a hallway mirror and loosened her hair from the barrette that held it at the nape of her neck. She swept the strands close around her face, hoping to hide the signs of her recent emotions. Leaving the house lights off, she opened a sliding door to the deck.

"Ian," she called out. "I'm sorry. I can't see you tonight."

His back still to her, he said, "Your voice is full of sorrow."

Alma retreated into the darkness and covered her mouth, trying to hold back the pulse of anguish that threatened to spill over.

He glanced over his shoulder quickly then returned his gaze to the mountains. "We Scots are good listeners."

"Another time, perhaps." Alma said, determined to avoid his attempts to talk his way inside.

"I brought ice cream. I'll just put it in the freezer."

Before she could stop him, he was in the house. She backed up until she was against a chair. Realizing he'd frightened her, he stopped, held out a brown paper bag, then set it on a bookcase.

"I would appreciate it if you'd respect my privacy," she said firmly.

"Alma, you've been crying."

"No, I haven't."

"Liar."

She turned away from him and stepped into the living room. The darkness made her tan leather furniture look like crouching animals. A mirrored wall reflected their shadowy forms, Ian's slightly behind hers. "I'm not strong enough to have this argument right now," she said to his reflection.

She heard the sound of a scratch followed by a soft

golden illumination as he lit a candle. "I didn't come to argue." His voice softened, increasing the inflection of his accent. "Don't expect me to turn away. It's not my way."

The silence that ensued created a vortex of images in Alma's mind: her father, her mother, herself as a young girl waiting at the window for a man who never returned. In her confusion she sensed other thoughts—painful images of Ian as if he spoke to her of his longing for a love he hadn't found. The vibration was as strong as a flooding river. But his longing seemed more intense, as if the love he gave had been slapped away in one brutal stroke, and the child part of him looked on the broken pieces and wept at what would never be.

She felt the light pressure of Ian's hand on her back. It slid up to her neck and came to rest on her shoulder. "Everything in life is a risk," he said softly. His touch tightened slightly. "Life, love, death. When teetering on that edge of choosing, do you stay with what you know, or risk crossing over into . . ."

He turned her around toward him. His eyes caught the candle's reflection and the spicy smell of his cologne wafted around her. Alma's legs felt weak. "How can you dare not to know what is on the other side?" he whispered.

Her breath deepened as she stared into his amber eyes. She started to speak but could not find words, much less her voice. Her hands rose and rested on his chest to keep at least that much distance between them. His full lips rounded into words she couldn't make out and ended in a gentle stream of breath he blew around her face. He leaned forward against her hands. The muscles in her arms trembled and threatened to give even though the pressure of his body was slight. With each expansion of his chest her barriers gave way. He touched her chin with one finger, tilting her face up to his. "I'll only hold you. I promise."

As his arms closed around her, Alma felt her energy drain. What movement there was between the two of them was his, as if he cocooned her in his depths, and she surrendered to let him take care of her. His lips pressed gently against her ear. "Trust me."

15

"Almmmaaa . . . Almmmaaa!" Her eyes opened at the sound of her name. The applelike scent of another body covered her in a warm sweat. She and Ian were lengthwise on the couch, his body partially on top of hers, their arms encircling each other and his head resting in the crook of her arm.

"Almmmaaa!" the voice called again, closer to the house.

Ian jerked and lifted his head. He looked at her, at first confused, as if trying to remember where he was.

"It's my brother," she said, disengaging her legs from his.

"Good." He rose on an elbow and smoothed back his hair. "For a minute I thought I was in a Tennessee Williams play."

An embarrassed silence followed as she sat up. Alma avoided Ian's eyes, looking anywhere but at him. The path across the living room was strewn with her high heels, his boots, his vest, and a silk scarf she'd worn the day before. Otherwise, they were both clothed. Thank God, she thought.

Whatever madness had possessed her the night before became an unnerving reality as she stared out the window into the gray sheet of sky. She glanced at Ian and looked away just as quickly, hoping her appearance wasn't as disheveled as his.

"What do you want me to do?" he asked. She heard him scratch his shadow of a beard. Melted ice cream had pooled on the bookcase and floor.

"Uh, clean that up" was all she could think to say.

The sound of Vernon's footsteps on the porch made her shoot up from the couch. A wave of dizziness unsteadied her as blood rushed from her head. She stepped toward the door, trying to reach it before Vernon walked in. When she briskly smoothed her skirt, she saw the wrinkled linen was hopeless. Her shirt was pulled out on one side and she tucked it in haphazardly.

Vernon jiggled the door handle just as Alma opened it. "Uncle Ames and Uncle George aren't working on the house this week," she said quickly. "They're hunting."

Vernon took in her appearance in one swift look. "I know that," he said with a hint of impatience. He stared at her as if to demand entrance, but Alma continued holding the door to close him out. "They ain't leaving till . . ." He looked past her. "Hey, who's that?" He pointed at Ian who was down on his knees, wiping up the melted ice cream.

Alma twisted backward and Vernon kicked the bottom of the door, jarring it from her hand. Her cheeks flushed and she frowned. Her brother's stare was trained on Ian like a hunting dog spotting prey. When Alma turned to face him, Ian came up beside her in three quick strides. He smiled tentatively, his eyes fixed on Vernon's with the tension of a boxer awaiting the first punch.

"Ian Corey," he said, holding out his hand.

Vernon examined the hand for a second then shook it. The two men held their grip in a mock test of the other's strength. "Known Alma long?" he asked, pulling back his shoulders as if to measure his own chest span against Ian's.

Ian was slightly shorter than Vernon, but Alma noticed he straightened his back to even their heights and cocked his head to one side as he assessed Vernon. "Your sister and I have . . . known each other . . . for a while." He touched Alma's shoulder in a protective gesture.

"What did you want?" she asked her brother.

"Uh . . ." Vernon hesitated and stared at Ian. "You need to go down to Mamaw's house, now."

"Why?" She knew her tone was curt.

Vernon kept his eyes on Ian. "Just go," he said. "Trust me."

The echo of Ian's words from the previous night made her feel uneasy. She turned to Ian. "I'll only be gone a few minutes," she told him. "Will you wait?"

"Of course."

Alma ran back to the kitchen to retrieve her car keys. Her father's letters, scattered across the table, caused a lump in her throat. She gathered them up and placed them in a cabinet. When she returned to the front of the house, Vernon had plopped down on the couch and was surfing through television channels with the remote. "Are you coming?" she asked.

"Naw," he drawled. "Think I'll wait here and get to know E-an."

Alma glared at him. Ian walked her to the door. "Don't worry," he whispered. "I can hold my own. I have a brother, too, you know."

"Not like this one," she said under her breath.

He smiled and touched her cheek. She was grateful for his humor and easy manner. "I'll be waiting," he said and winked.

*   *   *

The drive down the hill was very short but it would have taken a quarter hour to walk back and forth. The clock showed 9:15 although Alma was certain it ran fast. She quickly called her office on the car phone and said she'd be late.

A misty fog had settled through the hollow all the way to the main road. She saw some of the Bingham's grandchildren playing in their front yard at the mouth of the hollow. Next to it the Fletcher and Gilbert houses appeared to be closed up. She wondered if the two old couples living there just didn't care for the rambunctious Bingham grandkids.

An image of Jefferson came to mind and she deliberately pushed it away. Thinking of him and the push-pull tension between them was just too confusing.

The Bashears extended family occupied the back end of the hollow. Sue, her husband, Jack, and their children, Larry Joe and Eddie, lived at the foot of the hill. Farther up, nestled into a saddle-shaped piece of land were houses belonging to Uncle Ames, Aunt Joyce, and her husband, George. Mamaw lived across the road from them where Vernon slept in a trailer in the side yard.

A burgundy Buick Regal parked in front didn't look familiar. The trailer, angled beside a tattered barn that housed a pack of beagles, three feral cats, and a pet opossum named Albert, had all its lights on. The front doors of both her uncles' houses were open, which made Alma suspicious of Vernon's motives. If other family members were already up and around, then he'd have gone to them if something was seriously wrong. For him to walk a quarter mile up the hollow to her house meant there was a situation in which he didn't want to involve his volatile uncles, who were just as likely to grab a shotgun as a flyswatter. For a moment she wondered if last night's events had found their way to Mamaw's door.

She got out of her car, walked onto the porch, and rested her hand on the doorknob, trying to read the mood of the place. "Mamaw?" she called out as she entered.

Voices in the kitchen indicated a direction. Her grandmother said, "In here, Alma." At the mention of her name Alma noticed that the other voice ceased speaking. She decided the visitor probably wasn't a relative.

Nothing short of a bolt of lightning could have jarred her more than seeing Cassidy Fuller and a heavyset, brown-haired woman who stood as Alma entered the kitchen. "Hello," she said. "I'm Danielle Fuller, Reverend Fuller's wife."

Alma stammered a hello. She looked down at the woman's outstretched hand and shook it. The coldness of Danielle's skin snapped Alma to her senses. Cassidy Fuller stared down at the table and would not engage Alma except for a "hello" so quiet it was almost a whisper. Her long blond hair was parted in the middle, the sides combed so forward it obscured most of her cheeks.

The aroma of French roast coffee filled the kitchen. The pinewood table, which seated twelve and could squeeze in sixteen, was centered between Alma and the reverend's wife. Alma got a hint of her liking it that way, as Mrs. Fuller pulled back from the handshake and slowly lowered herself into a chair as adeptly as the Queen Mother.

"Get yourself a bite to eat," Mamaw said to Cassidy and pushed a plate of steaming butter biscuits toward her. "No need to be so shy."

The girl picked up a biscuit and it broke apart spilling butter onto the table. Her trembling hand pulled back, bringing the bread to her lap as if to hide it. She looked at her mother, then at Mamaw, her face coloring a bright cherry. Realizing the grease was staining her dress, she returned the biscuit to the plate.

"They're always that messy," Mamaw said, handing her a napkin. "Nothing to be so worked up over."

Mrs. Fuller's icy stare at her daughter appeared to indicate that this was an embarrassment she'd have to repair. To deflect attention, she swiftly arranged a spread of glossy, expensive brochures about the Mirror of Our Soul Congregation toward the center of the table. Pushing glasses up on her nose, Danielle picked one up and handed it to Alma. "It's our way of letting people get to know us."

Alma looked at the picture of the Tudor-style mansion. The right side had an inset photo of Harlan Fuller, his eyes intense and a half-smile on his face that looked ready to say the words "trust in me." Scripted across the bottom was *Experience the Wonder.*

"Mrs. Fuller is visiting all the families in the hollows, Alma," Mamaw said and pushed out a chair. "She says they can even get my wheelchair into every part of their building." Mamaw backed up and rolled over to a cabinet where she retrieved a coffee mug for Alma.

"Interesting," Alma said, "that a church with mostly downtown people as members is now targeting the hollows."

"We call it our day of bearing witness," Danielle replied. "All our members spread throughout the community to teach, inform, and share." She waited to see if Alma would respond then continued. "It's one of my happier duties to be able to tell others how my husband's work has changed my life."

"It's changed a lot of people's lives," Alma said, thinking of Cash McGee. She slowly lowered herself in place opposite the reverend's wife and focused on her intently. "And what is it that you hope to impart, Cassidy?" Alma asked the daughter but continued staring at Danielle, suspecting the girl was this woman's weak link. Cassidy sat as still as a domesticated parrot knowing its cage was being watched by a cat. Her arms were straight with her hands neatly folded across her lap under the table. She glanced quickly at her mother, the insecurity in her eyes indicating her fear of saying the wrong thing.

Danielle touched her daughter's shoulder and spoke slowly to her, though she was answering Alma. "The twenty-first century needs women like Cassidy. She bears witness to the fact that these years are spent preparing herself for her place in a troubled and evil world."

"A noble cause," Alma said. "But so much responsibility for one so young." Mrs. Fuller gave her a false grin. While Mamaw made a fresh pot of coffee, Alma whispered across the table, "What are you really doing here?"

The minister's wife sipped from a cup and peered up at Alma over her glasses, but she could not sustain the negotiated stare. As she lowered the cup her eyes stayed steady on the table like a child about to lie. Alma fought the impulse to jerk her up by the hair and shake her hard.

"Mamaw," Alma said, picking up one of the slick brochures, "while the coffee's brewing, I'm going to show Mrs. Fuller around the hollow. Some fresh air will do us a world of wonder." She dropped the brochure on the table.

Danielle stood swiftly. "Oh," she cooed, "I'd just love that." She reached for her daughter's arm to pull her along.

"Why don't we let Cassidy keep my grandmother company?" Alma said, sure that what she was about to say to Mrs. Fuller would not be pleasant for the insecure girl. "Besides, I'm smelling a new batch of butter biscuits from the oven and Mamaw loves feeding them to visitors."

Outside, Alma chose a gravel path that led through a grove of royal fern. The spiky-leafed plants were nearly five feet tall and the ground beneath was damp and spongy from the early-morning rain. Orange-red wood lilies grew interspersed through the green ferns. Fuzzy drooping sedge hung around the edges of the path. Alma walked at a quick pace and heard Danielle panting heavily behind her.

"Let me be frank," Alma said, turning around. "Your church is under investigation for harboring a criminal. A visit to my grandmother's home might seem coincidental to some . . ." She crossed her arms. "But don't expect me to buy it."

"I assure you—"

"I'll be blunt. You do not have permission to seek out any of my relatives, so do your membership drive in another neighborhood."

"Some days I just have plain bad luck with witnessing." Danielle smiled and continued in a soft but patronizing voice. "Permission is such a controlling kind of word." She touched Alma's arm. "The smell of dew on wood is like an invitation to say thank you to a glorious world." Sucking in a deep breath, she turned aside to exhale then clasped her hands and touched her fingers to her lips. "Your grandmother's very worried about you." Not waiting for a response, she stepped around Alma and headed toward a sickle-shaped patch of moss at the edge of a cliff overlooking a winding creek. The gurgle of the water prompted her to speak louder. "She's afraid she made a mistake having you come back to Contrary."

"My grandmother isn't inclined to confide in strangers," Alma shot back, following her up the path.

"She's afraid you're always going to be alone."

"That's enough," Alma said abruptly and jerked Danielle around by her arm.

"You look like you're scared to death." Danielle put a hand on Alma's and squeezed it in a caring gesture. "Is the prospect of being alone so terrifying to you?"

"What I find terrifying is the way you try to dominate

simple people with New Age crap in the name of God. What's amusing is that you believe you can run this line of bull on me." Three whippoorwills took flight from a bush when the irritation in Alma's voice disturbed the peaceful forest.

Danielle continued as if a harsh word had never been spoken. "You're not alone, Alma. I'm here. You can reach out to me, Alma."

"Will you stop using my name like it's a mantra?"

"You think very poorly of us, don't you?"

"What I think is immaterial," she said firmly, controlling her anger. "Let me make this clear, and don't you ever doubt my words. My family is off-limits, Mrs. Fuller."

"Curious," she remarked, her brows knitting together. "You put you and yours off-limits to our outreach program, and yet . . . you have no qualms about peppering my daughter with numerous personal questions about my church, which is *my family*. Doesn't that strike you as a double standard?"

Alma waited several seconds before responding. It amazed her that Danielle would use such a thick-witted argument. "Now, we get to the truth of your visit. Well, let me make my concerns clear to you. My interest in your organization is professional. If your members, who include your daughter, don't want to answer my questions informally, then they'll answer them at the direction of a subpoena. I'm investigating a crime . . . a crime that may be far more serious than a shooting at the Highland Toy Factory."

"Ah." Danielle caught on to the end of Alma's sentence as if following a dance step. "But our interest is professional as well." She leaned down and picked a purple wildflower growing at the side of the path. Waving it under her nose, she inhaled, seeming to pull the strength of the flower out from the root. Danielle opened her arms toward the sun and spoke in a restful voice. "Your soul is very important to us."

"Is there any talking to you without the threat of conversion?" Alma said in a frustrated huff.

A whinnying moan rose from a thicket of high weeds to their right. "Did you hear that?" Danielle turned and looked out over the field. She raised a finger to her lips and listened intently. "It's in pain." She squeezed her eyes closed and cupped a hand behind her ear. A high-pitched squeak, almost like a bird's chirp, rose into the air. "It's over here." She stepped off the path and into a thick mass of ferns and weeds.

"There's snakes all over these woods," Alma called out. "Stay on the path!" Danielle continued deeper into the thicket. "Come back!"

When the weeds reached her chest, Danielle leaned down and disappeared from sight. Alma half expected the woman had put herself in harm's way purposely. If she got bitten by a snake, twisted an ankle, or broke a leg, then the Bashears family would be responsible. Furious, but with no choice, Alma plunged into the weeds after her.

Burrs attached themselves to her skirt and she got three snags in her stockings before she was within ten feet of Danielle. The soft soil was rocky enough to walk on but Alma's heels sank into the ground several times. By the time she was behind Danielle, a layer of malice covered her fury. "What is it?" she spat out. "Oh, my God."

Danielle stroked the head of Star, one of Vernon's beagles. She'd given birth to a litter of pups. Two of them sucked at her stomach and three were nestled like chicks on her hind leg.

Alma knelt down beside Danielle. She petted one of the tiny newborns. Star gently nudged her hand away, licking her whiskers on both sides as she stared up with large, brown, almond-shaped eyes.

"What's that?" Danielle pointed at three round bulges in the weeds behind Star's back.

"More pups," Alma said. "They didn't make it."

"Oh, no," Danielle brought a hand to her mouth, realizing the dog had lain on them. "She couldn't tell that she smothered them."

"No," Alma said. "Sometimes it's necessary to weed out the litter."

"What?" Danielle asked incredulously.

Alma stood and motioned Danielle back toward the path. "Let's leave her alone right now. My brother can come and get her later today."

"I hardly think she'd kill her own pups."

"Animals do that sometimes."

Danielle led the way back to the house as if she needed to get away from the scene. "I don't believe you."

"Well, I suppose you could chalk it up to bad luck." Alma turned and stared at her instructively. "I'm not an expert on Mother Nature," she said, "I can only tell you that sometimes it happens—for reasons only the dog knows."

Danielle looked puzzled for a few seconds. "We would never turn anybody away from our family."

"Including Cash McGee?" Alma asked.

Danielle walked over to her car and rested her hands on the hood. "I hope you and your family will take some time to look over the brochures I left." She slowly turned to face Alma with a trapped expression, as if she might have to fight her way out of this engagement.

"I'm waiting for an answer," Alma said. "Cash McGee?"

Danielle touched Alma's arm, letting her hand slide down

until she held her palm. "We would so look forward to an honest visit from you to our congregation."

Alma shivered unconsciously. The gesture was almost sexual and she stepped back to break the grip. "I feel I've been clear about my insistence that you not visit my family again."

"Some days, it's just bad luck." Danielle nodded and glanced down at the grass then up at Alma again, staring into her eyes for several seconds. "As you wish," she said in a low voice that bordered on a whisper, "but remember, I'll be here." She smiled, winked, and reached into the window to blow the horn once. As if it were a subliminal cue, Cassidy ran outside, her long blond hair flying behind her. She jumped into the car, locked her door, and looked up at Alma with a tense, glazed expression. The darkness under her eyes was set off by the pale blue color of her irises. It occurred to Alma that her quiet, hesitant demeanor was the norm while their previous encounter at the church was more like an imitation of her mother.

"Remember," Mrs. Fuller called out. "I'll always be here."

"That's what I'm afraid of," Alma said to herself as she watched the Buick drive out of the hollow. "What will they try to pull next?" That they had an agenda was something she never doubted.

"You could have warned me about her," Alma said, entering through the back door of her house and letting the screen door slam.

Vernon sat at the kitchen table looking at models in advertisements of the latest issue of *Vanity Fair*. "I didn't want to say anything in front of Mr. Muscles. He might've thought we were a dysfunctional family or something."

He bit into a slice of toast then helped himself to a swig of orange juice directly from the bottle.

"Where's Ian?"

"E-an had to de-part."

"Vernon," she groaned and anchored a hand on her hip.

"I didn't do nothing!" He raised his hands, palms up and chest high. "If I ever run off one of your boyfriends, I'd admit to it."

Alma noticed that the cabinet where she'd stashed her father's letters now stood ajar. She looked over at Vernon, who continued to flip magazine pages and didn't react when she closed the door. "I don't think Mrs. Fuller will be returning, but if she does, you call me immediately."

"You got yourself in a mess on this one, Sis." He wiped his mouth with the back of a hand as he stood up and burped. "Those people are like fly tape once they know you exist."

"Religion by mailing list."

"Ahh, I don't know." He scooted the chair under the table, sliding her magazines under his arm to take with him, then stopped to lean against the doorframe. "Some do a lot of good . . . maybe even the Fullers do some good in the world."

"The Fullers are only thinking of how to keep me from prosecuting Cash McGee."

Vernon nodded his head. "I guess I know that."

Alma sensed his tentativeness. "Vernon," she said, stepping toward him. "This is not about God. It's about people who use God for their own agenda."

"When Momma used to take us to church as kids, I'd spend most of the time trying to keep my eyes open." He shook his head as if shaking off an uncomfortable feeling. "You sure lightning ain't gonna strike you, Alma?"

"Fear is what they're counting on, Vernon." Alma put a

hand on his shoulder. "If they can scare you and every-body else in these hollows enough, then they've bent God to their own purposes. They call themselves servants of the Lord and expect no one will ever question them—the Fullers are more interested in your wallet than your soul."

"Yep." He pulled himself up straight. " 'Sides, if there's anybody who'll prosper in Hell, reckon it'll be me." He waved his hands at his feet as if fanning flames. "Now, to the good stuff. Where'd you get Mr. Muscles?"

"Ordered him from a catalog." She pointed to the door, indicating for him to leave.

"He ain't gonna take you on a spin on that brand-new Harley?"

"None of your business."

"Ain't never stopped me before. 'Sides, if you don't ask questions, you'll never know the answers."

"And don't you mention him to Momma or Sue."

"Alma." He paused on the porch, letting the screen door shut between them. "Seriously, I know I've been the one telling you to get out more . . ." His hesitation betrayed his ambivalence, as if he questioned himself even as he spoke. He reached out, letting one of his fingernails scratch down the screen. "But I don't like him."

His opinion surprised Alma. An embarrassed flush spread through her body. "He's not in town for long." She forced a smile. "By the way, Star had a litter of puppies about halfway up the trail leading to the creek."

"I been waiting for them to turn up," he said. "I got a line on Danny-boy. Anything turns up, I'll call you." He hesitated then said in a soft voice, "Take care of yourself, Sis."

Near the curve of the hill she saw him picking up rocks from the edge of the road and throwing them into the woods. After he was out of sight, she returned to the living room and collapsed on the couch.

The tangy smell of Ian remained, but it didn't bring back the warmth of the previous night. The house suddenly seemed too big. She wondered why she had built such a monstrosity. Did she really believe she might marry some day? Had she pretended there might be children—grandchildren? Wasn't her home meant to be the center for family gatherings? "You idiot." she said, looking out the atrium windows at the oak trees in the side yard. "You'll be ninety living here all by yourself and too feeble to get off the mountain."

Danielle's words haunted her with a dreadful sense of reality she wasn't ready to admit. *Your grandmother is very worried about you . . . She's afraid you're always going to be alone.* The words sank into Alma reviving a fear she'd secretly harbored. They repeated inside her head until she squeezed her eyes shut, blocking them out. Her reason told her Danielle had twisted Mamaw's words, if not outright lied. She hated not being able to control her thoughts, but she knew Danielle had scraped a raw nerve. *Always going to be alone . . .*

16

The buzz of activity in the commonwealth attorney's outer offices not only told Alma that she was late but that details of her cousin's grisly death had leaked out. A group of secretaries was huddled around a desk, their hands moving as quickly as their lips. They quieted as she passed, but the eyes following her made her as uncomfortable as the attacks from the Highland's workers.

When she opened the door to her suites a slew of assistants flew at her. She answered questions as she walked through the reception room and approved memos with a quick initial. "Val," she called out to her secretary. "I have a special job for you."

"Your sister's waiting for you," Val said, pushing her coffee-colored hair behind one ear.

Alma paused and looked through the open door of her office. Sue was on the floor playing with Larry Joe and Eddie, a wobbly skyscraper made of Tinkertoys between them. She pulled Val aside to ensure her sister didn't hear. "Call the Detroit Police Department and find someone who's willing to talk to me about a twenty-year-old missing person case. I'm going to want all the files as well. You know this is going to be difficult."

"They're going to put me on hold till the year two thousand."

"Do the best you can. Also, I need an appointment with Charlotte Gentry. Make it through her son because she's in Contrary Miner's Hospital. She's very ill, so pronto on that."

Sue stood when Alma entered and shut the door behind her. "I know what you're going to say—" Alma began.

"I had to stay the whole night with Momma," Sue interrupted.

"The whole night," Larry Joe echoed. "Daddy had to cook." He scrunched up his face, put a hand to his throat, and mimicked gagging.

"Well, better you than me." Alma laughed, determined to sound nonchalant. "Did she say anything more to you?" For now, she decided it was best that no one knew of what she'd discovered about their father.

"Meaning what?"

Alma dropped into her chair, the hunter-green leather exhaling as she leaned back. Eddie sprinted around her desk and threw out his arms. Alma picked him up and sat him in her lap. "I don't entirely know right now, Sue." Her sister's eyebrows peaked in an expression of disbelief.

"She didn't go to work today. The condition she's in, I doubt she'll make it all week."

"I'll go by and talk to her tonight."

"No," Sue said sternly. "You stay away from her, Alma."

"Come on, Sue, you know Momma's more dramatic than Bette Davis in a close-up." Eddie squirmed and slid off her lap. She opened her palms toward Sue in a consoling effort. Her intercom buzzed and she gestured for Sue to wait. Instead, her sister stood and told the boys to pack up the Tinkertoys. "One minute," Alma said as she picked up the phone. "Yes, Val."

"Harlan Fuller's here to see you."

For a second Alma was stunned. "He has no appointment." She noticed her sister watching her.

"He says it's important." Val's voice had a dreamy quality, as if she'd been seduced by Fuller's smile.

"I'll be right out." Alma hung up the phone and shrugged at her sister to indicate the interruption couldn't be helped. The intercom rang again. She punched the speaker button and said impatiently, "I said I'll be right out, Val."

"No," Val said. "I have a Detective Grady Forester from Detroit waiting to talk to you about that—"

"Great timing," Alma said quickly and cut off the intercom. She rounded her desk and took her sister by the arm. "If you can take care of Momma right now, I promise you, I'll have some answers soon." Sue motioned to her sons and stepped toward the door. "Sue," Alma said. "I can't promise they'll be the answers we want to hear."

Sue looked deeply into Alma's eyes, curious, questioning, but did not push her further. She picked up Eddie, securing him on her hip and held Larry Joe by the collar of his shirt. "By the way," she said at the door, "who's that man who spent last night at your house?"

Alma turned quickly to her desk and picked up the phone. She smiled tentatively and shooed Sue away with a wave of her hand, making a mental note to wring Vernon out the next time she saw him. "Detective Grady?" she asked.

"Detective Forester," the man's voice replied in a flat, unimpressed accent.

"Sorry," Alma said. As she began explaining what she wanted from him, she noticed a file marked CONFIDEN- TIAL in her priority basket. She stood up and stretched as she spoke then opened the file and thumbed through it. A picture of a nearly decapitated woman fell out. She dropped the phone. "Jesus!"

"Anybody there?" Detective Forester asked.

"I'm sorry," Alma said, picking up the phone with one hand and turning the picture facedown with the other. "Some friends left me an unexpected surprise." Across the back was written *This could be you.* She shivered, the image of the cut throat too conveniently like that of her cousin.

"Here's what I think," the detective said. "This is a hell of a lot of work and chances are the file's been shredded."

"But the case is unsolved." Alma fought to keep defensiveness out of her voice. "I realize how much I'm asking, but it's very important."

"Look, we get crackers from Appalachia into Detroit every day of the year. Some get killed. Some disappear. Some stay and some move away. Their kinfolk never hear from them again because they get sick of supporting twelve million cracker relatives who are too stupid to apply for welfare."

Alma bit the side of her mouth. "That's a rather bigoted stereotype, don't you think?"

"Bigoted, hell! I live in Detroit, lady! Don't talk to me about intolerance!"

"Detective Forester," she said loudly, intending to break the line the conversation was following. "We both know I could call your superior. It might take me a while, but eventually you'll have to go find the file I'm requesting. So—"

"Hardball with a girl-cracker—not bad. Guess I'll be enjoying my favorite way to spend a crappy weekend, going through twenty-year-old files that the cockroaches have half-eaten away."

Alma inhaled a deep breath and held it. She could hear

him slapping down papers and wished there was a way to make all of this more agreeable for him. "I'll be happy to return the favor some day."

"What's this yahoo's name? Egypt?"

"Esau," Alma said, softening her voice and trying to sound grateful. Even though she would like to slam down the phone on this rude man, she needed him. "Esau Bashears."

"Fine. And you are again?"

"Alma," she said and spelled it. "Alma Bashears." The silence that followed was tense. She knew he'd made the name connection and wasn't sure how he'd react. She hoped he wouldn't erupt again. "I realize," she said trying to sound sympathetic, "this is a lot to ask." The silence continued and she could sense him thinking.

"You got E-mail down there in the sticks?"

She swallowed her growing anger and replied politely, "You can reach me at bashears@falconer.com."

"Great," Detective Forester said, "you can get me at ignoramus.jerk."

The phone disconnected. Alma couldn't decide whether he would help at all and wondered if she'd ever get the file. Her father was nothing to him. For now she could only wait.

She turned the picture over and examined it for identifying marks. It was a black-and-white 8 x 10, and Alma knew whoever sent it had been too smart to leave fingerprints. What bothered her most was she couldn't tell if it was doctored, faked, or perhaps a real photo taken by a killer. This body could be out in the woods decaying and they just hadn't found it yet. One thing was sure. It would be pointless to hand it over to Chief Coyle.

She quickly jotted down the details of how she received it, resealed the information and picture in a fresh envelope, and printed Nathan Deever's name on the front. If this harassment exploded in a way she couldn't control, it seemed best to leave the evidence with someone she could trust. Once she had more evidence, she'd call the State Police. Inwardly, she prayed she could connect Coyle with everything that had happened, even if through his drug dealing brother-in-law. A new police chief would suit Contrary quite well.

When she exited the office, Harlan Fuller raised a hand and waved tentatively to her. He sat on the edge of the bench, smiling slightly. She'd forgotten about him and was sure her face must have shown an embarrassed flush. Cassidy stood behind her father. Alma couldn't help noticing how much more at ease she appeared than this morning with her mother. She was like a girl who'd broken the puppet strings. The top buttons of her shirt were open, her eyes were brighter despite some darkness underneath, and her hair was brushed into a fuller style that gave her narrow face more width. "Good afternoon," she told Alma. "I'm so thrilled to introduce you to my father."

"Mrs. Gentry isn't in the hospital anymore," Val said, stepping in front of the girl as if territory needed to be defended. "And they won't give out information to anyone who's not family."

Alma acknowledged the information and gestured to Fuller. "Hello, Cassidy," she said to the girl. "No introductions necessary."

The circles under Cassidy's eyes were evident despite heavy makeup. The girl's hollowed cheeks and pale skin betrayed an anxiety that she'd taken great pains to hide from her father. She was an adolescent ready to explode. "We felt this might be a good time to stop by for a talk," she said. She held her father's arm as if promoting him.

"Mr. Fuller," Alma said to the reverend. "Can't talk

right now, but please . . ." Alma smiled, opened the door and indicated the hallway. "Walk with me. I have a few things to say to you about your wife."

Both followed her into the hall. "I came to see you," he said, the richness of his voice mellowed in its softer tones. "I knew you'd want me to—"

"If your wife ever," Alma interrupted, "I mean, *ever* goes to my grandmother's house again, I will have every city, county, and state department devour your building looking for violations."

"I—I don't understand," he stammered.

They walked outside into the midday sun. It was as hot as June was going to get, and Alma let the heat build her anger. She stopped and faced him. "And when that is finished, the IRS may have to take a close look at your tax-exempt status. Chief Coyle might be too much of a chicken to take you on, but I'm not, and I have no sympathy for people who hide lawbreakers."

Fuller's eyes widened, almost puppy dog–like, and his lips parted the slightest bit, but he did not interrupt. He looked at Cassidy and his stature seemed to grow small and humble.

"I'll tell you about it on the way home, Daddy," his daughter said. "Mother went up into the hollows."

Alma realized that Fuller didn't know about Danielle's visit. A splash of guilt filled her, but she shielded her conscience, certain he was hiding Cash McGee.

"Uh . . ." He hesitated and looked down at the sidewalk. "I thought you would want to know," he said in a quiet, controlled voice. "I tried to find Chief Coyle but he's evidently out or he won't take my phone calls." Fuller's tongue flickered over his lips and he gestured with his hands as he spoke. "I didn't feel comfortable talking to anyone else there, so I came here—to speak to you."

Under pressure his facade failed him. It was almost as if without supporters praising him, his glowing charisma faded and he was as ordinary as the next man. She couldn't help thinking how much he seemed like a little boy. Even his daughter seemed embarrassed for him, and Alma noted how opposite she acted around her father than with Danielle. Cassidy had walked over to a helmeted man who sat on an idling motorcycle some yards away. Her lips moved in a whispered conversation with him. She glanced sparingly at her father, acting as if it pained her to see him in such circumstances. Alma closed her eyes, told herself to be kinder, and looked again at Fuller. "There is a great deal of pressure on all of us—"

"Cash McGee can be found at his brother's cabin," he interrupted. "At a place call Warrior's Pass." He glanced aside then back at Alma. "I hope this is helpful to you."

Alma put one hand on a parking meter to steady herself, processing again what she'd just heard. She watched Fuller walk away, his body shifting from side to side, stooped like an elderly man unsure of his direction. Cassidy ran after him without looking back at Alma or her friend on the motorcycle. In her own mind, all Alma could think were the words Grady Forester had used when he realized he'd attacked her without provocation—ignoramus.jerk.

17

"We should call in the National Guard," Chief Coyle argued and kicked the tire of his police cruiser. "At least the ATF."

Alma motioned him toward the back of the car so the other officers wouldn't hear. Alcohol, Tobacco, and Firearms, she thought—wonderful way to turn this into a disaster. Before she could speak he launched into a tirade about Derek McGee.

"He's a known neo-Nazi, a Klansman, a member of several militias advocating anarchy, and we got intelligence saying he's got enough fire power up there to blow off the top of this mountain." Coyle wiped a wall of sweat off his forehead. "I should never have told you the only person Derek ever talks to other than his brother is your brother."

"It's not a picnic for me either, Chief. I don't relish the idea of asking Vernon for a favor. Payback is usually everlasting." Alma stared up at the clapboard cabin set at the edge of a creek and backed by giant boulders that had tumbled down the mountain ages ago. A patch of corn grew in the side yard, laced with string beans and rows of bright red tomatoes. From their position on the dirt road below, they were sitting ducks if the McGee brothers got it in their heads to start shooting. Even if half of what Coyle said about Derek was true, Alma felt the situation could deteriorate into another Ruby Ridge. She didn't typically accompany the police on their missions but was terrified that Coyle would violate every civil right in existence. "Cash McGee is our objective," she said. "Whatever Derek may or may not have on his mountain is not our concern at this time."

"If that damn shack had been twelve feet to the north, this would be the county's problem." Coyle huffed, cursing his bad luck. "I guarantee you, they'd call out the National Guard."

Alma looked up at the cabin and wished Vernon would come out. He'd begged her to let him try to get Cash to give himself up, promising that Derek was not the lunatic people made him out to be. He had assured her that Derek probably didn't realize why his brother was visiting, and to go in with guns aimed would surely provoke violence. Only his promise to beat the police to the cabin with a warning for Cash had persuaded her to let him try it his way. Chief Coyle was not so convinced of Derek's integrity, and Alma fought her own doubts as well. If anything happened to Vernon, how would she ever live with herself?

Coyle paced beside the car and chewed up one toothpick after another. His cheeks were a fiery red but Alma couldn't tell if it was from the stress of the situation or because the sun beat hotly on their position. "Chief," she called out. "I received an interesting photograph at my office today."

"I'm not some fricking god," he said abruptly. "There are things in this world—the weather, the stock market, relatives—that even I can't control." He threw down his chewed toothpick, mashing it with his foot as if it were a cigarette.

"Well," Alma said, caught off guard, "after this is over,

let's sit down and talk about that photo. Maybe if you'll tell me more about these things . . . or people—relatives you can't control—we can find a way to deal with it." She watched him carefully to see if he recognized that she was referring to his brother-in-law, Jimmy Blackburn.

Coyle turned his back on her and looked down at the dozen other officers waiting at various points on the road. "Damn it," he said, as if her offer was a gesture he was not capable of accepting. "I would think you of all people would understand how things work in the mountains."

Alma remained silent and watched as he unholstered his gun and checked the chamber then, using the back of his arm, wiped sweat from his forehead. In a way Coyle had been ensnared by a trap of his own making. In allowing his family to run the mountain drug trade, he'd spent too many years looking the other way and now faced a decision he couldn't avoid—would he look the other way for murder?

The slam of the cabin door broke her trance. Vernon waved at them and jogged down the hill. All the policemen jumped into position behind cars, trees, boulders, and on the ridge behind the house. A flock of birds took flight from the surrounding pine trees as if sensing a sudden increase in tension. A rush of adrenaline shot through Alma and her arms tingled, adding a tremble to her muscles. She leaned against a police car to control the shivering.

Vernon came straight to Alma. "Derek says you can come and explain to him what his brother did. If he agrees with you, then he'll send Cash down."

Coyle slammed his hand on the car hood. "This is not a negotiation. The mayor says to bring McGee in no matter what and I'm not putting my rear end on the line. I've a mind to order these men to open fire on that cabin and blow it to kingdom come."

Alma touched the chief's arm to calm him. "Vernon, that is highly unusual. I don't usually come to these situations at all. And the chief's correct. Cash McGee is a fugitive. It's not negotiable."

"Give him a break," Vernon said. "If you just talk to Derek and tell him the facts . . ." Seeing that his argument was not convincing her, he added forcefully, "Derek's the key to getting Cash."

"He got any dynamite up there?" Coyle pointed at the cabin.

"Just a couple of hunting rifles," Vernon said angrily. "You know, it's a little hard to get down to the store in the middle of winter, so ammunition comes in handy."

Coyle sneered at Vernon. "Alma, I can't let you do this."

"It's the only way, Alma." Vernon's expression pleaded as if he were a starving man asking for food.

Her doubts fought with her logic and tangled even more with her need to follow procedure, to ensure the law was not skewed. She couldn't afford mistakes. This had to be done right. Under the circumstances, what did she have to lose?

"I can't guarantee your safety," Coyle argued.

"Vernon?" Alma looked at him, hoping for some reassurance.

"I'll do it," Coyle said. "It's my place to go."

His words sent a chill through her. Maybe she should have let him call the National Guard.

"I would never take you into an unsafe situation," Vernon said. "It has to be you, Alma. Since Vietnam, uniforms make Derek nervous." Vernon gave the chief's clothes an up-and-down glance.

"All right," she told Coyle. "I'm going up there."

18

Alma didn't see any dynamite, hand grenades, or the arsenal of weaponry Chief Coyle had described. What caught her gaze as she stepped into Derek McGee's cabin was a framed Silver Star hung beside a picture of him in army fatigues of the Vietnam era. She stayed slightly behind Vernon. The heavy smell of pinto beans filled the main room. Except for two half-eaten bowls of beans on a TV tray, the cabin was meticulously kept. Every stick of worn dime-store furniture seemed to have its place. Two hunting rifles rested on shelves above a fireplace, and several half-burned candles appeared to be the only source of light. A white sheet nailed over a doorway blocked her view into the only other room.

Vernon pulled back the covering and said, "They're in here."

She ducked under the material. Cash McGee sat in a wicker chair tilted back against a shelf of canned food that was anchored against the side of a cast-iron stove. A pot of soupy pinto beans sat on a burner and had cooled until the top crusted. In the opposite corner Derek McGee stood straight as a soldier with his arms crossed over his chest. He was slimmer than his brother, with short-cropped brown hair touched with gray at the temples. He looked directly at Alma, and his head jerked three times to the right. A rifle leaning in the corner behind him made her nervous. He noticed her staring at it and stepped in front of the gun. She wasn't sure if he meant to block her view or position himself where he could get to it easily. Her heartbeat raced and her mouth was dry with anxiety.

"My brother didn't kill nobody," Derek said. "That's what he's told me and I believe him." He kept his body turned to the side. His arms shook and he seemed to be holding on to them to keep them crossed.

"He's not under suspicion of murder, Mr. McGee," Alma said. "The factory owner didn't die. But your brother did shoot him."

"It was an accident!" Cash burst out. "That fool was swinging a baseball bat at me."

"Every man has a right to defend hisself," Derek echoed, his head jerking to the side.

"That's for your attorney to argue, Mr. McGee," Alma said quickly and insistently. "What are we going to have here, gentlemen—a standoff? Or do we bring this to a conclusion?" She waited.

Derek McGee's arms came uncrossed and the fingers of one hand wiggled and twisted in an odd fashion. He held it with his other hand to keep the gesture from repeating itself. His head snapped sideways and with much effort he turned to face her. She kept her eyes on his and didn't react to what she suspected was Tourette's syndrome. He stared at her as if assessing her opinion of him. She fought the urge to go closer to him, recognizing that he preferred distance. "I can't change the facts of what your brother did. I can only tell you that he can't walk away like it never happened."

Derek kicked the side of his brother's chair so the front legs came down and hit the floor. "How many times have I told you," he shouted. "Save it till it counts!"

Cash didn't speak, just stared at his feet. A few seconds later he panted out short little breaths and fought to control his emotions. He raised his hands to speak but then let them fall into his lap as if the futility of his position consumed him.

Alma took her opportunity. "Do you really want to bring this down on your brother?" She knelt and looked up into Cash's face. "Vernon and I will walk you to the road. You'll have to be handcuffed."

"I ain't gonna let my brother be mistreated," Derek said grimly.

"I got him a lawyer," Vernon said. "Name's Jefferson Bingham."

Alma realized that her influence was essential to ending the dialogue. "It bewilders me, but I've got to admit it," she said, and glanced sideways at her brother before looking directly at Derek. "Since I've been commonwealth attorney, in all the cases where I've gone up against Mr. Bingham . . ." She just about bit the words. "I've yet to win." She swallowed hard, the confession difficult. "That, of course, is not in the spirit of making you any promises, you understand."

"Cash," Derek said. "This is about all I can stand." His voice was low, his tone flat and without emotion. "Make your call."

Alma looked quickly at Vernon. His eyes seemed anxious and the uncertainty unsettled her. There was a feeling of menace in the air and the cabin temperature seemed to rise a few degrees. She walked over to the stove, picked up a ladle, and stirred the beans. "This is such a peaceful, serene hillside," she said and sipped some of the soup. "Your brother carved himself a place where life is truly what he wants it to be." She set the ladle down and held her breath. As she turned Cash was staring at her. His eyes were wide and the irises deep blue. "You do need to decide," she said. Vernon and I are leaving. Are you coming with us, or is today the day this mountain runs red with your blood?"

Cash stood up and hugged his brother. "I don't know when I'll see ye again." He buried his face into his brother's shoulder.

Derek's eyes blinked several times, then both men led the way to the front of the house. Vernon and Cash went outside.

Alma followed them. At the door she turned and looked back at Derek. He stood as straight as he might have in the military. Behind him was the Silver Star and the picture of himself as a youth—smiling and thin, his arm around a fellow soldier. The dimness of the room made him look like a scarecrow beaten apart by foul weather.

"Thank you for not bringing them up here," he said, indicating the police with a nod of his head. "I go to town twice a year. Once in April to pay my taxes and once in July to stock up for winter. That's about all I can stand."

"Well," Alma said, struggling to keep her voice even, "when you come in July, make sure you stop by and say hello to me." She raised her hand to acknowledge him then watched as he closed the door behind her.

19

Alma tapped the lion's head doorknocker on Charlotte Gentry's front door. Postcard-size windows jiggled in the center of the door frame. When there was no answer, she rapped on the glass. She could hear a melodic Mozart playing in a third-story room on the north side where a round gray stone steeple made the house look like a castle. Walter was inside, ignoring her, and that heated the smoldering fire in her belly.

Alma knew his wife had left him and taken their children to New York. After closing down their house, he'd moved in with his mother during her illness. Since losing the commonwealth attorney election, his stature in the state had fallen considerably and he blamed Alma for all his troubles. When Val told her that Charlotte had been brought home, Alma hesitated about encountering Walter on his turf, especially while caring for his mother.

Savage thoughts clawed at her mind as she wished for one hour of remission for Charlotte Gentry. That's okay, she thought, annoyed that the old woman had the safety of her illness. She'd have no problem venting her anger on Charlotte's son. She banged on the door and finally saw Walter's figure through a thin chiffon curtain, stomping down the staircase.

"Allafair Adair," she shouted at him. "You're going to tell me who she is!" She held up the snow globe.

He stood on the other side of the door, looking at her through the glass panes. He was dressed in a gray suit, and his beard had been trimmed since she last saw him. His forehead and bald scalp looked dry, almost powdered. He frowned, trying to control his irritation at the sight of her. "Go away," he said.

Alma jiggled the door handle. She had no intention of allowing him to use his mother's illness as an excuse. "I listened to your mother's vicious ranting. I stood there and took it. Now, you're going to give me answers, or I'll knock this door down and get them from her."

Walter parted his lips and sucked in a deep breath, closing his eyes at the same time. He opened the door halfway. His dark suit was immaculate, set off by a yellow Yves Saint Laurent tie. A floral smell wafted toward her from inside the house. "I don't know Allafair Adair," he said flatly and with no emotion, simply staring at Alma impatiently, then started to close the door.

"But you've heard the name." Alma placed a hand on the door. "Do you know what this is?" She held up the snow globe.

"Do you think I'm lying?"

"Yes. I think you'd lie about anything you had to if it involved some trouble your mother had stirred up." She moved forward, opening the door another inch. "There's a connection between your mother, Allafair Adair, and my family. Tell me what it is."

"Mother was sick. Just let it go."

"She wouldn't have had such a good time rubbing it in my face if there wasn't something to it." Alma stepped into the house, causing Walter to let go of the door. She set the snow globe on a hallway table and watched the flakes flurry around the doll's face.

He stared at it, covered his face with his hands, wiped his cheeks, then let out an exhausted huff. "I was a kid. I can't be sure of what I heard." He rubbed his forehead over the right eye as if he had a headache.

"You do know . . ." Alma's throat constricted, cutting off her words. She steadied herself against the table. The years of manipulation this family had heaped on hers flooded around her like an eddy. She'd found out about each piece of treachery like some million-piece jigsaw puzzle that slowly formed a horrifying picture: Walter's father had blackballed Esau Bashears from securing employment and forced him to leave town; Mrs. Gentry had planted newspaper articles to try to convict Alma's brother of first-degree murder; she'd given campaign contributions to politicians in an effort to make Alma quit the case. What persecutions she hadn't discovered she had experienced firsthand—the sting of twenty-five thousand dollars slapped against her face, a bribe to make the seventeen-year-old leave town and protect her son's honor. Walter's honor, she thought. This family had less honor than most of the criminals she'd prosecuted.

Walter reached out and touched the edge of a Tiffany lamp. He stared into the deep-toned shade as if his thoughts were as fragmented as the pigments of color. "Did you ever think it might be best to leave things alone?"

"Like forgetting what happened at Jesus Falls? Forgetting how a teenage boy held me down while his friends raped me?"

"Stop it." He turned away from her and walked farther into the house.

Alma followed, raised a hand and smacked him hard on

the back. "Face me, you coward!" She grabbed his arm and pulled him backward even as he tried to jerk away from her. "You owe me! Your family owes me! And, by God, you'll tell me the truth!"

"All right!" He walked around her. His teeth gritted as he spoke and his eyes bulged angrily. "When I was a kid, sitting at my dinner table, I do recall the name of Allafair Adair being brought up in conversation."

"Go on," Alma demanded.

"Every man in the county knew Allafair Adair. I believe my old man even had a go at her."

Alma stepped back and turned aside. "Wait," she said. Some survival instinct activated deep inside her. She picked up the snow globe and moved toward the door, but each step was a frozen action.

"Your father ran away with her," Walter said, circling around and shouting in her face. "He deserted his family and ran away with the town whore."

"That's not true."

"You wanted to know, Miss High-and-Mighty, now you live with it." Walter hung over her. "You've always clung to your moral superiority like a badge of honor. Thinking you were better than me because you were a victim. Do you think I'm the only one to make a mistake in life? Do you think it even possible that a Bashears might be a scumbag, or is that a title you reserve for the best of families who value respectability but on occasion fall short of it? We paid for our mistakes. We made up for them the best we could. I suffered for what happened to you, and it cost me everything! And in losing to you I am clean. I'll go to my grave redeemed. Redemption! That's more than I can say for a father who deserted his family."

"This is one of your mother's lies," Alma shot back. 'I'll drag the truth out of her. I don't care how sick she is."

She hurried toward the staircase. Walter grabbed her arm, holding it so tight it hurt. "No, you won't," he said in a calmer voice. "You'll never hurt my mother again."

"Take your hand away or I'll break it off at the wrist."

He let her go but extended his arm out in front of her and pointed to the living room. The hunter-green wallpaper had faded, no longer matching the overstuffed couch heavy with indentations. The book-lined shelves gave the room the musty odor of decaying paper. The curtains were drawn and the room was dark except for the glow of candles from the far end. She looked up at Walter, who still pointed to the part of a room she couldn't see. His eyes were squinted tightly, still glaring at her with the full anger of his previous outburst.

Alma entered the room. Her hands sweated on the coal base of the snow globe, and she gripped it tightly to secure her hold. A purple drape had been fashioned around the fireplace. In front of it was an open coffin. She stepped toward it. Part of her shook inside from the information she'd just heard, part of her couldn't believe that she stared at the shrunken body of Charlotte Gentry. She was dressed in a teal-blue suit, and her white hair was so thin the scalp showed through. Her slender white hands were crossed over her stomach, a single silver wedding band her only jewelry. Dead. Charlotte Gentry was dead.

One of the candles fluttered out. Shadows stretched across the room in long, dark bars. She was right, Alma thought angrily. This snow globe held a key to her father's life, and only Charlotte Gentry knew the secret. The old woman's bitter words saturated her mind: *I just might have my revenge after all.* She could sense Walter behind her.

"So you see," he said in a quiet voice, "you have my job. You have the town's confidence. The people respect you, trust you, depend on you to lead them into the next century. It will be you who shapes their destiny, you who protects them, and you who sets the standard of what is right in their world. You. Alma Mae Bashears, the little white-trash girl from the hollows, now has everything that was mine. So you carry that flag of purity like a knight in shining armor, and you see how easy it is." His voice lowered to a whisper. "And I have nothing. Most of all, I have nothing more to lose."

The hurt Alma heard in his voice was tinged with hatred, and she knew her enemy had returned—returned with a vengeance.

20

A friend was what her heart called out for. Not family, or a lover, but someone who knew her better than she knew herself, someone who'd been there when she'd made mistakes, someone who'd seen her vulnerable, held her when she cried, and knew when to encourage her. Alma knocked on Jefferson's door and prayed that he'd be home. He opened the door almost immediately and she rushed into his arms. "Thank God, you're here," she gasped. "You're not going to believe what Walter Gentry just told me."

"Alma?" he said, surprised, yet his arms wrapped instinctively around her. "Uh, I have company."

She looked around Jefferson's shoulder at an attractive blond woman sitting on the couch. Alma dropped her arms from embracing him just as the woman stared uncomfortably at the floor. She was at a loss for words and felt her cheeks flush.

"Come in." Jefferson pulled her inside. "This is Jennifer Henderson. She's a professor at Kingsley University over in Liberty. Alma Bashears," he told the woman. "My former law partner."

"And childhood friend," Alma said quickly, with the emphasis on friend. "I'm sorry I interrupted. I'll call you later."

The woman stood up and shook Alma's hand. "That's not necessary," she said smoothly. "I'll finish up the salad in the kitchen." She kissed Jefferson on the cheek and took his wineglass. Alma noticed she was barefoot and, in a casual one-piece halter suit, she looked as if she were well at home.

"Jefferson, I'm so sorry," Alma said.

He steered her to the couch, sitting beside her as she talked.

"A long time ago," she said nervously, "you told me that when you were a kid you heard rumors that my father had deserted his family."

"They were just that, Alma." He cupped her cheek in his hand and studied her features. "Rumors started by the Gentrys. Why would you listen to them now?"

"Have you ever heard the name Allafair Adair?"

"No."

"You're sure?" She bit the inside of her mouth. "Please," she said, wishing her voice didn't sound so desperate. "Don't spare my feelings."

"I don't remember hearing the name," he said softly.

She let out a distraught breath, aware that she clutched her hands so tightly her fingers were white from the pressure.

"I was only eleven years old," he said, aware that his answer did not satisfy her. He stroked her hair and held to her shoulder with the other hand. "Alma, you need to calm down."

"This could change everything." Hardly sensing what she said, her thoughts were a confused mass of knots.

"Why would you listen to anything Walter Gentry said in the first place? He'd tell any lie if he thought it'd get a rise out of you."

She looked at him as if she'd been suddenly shaken back to her senses. "Yeah." She chuckled nervously. "I guess I should know that by now." She glanced toward the kitchen and heard the oven door open and close. The smell of lasagna filled the air. "I feel a little silly."

"You can stay for dinner."

She rose. "No, but thank you. Another time." She smiled at him. "I'd like to get to know Jennifer." Alma hugged him. "I want so much for you to be happy," she whispered in his ear, at the same time fighting a feeling of loss that rose up inside of her.

As he walked her to the door he inquired, "Any word on Danny?"

Alma hid her surprise and casually asked, "Do you mind if I ask why you keep bringing up Danny?"

"Nothing important. There are some legal issues I need to inform him of regarding his mother's will. That's all, okay?"

She couldn't help noticing his frozen smile. "You realize that we don't know yet if he might be the perpetrator."

"He would never have killed his mother," Jefferson said firmly. "I sure hope he's okay. He was a cute kid."

Alma stepped out into the hallway, turned, and stared past him back to the kitchen. "She seems nice," she said. "I hope . . ." Her voice broke and she was filled with a regret that she hadn't expected to feel.

"Where are you going now?"

"To the office. There's a lot to do."

"Alma," he said, his arm slipping around her shoulders, "for the better part of the last year, I'd hoped something would come of you and me—but it didn't. Maybe it wasn't meant to be, maybe I pushed too hard at the wrong time, I don't know, but . . . don't spend your life working. You need someone, and if it's not me, then find somebody else because . . ."

"If you're about to say I'm not getting any younger . . ."

She tried to smile but couldn't keep her lower lip from trembling.

Jefferson pulled her close and kissed her on the forehead. He touched her cheek with his finger and stepped back inside his door, looking deeply into her eyes until he closed it.

Outside on the street she looked up at his window. A breeze blew the curtains outward. The image seemed relaxed and comfortable. She walked to the car, partly aching over the loss of a romance she herself had rejected and partly questioning his interest in Danny that seemed more than casual, more than professional. At least he'd calmed her down about Allafair Adair. It was all a Gentry lie—started by Charlotte and repeated today by her son for no reason other than to hurt her.

She drove toward the office, but at the traffic light steered the car in a different direction. The sun, low in the sky, had begun to color the horizon a pinkish hue. Ian would be in town one more night. Jesus Falls was the last place on earth she wanted to be, but if she was going to find him, it was where she'd have to go. And Jefferson was right about one thing—she needed someone, if only for this one night.

Alma parked in front of the sign JESUS FALLS PARK AND RECREATION AREA. She exited the car and listened. In one direction she heard the sound of people enjoying themselves as if a party were in full swing. In the other direction the gentle sound of water against water—Jesus Falls. Alma reached into her car and turned off the headlights. She walked past the sign erected by the town to honor the Gentry family who'd cut the ruggedness out of the mountain and built this sanctuary of hiking paths, picnic tables, barbecue pits, a baseball diamond, tennis and basketball courts, and campgrounds around a natural waterfall.

What the town didn't realize was all this beauty was stitched together with Alma's pain. She looked out across the water. The falls was a gentle stream, clear as crystal and flowing as evenly as a cloth spread on the ground. After a spring shower or summer storm it could roar with fury and billow out mists as strong as rain.

The edge of the large pond below the falls was often used by local churches as a baptismal pool. A road had been paved up to it and down into four feet of water, painted golden and embedded with a spread of glitter. Even now Alma could see the reflecting sparkling path. It gave her a shudder—this place now revered by so many people who didn't know what had happened to her here. This wonderful place had been created to assuage the guilt of Walter Gentry for the violation of a teenage girl. Alma turned away from the scene, fighting suffocating memories she could not allow herself to succumb to.

She walked along the path farthest from the falls to the campgrounds. The evening air was flavored with the smell of barbecue, and as she rounded the rocky path she could see red coals burning in the pits. Laughter rocked with the sound of an old Van Halen tune while figures standing in groups swayed to the beat of the music. The heavy smell of beer drifted past her.

She looked around but didn't see Ian. Several tents were set up next to each other with about a dozen sleeping bags laid out in the open. The cluster of people nearest to her quieted, their talk draining from them as she approached. They were young—late teens, early twenties—four boys and three girls. She hesitated to speak to them, some part of her wishing to keep her familiarity with Ian a secret.

"Well, look what the cat dragged in," a female voice said behind her.

Alma turned and faced the blond-haired woman she'd first seen at the jail. The man who'd been getting arrested stood with her. Kevin, she repeated his name to herself.

"Meeoow," he said and sniggered. "Just a little pussy. You're not jealous of a little pussycat, are you, Julie?"

The sense of alarm that suddenly spread through Alma was more than her history with Jesus Falls. The man eyed her up and down even as he draped an arm around Julie's shoulders. Alma stared at him, trying to give the impression that she was unaffected by his words. "Where will I find Ian?" she asked.

"Probably that way," Julie said and pointed toward a line of tents about twenty yards down the path.

"Or maybe that way," the man said with a deep Scottish inflection. "You take the high road and I'll take the low . . ." he sang.

"Kevin," the girl whined, "you know Ian is over there." She indicated a different direction from her first instructions.

"Or maybe he's not here at all," Kevin said.

Julie giggled and pointed at Alma. "Maybe you're here all alone—would that scare you?"

"Or titillate you?" Kevin asked.

Alma turned sideways. "I'm seldom frightened by childishness." She walked away while the couple broke into a spasm of laughter then approached a group of girls sitting around a barbecue pit. They held marshmallows on sticks over a rising fire, roasting them to a crispy brown. "Are you part of Ian Corey's group?" she asked.

"We be," they answered almost in unison. "You find him in the corrie." One girl pointed at a bowl-shaped indentation behind a hill. "Cry his name and he'll answer ye."

Relieved that they were friendlier, Alma thanked them

and stepped off the path to climb a steep incline. The slope smelled grassy and dandelions covered the ground. The sun was setting and the bluish darkness made it difficult to see. "Ian," she called out. There was no answer. She slid partially down the hill on the other side and called out again. The fading voices of the campers made her nervous. She didn't want to get too far away from them in case she had another unexpected meeting with Kevin. Farther down the hill, her foot caught on a vine. She untangled herself and realized she'd have to go back because she could no longer see. "Damn," she said to herself.

She held a hand out in front of her and started back up the hill. A rocky cliff to the left made her think she'd gone too far. Her heart beat faster as she realized she'd lost the path. Muscles in her back tightened and her breath caught in her throat. Behind her she heard footsteps through the weeds. She froze. Let it be Ian, she prayed. Her heart pounded like a workman's hammer. She stepped a few feet farther. The footsteps followed her. She turned her head to the side, too afraid to revolve completely around. "Ian?" she called out tentatively.

"Alma." He spun her around, pulling her into his arms. Before she could speak, his mouth covered hers and he kissed her deeply.

The taste of him was warm and she responded. When he broke away, she pulled him back and kissed him again. Her hands wandered over his back muscles as his arms closed around her and he lifted her from the ground. Her hands touched his face, feeling the roughness of the day's beard that he had yet to shave.

"I'm glad you did that," he said, holding her tight. "I . . . I feared being forward."

"I told you not to leave the other day, didn't I," she said.

He rubbed the back of her neck as he hugged her to him. "That's about all I've considered since then." He lifted her onto a large boulder that jutted out of the side of the mountain, anchoring himself between her legs and resting his hands on her thighs. "I knew I had to leave on the morrow and we'd probably never see each other again. Part of me didn't want to cause you any trouble. Part of me . . ." His voice trailed off.

She circled her arms around his neck and held him close to her. "If there's only tonight, then I guess there's only tonight." The full moon peeked over the mountaintop. Crickets chirped whenever they stopped talking and ceased if they made a sound. In the surrounding woods the iridescent glow of fireflies flashed off and on. The sound of the waterfall seemed so far away, as far away as a dim memory of a childhood scolding.

She slid off the boulder, letting her legs encircle his while he still held her. He pressed her back against the rock, then turned the two of them sideways and dropped to his knees. Holding her against him with one arm, he lowered her into the soft clover that surrounded them with a tart grassy smell. She stared at the moon over his shoulder. A hazy cloud passed over it, causing a golden halo to light the dark sky. She clung to him with the hunger of a woman who needed to be touched, and he kissed her gently as if she were fragile enough to break.

Suddenly the long whining sound of sirens bit into the hum of the night. For a moment Alma banished them, too happy and satisfied to be dragged back into the real world. But Ian lifted himself up from her and stared in the direction of the sound.

"Let's get over there," he said.

As they crested the hill, Alma was shocked to see the entire campground surrounded by patrol cars, flashing lights, police dogs barking and straining against their leashes. Floodlights lit the center of the camp. She and Ian ran toward them.

"What's going on?" Alma headed directly to Chief Coyle, who held up a grainy photograph next to Kevin's face. Two officers held him on both sides even though he was already handcuffed.

'I got him, Alma," Coyle said, his expression registering surprise at seeing her. "I can prove he killed Kitty Sloat."

"We didn't kill anybody!" Ian burst out and stepped in front of Alma. "Haven't we been through this already?" He stood face-to-face with the chief. Kevin stayed silent and watched with a spiteful smile that Alma found disturbing. He gave a low chuckle and even the two policemen who held him appeared spooked.

"Chief," she said, "give me the warrant." She held her breath, hoping he was on firm ground.

"I got this file here." Coyle waved a manila folder in the air. "All the way from Scotland Yard. This one," he said, pointing at Kevin, "has an arrest record long as the Cumberland River. They charged him there for murder—and now we have a body."

"That charge was dropped," Ian said coldly.

Alma looked at him, taken aback. "Ian, we do have a murder. That information is relevant."

The expression in his eyes broadcast a sense of betrayal. "Alma, why are you letting this idiot make a fool of you?"

She answered defensively, "Why aren't you letting the police do their job?" She indicated Kevin with a sharp glance. "That man is nuts! Why are you defending him?"

"Because he's my brother!" Ian yelled.

Alma's muscles froze. The distress of the connection made her feel like she'd been grabbed and shaken. She stared at Ian.

He stepped closer to the chief and shouted into his face, "Let's hear your evidence!"

Coyle's eyes bulged out. "See them motorcycles? At least two of them are new. So, what happened to the old ones?"

"That's it?" Alma asked in a low voice, hoping he had more.

"As soon as I get him into interrogation," Coyle said, pointing at Kevin, "I'll have your case for you."

Alma felt sick to her stomach.

Ian's eyes flashed and the nearby fire held the flaming image in his pupils. "I've had about enough!" He knocked the file out of Coyle's hand, scattering the papers on the ground. Two policemen jumped toward him. Coyle fell into the brawl.

"Stop this!" Alma yelled. They ignored her. A crack rang out and she jumped, recognizing the sound of a gunshot. For a few seconds all activity ceased.

Kevin strained against his captors and yelled, "Ian!"

The policemen spread out. Coyle held a gun over Ian as he lay on the ground clutching his arm. His face grimaced in pain. Alma dropped to her knees beside him. "Oh, my God." She put a hand against his bleeding arm and called for a first aid kit. "Ian, hold still," she said when he started to get up. She ordered a police car to take him to the hospital rather than wait for an ambulance.

Ian was moved to the back of the police car. As he waited he glared at Coyle and waved away an officer with a first aid kit.

"I'll come with you," Alma said, leaning down to the window.

"No," he muttered, unable to look into her eyes. "Stay away from me." His cold voice penetrated her like a knife.

As the police car sped away, she turned toward the two policemen restraining Kevin. "Uncuff him," she said.

"What?" Coyle asked, his mouth hanging open.

"You don't have probable cause to even question him, much less hold him."

"Alma, you have to see this file . . ."

She took it from him, now a disarray of papers. "Chief!" she said in a huff of frustration. "You don't even know if they were in the area at the time of the murder. For god-sake, think!" She noticed that he was staring at the left side of her hair. Unconsciously her hand went through it and pulled out a stray leaf.

"I am thinking, Alma." He surveyed the campground with the sleeping bags, tents, and again eyed her slightly mussed appearance. "If you're not careful, you might end up in the same condition as your cousin, young lady."

"Dead?" she growled.

His eyes lowered to her stomach. "I hope you used protection."

Rather than respond to his condescension, Alma broke away. She nearly knocked over Julie who'd planted herself in front of Alma's car.

"Good thing you made your lap dogs heel," Julie said. "You don't want to see the boys when they're mad."

Alma slid into the car and turned on the ignition. Julie hiked a foot onto the car bumper. "Move your ass," Alma said out her window. "You don't want to see *me* mad."

As she drove away, Coyle's words hammered in her mind. What did he mean—her cousin's condition? Could

he have been the one to send her the picture of the corpse?
Or did he mean something else? Something more subtle—
a clue that might solve the crime. Damn him, she thought.
Kitty had been pregnant and he purposely hadn't told her.

21

Mayor Hudson slapped a folded *Contrary Gazette* on the edge of Alma's desk. He rubbed his forehead as he took his blue medicine bottle from his pocket and drank deeply. "It's only a flesh wound," he said. "Why's everybody so upset?"

She scanned the headline: POLICE CHIEF SHOOTS TOURIST. "Doesn't this convince you of the right thing to do?" she asked, raising one hand in a frustrated gesture. "I've been telling you that for months."

"You ain't been telling me nothing!" he exploded then paced back and forth across her office as if it were his own. "I can't fire Coyle." He proceeded to list the reasons.

"Mayor," Alma said over his talking, "you can certainly do what you want with your police chief—but remember, if your only reasoning is that he knows where the bodies are buried, then I suggest you start counting what bodies might lie in your future because of his inaction and incompetence." As annoyed as Alma was, she knew her opinion counted for little. She pulled loose an eight-page center section of the paper devoted to the passing of Charlotte Gentry. An 8 x 10 color photo was centered within a full-page obituary. Alma studied the picture of a much younger, seemingly kinder Mrs. Gentry.

"He just got overconfident after capturing Cash McGee,"

the mayor said. "Thank God for McGee." He opened the window and took out a cigarette. "We ought to write a thank you letter to Harlan Fuller."

"That might be a bit hasty," Alma said, holding her breath as he lit up. "McGee does have ties to Fuller's political group." She put aside the Gentry memorial section and retrieved the front page. The McGee capture was written up in a small corner column. The rest of the front page had articles about Kitty Sloat, her dubious background, and her still missing son who was considered a suspect. Details of the grisly murder had leaked out and one article speculated about the possibility of a serial murderer passing through the area. It briefly summarized three other murders of young women from New Jersey, Pennsylvania, and West Virginia. The editorial page criticized Contrary police for not yet making an arrest and the commonwealth attorney's office for not releasing enough details to keep the public informed.

"Is this motorcycle man gonna sue?" Hudson asked through a series of puffs.

"I don't think so," Alma replied. "The students left this morning, and I believe Ian and Kevin Corey simply want to leave town as soon as Ian is able."

"I thought it was just a flesh wound."

"The doctor kept him overnight. I expect he'll be leaving town today."

"I'll tell you what. You ought to watch yourself a little better, Miss Commonwealth Attorney. Cavorting around in the middle of the night with a bunch of roughnecks could get you a reputation."

Alma dropped the newspaper on the desk and stood, holding back the rumbling that the insult provoked in her. She snatched the cigarette from the mayor's lips and dropped it out the window, which she then closed. "I suspect my friendship with Professor Corey is all that stands between this town and a multimillion-dollar lawsuit." She marched around her desk to stand directly opposite the mayor. "If you want to do yourselves and Contrary a favor, then make sure that the next police chief is versed in the law—particularly of what is and isn't probable cause. And in case you don't know, simply owning a motorcycle isn't!"

"No need to get huffy, Alma," the mayor said. "I'm just looking out for you. This ain't the big city, you know. People around here watch what you do."

"And you, Mayor Hudson, are not my father." Alma fought the angry tone in her voice but knew it was pointless. Every way she turned she encountered men who believed they knew the law better than she. They would never have done this to Walter Gentry, she thought, and the insight made her even angrier.

"Maybe not," the mayor said, "but don't forget that you need me to get elected." He pulled out the pack of cigarettes and swore when he saw it was empty. "I've had about enough of this. It's not the commonwealth attorney's place to tell me how to run this town. I was running it when your clan was digging 'taters for evening supper." Hudson crumpled the empty packet, tossed it at the trash can, then pulled a new pack from an inside pocket of his jacket. "Reality, Miss Bashears, is that nobody gets elected in this county without my backing, so you think about that come November." He ripped open the pack and pulled out another cigarette. "What I'm here to say is your office better come up with some convictions or everybody is going to suffer."

The intercom buzzed and Val told her that Grady Forester was on the line. "I'll call him back," Alma replied.

"Let's not have things get out of hand," the mayor said, using the best conciliatory tone of a politician smart enough not to burn his bridges. "All I'm saying, Alma, is . . . Oh, heck, let's let it go for now. What's important is we got one criminal in jail, which will soothe the feelings of management at the Highland Toy Factory, and I assume another one under surveillance?" He gestured like a candidate making a speech.

"No," Alma said, and he groaned. "There is no reason to put Professor Corey's group under suspicion."

"Has Kitty's boy been found?"

"No," she admitted.

"You need to locate that boy." The mayor fumbled with a match but couldn't get it to light.

"Chief Coyle's suggestion that Danny might be a possible suspect is as unfounded as his allegations against Corey's group."

"Yes, unfounded." Hudson bit into the filter of a cigarette. "That boy should be located," he said, not listening to her opinion. "Does any law enforcement in this town have a lick of common sense?" He looked at Alma, including her in his assessment.

"If Danny's running, I suspect he's running for a reason," she said.

"Why would you accuse your own kin?" the mayor asked, holding on to the cigarette without lighting it.

"I'm not. I'm just saying it looks like he's afraid of something—law enforcement, perhaps." She waited to see if he'd respond. "Maybe people he knows in Quinntown? Maybe Coyle knows these people?"

"Maybe the kid's afraid of this motorcyclist the chief wanted to arrest?" The mayor leaned forward, tapping a finger on her desk.

"It could be anybody," Alma said, slowly, wondering

why he'd try to direct her away from the Quinntown connection. "It could be me, you, one of this motorcycle group. The evidence isn't leading us anywhere right now, and it's simply too early to make unsubstantiated accusations."

"You better be sure before you let them ride out of these mountains, because if this man gets away, you'll be held responsible."

"Mayor," Alma said, "it would deflect a lot of criticism if you and the council started filling our police force management with some competent individuals. The rank and file are as good as they come, but they need leadership. In the meantime, I'll shepherd Coyle through this case, but I'm more than a little resentful for having to do his job and mine, too."

Mayor Hudson walked toward the door and looked back over his shoulder. "I'd worry more about what I said just now than about who does the job. Life may not be fair, but it is exact." He smoothed his white hair with both hands. "Now, I've got to get to Charlotte Gentry's funeral. See you there?" He closed the door behind him, not waiting for an answer.

Alma dropped into her chair and stared at the wall. Her law degree hung beside her diploma from UC Berkeley. She wondered what her highly educated professors would say about small town politics and doubted that they'd be able to keep score.

"Get Detective Forester back on the phone, Val," she said to her assistant. While Alma waited she took several deep breaths and braced herself for more bad news. If he'd been able to find a file at all, there'd probably be little in it.

"Bashears," Detective Forester said, his voice full of amusement. "Your little hamlet made the Detroit papers." He chuckled.

"My file," she said, "do you have my father's file?"

" 'Course it was the back page of the cracker corner, but it's not every day that the sheriff shoots it out with a bunch of college kids." He broke out into a rich belly laugh.

"Police chief," Alma said tightly over his laughter. "I'm sure if Detroit law enforcement had such twenty-twenty hindsight, then Halloween might be the pleasant celebration that it is in the rest of the country."

He stopped laughing. "I never work that night," he replied. "So tell me, did the schmo get canned? I'm looking for a job." He broke into another round of laughter.

She heard more boisterous laughter in the background and figured he must be grandstanding for his colleagues. "I can't imagine that our little hamlet would hold enough interest for a big city flatfoot like you." Some of the frustration from her previous conversation eased. "Now, my father's file."

"Oh, yeah. I scanned it and attached it to an E-mail. You'll have it in a millisecond."

"Thank you," she said coolly. "When you get a job offer, be sure to put me down as a reference." She could certainly say plenty to a perspective employer about his arrogant attitude.

"Alma," he said, his voice a bit warmer, "there's not much information. It was a long time ago. I'm sorry."

His words were the first kind ones she'd heard that morning, but she found herself unable to acknowledge them. She hung up and opened her computer to download. While she waited, she pulled the packet of her father's letters from her law bag. It was time, she told herself. She held them to her chest, then savored them, one at a time, reading as if his words would bring him back to life. And in a way, they did. She slowly opened one and read:

Dear Merl,

 My bones are so weary I sometimes think I'll fall to dust. If I did I pray my soul would ride on the wind and find you. Until then I'm grateful for tender graces that God sometimes grants us—a night that's not so cold as the one before, the softness of a newly washed blanket, an unexpected memory of my children. They make my troubles bearable and remind me that I'm a day closer to being home. When you see the next sunrise, remember that it shines on me, and at that same time, I'm thinking of you.

Love, Esau

Alma was embarrassed to experience such an intimate moment. An instant that belonged to her parents. His love for her mother was so evident it made the Gentry claims seem like sacrilege. She thought of Charlotte Gentry being lowered into the cold earth as she read. Buried with her was a lifetime of manipulation and hatred. Alma could feel no remorse—only relief that there was one less Gentry in the world.

She turned back to the computer and started scrolling down the screen. After fifteen minutes of staring at the file, all she could see was the address on the missing person's report: ESAU BASHEARS, 646 SANDUSKY ROAD, DETROIT, MI; C/O ADAIR. The letter fell from her hand.

22

The cold air of the county morgue rivaled the chill of winter, making Quinntown General Hospital seem an appropriate location for the coroner's office. Unlike the more modern facilities in Contrary, Quinntown General had been built as a WPA project in the 1930s. Its gray tiled floors were yellowed and the peeled wall paint showed a multitude of underlying colors. A tree-shaped air freshener, hanging on the handle of a brown, rusted radiator, scented the air with a strong pine odor. Two rear rooms had been set aside for law enforcement.

While Alma waited for Nathan Deever she dodged his assistants who rolled in gurneys, sometimes with a bagged or covered body, and made a macabre game of coasting them beside each other like pool balls aimed for the corner pocket. She found a safe place by a window so small only her face fit in the opening. From the third floor she could see a back section of the round hamlet of Quinntown. One building in particular held her interest. A video store. Customers went in and out so fast, she knew they couldn't possibly be shopping for tapes. She counted the people who left empty-handed and stopped at fifteen. It had to be one of Quinntown's notorious drug dens. If these were the people who killed Kitty as a warning to her son to keep his mouth shut then they'd stop at nothing to get their hands on the boy.

When the death of her cousin was solved, she would ask the state and the Feds to launch an investigation on the local drug kingpins. To fight this kind of crime, she needed stronger forces than what was available here. She hoped she'd be taken seriously. About now Kentucky's attorney general would be receiving the hodgepodge of recall petitions that had circulated around town. She wondered how he'd react and how she'd explain.

"I bet you came for this," Nathan Deever said behind her.

Alma turned and took a security-sealed, brown paper bag he held out for her. "I came to find out why the autopsy report didn't inform me of my cousin's pregnancy," she said in a grave tone. "Do you know how humiliating it is to find out via Coyle's insults?"

"Alma." He sat in a chair and pulled one up for her. "I haven't issued an autopsy report, only a preliminary cause of death." He paused and made firm eye contact. "And I won't until I get toxicology reports back from the state."

"But an unwanted pregnancy could be a motive."

"It's the reason I held the body an extra day. When you get a suspect, I'll have the fetus's DNA. I informed the detectives of that."

"Of course," Alma said, feeling like a perfect fool. "I'm sorry, Nathan."

He rubbed his forehead then made a quieting gesture with the same hand. "When I started this job, I got sent to at least six sites where there were no bodies, and another dozen where the victims were still alive."

"I don't have the patience for that level of fun and games." She started to get up.

"You don't have a choice," he said, pulling her back down in the seat. "They're gonna do what they're gonna do. And you have to play the game." He removed a pair of low-slung glasses and rubbed the bridge of his nose. "It's like that awful picture you got. If they can scare you into doing nothing, then they've done their job."

"All the more reason for us to do our work thoroughly," she said, almost as a plea.

"Alma, perhaps it's time for you to turn this case over to the commonwealth attorney who will prosecute it." He shook her arms slightly as if to be sure he had her attention. "That woman over in Cherokee County is top-notch."

Alma knew that because of her relationship to Kitty, a commonwealth attorney from another county would take the case to court, but until an arrest, she'd put off thinking about it. "I haven't lost my objectivity," she said, unable to keep a hint of defensiveness out of her voice.

"How can you keep your objectivity when you're sent a threatening picture of a corpse?"

"I can't let them intimidate me."

"Well," he said, somewhat hesitantly, "I halfway wish they would've scared you off. Your safety may be more in question than you realize."

"What do you mean?"

"I tracked down the body in that picture." He got up and went to a file cabinet, returning with the envelope she'd sent him for safekeeping. "It's from the files of a University of Tennessee forensic anthropologist who works at a body farm. That's the good news—there's no new dead person out there in the woods."

"A body farm?" she repeated.

"It's located a little north of Knoxville. They take bodies and leave them out in the open—sometimes in the woods, in trunks of cars, in water. They study how corpses decompose. The information they've gathered is invaluable to the forensic science. Anyway, his office was broken into and a number of stolen photos are circulating on the black market. Whoever is into this is one scary person."

"At least it wasn't another murder," she said. "Just a warning, but from who?"

He tapped on the secured bag. "This is death with implications."

"Contrary police don't want to solve this crime, and I can't help feeling it's because she's related to me." Anger surged through her veins, making her skin hot even in the icy room. "Or because I won't intervene in that damn strike."

"Or Kitty had a relationship with somebody important." Nathan pointed again at the bag. "The detectives forgot it when they took Miss Sloat's personal effects. I thought it was what you'd come to get."

Alma opened the bag and emptied it onto a steel tray. Nathan handed her a pair of gloves, but she didn't have to touch the items. She saw what he wanted her to see. A business card printed with the logo of the Quinntown satellite office, Mirror of Our Soul Congregation. "They didn't forget it," she said. "They dismissed it."

"It was deep in her jeans pocket," he said. "Looks like it went through the washer a time or two."

"I'll be glad to deliver this to Chief Coyle."

Nathan resealed the bag and initialed it. "I know what you're thinking. This address is around the corner in a bad part of town, so I better go with you."

"I'm not going to the satellite office, " she said. "I'm going to the promised land."

23

As Alma drove, the words *tender graces* repeated in her mind. A beautiful phrase from one of her father's letters. She couldn't remember a time when she'd felt so confused. Poor Kitty, pregnant. Could that have been the motive for her death? Were the drug dealers a red herring? Tracking down all of Kitty's clandestine and known boyfriends would be almost impossible. About as impossible as finding Allafair Adair.

There could be a hundred explanations for why her father's Detroit address was in care of the name Adair. It didn't make sense that his letters were so loving and lonely and yet his life in the city had been with another woman. Was Allafair Adair simply an answer to his loneliness?

Alma thought of Ian, probably somewhere on the road by now. She barely knew him and had fallen into his arms because it was what she needed. On some levels didn't she understand how easy it could be to reach out for someone? But as a ten-year-old child who'd been left behind, she'd felt deserted and betrayed, and those feelings still crept up inside her despite how much she loved her father. Maybe it was best not to know what had happened to him. Better to be satisfied with *tender graces*. She could use some grace right now. Idling the car just short of the Fullers' driveway, she figured she could give some as well. On the car phone she dialed her mother's number but heard only the answering machine message.

"Momma, pick up. I know you're there." She waited. Her mother didn't answer. "Momma, if it's what you want, I'll drop trying to find Daddy. I'll give you back these letters and we'll never speak of them again. For the rest of my life, we'll act like this never happened. Call me. Let me know what will be best for you." She disconnected the phone and gunned the gas up to the Fuller mansion.

Reverend Fuller sat on a couch in the Living Room. From a distance it appeared as though he was praying. His head was bowed and one hand rested on his forehead, shielding his eyes. As she approached she realized he was reading the newspaper. He looked up, his expression registering a surprising openness, considering her last unpleasant encounter with him. He lay the paper across his lap, and Alma picked it up as she sat beside him. She saw the *Contrary Gazette*'s analysis of her first year in office with a summary of reasons for the recall petitions. Then she noticed a reddish copperhead coiled restfully on the reverend's lap. Alma shot up from the couch and stepped back.

"Don't be afraid," he said, slowly rising and holding the snake in his arms like a baby. He turned aside and gently placed it in a cardboard box, sealing the top and covering it with a dark towel. "Sometimes testing my faith is as important in daily life as it is when filled with the Spirit."

"Carrying around a snake tests more than faith," Alma replied. She clutched the newspaper tightly in one hand, and he reached out and took it, smiling slightly as her adrenaline returned to normal. The articles about her unfolded in front of them. "I seem to be as popular as a crop virus these days," she said.

"These articles are slanted." Fuller smacked the paper against his knee. "How can they compare the twelve years Walter Gentry held the office with your first year?"

Taken aback by his defense of her, Alma smiled involuntarily, and he responded by patting her shoulder. "It comes with the territory," she said with a dismissive wave of her hand.

"I've never had any use for rudeness, and freedom of the press is little excuse."

"That's a kind thing to say." She forced warmth into her voice and expected him to respond.

"You should smile more often," he said.

Alma shook off the girlish feeling he invoked and pushed herself forward on the couch. "I came to thank you for your help in locating Cash McGee." She bit into her words, swallowing hard. "He's in custody without incident, and without your information it might have been months before we found him."

"Mr. McGee is a confused man." Fuller touched an index finger to the center of his heart-shaped lips. "I pray that your office will follow the path that helps him rather than punishes an errant child."

"We're looking at that closely. For now I'm more focused on Kitty's Sloat death, and I have a lot to do." When she rose to leave he reached out, touched her arm, and pulled her back down.

"Alma," he said, "if I'm speaking out of turn, I apologize, but I sense some confusion in you." He looked down at the articles still between them. "It's more than this," he added and tossed the paper on the floor. "Tell me about it." His voice was gentle, comforting, almost mesmerizing.

Alma stared at the floor, her eyes resting on the box containing the copperhead. She kept her eyes lowered. "I've questioned Mr. McGee with every skill I have as a prosecutor. I don't believe he killed my cousin." She let feeling infuse her voice. A strand of Fuller's silver hair fell onto his forehead and he pushed it back into a wavy lock. "Right now, I'm building a trail of evidence that covers every place Kitty went that last day."

"Is there anything I can do to help? We have many resources among our flock." He smiled like a dear friend, reached out, and caressed the back of her hand. "Tell me more."

"Well," she said, softening her voice and trying to appear vulnerable. "It appears she and someone, possibly the killer, may have some connection to a video store in Quinntown." Alma cleared her throat and waited for a response. His eyes blinked a few times, but he said nothing. She ventured further. "It's the one that's around the corner from your satellite office, I believe."

"I know that store," he volunteered quickly. "It's owned by one of our members, Jimmy Blackburn." He leaned into her, one hand wrapping around hers and squeezing gently. "I could ask him to inquire if his employees saw her that day."

"One of your members?" she repeated, surprised that he'd volunteered the information so quickly and helpfully.

"An important member," Fuller said. "Mr. Blackburn heads our finance committee."

"Really," Alma said as innocently as she could. She couldn't wait to submit her report on Crimson County drug dealers to the attorney general. Her gaze floated around the room and suddenly she saw the opulence of the house in a different light. The gold leaf around the fireplace, the two velvet, kingly chairs, expensive carpeting, silky curtains, and oversized vases at every door. The affluent townspeople who came here also gave to their own churches and the hollow folk didn't have that much to give—the Fullers had to pay for all of this somehow. Drug money, she thought. No profit like nonprofit laundering. She wondered how much Fuller knew. He was volunteering too much information to be completely in the loop. Then again, she knew better than to try and out-fox a fox, so she decided to conclude their meeting with a more direct allegation. "You knew my cousin, didn't you?"

His Adam's apple floated up and down his throat as he stared at her, his open smile freezing. "Why, no. I never had the pleasure."

"Among her effects was a card for your satellite office in Quinntown."

"Ah." He raised a hand and pointed a finger at a poster with rainbow-colored words: BEGINNING NOW. "Our membership drive, most likely."

"There really was such a thing?" she asked. The uncomfortable silence that followed made her aware that she'd given up more than she intended.

"I'm an honest man," he said in a deep-voiced whisper. "I'd never say anything to mislead or manipulate."

Alma's cheeks flushed. She knew she'd overplayed her cards. She started to turn away but realized he was still holding her hand. The warmth between their touching flesh had become moist, and he leaned in closer to her until his face came within inches of hers. His white-shaded pupils were like blinders hiding his thoughts, but Alma knew he was on to her.

Before she could stop him he touched her cheek, letting his hand travel back into her hair. "You are under such pressure, " he said. "I understand."

"Have you seen Cassidy?" A sharp voice came from the doorway behind them. Danielle Fuller stepped into the room, heavy-footed in muddy boots and gardening gloves. "I'm digging out that koi pond she wanted." She strode across the room, but her eyes never left Alma. "Cassidy's good with fish. I've always had bad luck with them."

Alma had jerked away from Fuller at the instant of hearing her voice, and she regretted the impression of impropriety. She looked up at Danielle and couldn't help thinking that the expression on her face was a subtle, knowing one, as if she'd caught her husband in this situation before.

"Dani, look at what you're doing to the floor," Fuller said, pointing down at mud caking off her boots. A distasteful expression lined the reverend's face.

"I told her to stay with you." Danielle pulled off a glove and anchored the hand on her hip as she observed Alma then focused again on her husband. "You were the one who said she needed to learn more about the daily operations. Didn't you say that?"

"I thought she was helping you," Harlan said in a soft yet patronizing voice. He watched his wife open a side door onto the playground and survey it. "Have you checked her room?"

"Daughters can sometimes be so worrisome." Danielle closed the door and slowly moved toward them, pausing a good twenty feet from the couch. She pushed her glasses up with a wrist then wiped her cheek. "Isn't there a murderer you should be chasing?" she asked Alma directly, emphasizing the last word. "I'm keeping Cassidy close to home until there's an arrest."

"Alma came to thank us for our help in locating Mr. McGee," Fuller said indifferently. "I was about to invite her to stay for dinner." He scooted an inch closer to Alma and Danielle smiled stiffly.

"As your wife pointed out," Alma said with emphasis on the noun, "I've work to do elsewhere."

"I'll walk you to the door," he said.

"That's not necessary," Alma quickly responded, but he circled her as she stood and clasped her arm just above the elbow. She looked at Danielle, knowing she'd triggered an explosive anger the woman tried desperately to hide from her husband.

"It's amazing," Danielle said, studying her with magnified eyes behind thick glasses and pretending not to notice her husband's obvious slight, "that such a thing could take place in Contrary. I thought death like that only happened in the cities." She didn't wait for Alma and Fuller to exit but instead hurried ahead of them, calling out Cassidy's name as she mounted a staircase.

The silence between them grew awkward as they continued to the door. Alma wasn't sure how to extricate herself from the bond she felt him trying to create. She held out a hand to shake his.

"Some day," he said, holding her hand, "you'll see us from the inside, and when you do, you'll know my caring is pure." Before she realized what was happening, he hugged her, squeezing her tightly and whispering in her ear, "And then, I hope to see that smile of yours more permanently." He stepped back and gave her a penetrating stare. "If these forces that reproach you become too much—know that you'll find a haven here."

As Alma walked to the car, she began to understand how intelligent people were drawn into Fuller's spell. He gave such comfort in times of distress; he was the lifeline for those drowning in their own loneliness; he gave acceptance when the rest of the world condemned. She wanted very much to believe that he was manipulative and underhanded. And yet, with each and every dealing with him, she hadn't sensed the conspiracy she expected.

Perhaps her suspicions were groundless. Even if not, his involvement in money laundering for a drug lord would be hard to prove. He was a figurehead, so wrapped up in his creation of a doctrine that the details were always left to someone else. His job was to provide love. The one emotion that everyone craved. It gave Alma a chill to think of what he could do with all that power. San Diego's Heaven's Gate cult came to mind. As well as Waco. Jonestown.

24

"Coyle!" Alma yelled across the parking lot, letting the name drop like a stone. She aimed herself through a puzzle of cars to pursue him. He continued walking out of the parking area and toward the station although Alma was sure he'd heard her. Rather than yell again, she picked up a half-dollar-sized rock and threw it at his back, nailing him between the shoulders. That might have been a mistake, she thought, almost expecting him to turn with his service revolver drawn.

Instead he stood still, took off his cowboy hat, and tossed it on the nearest auto, a black Taurus. "Okay, Alma," he said without turning around. "You got my attention."

She came up behind him and dropped the bag of evidence into his hat. "I would say it's a gift from Nathan Deever, but that would imply you'd done your job."

"I know about these items," he said, facing her and picking up the bag. "The detectives forgot it. Everybody makes mistakes."

"Did you also forget to tell me about Kitty's pregnancy?"

He grabbed her arm and pulled her sideways into the nearby alley behind the police station. "Keep your voice down," he said in an angry tone. "We don't want that information getting out."

"If you think it's the motive, why are you taking shots at

Kitty's son?" She jerked out of his grasp and anchored both hands on her hips. "And don't manhandle me."

"We figured it's just a matter of time before the father of the child comes forward and shows his hand."

"Let's stop these stupid games," she said, not believing his reasoning for an instant. "I know about the video store in Quinntown. I know who owns it. I know he's one of Harlan Fuller's biggest financial supporters, and I know he's your brother-in-law."

"There's no law against peddling videos or being a religious crackpot." Coyle's eyes narrowed and watched her closely as if to ascertain just how much she knew. "Every family has one."

"What is Danny's involvement?" She waited, letting it sink in just how much she knew. He didn't answer. "I can guess a few things. His motorcycle is very important to him—is he a drug courier? Did you let him ride through this county unnoticed, giving tickets only to red-light runners?"

"You're treading dangerous ground," he said, his eyes narrowing.

"Trying to scare me off?"

"Maybe a little bit—for your own good."

"Is that why you sent me a picture of a dead body?" She started to walk around Coyle, determined to blast him with a more forceful allegation of collusion when he slammed her body against the back wall of the police station.

"You don't know who you're dealing with, lady," he said, holding her by the shoulders.

Alma grabbed on to his shirtsleeves but was so stunned by his attack that she couldn't struggle against his firm grip.

"And I'm not talking about me," he said in a tone so desperately sincere that she didn't call out for help. "These people will walk into your hollow at night and kill your entire family before you can finish dialing the area code of the DEA."

"I don't take threats easily," she said, mustering the strength to push against him.

He pushed back, not letting her gain an inch, then swung her around so hard that she sprawled on the ground. He dropped to his knees beside her and pleaded, "I've been trying to save your life from the first day you opened your big mouth about Danny Sloat." He sat in the dirt. "You think people didn't hear you? You think they're not watching what you do? The minute you get your hands on that boy, you're both dead. I've been trying to scare you off because you need to be scared off." He wiped a hand across his face, staining one cheek with grime from the ground. "Let it go, Alma. You don't know the kid. You're barely related to him. I can't do nothing about it." Letting both hands fall listlessly beside him, he gave up some of his righteous superiority. "It's not in my power to prevent. I tried to help you but you think you're too damn good for me."

Alma swallowed and rubbed her arm, which throbbed from her fall. "Did they kill my cousin?" she asked.

"I don't know," he said. "I don't know."

She pushed herself up and limped to the edge of the alley, stopping only to dust off her pants. She could feel a scrape underneath the material and knew her back was going to be badly bruised. Looking around at Coyle, she was surprised to see him still sitting on the ground, his forehead resting on his knee.

"If they tell me to blow you away," he said after her, "it'll be a choice between me and you. And that ain't no choice."

The words made her shudder despite the regret in his voice. She exited the alley and slowly made her way toward her building. Every person who passed her seemed suspicious. All she could think was that Danny had gotten into some kind of trouble with his bosses and it had cost Kitty her life.

She paused at the bottom of the stairs, wiggling one foot around to see if the ankle might be sprained. Coyle was right about one thing, she decided. Whether they killed Kitty or not, Danny was a problem for them. Danny was dispensable and apparently she was, too.

25

When Alma drove up the hill to her house she saw her mother waiting on the porch. Curled up in a lawn chair, her arms were wrapped around her legs and her chin rested on her knees. She parked beside the red-and-white Plymouth and sat a few seconds, trying to read the mood. Merl stood, walked to the edge of the porch, and held on to a railing. Alma squeezed her eyes shut, readying herself for who knew what. Her mother could disown her as easily as forgive her, and then change her mind the next day.

As she walked toward the porch, she quickly called her office on her cellular phone and told Val she'd be longer at lunch than she'd planned.

"You're not still with Reverend Fuller, are you?" Val asked.

"Why would you ask that?" Alma frowned.

"Everybody's looking for him. Mrs. Fuller is in the chief's office now."

"I left him and Mrs. Fuller together—early this morning. Any idea what's up?"

"You're supposed to tell me," Val complained.

"Maybe their fishpond is leaking." Alma disconnected before Val could ask more questions.

She sat in the porch swing and gently rocked, waiting for her mother to speak. For the longest time, Merl stared at the view—the mountains a carpet of deep jewel-green with only the folds of earth against earth colored deeply black. She pressed a thumb and forefinger to her eyelids, her mouth a flat grimace as she struggled with her emotions.

"I never did any of this to hurt you, Momma." Alma waited for her to respond, but Merl kept staring at the woods as if the trees might give her an answer. The silence became a brick wall and communication like sweet fruit trees on the other side. "Okay." Alma stood. "I'll get the letters."

"No," her mother said, turning around to face her. "No, you find him. If he's alive, you find him."

Alma lowered herself back into the swing. She studied her mother with care, unsure that her words were as sincere as she would have wanted them to be. "Have you spoken to any of the family?"

"No need for them to know." Merl plopped down on the swing next to Alma, causing it to bounce. "I'll pull myself together and say it was a love spat with J.D." She stared down at the reddish wood of the porch and rubbed her hands together. "They'll all believe that. I held this inside me too long. I don't want you doing what I did." She let her legs spread out in front of her and cackled a cynical laugh. "Hell, if I'd've dealt with my own troubles I probably wouldn't go around trying to run my children's lives." She rubbed Alma's shoulder and squeezed it as if she were a little girl getting a tickle. "You must understand—the way you put people in jail and all."

Alma couldn't help a smile. "Yes, I'm told I don't have much of a life outside of my job."

Merl started for the steps then turned and hugged her daughter. Alma held on to her, feeling the warmth of her mother's arms and chest against her. The tremble of muscles held them together and the connection of family deepened in ways that couldn't be expressed in words. "Momma," she said into her shoulder. "What if I find Daddy's alive?"

Merl stepped down the stairs. "If it's any help to you, there's something Mamaw told me when Esau first disappeared." She wiped her eyes and nose with the back of her hand. "She said that I just had to have faith in my husband, 'cause that might be the only answer I'll ever get. You have to have faith that your father was not the kind of man who would desert his family."

Alma nodded and waved to her mother as she got into her car. She watched until the Plymouth disappeared and swallowed the emotion of their newfound connection. Faith, she thought. Yes, she had to have faith.

She retrieved her bag from the car and sat on the porch steps, pulling out a manila envelope. Inside was the Scotland Yard file on Kevin Corey. She opened it and looked at the personal information sheet. The motorcyclist was described as 5'11", 190 lbs, raised in Edinburgh, Scotland, by his brother. She wondered where Ian might be right now—the Smoky Mountains, Georgia, the Carolinas. The thought of him spurred as warm a set of memories as it did a harbor of regrets. In defending her town she'd lost him.

As Alma read through the file, Kevin's life became more sinister with each page. Details caught her attention: as a child he'd tortured cats by hanging them and setting them afire before they were dead; he was suspected of burning down his neighbor's house. The final section summarized his juvenile and adult arrest record and reviewed his mother's suicide. Kevin had been detained for the death then released without being charged. The report was sketchy and Alma wished she had more information. Could it have been a slick lawyer's trick, or was he a troubled boy who'd ended up at the wrong place at the wrong time? Kind of like Danny, she thought.

The phone rang. She prayed it was Vernon with some information about her young cousin.

"I need you to come to my office right away," Chief Coyle said urgently.

"Should I bring Muhammad Ali?" she asked flippantly.

He didn't answer. She could hear sobbing in the background.

"Okay," she said, inferring from his silence that a crucial matter was at hand. "I'll be right there."

As Alma drove she called Val again and asked her to E-mail Grady Forester. "He's going to be grumpy," she cautioned her.

"I'll sweet-talk him for you," Val said.

Alma hoped she wasn't making a mistake by letting Val handle such a personal matter. "I need to find out if an Adair family still resides at Six-Four-Six Sandusky Road. In particular, an Allafair Adair."

"If she ain't at that address, me and Mr. Grady will find her for you."

She thanked Val, parked as close to the chief's office as possible, and hurried inside. These days, she didn't like the idea of being out of view of a crowd.

Sitting across from Chief Coyle was a tearful Danielle Fuller. The reverend stood behind her with his hands resting on her shoulders. The three looked at Alma as she closed the door. Fuller's face was pale and his expression confused. Danielle blew her nose and sniffed, looking up at Alma with red-rimmed eyes.

"You know the Fullers," Coyle said.

Before Alma could respond, Danielle burst into sobs.

Her husband stroked her shoulders and handed her more tissues as he tried to calm her.

Alma sat in the remaining chair and looked from the Fullers to Coyle, waiting for an explanation.

"You've got to help us," Fuller said to her, his eyes bloodshot as if he'd also shed recent tears.

"My daughter," Danielle blurted through congestion she wiped away with an overused tissue. "My daughter is gone. She's been kidnapped. She could be dead by now. That killer must have murdered my daughter!"

26

"She didn't run away," Danielle said, as if she could sense what Alma was thinking.

"We should check all possibilities," Alma suggested to the chief, hoping he'd take the hint and not allow the parents' hysteria to drive the conversation. Her memories of Cassidy Fuller were of a teenager who hid a great deal of dissatisfaction underneath a sugarcoated smile. Twice she'd seen her with a young man on a motorcycle.

As aware as Alma was of Kitty's murder, Cassidy didn't fit the profile of a stranger abduction and it seemed more likely that she'd run away. Still she knew special care needed to be taken in the case of a missing child. "The detectives will be here soon," she said softly to the Fullers. "Try to think of names of Cassidy's friends, where she liked to go to be alone, her regular hangouts, anything you can think of that might—"

"You talk like we're going to find her having a chocolate sundae at the mall," Danielle interrupted her through sniffles. "Don't you think we've done that already?" She scowled at Alma as if correcting a student then turned to her husband who stood silent and stoic.

"The good news is there is no obvious evidence of foul play, but we'll still involve the FBI if she's not found in twenty-four hours," Alma assured them. She waited for the chief to take the lead, but he fiddled with the toe of his worn boot and avoided engaging her. "The detectives are trained in a way that the two of you are not," she said firmly, although with compassion. "If she's out there, perhaps angry, perhaps hiding, maybe simply having lost track of time—they'll find her. It's only been six hours since you saw her last, and while we treat a missing child very seriously, Cassidy is a teenager. It is difficult to say what is going on in her head."

"My mind is going a million miles a minute." Danielle covered her tear-swollen eyes with a hand and leaned into her husband. "I just can't think."

"Dani," Fuller said, kneeling by his wife's chair. "Calm down. We have questions to answer." He held one of her hands and rubbed her shoulder soothingly.

Alma couldn't help thinking his reactions seemed more guilt-ridden than heartfelt. "Start with simple things," she said. "What were the names of her friends? Her boyfriend?"

"My daughter didn't have a boyfriend! She was a child!" Danielle broke into watery tears and buried her face into her husband's shoulder.

Alma realized they were getting nowhere and turned to Chief Coyle. She motioned to speak with him out in the hall, but he ignored the gesture. She wrote on a pad on his desk: *They need to take a lie detector.* The chief tore the sheet off, crumpled it, and tossed it in the trash can. Alma fumed.

"I have detectives combing her room," he said in a quiet, understanding whisper. "There is a backpack missing, but it could be misplaced."

"Mr. Fuller," Alma said, hoping to avoid another of Danielle's outbursts but knowing it was unlikely. "I've seen your daughter with a young man who rides a motorcycle. We should talk to him."

"That's impossible," Danielle blurted, jerking away from her husband. "I knew all her friends. She only went to chaperoned events."

"We need to look into the possibility of running away or the involvement of a friend."

A shrill cry escaped Danielle's throat. "How can you let her talk to me this way, Harlan?" She held on to her husband's shirtsleeves, imploring him for protection. "Next she's going to accuse us of having something to do with this."

"We're not accusing," Alma explained. "We're eliminating. Chief Coyle has spoken to you about the necessity of clearing yourselves—"

"Please, Alma," Fuller interrupted, stroking the back of his wife's head to comfort her. "Please help us."

"That woman had her throat cut." Danielle sobbed. "My baby could by lying out there somewhere bleeding to death."

Alma paused. "You had been keeping her close to home because of Kitty's murder. How did Cassidy suddenly get out of your sight?"

Danielle turned and spoke angrily into her face. "Are you capable of doing anything other than attacking my mothering skills?"

"Her throat cut," Fuller repeated as if the image was stuck in his mind like a repeating song verse. He walked to the window and covered his mouth with one hand.

Alma moved to his side. "It's not going to do either of you any good to think that way."

"That poor woman," he said. "That poor woman."

Alma looked over at the chief but his face was as pale as the Fullers' and he seemed to be focused inward. Part of her wanted to shake him to attention and reprimand him for bringing her into this situation. But now that she was here, she couldn't walk away without seeming cold, and the Fullers' suffering was as real as her own was for Kitty. It was impossible not to be sympathetic.

After an hour had passed, the room was hot with body perspiration. Danielle sat in a corner chair with Harlan alternately standing or kneeling at her side. Their quiet prayers were the only sound in the room. Alma and Chief Coyle were taking turns trading annoyed glances when a detective burst into the room, waving a handful of papers. "Here it is," he said. "I tightened the noose around Corey's neck."

"You've had them investigating Kevin Corey?" Alma asked Coyle. "Based on what?"

"This," the detective said, and laid a missing-person poster in front of her of Janelle Julie Blackard, the blond-haired girl traveling with Kevin Corey. "She used her middle name—that's why she was so hard to track. She is missing from upstate New York, listed as a possible runaway, but law enforcement and her parents are unsure. And I've got death reports here of young women killed in New York City, Pennsylvania, and Ohio. Their throats were cut and their faces peeled back from their heads. The pattern of deaths follows the same route taken by Corey's motorcycle group."

Alma immediately tried to lead the Fullers from the room but didn't move fast enough.

"Oh, my God!" Danielle broke from her husband's arms and stood up to face Alma. "My daughter has been killed! I know it! She's dead! And you've let the murderer get away!" She collapsed on the floor, her arms and legs sprawling uselessly. Fuller dropped down beside his wife and cradled her in his arms. He looked up at Alma, then gazed out the window at the blue sky as if his thoughts were far away.

Alma followed his line of sight—but her thoughts were of Ian and his brother, Kevin. Could she have been so wrong? Could she really have been that wrong?

27

"I couldn't get a charge to stick on him if I'd had a truck of superglue." The assistant commonwealth attorney, Craig Carr, was as pale as ash as he sat across from Alma. In his hands was all the paper evidence and a stack of depositions against Cash McGee. "The grand jury is against you, Alma," he said, flipping through a mountain of testimony. "This is one of the best evidentiary cases I've ever handled, with a dozen eyewitnesses and a blasted videotape." He snapped down the lid of his briefcase and shook his head. "I wasn't real happy asking for a reduced charge in the first place, but I did it for you—"

"This wasn't a case of attempted murder," Alma defended herself. "The charge we asked for was fair."

"We should have stuck with attempted murder. If I'm going to go down at least I don't look like a sellout."

"It's not you. The grand jury has lost faith in me," Alma said, depression weighing on her as she slapped down a yellow pad of paper. She held a half dozen pink message slips but had been unable to return the calls, feeling too embarrassed and inadequate to speak intelligently to anyone. She noted one from Jefferson asking if there was any word on Danny Sloat. A time like this and he's only thinking of his own cases, she thought, wondering why after all the pressure she was under he didn't call to give her just a smidgen of support.

"We could drop the case now and try again later."

Alma held up a stack of letters. "The ones who aren't calling me a defender of the rich and corrupt are suggesting I donate all of my salary to the Highland workers' strike fund to prove my loyalty."

She held up her uncashed paycheck. "If I thought it would prove something, I might." The *Contrary Gazette* lay faceup on her desk. It was full of critical articles about the missing girl and the unsolved homicide at Silver Lake. Speculation about links between the two were as rampant in the community as they were in the press. Various journalists stated that Alma had stood by while a mysterious motorcycle group, of which one member was the main suspect, rode away; such behavior was unforgivable as well as incompetent. She turned to Craig, knowing he would not like what she was about to say, and bit down as she spoke the distasteful words. "Call McGee's lawyer. Tell him we'd be willing to entertain a guilty plea to misdemeanor assault and kick it down to the county attorney."

Craig looked like he'd rather drink poison than reduce the charge again. "This is not why I became a prosecutor." He spat out his reply as if it were sour food. "I prefer a little salt when I have to eat crow."

"The grand jury is going to let him walk," Alma said, trying to keep the despair she felt from filtering into her voice. "Better a victory on the lesser charge than more of this." She held up the newspaper and pointed to small articles which reported break-ins at the local hardware store and a food market. A teenage boy had been seen running away, but the police had not been fast enough to catch him. "I don't think I can stand one more example of how we're not even good enough to stop petty crime."

Craig looked down at the floor, acknowledging the defeat. He stood and picked up his briefcase. "I'll take care of it," he said without looking at her. His avoidance spoke volumes and Alma knew it. He had lost faith in her as well.

Alma sank into her desk chair with a sigh. Twenty-four hours had passed and no Cassidy Fuller. Everything that could be done had been: the FBI, and the Polly Klaas foundation notified; the National Center for Missing and Exploited Children had given the community resources on which to draw; local churches were mobilized to send out flyers to police departments around the country; the National Guard was still combing the woods around the church and the local state parks.

Alma sat in her office with the door closed, staring out the window into the leaves of a spruce tree. Last summer a cardinal had made its nest in the crook of two branches. The tattered remnants looked like a mud pie one of her nephews might have made. One by one the baby birds had flown away but the mother had stayed long into fall as if watching to see if they'd come back. Little birds deserting the nest, she thought. Wasn't that what baby birds did? In her gut, Alma was sure Cassidy had run away. If she could figure out why, it might help locate her, but the Fullers had offered no assistance, and the chief was reluctant to treat them as anything other than faultless parents. Her lone supporter had been an FBI profiler who looked at Cassidy's and Kitty's cases and wrote a one-page report stating the teenager was probably a runaway. But he was in Washington, D.C., and an outsider, so his views had been quickly dismissed.

Alma's computer beeped, indicating she had E-mail. She downloaded the message and saw that it was from Grady Forester. With all that had happened, she'd hardly had time to think of locating the Adairs and was grateful that Val had taken care of the correspondence with him. His message read: BAD NEWS, WONDERGIRL. NO ADAIRS AT THAT ADDRESS AND NO ONE REMEMBERS THEM. THE HOUSE IS IN A PART OF TOWN THAT'S SET AFIRE EVERY YEAR ON DEVIL'S NIGHT. I NEARLY GOT MUGGED. DON'T ASK ME FOR ANY MORE FAVORS.

"Wondergirl?" Alma said. She filed the message and leaned back in her chair. It had been optimistic to hope to locate the Adairs in a city like Detroit. In twenty years they could be anywhere. She wished she had the time to fly to Detroit and check voter registration, DMV, and tax records, but it would have to wait until the current crisis was resolved, or she got bounced in a recall election.

With the heel of one shoe she pulled open the bottom desk drawer. Her father's letters were there, tied up nicely with a faded pink ribbon. Every cell in her body said that now was not the time to read a letter. It would only depress her more, make her wish for a time when someone watched over her, when responsibilities had been few and the future seemed hopeful. Out the window she saw Craig walking across the triangle between the courthouse and the town. He was headed to Jefferson Bingham's office, McGee's attorney. "To eat crow," she said to herself. She had certainly been served a large enough portion of her own.

She reached down and pulled out one of the letters.

When I'm home, Merl, let's you and me go over to that honky-tonk in Harrogate. It's still there ain't it? We can eat and drink and dance till we drop. My nights are filled with thoughts of you—dancing real close to "Blue Suede Shoes."

A wall map of Kentucky, Tennessee, and Virginia attracted Alma's attention. The song played in her head and she considered the incongruity of dancing slow to it. Only a thing people in love would do, she thought. She focused on Elvis Presley. Memphis. Graceland. She dropped the letter, and as she leaned down to pick it up said, "Of course. That's where Ian is."

She knew that her hunch had to be right. Her heart beat faster with excitement and a feeling of certainty. She held her breath as she called the State Police. They'd have the connections to initiate a search in Tennessee. He was there. She knew it. He was in Memphis. All she could do now was wait.

28

"Got 'im." Chief Coyle's announcement made Alma feel like she could breathe again. She sank onto her desk, setting the phone gently in its cradle. The sourness in her stomach eased like the spread of sweet milk into a butter biscuit. The group of Scottish students had been easy to recognize, and Kevin was picked up yesterday. He'd been flown to the Knoxville airport and passed on to a transport company that was bringing him to Contrary for questioning today. It wasn't over yet. The prosecution had nothing to connect Cassidy with this group, other than that the girl had been seen by several people riding on the back of a motorcycle.

Alma decided to go to the police station and wait, then her E-mail beeped. Grady Forester had left a message. DO YOU THINK I'M A MASOCHIST? I'D BE IN LINE ALL DAY AT VOTER REGISTRATION LOOKING UP ADAIR NAMES. SHE MIGHT AS WELL BE NAMED SMITH. GRADY. P.S.: I'M TOLD I LOOK LIKE SEAN CONNERY. AND YOU?

For a moment she was tempted to smile but then realized that his message was too flirty. "Val," she said on her way out the door. "Did you ask Grady Forester to look up the Adairs at voter registration?"

"And DMV, Social Security, and—"

"Val!"

"We peons who work on Saturday have to keep busy." She gave a little jerk to her shirtsleeves and positioned her hands over the computer.

"I'll remember that when I okay your overtime. Now thank Mr. Forester for his help but ask him not to go to any further trouble."

"Yes, ma'am," Val said smugly.

"Let's bring his involvement to a conclusion. His messages are becoming strange."

"Just forward them to me, Miss Bashears. I'll handle everything."

"Val, has anyone ever told you you're a smart aleck?"

"My momma used to threaten to smack this grin off my face every other day. Now let me get back to work—Saturday work, that is."

As Alma walked to the jail nearly every store window was posted with a flyer showing a picture of Cassidy with MISSING in large letters across the top. The word made her feel guilty. She tried to keep from staring at it, but groups of people gathered in various spots to examine the flyers were impossible to avoid. Some of them looked at her. They were silent. Their stares were as painful as if they'd attacked her verbally. A man held his hat in one hand, then put it quickly on his head and walked away, growling as he turned from her in disgust. Other men's eyes searched the ground, but the women's expressions bore down at her—their glares an accusation that she could not answer. She wished she could say something to ease their suspicions, yet any attempt would only seem to be a defense of herself rather than concern for the missing girl.

At the jail Alma paced in front of the main desk, the unspoken judgment of the townspeople weighing heavy on her mind. A representative of the transport company reviewed the paperwork he would be asked to sign. She was glad that Kevin had been located far from Contrary. At least this way, she didn't have to face Ian.

"Alma," Chief Coyle said, breaking into her thoughts. His voice wavered when he said her name, and as he started to speak he stammered several times. Finally, he was able to get out the words, "There's a letter."

She turned toward him and when he moved to avoid her, she knew he had more bad news. He wouldn't look her in the eye. "Relax," she said, "I have no intentions of complaining about our tussle in the alley. Right now, I have bigger bruises."

"It's addressed to the state's attorney general . . . asking for a special prosecutor to be appointed."

"What?" She stiffened in astonishment.

"It's been signed by several leading citizens."

"I can guess which several."

"After letting Kevin Corey get away—"

"But the state police found him," Alma interrupted.

Coyle just looked at her.

"Well, the recall petitions should make interesting reading." She tried not to sound concerned.

"It goes on to ask that this special prosecutor take over your duties until a recall election can be mounted. They've summarized everything that's happened lately and much of it—even Cassidy Fuller's disappearance—points to being your fault. It never would've happened if you'd listened to me."

"I'm surprised they didn't manage to get the Kennedy assassination connected to me."

"Alma," he said, letting out a deep, satisfied breath. "I signed the letter, too."

She was too stunned to respond. All she could think was the number of times she'd covered this man's mistakes and the flack she'd taken for his inept actions. The complaints she could have made and didn't. His lack of respect for the law was simply indefensible. He ignored the letter and spirit of the law, thought nothing of beating a confession out of an inmate, letting an abusive husband out of custody because it was simply his wife who'd been hit, or looking the other way as long as the bootleg and drug money lined his pockets.

"I just thought I should tell you to your face." He gave her a cold, hard stare, a demonstration that he had her; he was the power structure. She—despite being common-wealth attorney in her own hometown—was still the out-sider, the interloper who had to be taught a lesson.

She swallowed, knowing she needed to control her emotions in front of him. "At least that is more courageous than the other signees."

"It's not too late," he said. "Things could be turned around if you'd just—"

"I never realized the depths of your feelings for me," she interrupted. "Don't be expecting me to pull in line anytime soon. I have no intention of looking the other way for your brother-in-law, especially if I find out there's a connection to Kitty's death."

He pointed down the street at an armored van. "Fine," he responded through gritted teeth. "I'll stop asking you out on dates and leave you to more suitable company."

The van pulled up in front of the station. Alma felt a rush of uneasiness through her body as she walked outside. Kevin emerged from the back. He wore ankle and wrist shackles. "Glad to get rid of this one," the escorting officer said.

Kevin stood with his feet as far apart as possible. His straggly hair looked as if it hadn't been combed in several days. She could smell the sweatiness of his clothes that had not been changed. When he saw Alma his lips curled into a slight smirk.

"Mr. Corey," she said. No trace of apprehension in his eyes. "You're being held for questioning in the disappearance of Cassidy Fuller and the death of Kitty Sloat. Chief Coyle will read you your rights."

She stepped back as Coyle began. "You have the right to remain silent . . ."

"Hello, Alma," a voice said from behind her.

She felt like she'd been speared. "Ian," she said and turned around. He looked tired and the lines around his eyes had deepened. Her heart went out to him. "I wasn't sure you'd come."

"I came for my brother," he said, his guarded expression preventing any warmth from opening between them.

"Of course." The tremble in his voice touched her. She knew that ultimately he would hold her responsible for whatever happened to his brother. "If he's done nothing, this will be over soon," she tried to reassure him.

"Don't justify what's happened with the excuse that you're just doing your job."

Alma knew she had no answer that would be acceptable to him. It hadn't been that long ago when she was in his position, defending Vernon against charges in a murder case that seemed airtight. For Ian the circumstances were even more precarious. He was a foreigner, in a strange town where it seemed everyone was attacking him. She could relate to him more than she could ever admit, but she couldn't let him know that—she was the prosecuting attorney in Cassidy's disappearance, and that bound her to legal principles. The best she could do for him now was leave him alone. "If you need anything, the officer at the desk will help you."

"I do need something," he said, his tone and attitude mellowing as he stepped closer. He spoke in a whisper. "I need you to recommend an attorney."

"Ian." She lowered her voice and looked up into his eyes. "It's not my place. There are several good lawyers in town who you could interview in an afternoon, and plenty others close by in Knoxville or Lexington."

"I don't want to go to the phone book to get an advocate," he pleaded. "Alma, this is my brother. You of all people ought to know what I'm going through."

His voice tore at Alma and she let her hand slip into his. What responsibility her job thrust on her struggled with the protective instincts he invoked. She wished she could guarantee that everything would be fine.

"I'm all alone here," he said. "I know no one. Just a name. Who's the best attorney in town?" He looked at her imploringly. "Please, Alma. Please help me."

"Jefferson Bingham," she said. "He'll be a strong and fierce defender. If I needed an attorney, he's who I'd call."

"All right," Ian said, some relief softening his face. "Thank you." He touched her shoulder, squeezing it gently. "Alma," he said. "Just so you know . . . this isn't what it looks like. The girl, Julie, is eighteen. She was having problems at home and wanted to get away for a while. As for the others—Kevin's committed no crime."

"We're taking him into interrogation room two," Coyle yelled from the top of the stairs. His voice jarred Alma and she glared up at him, realizing he'd been listening. Ian stepped away and their closeness immediately vanished, but his expression acknowledged her. "You coming?" Coyle called out.

As Ian walked away his broad shoulders slumped as if the weight of his circumstances was too heavy for even such a strong man. If she could have shouldered that weight, she would have, but she was responsible for causing it. The sight of him standing all alone inside a corner phone booth, counting out change, tugged at her heart.

Coyle came down the steps behind her. "Well," he said, "he played you like a prize fool."

Alma looked up at him. "What gives you the right to say something like that?"

"Expert opinion," he said and rolled his eyes. "It's the way of one man recognizing another—women are either babes or they're useful, and to him, you are both." He turned away from her then said, "You see, it's like running a horse into danger. Keep the blinders in place and even a thoroughbred will run a ring of fire until it's too late."

The police station door slammed in its frame. Alma did not follow Coyle. She stared at Ian as he dialed the pay phone. An uncomfortable realization fought with her feelings for him. Her gaze lifted to scan the town, then to the horizon and the mountain ridges against an azure sky. Even when she'd stood among skyscrapers in San Francisco, she hadn't felt this crowded. Having reconciled herself to come home, live among people who saw her as a hollow girl—someone not quite good enough—she accepted that her experience of the world isolated her from this community. Had that isolation made her vulnerable to a con man who represented the sophistication that she'd abandoned? Had she been alone so long that she'd indulged in a blind trust? The thoughts made her doubt her own judgment, and in her mind, she formed that distrust into a ring of fire that fed her concentration. She turned and entered the station to face Kevin Corey.

29

A loud bang against the wall told Alma that Kevin Corey was getting impatient in the interrogation room. "Let him wait five more minutes," she said to the detectives.

It was a tactic she hoped would pay off. She'd noted that when Kevin didn't get his way, he became frustrated and made mistakes. She counted on him making another. He hadn't requested an attorney, nor had Ian returned with one, so there was no reason she should not take advantage of that situation. She wished the Contrary jail had rooms with one-way mirrors, but funding had fallen short. She could either go into the room or stay out. Another loud bang shook the wall. There was no way she was going to miss this initial questioning.

She looked at her watch, the five minutes passing slowly. A patrol officer barged through the outer office door, holding his shoulder in pain while dropping a leather jacket on the counter. Alma barely noticed as he slammed paperwork on the desk and began to fill it out in a frustrated scrawl. Chief Coyle paced nervously as another slam jarred the wall. "Alma," he said, "he's already broke one chair."

"He's about ripe." She motioned to the two detectives Coyle had chosen to question the suspect. One detective fiddled with a skull pin on the jacket brought in by the patrol officer.

"Not that damn shoplifter again?" the detective said.

"I had him by the coat," the officer said. "Little crapper pulled hisself right out of it. Run like a hare through a thicket."

"Gentlemen," Alma said, focusing on the job at hand. "Kevin Corey has an IQ of one hundred forty. That'll make him a little arrogant. He'll think he's smarter than you, so let him think that. Don't get in a verbal contest with him." She steeled herself for battle though her eyes followed the jacket that the patrol officer folded to place in an evidence bag. "If we're careful, he'll even admit his crime and think we're too stupid to realize . . . Where did you get that jacket?" she asked, the familiarity of it flipping pages in her memory.

"Off a shoplifting suspect," the officer said, surprised at her sudden interest.

"The one who's been breaking into the food markets?" Her mind clicked, remembering the newspaper articles.

"This was a car dealership. Actually, looked like he was trying to get some motorcycle parts, but—"

"Was he about six foot tall, blond hair, kind of a baby face?"

"He steal something from you?"

Alma reached out for the coat and spread it before her. It was the same jacket, she realized, that she'd seen on the boy scaling the fence behind Kitty's house. It was Danny's jacket. "Interesting design," she remarked to the officer, not wanting to draw the chief's attention. "Where did you say you saw him?" She knew the industrial area the officer described but let the discussion drop when Coyle moved closer to them. "Gentlemen," she said to the detectives, "let's dance."

"A woman who leads," one replied. "I admire that."

Kevin anchored himself in the corner of the room, one foot jacked behind him on the wall. As Alma and the others filed in, he yawned. "This crap's for bad American TV," he said. "So why's Miss Lucy here?" He looked Alma up and down, then pushed himself away from the wall with his foot. "You know, Lucy from Charlie Brown?" He slowly lowered himself in a seat beside a detective and joked bitterly. "Hey, Charlie Brown."

"I'm going to ask the questions," she said, thinking of the citizens who blamed her for Cassidy's disappearance. The two detectives looked at her, at each other, then at Coyle who nodded to them to let her continue. She could tell both wanted to object, but rather than appear divided in front of the suspect, they stayed quiet. Coyle probably figured she would screw things up and he could then blame her. She figured just the opposite. Her gamble was that Kevin would consider her less of a challenge.

"Oh, boy," he said and kicked the chair opposite him. "Let's play horsey."

Alma let one side of her mouth curve into a satisfied smile and slowly lowered herself in the chair. She crossed one hand over the other in the same manner Kevin had his, and when he leaned a bit to the left, she did the same. "We know from members of your group that you disappeared for a few days just prior to them all arriving at Jesus Falls," she said. "Can you tell me where you went?"

"I can," he answered but said no more.

Alma opened her hands palms up as if to inquire.

Kevin's face faked a confused look. "Oh," he said. "I thought I was only to answer the questions you asked." His deep brown eyes, shades darker than Ian's, were menacing when he stared at her. She thought of coal when she looked into them, but they lacked the sparkle of mineral.

She remembered the Scotland Yard file had described him as having adopted pets from an animal shelter in order to set them afire. The information stuck with her because it pointed to the two sides of his personality. Here was a man who burned kittens, but could make a good enough impression to secure possession of them. Yet she wasn't seeing his charming side—the side that manipulated, and the lack of it was confusing.

"You're right," she said. "Thank you for correcting me." He shifted in his chair as if bored with her small talk. Alma let her body language follow his and shifted as well. "Where were you during those days?"

"Disneyland."

"Got any receipts?"

He rolled his eyes and huffed.

"So you weren't at Disneyland." Alma stood up and circled the table. Time to get into his space, she thought. "Mr. Corey," she said with a drawl and leaned down next to his ear. "My VCR is set, so I can stay here all night and ask this same question. But I would hate to inconvenience you."

"You're not going to like the answer." He sneered.

"That's not a requirement."

"I was with my brother at Silver Lake."

She knew her upper lip was sweating but didn't dare wipe it.

"Ian will tell you. You'd believe him, wouldn't you?"

Alma hardened her voice. "What I'd like to hear is the truth." She returned to her chair and leaned toward him. "And that's not what you're telling me."

"He was meeting somebody up there. She looked a lot like you." He paused and squeezed his features in a pondering expression. "Maybe it was you."

Anger bubbled in Alma's veins. He was playing her for

an innocent, and it amazed her that he'd implicate his own brother so directly—after all Ian had done to help him. She was certain he was lying, but the detectives wrote down every word.

"How long have you known Cassidy Fuller?" she asked, biting back her irritation.

"Who?"

"You heard me."

"Thirty years," he answered. "Give or take a decade."

"You don't even know who she is, do you?" Alma leaned forward and spoke more harshly. "You don't care to know any of your victims, do you?"

"I know a lot of girls. So does my brother. He gets laid in every town." He laughed in a low gargle. One detective made a move toward him, but she raised a hand to stop him.

Ian's friendship was the one weakness he could use against her. She moved in for the kill before he had the chance. "You prefer them anonymous. That way when you kill them they are like prey, no more important than swatting a mosquito. If they were individuals to you, you'd have to wrestle with what little conscience you have." She stood up and rested her hands on the table. "Tell me, do you keep souvenirs?"

"Do you screw every Scotsman that passes through town?"

"Kitty Sloat looked like somebody you knew?"

"So, is my brother good in bed?"

"Scotland Yard says your mother hanged herself. Do you think it was a suicide?" Kevin didn't answer. "Did Kitty look like your mother? Do I?" His eyes took on a glazed look, and he stared at the wall behind Alma's back. She had him on the edge and pushed. "Where were you when your mother was killed . . . Excuse me, when she died?"

He stood up quickly, knocking his chair backward. The detectives rushed him and slammed him against the wall. They picked up the chair and jammed him back down on it. "Do it again. I'd love to cuff you to the chair," a detective said.

"Why don't we stop playing games?" Alma asked. "Tell me where to find Cassidy Fuller."

Kevin stood up carefully this time and leaned into the table, matching her stance inch by inch, and whispered, "Follow the yellow brick road, bitch."

There was a knock on the door and then it swung open. Ian walked in with an agitated, wide-eyed expression. "Don't say anything, Kevin," he insisted. Beside him stood Walter Gentry.

Walter marched into the room as if he owned it. "Gentlemen . . . and Miss Bashears," he said stiffly. "I would appreciate all questioning of my client to cease this instant. I am now Mr. Corey's attorney."

"I was having such a good time," Kevin said, a hyena-like laugh escaping his lips. "Sure you want to represent me? I've killed thousands of people." He leered at all of them, moving his head in a semicircle. "I've smothered babies and gutted their mothers. I've gassed families in their sleep and decapitated priests as they prayed."

"Shut up," Walter said.

"You shut me up!" Kevin yelled back, bouncing around as if he couldn't control his body. "I'm a rapist, an arsonist, a God who'll send lightning to your grave to burn your rotting bodies! You should be shaking in your boots, old man. You better pray! Call out to God, mister. You should be afraid of me! I'm the Devil!"

Walter slammed his hands on the table in front of Kevin.

"I haven't prayed in ten years. I've taken on murderers who threatened my family and terrorists who bombed my office. I've eaten at the table of politicians who'd sell out their mothers for a nickel and watched as they did it. I'm not afraid of them. I'm not afraid of anything. I'm not afraid of the Devil, or God, or Alma Bashears, and I sure as hell am not afraid of you!"

Alma stood back as Walter ranted, getting control of his client, and oddly, restoring order to the room. She had to admit—for the first time that she could remember— watching Walter put Kevin in his place, she was impressed. And a bit afraid.

30

How could Ian do it? The question repeated in her mind as she slowly walked back to her office. Walter Gentry represented Kevin Corey. Part of her wanted to scream and part of her wanted to move out of the state. She cut through the park centered between the police station, courthouse, and city hall, slowing down by the fountain. The water cascaded down a concrete pyramid and the bubbling sounded almost like words. She wished they could give her an answer to what she should do next.

She sat on the edge of the structure, dipping her fingers in the cold water. On the far side she spied Patrick Kingsley, a folklorist and founding professor of Kingsley University. A crowd of kids gathered around him. During summer months he traveled from town to town telling Appalachian Jack tales. The children's laughter mixed with the gurgle of the fountain as Patrick let his voice slip into a deep bass tone that sounded as gnarly as a tree branch. "Then Jack realized the giant had lied to him, and he was mad as fire . . ."

"Miss Bashears!" a sharp voice called out. "I insist on speaking with you."

Alma turned to see Letitia Whitcomb marching toward her like an armor-wearing matron ready for battle. Near sixty, her fiery red hair was cropped closed to her face, giving her a birdlike appearance. "I am appalled at how you're mistreating the Fullers," she said, shaking her finger in Alma's face.

"Mrs. Whitcomb, I'm sorry you feel that way, but these are legal matters I can't discuss."

"There's nothing legal about trying to force those poor people into lie detector tests!"

As the woman's voice rose, Alma patted her shoulder to try to calm her down. Instead she jerked away.

"They aren't like that Susan Smith. These are religious people."

"With every missing child," Alma said, "a parallel investigation must be conducted and—"

"You've more than conducted your own tragedy, haven't you?"

"Excuse me?" Alma said.

"Diverting attention to the Sloat case every chance you get."

"That isn't true," Alma shot back, beginning to get angry.

"We didn't elect you so you could turn this into your own private kingdom." Mrs. Whitcomb crossed her arms and shifted her weight backward. "Without the downtown support you would never have been elected."

"I think demographics will show I had just as much hollow support, but that really is beside the point."

She laughed out loud. "And you won't have that by the time the Highland Toy strike is done."

"I have nothing to do with that strike."

"You're part of everything that goes on in this town, Alma Bashears, and so is your family." Mrs. Whitcomb's cheeks colored scarlet with her tirade.

"That isn't fair." Alma defended herself.

"I'll tell you what isn't fair—having your daughter disappear for no reason isn't fair. Not knowing what happened to her isn't fair. Kitty Sloat—this whole town could have foreseen she'd turn out like she did 'cause that's the way most hollow sluts end up!" She bobbed her head in a gesture of finality and stormed away.

Alma watched after Mrs. Whitcomb. Her heart pounded like a drum in her chest. "Well, does anybody else want to tell me off today?" she asked aloud.

"And Jack realized a very important thing that day," said a voice behind her. "When he sought his fortune in the land of ogres and giants, 'twas best to remember he couldn't always play by the rules."

Alma turned and saw that all the children were gone. Patrick Kingsley stood opposite her, staring up at the peak of the water spout. One thumb was looped through the strap of his costumed overalls and he held an oak walking stick. His gaze lowered to where Alma stood, but he didn't look directly at her. Taking a corncob pipe from his pocket, he bit down on it with the side of his mouth and nodded in her direction before turning and walking steadfastly toward the next town.

Alma watched after him, contemplating his words. The familiar ring of them came back to her in all the warnings of the past weeks. Jefferson's words rang in her head: *Contrary will follow its own path and play its own cards in its own way.* Vernon had said: *Your manner of thinking ain't always caught up with the rest of the town.* Mamaw had warned her: *No use locking the front door when the Devil has the key to the back.* Even Nathan Deever had reminded her: *They're gonna do what they're gonna do. And you have to play the game. If they can scare you into doing nothing, then they've done their job.*

They were all saying the same thing. She'd been trying to play by the rules, do what was legal and think she could mother this town as if it were a babe in diapers. She was still relearning how to live here. She was still remembering all the things she'd forgotten. How arrogant she'd been to presume the town needed protection. The mountains have their own ways and she'd have to adapt to them, not the other way around. She had to understand the people on their own terms. The rules were the last thing she'd follow from here on in.

31

Kitty's trailer had a stuffy sweet smell like the lingering odor of cheap perfume. Alma hadn't noticed it the first time she came, but the scent permeated the entire residence during a quick walk through. She returned to the couch and studied the living room, trying to see it as Kitty might have. The quiet offered an escape from everything going on in Contrary. Yet this was not a quiet house. A red feather boa draped around photos of friends with the logo of some bar pressing down on the top of the pictures, shelves were filled with coffee mugs and tacky souvenirs from Gatlinburg, the Smoky Mountains, and Dollywood, an unopened Garth Brooks CD lay on the coffee table. Danny's life didn't seem to exist in this room except in photos as a child, graduation from kindergarten, Little League; the picture where he seemed the oldest was in a junior high play dressed as a dragon. After that there seemed to be no documentation of his life.

In Kitty's bedroom a pile of *People* magazines had slid from their stack against the wall. Alma stepped over them and took in the sexualized decor—leopard-print sheets, a drawing of entwined lovers, candles surrounding the headboard, and scented sachets hanging from the ceiling. Where to start, she asked herself. What kind of woman were you, Kitty? I need to know you, if I'm going to find out who killed you.

On a dresser was a snapshot of Danny as a baby. Other photos showed his mother as a redhead, a brunette, and finally a blond, always with a full leonine mane that draped all the way to her waist. Her eyes were consistently her strongest feature, slightly grayer than Alma's, but just as intense.

She looked around and noted that the worn living room and overused kitchen were out of sync with the contents of the bedroom. It was as if Kitty's essence had drawn its strength from this room, where being female was all-important to her—but this woman seemed more girlish than grown-up, despite her age.

Out the window Alma could see an abandoned, stripped car, looking as if it had sat in the backyard for the last five years. On the hillside just beyond the property line was a grove of tulip trees. A man sat with his back propped against one tree. Both legs were jacked up against an adjoining tree and a oversized cowboy hat shaded his eyes. Alma watched him for several minutes. She realized he wasn't enjoying the afternoon sun. He was watching this trailer. A knock on the door startled her.

Through the window she saw Vernon. When he caught sight of her, she motioned to him that the door was open. He followed her to the bedroom and she pointed out the man on the hill.

"Probably Blackburn's people," he said. "They know I'm looking for Danny, but they can't keep me in sight but half the time."

"Vernon, you've got to be careful."

He shrugged off the warning. "Uncle George shot out a feller's tires last night." He chuckled as though he enjoyed the game. "They won't come into the hollow now without thinking on it real serious."

The discord worried Alma. She hadn't intended to put her family in more danger. "The only way to end this is to get that boy." She looked across the hall at Danny's room, which resembled the remains of a sale table at a department store. "I thought if I went through the house, I might find something."

"Did you find his box?"

"Box?"

"His secret box."

"I haven't searched his room yet, but . . . secret box?"

"Every boy has a secret box. It's where he keeps his stuff."

Danny's room was so crammed that they could barely find a path to walk. Posters of rap groups and half-clad starlets covered every available wall space. Desks and tabletops were covered with tools and engine parts. His clothes were bunched in piles, most at the bottom of the bed. "He's got a whole roomful of stuff," Alma said. "It doesn't look to me like he needed a separate place to keep anything."

Vernon rolled his eyes as he stepped over a large greasy motorcycle part that was so torn apart it was unidentifiable. "You need a place to hide stuff from your mother—and sisters, if you're unlucky enough to have them."

"I bow to your higher expertise." She opened her arms wide as if to offer him the room.

Vernon looked around and turned in a circle. He lifted up the bedsprings, dropping them with a thud when he found nothing. Tapping on several loose floorboards and knocking on the wall also brought no results. Amused, Alma couldn't help laughing when he pushed up a loose ceiling tile and down fell a *Playboy* magazine. Much to her amazement, there was a space above the ceiling. "Ah-ha," Vernon said, reaching in and feeling around. He grinned and pulled out a metal army surplus ammunition case. "See," he said triumphantly. "His box."

They sat on a pile of dank-smelling clothes on Danny's bed and emptied the box. They found a skeleton key, a sterling silver cross, a tiny metal plate with the logo LARRY-BOB LAZZARA'S FRYING PANS, a length of long blond hair bound with a rubber band, and a half dozen school pictures of teenagers.

"Oh, my God," Alma said, picking up one of the photos.

Vernon was focused on the metal logo, holding it closely for inspection.

She also picked up the lock of hair, then showed him the picture. "Do you know who this is?"

"Girlfriend?" he asked.

"Cassidy Fuller." She held the hair next to the picture. "And I would bet this is hers. Now, who do you give a lock of your hair?"

"Boyfriend?"

"Do you realize what this means?"

"It could mean many things, Alma," Vernon replied. "We used to trade school pictures all the time."

"But not hair," she said, the discovery beginning to excite her.

"What it doesn't mean is that we're any closer to knowing where Danny is."

"Well, I'll make one bet that I'm confident on—wherever he is, you'll also find Cassidy Fuller."

Alma leaned back on the pile of clothes. Suddenly the helmet-clad motorcyclist she'd seen at the church and in town talking to Cassidy made her wonder. Could that have been Danny? She looked over at Vernon, who was tapping the metal plate against his palm. "What is that?" she asked.

Shaking the plate until some of the rust fell off, he appeared deep in thought. "They used to make these frying pans in the eighties at the old factory on Highway Ninety-nine."

"It's been abandoned for years," she said. "An industrial area," she added, beginning to catch on to his line of thinking and remembering the patrolman in Contrary who had chased Danny in the same area.

"A good place to hide."

Alma looked out the window at the hillside. The man had been replaced by a woman in a sundress reading a magazine and talking on a cell phone.

"I can get there," he said as he stood.

"Wait for me." She rose, eagerness filling her for the first time in many days. "I'll go to my office for a few hours to throw them off. I'll make sure everybody sees me, then slip out the back way."

They agreed to meet in two hours on a service road behind the factory. Alma took the picture of Cassidy and the strand of hair. She needed answers, and needed them from people who wouldn't want to give them.

32

"Val," Alma said into her car phone as she swerved around a double-parked car. "I need you to locate the Fullers and Chief Coyle and get them to my office ASAP." If she let these key people see her, she figured that they would not bother her the rest of the day, leaving her free to meet Vernon and search for Danny.

"That's not hard to do," Val answered. "The whole building is buzzing . . ."

"About what?" Alma steeled herself for the latest news.

"The Fullers and the press are with Kevin Corey. They're over at the jail now."

"Is this being televised?" Alma asked, but she already knew the answer.

"Uh-huh," Val muttered. "Wonder how much of a donation this escapade brought?"

"I'm at the jail," Alma said, making a U-turn behind the station and pulling into the zone marked for police units only. This wasn't what she'd intended when she'd thought of making sure everyone saw her in the office in order to throw them off her trail, but it would work just as well.

"Wait," Val squealed. "You have E-mail from Grady."

"Who?"

"Detective Forester," she said.

"You're on a first-name basis with him?" Alma asked with some amusement.

"Uh . . ." Val hesitated. "Yes and no. I'm not, but you are."

"What do you mean, Val?"

"Well," she drawled, guilt filtering through her voice. "I never got around to canceling that request. You know, the DMV records, voter registration. I used your password, so . . ."

"He still thinks the request came from me." Alma put the phone on her shoulder to take a deep breath. "And what is this going to cost me, Wondergirl?"

"Just a letter of recommendation for a job he's applying for."

"Oh, that's all." Alma cursed to herself. "Val, he could be an incompetent dolt for all I know."

"But he's not. You should see the databases he's come up with, not just in Detroit but nationally. I bet he finds your Allafair Adair."

"Okay," she said, "where's the job he's appling for?"

"Police chief in Chattanooga."

"Well, I guess that's far enough away from me."

At the front entrance of the jail, vans from various television stations and a Knoxville tabloid show were parked in the handicapped section. Alma motioned to an officer and told him to ticket all of them. A handful of reporters waiting around the front desk shouted questions to her until she was out of their line of sight. All the interrogation rooms, meeting rooms, and holding cells were empty. Alma pondered the situation. Surely Coyle wouldn't let the media into the cell block. She went up a back staircase and came to the first guard station.

"Is Chief Coyle back here?" she asked.

The officer rolled his eyes and drew Alma aside. "Miss Bashears," he said, a worried tone in his voice, "I'm as loyal a man as there is in this department, but I can't understand why the chief would do something like this."

"Get someone to take me to them."

A few minutes later her request was accommodated and Alma could hardly believe the scene. The glare of camera lights struck her as she marched down the hall. Danielle was on her knees praying while Harlan spoke to a reporter. As Alma came closer she saw that Kevin sat on the end of his bunk staring through the bars at three different video cameras.

Danielle opened her eyes but stayed on her knees. "You seem like a spiritual kind of man," she said to Kevin. "Do you understand how I feel?"

He swung his legs back and forth, a nasty smirk on his face. "Why don't you tell me?"

"I loved my daughter with all my heart." Danielle reached out and leaned on the bars.

Alma waved frantically to Coyle, who stood on the other side of the group behind the camera crews. There was no way she could reach him without being caught on tape.

"Can you find it in your heart to feel our loss?" Harlan stepped behind his wife, letting a hand rest on her shoulder. "All we ask is for you to tell us where she is—even if—" His voice broke and he bowed his face into his hands. Danielle reached behind her and held on to her husband's legs as tears streamed down her face.

"I beg you," Danielle said. "I know we can work together on this."

Kevin exploded with laughter. His cruel outburst was taken in stride by the Fullers, but Alma felt disgusted by the scene. "Talk to me," Danielle said, "Christian to Christian."

Kevin jumped off the bunk and went down on his knees to Danielle's level. "How 'bout killer to killer?"

"Chief Coyle!" Alma called out, knowing she had to bring an end to this. A camera swung toward her, its bright light blinding. She knew she had to act carefully. "I'd like to speak with you . . . privately."

A series of slamming gates behind her carried the sound of more trouble.

"Stop this! Stop this at once!" Walter Gentry yelled as he hurried toward them. He came up beside Alma into the camera light. "You have no right to do this to my client. Turn that video off at once."

The camera kept rolling, but Alma stepped forward and put a hand over the eye. "Chief Coyle, get this crew out of here now, and take the Fullers to your office."

"Please," Danielle pleaded. "He can help us." She turned back to the cell. "Have you buried her? Burned her? Is she in water? Just tell me. I will help you, and I will forgive you with all my heart!" Harlan wrapped his arms around her and she sank against him.

Several officers arrived and Coyle slunk back into a shadowed area as they hustled the camera crews out.

"How could you let this happen?" Walter accused Alma.

"I didn't," she tried to explain.

"Mr. Gentry." Harlan stepped away from his wife and put his hand on Walter's shoulder. Walter immediately wiped it off. "Can you not see our desperation?"

"Grabbing at straws isn't going to locate your daughter," Walter retorted. "Find another way."

"Alma," Harlan implored. "Help me."

She knew she had to remain sympathetic to the parents of a missing child but also make it clear that this kind of exploitation could never happen again. "In this case, I wholeheartedly agree with Mr. Gentry." She got in between

Danielle and her husband, intending to separate them and prevent their unified stand. "You may have jeopardized the prosecution of this case—that is, if Mr. Corey is the one responsible for your daughter's disappearance."

"I'm responsible for the whole wide world," Kevin called out from his cell and kicked the bars. "From the shores of Montezuma to the cliffs of Silver Lake."

"Don't you see what an animal he is?" Danielle whispered in a trembling voice. "Think of what he might have done to my beautiful daughter."

"Where's all that forgiveness you promised?" Kevin asked and laughed as he bounced onto the lower bunk. "Don't you know I can predict the future?" He pointed at Danielle. "And I see you forgiving me. Is that what's in your heart?"

Walter ignored him and asked Alma, "What did you mean, *if* he's responsible?"

She looked up at Walter, figuring she should not be surprised that he'd caught her words. She pulled out the picture of Cassidy and the lock of hair and held both up in front of the Fullers. "These were in Danny Sloat's room. They knew each other . . . very well." The silence of the next several seconds was broken only by a low chuckle from Kevin Corey. Even if he were innocent, Alma thought, it was an evil sound. "Now Danny is hiding. Tell me if it's possible that Cassidy is with him."

Danielle's expression hardened. "I tried to be friends with you, Alma. I wanted to be. But you're like that thief that steals in during the night and you've stolen my daughter's integrity."

"See," Kevin said, rising up and pressing his face against the bars. "Danny killed her. Danny killed her. Danny. Danny. Danny." He repeated the name over and over.

Danielle began trembling and Harlan pulled her into

his arms. She jerked away and backed toward the exit. Her eyes were wide, almost wild. For a moment Alma thought Danielle might run forward, throw herself against the bars, and attack Kevin. Danielle pointed at him, her finger shaking so hard she could barely sustain the gesture. "I'll be back," she said to him. "I'll be back, and we'll pray together."

Kevin's cackle was so wicked it made Alma want to slam him against the wall. She couldn't believe he was the brother of a man she had come to care about. As she left Walter with his client, she could hear him chanting, "Danny did it. Danny did it."

33

Alma turned up the radio as the voice of a tearful Danielle Fuller pleaded for the safe return of her daughter. Harlan echoed the request and gave an 800 number for donations to the Find Cassidy Fund. "Why do I have such a slimy feeling about such a good cause?" she asked herself.

When she saw Vernon's Jeep Cherokee coming up the road she switched off the radio and got out of her car. He stopped about twenty feet away, leaned across the seat, and came out of the Jeep with a pair of binoculars. By that time, Alma was beside him.

"Sure you weren't followed?" he asked, scrutinizing the road behind him.

"Well, I'm no double-oh-seven, but I don't think so." Alma walked to the shoulder of the road and looked down an embankment at a deserted factory. Each floor of the four-story redbrick building was lined with large windows formed of postcard-size panes, most of which were broken. "So you think he's hiding there."

Vernon pointed to one side of the building. "Look," he said, giving her the binoculars.

Overgrown weeds and rusted barrels were scattered across what used to be a parking lot. Alma adjusted the lenses then let her gaze coast over the broken windows, metal doors hanging by their hinges, and fallen-down signs of a more successful era. Graffiti spattered nearly every wall. She thought she even saw something from the class of '82—her class.

"Over by the loading dock," Vernon said.

A large concrete loading dock jutted out from the building and slanted at an angle. "I see it," Alma said. Near the door was a skeletal motorcycle. Strewn around it were a wheel, motor, and a set of handlebars turned upside down. "Someone's doing their best to repair it," she said. "Okay, how do we do this?"

Vernon had the glint of a hunter in his eyes. "It's called skunk and flush." He grinned. "Me and Star go after squirrels that way."

"Well, let's just try to catch a boy." Alma slid down the hillside and told him to pull up his Jeep next to the loading dock. "I'll flush," she said. "You skunk."

"Wait," Vernon called after her. "Don't go in till I get there."

"I don't want to scare him," she called back. "Stand guard near that motorcycle. That's the way he'll go. In case he runs . . . just make sure you get him."

Alma entered the building through a side door left ajar so many years ago that the bottom was caked into a mound of dirt. She tightened her grip on her unlit flashlight. The hull of the building was like a fractured eggshell, light leaking into the large auditorium from hundreds of broken windows and cracked walls. She surveyed the area quickly then listened. The tinny sound of music came from upper rooms on the north side.

Across the dusty floor she watched for footprints to follow. Several wobbly metal staircases led to higher floors but didn't look safe. She stepped onto the one just below the rooms where the music played and it swayed under her weight. She'd have to find another way up or . . .

maybe she could get him to come down. "Danny?" she called out, her voice sounding hollow in the vacuum of space. No answer. "Danny," she said louder. "It's your cousin, Alma. I'm here to help you." The music continued to play.

She touched the handrail of the staircase and stepped up despite the swaying and disjointed creaks of the metal. When she reached the next level, she followed the music down a hallway. The hall was dim and only a few dusty, cobweb-filled rooms had windows. In several cubbyholes rats scattered when she shined her flashlight. At the end of the hall, she came to the room with the music. She turned off her flashlight and peered around the corner.

A blond-haired boy, his back to her, beat an imaginary set of drums to the rhythm of grunge music on a tape recorder. His hair swung and shook all around him in the dim light. Alma reached out to touch his shoulder. "Danny?" she asked.

He spun around at the sound of her voice, knocking over the tape player. Before she could speak he darted into the next room. Alma ran after him. "Danny!" she screamed. "Wait!" He scrambled down corridors and through dark rooms. A wisp of cobweb clung to her face and she flinched. Before she knew it, he was out of sight and she was lost. She hadn't heard any of the staircases creaking so was fairly certain he was still on her level. If she could only get him to listen to her.

"Danny," she called out. "I'm your mother's cousin. Alma Bashears. She must have told you about me." She stepped onto a creaking board that gave with her weight and moved in a different direction. "I'm here to help you. Danny, you know you need help. I understand the kind of trouble you're in." A shove against her back sent her sprawling. She lost the flashlight and stumbled against a pile of lumber, which cascaded over the railing onto the concrete floor below. The boards beneath her gave way. She grabbed for whatever she could but momentum carried her down. Her shirt got caught on a rafter. The material ripped. Alma looked up and grabbed for the piece of wood.

Swinging by one hand, she struggled to get a firm hold with the other. Only then did she look below and see that the drop was nearly twenty feet. A steel pipe jutted out of the wall next to her and she tried anchoring a foot against it so she could jimmy herself up onto the upper-level floor again.

"Give me your hand," said a voice above her.

She looked up and was stunned to see Walter Gentry leaning down toward her with his hand extended. Distrust filled her stomach like a full-course meal. The drop beneath her was serious. She might break a leg if she fell, but nothing inside her was going to rely on him.

"Come on," he insisted and bent farther forward, holding on to only the metal railing that outlined the upper levels.

"I have nothing against a helping hand." She stared up at him. "But I'm not entirely certain yours wasn't the one that pushed me."

He rolled his eyes and pursed his mouth in annoyance. "Don't be a fool. You could kill yourself."

"Or you could conveniently drop me." The board she held on to cracked like a breaking twig. "What the hell are you doing here?"

"Cross-examination is probably not a prudent exercise at a time like this."

Behind him came the rhythmic sound of footsteps. "Alma," Jefferson Bingham's voice rang out. "Oh, my God!" He stood behind Walter and gripped him around the waist. "Grab on," he told Alma.

She reached up and seized hold of Walter's hand. Together they hoisted her up, landing in a sprawling pile of arms and legs.

Alma quickly struggled to her feet. "Do you want to answer me?" she asked Walter. "What the hell are you doing here?" She looked over at Jefferson as well. "Both of you?"

Walter dusted off the legs of his pants and took his time. "Obviously, I'm following you." He turned to leave.

"That's all?" she yelled at his back.

"You're after that boy, and so am I. I don't trust you to turn him over. You find him—and you'll find Cassidy Fuller." Walter continued to walk away with the disinterest of someone who had no further use for her. "Then my client can get out of jail. A simple explanation, I would think." He carefully traversed a wobbly metal staircase to the ground floor. "Did you expect a conspiracy?" He disappeared into the haze of dust but his voice finished out. "Don't bother thanking me for saving your life. It's the least I could do."

Alma glanced over at Jefferson, who looked like a sheepdog that had chased the herd instead of guarding it. "And you?"

"I was following Gentry," he said. "I had no idea where he was going. I saw him following you . . . and—and . . ." He stuttered and his face flushed.

"I don't believe you," Alma said and crossed her arms over her chest. "You were following me, too, weren't you?"

Jefferson bit his bottom lip, the pink in his cheeks growing redder. "Danny isn't still a suspect in his mother's murder, is he?"

Alma shot him a look of disbelief. "I suppose it depends on who you ask." Jefferson looked after Walter and stepped in that direction as if to leave. "Just a minute," she said sternly, stopping him in his tracks. "You don't spend your time shadowing Walter Gentry. Every time I'm close to finding Danny or have some information about him—there you are, snooping in the background." She circled around and got in front of him. "What is your connection with this boy, Jefferson?"

He shrugged his shoulders and held out his hands with a look of innocence. "I've answered you, Alma. What more can I say?" He shrugged again.

Alma still didn't believe him, but she knew him well enough to know he wouldn't reveal any more. "Let's get out of here," she said and took his arm. "Danny's gone."

"Are you sure you're okay?" he asked as he helped her down the stairs.

"I'm glad you followed Walter," she said, holding on to his arm. "I wouldn't have grabbed his hand if I hadn't seen you."

He circled an arm around her shoulders. "Call me your guardian angel."

She hugged him and they held each other. She leaned into his neck and whispered gently in his ear. "Tell me what your interest is in this boy."

Jefferson pushed back. "You play me every damn time!" He walked a wide circle around her, dust kicking up from his heavy-footed march. "It's all a puzzle to you—and you can't be satisfied till you know the answer to every question. Sometimes you're as big a busybody as your mother."

"That's why I'm such a good prosecutor," she teased, enjoying his discomfort. Alma watched as Jefferson followed Walter Gentry down the road, and one after another both men got into their cars. Once they were out of sight, Alma ran as fast as she could to the back loading dock.

"Did you get him?" she yelled frantically at Vernon who leaned against the back of his Jeep.

He opened up the hatch and said, "Uh-huh." There on the floor was a hog-tied Danny Sloat, struggling against a piece of duct tape across his mouth as if he were calling them every obscenity he knew.

34

A single candle illuminated the room. Alma wiped a band of sweat from her upper lip and sipped lukewarm water from a jelly jar. Across from her a hostile Danny Sloat did everything he could to keep from looking her in the eye.

"Where am I?" he said defiantly.

"A safe place," she answered. "A place where no one will find you."

"Aren't you supposed to arrest me?" He shifted sideways as much as his restraints allowed and kicked the legs of the table. "At least the jail has electricity."

"Yes, I should take you to the police," Alma said and leaned toward him. "That I haven't—thus breaking the law by harboring a criminal—should convince you that I'm protecting your best interest." She spoke firmly. "Jail would be too convenient a place for your drug buddies to get their hands on you. And I think you know what would happen then."

He was quiet and stared at the floor. "I don't got nothing to say—either here or at jail."

"I can sit here another twenty minutes," she said to him. "But I'll be back, and then I can sit here all night." She reached out and squeezed his chin between her finger and thumb. "You're not going anywhere, Danny, and I'm not the enemy."

"You're holding me against my will," he spit back at her, jerking from her hold.

"It's for your own good."

"Yeah, right."

"If you don't care about yourself, then think of Cassidy," she said, appealing to his sense of loyalty. "That factory is dangerous. Cassidy is alone out there. If she's at the factory or you know where she is, let me help her before she gets hurt."

"Like you've helped me?" he growled, straining against the ropes.

She stood up and hovered over him. "Do you know how much danger you're in?"

"Anybody messes with me will know they been in a fight afterward." He shifted the other way as much as he could. "So untie me."

Alma looked down at the rope securing him to the chair. "Well, if you hadn't vaulted for the door twice and tried to jump out the window, you might've fostered a little more trust in me." She fingered the rope, tight around his chest. "You can stay tied up for now."

He let out a huff and sneered.

"Don't you understand I'm trying to help?"

"Why would I need it?"

"Because you don't have anybody else!" She slammed a fist down on the table. Her outburst quieted him and she was surprised that he didn't respond.

He looked down at the table and his expression crimped into a pout. After a moment he asked, "Did you arrest my mom because of what I do?"

Alma rested her elbows on the table between them and laid her face between her hands. The candlelight flickered.

Of course, she thought, he's been on the run, no radio or TV, he doesn't know what happened to his mother. She reached out and untied the rope holding his hands together. "Danny," she said. "I want you to remain calm." She leaned over and touched his shoulder. He didn't flinch or pull away like she expected. "I have some tragic news."

She inhaled deeply, trying to keep her voice from shaking. "Last week . . ." She swallowed. "Kitty went to Silver Lake. We think she was meeting someone."

"Mom hated the lake. She thought it was haunted." His eyes narrowed and he kept them averted from hers. "I figured the cops got her because I ditched 'em the last time I ran drugs over in Quinntown. They'd been questioning her a lot lately—about me. Mom is hurt? In the hospital?"

"Danny," she said to halt his talk. "Danny, I'm sorry." Her nose burned and she sniffed.

"No," he said.

"Your mother died at the lake." Alma wrapped her arms around his shoulders. "She was murdered. And I'm trying very hard to find out who is responsible."

Quietly he brought a hand up and covered his mouth as if in disbelief. The boy looked past her with a frozen expression, processing information that had cut him to the core. She touched his cheek and wiped sweat from his brow. He pressed his forehead to the table and silently stared at the wood. Alma stayed next to him, rubbing his back and telling him stories about when she and his mother were young girls. Before long the room felt full with Kitty's presence and then she sat silently, waiting until the boy was ready to speak.

"There's nowhere to go," Alma said when Danny finally lifted his head and looked at the door.

"Who killed her?" he demanded. "How did she die?"

He sat quietly as Alma explained. She left out the horrific

details, and when Danny said he had no idea who she was meeting that night, she took the opportunity to ask about Cassidy.

"I can't say where Cassidy is," he said, staring at the table. "We were supposed to meet at Jesus Falls . . ." He sniffed and his voice shook. "Blackburn did this?" he asked. "I'll get him . . . I'll get him."

"Which is why you're staying tied up right now." Alma grabbed the boy's hands and shook them to get his attention. "Leave Blackburn to me."

"I'd never turn on him . . . Why would he do such a thing?"

"He's only one suspect, honey." Alma knew she needed to draw his attention away from Blackburn. "How did you and Cassidy meet?" she asked.

"Mom trains her father's snakes." He folded his hands on the table and bit into his lower lip. "Trained the snakes. The Quinntown office . . ." He hesitated and drew in deep breaths. "Mom used to laugh about it—her and Reverend Fuller making time in the back room with the serpents, and me and Cassidy making out in the front room."

Alma thought back to her mother saying that Kitty had gone to a Pentecostal church at one time. That would have given her some experience with snake handling. "Let me understand this clearly," she said, stepping closer to the boy. "The snakes are trained?"

"Well, handled," he said. "The more you handle them, the more they become like pets. Then you can use them in the sermons and never get bit—well, almost never."

"That Fuller is such a con man."

"Naw," Danny said. "He was good to Mom. Better than most."

She stared out the window at a tiny willow tree, just barely breaking four feet. The same kind of tree that had hovered over Kitty's last breath, Alma thought. Her child died that night, too, and that pregnancy may have been the motive. "Just how good was Reverend Fuller to your mom?" Alma asked, careful not to let her voice or expression appear judgmental.

"I can't believe she's dead," Danny said, crossing his arms over his chest. "I can't believe somebody would do that to her." He looked up at her, staring deeply into her eyes. "Alma, when can I see her?"

"I'll make the arrangements, but for now, I have to keep you out of Blackburn's hands. You'll be safe here." She waited, and he didn't respond. "I'll have the ropes untied."

Alma walked outside on the porch and sat on a wood crate in between Vernon and Derek McGee. The air was hot even though the sun had set. "He may try to run away," she said to Derek.

"He won't get far."

Vernon stood up and stretched until his back cracked. "Best I go show my face in town and let Blackburn's boys start tailing me again."

Alma shook Derek's hand. "Thank you. There was no way I could safely hide him in our hollow without—"

"You did me a good turn," he interrupted and nodded knowingly, "and now I'm doing you one."

Alma followed Vernon down to the hill. Scores of fireflies illuminated the forest like twinkling stars and some distant foxfire glowed. It might be called beautiful, but as Alma took it all in, Danny's story of Kitty and Harlan swirled in her mind. She could think only one ugly thought. Harlan Fuller had reason to kill Kitty. It was the only explanation that made sense. Harlan Fuller was the father of Kitty's unborn child.

35

On the drive back to Contrary, Alma reconstructed everything she knew about Kitty's murder from the point of view of Harlan Fuller. He had a family and a ministry to protect. If her suspicions were correct and the church was being used as a front for laundering drug money, Fuller would have felt tremendous pressure. A bombshell like Kitty's pregnancy could have blown his reputation to the doorway of Hell and brought such unwanted attention as to make his benefactors nervous.

She wondered how Cassidy figured in. Could the girl's disappearance be a stunt meant to create a vortex of sympathy around the Fullers? It bothered Alma that Danny had said he *couldn't say* where Cassidy was, not that he didn't know her location. It could be that the two kids had their own agenda. All the more important to make sure Danny wouldn't run away again, hide out, and work against her, either on purpose or out of ignorance. But Vernon would take care of that—the hiding place was better than her cave up on the mountain.

On the outskirts of Contrary she slowed down when she saw Walter Gentry's white Porsche parked at the Indian Creek Motel. She pulled into the lot and drove up close enough to see a blue Ford rental car beside it. Most likely he's with Ian, she thought, parking her own car around the side of the motel. Several times she started to leave, but each time a pull inside of her made her turn off the ignition.

After twenty minutes she saw Gentry exit an upstairs room. He left without seeing her and she headed for the room. Her heart thumped rapidly and a tingle of dread and excitement spread through her. At the door she raised her hand to knock then stopped. Why was she here? What would she even say? To keep from changing her mind, she quickly tapped on the door.

Ian opened the door without welcoming her and his sidelong glance betrayed a mixture of hurt and confusion. He motioned her to enter. The air-conditioned room was icy and sterile. Two chairs were stacked with backpacks, books, and copies of legal documents that Walter had probably left. Alma sat on the side of the bed. The pillows were propped against the headboard and indented from where he'd been sitting. In the center of the bed were tiny strands of yellow cord and a thin gold metallic thread. They were braided in the most unusual crisscross pattern Alma had ever seen. She picked it up and noticed that it matched the tie holding back his ponytail. Within the unfinished piece he had imbedded yellow topaz rhinestones. "This is beautiful," she said.

"A silly hobby that helps in times of stress." His cheeks flushed a pinkish tone. "It's one of those craft things we do in Scotland." He took the piece from her and began to finish the last of it. "My mother taught me."

"I came by," Alma said, " to tell you that I don't think your brother killed my cousin." He looked up at her quickly and watched her face with the intensity of an artist searching for meaning. "Other suspects are being identified and we will investigate those."

"And Cassidy Fuller?"

"I don't know what to tell you about that yet, but . . ." She stopped. "Ian," she said hesitantly. "My position . . . There's only so much I can disclose."

He reached out and looped the gold band around her wrist. "Before all this happened, you gave me some of the best memories of my life." He tied the end, making it a bracelet. "This will be over soon, and I hope we'll find each other again. Until we can meet and not have to hide anything, let this gift say that there is a connection between us that is beyond this present reality."

She touched the bracelet and squeezed the material between her fingers. "I don't think anyone's ever given me something they made with their own hands." She laughed then touched his shoulder. "Unless you count the powder-blue polyester pantsuit my sister sewed for me last Christmas."

He chuckled along with her then reached out and caressed her cheek, letting his palm slide down the length of her arm and holding one of her hands, then both. The warmth of feeling was as if nothing negative had happened between them. She almost felt they were back in the cave. Part of her wanted to kiss him, fall into his arms and stay the night. She stood up to break the vision forming in her mind. Moving toward the door were the hardest steps she'd ever taken. "Can I ask you one question?" she said, firmly placing her hand on the doorknob in case her resolve weakened. "Why Walter Gentry? You asked my advice and I recommended Jefferson Bingham. You hired Walter Gentry."

Ian shrugged and looked briefly at the floor. "I was dialing Mr. Bingham's number when I remembered reading the articles about your brother's murder trial."

Alma thought back to the first time he came to her office. He'd mentioned having checked up on her.

"The library had most of the information. I saw Mr. Gentry's name there and found him in the phone book." He stood up and stared down at her, his composure showing no hint of apology. "Alma, I know how good you are. I knew I had to have someone who could beat you." His hands curled into fists. "From what I read and after talking to him, I realized I had to hire Gentry. This is my brother, Alma. You've faced these same circumstances. Would you do any different?"

She shook her head. She did understand. When Vernon had been in trouble, she would have done anything to save him. Why should she expect Ian to be any different? She opened the door, stepped out, and looked back at him. He leaned into the pillows, and his aloneness touched her. The bleakness of the motel room made her long to take him out of it and give him the comfort of a home.

"Alma," he called after her. "Gentry harbors a lot of resentment toward you. Something more than professional hatred."

She felt her face heating with shame. "Don't go there," she said. "It's ancient history and a deadly story." She turned and left, wishing with all that was in her that she could have stayed.

When she got home the ache of the incident gelled in her chest. She opened a bottle of sauvignon blanc and drank half before realizing it. Opening the glass door onto the side porch, she sat outside in the darkness, the starry sky reflecting the golden color of the wine. Drunk enough to wallow in her emotions, she wept and gulped down another drink. She stared into the oval pool of wine at the bottom of the glass. "If only you were tea leaves I could read," she said.

If she was right about Fuller, then half the puzzle was solved. But what of Cassidy? Her stomach cramped and what had been a pleasant warm buzz became a sick nausea. There were far too many possibilities to commit to one—Cassidy could be hiding and Danny knew where; she could have left willingly with Kevin or someone else; her disappearance could be a publicity stunt staged by the church. Alma rose from her chair, reaching up to the sky as if it would help her stand. Everything around her spun. She tripped over a table and crawled out into the yard, landing in a full-length lawn chair.

Curled into a fetal position, she thought that if she got sick, it might as well be outside her new house. She twisted onto her back, opened and closed her eyes waiting for the nausea to end, the stars that she so loved shone down, offering no comfort. This was what she wanted in a home—comfort. "Home," she said. "Maybe I misunderstood the concept. How will I ever get home . . . Follow the yellow brick road." She sat up, a clearness coming over her. *Bitch.*

Her stomach cramped and she pitched forward on her knees and threw up. When she managed to get back to the seat, Kevin's words repeated in her mind. *Follow the yellow brick road, bitch.* There was one possibility she was not considering. What if Cassidy Fuller was dead?

Alma had the awful feeling that as despicable as Kevin was, his honesty might be his only natural gift. *Follow the yellow brick road, bitch.* Oh, God, she thought, not there. Anywhere but there.

A clear picture of the gold-colored walkway leading into the baptismal pond at Jesus Falls formed in Alma's mind. Danny was supposed to meet Cassidy there. That placed the girl in the area. Ian's students had left early while Kevin remained behind, waiting for Ian to get out of the hospital. The park would have been deserted, except

for Kevin and an innocent teenager waiting on her boyfriend. She's there, Alma thought. I know she's there. But
if Kevin was telling the truth . . . he'd also said, *Danny
killed her. Danny killed her.*

36

By six A.M. the diver from the state police was suited up and ready to enter the water. Alma had instructed Chief Coyle to seal off the park. She realized he'd agreed only because he hoped she'd make a fool of herself. The fog through the trees was so thick it looked solid and the sun wouldn't break over the mountaintop for another two hours. A slight mist rose off the water and reflected an eerie blue under the spotlights anchored on top of police units. A dozen officers walked in line formation examining every inch of the park. Several cast quizzical glances at her. No doubt they shared Coyle's opinion that she was nuts.

The Fullers had been notified of her suspicion, but only Harlan had come. He stood near the edge of the water and stared into the baptismal pool with a vacant, weary expression. He seemed to have aged ten years overnight. She hadn't expected to see Walter Gentry. He hiked up the path just as the diver began walking into the water.

About waist-deep, the diver pulled down his mask, bit into the mouthpiece of his snorkel, then swam out until he dove into the deepest part of the pool. The waterfall curled in a horseshoe shape and cascaded from a height of forty feet in a clear, inviting sheet into the creek below.

Alma stepped back when Walter turned around. They faced each other like gunslingers, and for a moment she felt as if she had no breath. His lips were slightly parted and he, too, seemed to be struggling for air. He turned away and leaned against a police car. Alma lowered herself onto the bench of a picnic table, her strength ebbing from the nonspoken encounter.

"Why is that man here?" Harlan Fuller asked, coming over to sit next to her and pointing at Walter.

She cleared her throat to give herself some composure time. "He's representing the interest of his client," she said, staring straight ahead.

"It is difficult for me to understand how someone can defend such a despicable character as Kevin Corey."

Alma looked over at Fuller. His features were twisted in disgust.

"I know," he said before she could speak, "these are words you never thought you'd hear from me." He let out a short, curt laugh. "Imagine. Me—who has forgiven the sinful of their transgressions, taken in the scum of the earth, and loved the weak for their weakness. But I'd kill anyone who'd hurt my daughter." He clasped his hands together as if to keep them from shaking. "You must think me quite a hypocrite."

Alma studied him as he spoke, noting that the tear he wiped from the corner of his eye seemed as real as any she had shed. "I believe you'd do anything to protect what's yours," she said evenly. "That's only human nature, something all of us would do." She couldn't help remembering Danielle's disbelief that Star had pushed out her own pups. The differences between this husband and wife were like dream and nightmare: one offering glittery salvation while the other made the world into a version of her own skewed reality. Alma shifted toward him. "I hope I'm wrong about this," she said.

"Do you really think she's there?" he asked. "She was

always with one of us . . . She didn't drive . . . How would she have gotten here?"

"You see that ridge," Alma said and pointed beyond the waterfall at a hill that framed its far side. "On the other side is a hollow that ends in the back of your property. It's probably less than a twenty-minute hike."

He stared at the tree-lined mountains as if their beauty were now a puzzle to him. "But why would she come here?"

"Perhaps to meet someone." She watched to see if he'd react. "Someone she couldn't see anywhere else." Alma waited, noting that his breathing had deepened and his eyes were slightly out of focus as if he relived a memory. "If your daughter was usually with either you or your wife, then it is possible she was meeting someone one of you knows."

Fuller was silent, raised his hand as if he were about to speak, then did not.

"You know," she said deliberately. "I've been trying to find my cousin's son, for some days now." He leaked out a controlled breath like a man who needed time to process her words. "Why would he run from those who want to help?" she asked in a musing tone, so as not to challenge him. "He's too afraid, just doesn't trust—"

Fuller interrupted her as if his thoughts were a revelation to him. "You have to have faith in your children, just as they have to have the security of faith in you." He stood up, running his hands through his thick silver hair with the intensity of wiping guilt from his person. "I've failed her. I've failed my daughter."

"Then don't fall short of her now." Alma rose and stood beside him, one hand on his shoulder to support him. "Cassidy would want you to be the honest, upright man she believed in."

"I lied to you about knowing Kitty," Fuller said, one hand smoothing down the front of his yellow cotton shirt. "I did try to find the boy after his mother was killed." He glanced at her once but could not sustain eye contact, and his embarrassment reddened his cheeks. "I knew he'd need someone."

The response surprised Alma. She'd expected he would continue to deny any association with her cousin. "You're going to have to come to the station and answer some questions about your relationship with Kitty," she said. He nodded and closed his eyes. She started to move away, but he grabbed her arm and pulled her back down to the bench.

"I have nothing to hide. I have prayed to God that if he'd give me back my daughter, I'd own up to my responsibility to Kitty." He folded his hands at his waist. "The truth is in my faith."

"Faith is often a misapplied concept when it comes to the law," she said, a seed of unexplained bitterness planted in her voice.

"In the end, Alma, faith is all we have. There is no assurance in words, trust in books, or truth in actions without our faith that they are to us what we believe them to be."

An image of her own father flashed through her mind and she knew where the bitterness had been born. Misplaced, was all she could think. Misplaced faith.

A gurgle of bubbles emerged from the pond and the diver stood, pushing his mask onto his forehead. "It's about sixty feet at the deepest," he called out.

Alma hurried over to the edge of the pond. The diver walked toward them until the water was at his knees. A group of policemen, Walter Gentry, and Chief Coyle surrounded her.

"There's nothing, Miss Bashears," the diver said.

Alma raised a fist to her mouth and bit on the knuckle of her thumb. She had been so sure. She was positive Cassidy's body was here. He took off his flippers and walked out of the water.

"Waste of money," Chief Coyle said. "Biggest damn waste of money this county's ever seen." He strutted like a rooster about to crow.

"Try again," she told the diver. "This time . . ." she struggled with a thought she wasn't sure of. Her vision seemed to blur in front of her and she saw the sandy, grit-filled water rising around her. "Go underneath the falls," she said. "There's a . . . a shelf—a ledge of some kind. The body could be caught there."

The diver stared at her and wiped water from his nose. He turned back and looked at the pond, then at her again. "How would you know that?"

"I—I don't know," she stammered. "I just know."

"Our commonwealth attorney is psychic." Coyle laughed and slapped his knee.

"Do it," Walter Gentry said, in a low, firm voice.

Alma glanced at him and saw that his face was pale as the distant fog. She quickly turned away.

"Mr. Gentry," Chief Coyle said. "This is crazy."

A glare from Walter shut him up. The diver pulled down his mask and submerged himself beneath the water. Coyle marched along the shore. Behind her Alma felt Walter's presence. He stepped closer to her and she raised a hand to stop him without glancing at him. "Don't," she said angrily through gritted teeth. "I can't even look at you right now."

She heard his footsteps as he walked away, then a few moments later the motor of his car started. If she could thank him for anything, it would be his absence at a time like this. She looked up at the top of the falls. The water rolled over the crest like a clear bolt of silk. She could never tell them how she knew about the underwater ledge. She could never let them know that she'd once jumped from the cliffs of the falls. She'd jumped to get away from Walter Gentry and his friends—the friends who had raped her. She'd felt the sandy bottom, she knew the metallic taste of the water, the hazy depth that was brown and silver at the same time. She'd been there. That's how she knew what was underneath that waterfall.

An eruption of bubbles broke the surface, followed by the diver. He waved one arm over his head and spit the snorkel out of his mouth. "Got her," he yelled. Alma turned to look at Harlan Fuller. He stepped backward, then sat down hard on the bench of a picnic table, his mouth slightly ajar and his nose red as if he might cry. He licked his lips and closed his eyes as if in prayer, then folded his hands chest level to prove that he was.

37

Walter Gentry slammed his briefcase so hard against the bars of the jail cell that Alma flinched. The frustrations of the last half hour's negotiation were straining everyone to the breaking point.

"I agreed to this only on the condition that it be a civilized questioning," he shouted at the detective who stood next to him looking into the cell at Kevin Corey.

Kevin had been so violent that the detectives recommended not taking him to a conference area. The only way they were sure of being able to control him was to leave him locked up. The ripped-apart mattress on his bunk and a sink kicked half off the wall supported their conclusion. Out of the corner of her eye Alma saw Ian surveying the damage.

The detective turned around and blew through his lips. "There's nothing civilized about your client."

Walter said, "I've given you a copy of the sales receipt for a ninety-eight Harley from Corbin Motorcycles showing Kevin Corey was at that office on the evening Miss Sloat was killed. Once the detectives talk to the salesman, accounting office, and the receptionist, you'll have the proof that he could not have been at Silver Lake. This interview is at an end."

"Wait," Ian intervened. "The point is to show these

people that my brother had nothing to do with the Fuller girl's death." He looked over at Alma, his eyes pleading. "Can't we simply talk in a straightforward manner instead of resorting to these provocations?"

"You don't have to prove your brother's innocence," Walter said. "It's up to them to prove his guilt." He crossed his arms over his chest and marched up and down the cell block. "Miss Bashears knows that Cassidy was there to meet Danny Sloat. Her father has already admitted the two kids had an involvement of sorts. And yet you," he said sarcastically to Alma, "are not bringing Mr. Sloat in for any questioning. That indicates to me that you not only know where he is, but that he is just as likely a suspect in this girl's death." Walter walked to the other side of the group and leaned against the bars of the cell. "Well, Miss Bashears, when are you going to produce Danny Sloat?"

She smiled, parted her lips slowly, and spoke deliberately. "If you can prove I know Danny's whereabouts, then go ahead, Mr. Gentry. You can add it to the petition going to the governor. Until the police have located the boy, we obviously can't question him as to the validity of your alleged facts." The silence indicated to Alma that they knew the rules were being broken but also realized there was nothing they could do about it. Alma used it as the tool to distract them. If she brought Danny in, Coyle would turn him over to the drug dealers. The boy would be dead before he had a chance to answer a single question.

Time for redirection, she thought, and stepped up to the bars of the cell. "Back to the body we have," she said to Kevin. "The students were gone, your brother spent the night in the hospital, so that leaves you. You, for certain, were in the park. You were the only person at Jesus Falls besides Cassidy. Now what does that say?"

Kevin stepped closer to the bars. "Well, maybe not the only person."

Alma whispered, "So, you saw someone else there?" His lips curled into a smirk that pushed into his left cheek. The smile looked like Ian's and for several seconds it unnerved her. "Okay," she said. "Let's say you didn't kill Cassidy, but you saw who killed her. Now I can think of only one reason why you're not spilling your guts right now." She grabbed hold of the bars and pushed her face against them. "That person have something on you? What is it, Kevin? What could it possibly be? A rather implausible theory."

Kevin faced away from them and leaned his forehead on the wall. He spit out a half-laugh, then looked over his shoulder toward Alma, but not at her. He looked beyond her toward the entrance. "Danny killed her."

"You saw it?"

"He stabbed her."

"Where?"

"In the heart."

The men shuffled behind Alma. "That's not how Cassidy died," she said in a clear voice. "There was no one else there—no one but you."

He answered louder than necessary. "Maybe. Maybe I did see someone else there."

Alma flinched at the blare of his voice. "Maybe's not an answer. If someone else was there, obviously he might be able to clear you. So why not tell me who he is?"

He stared past her again. "Yeah, why not?"

A gasp from several yards away broke the intensity. The group turned and Alma saw Danielle Fuller. The guard behind her said, "Sorry, folks. I thought you were finished."

"What's she doing here?" Alma asked the detective under her breath.

"Gentry made special arrangements for her to come during visiting hours to pray with Corey. The guard shrugged his shoulders as if to say he didn't understand it. "Gentry said it was his client's request."

"I think Kevin Corey is about to find God and get real cooperative," Alma whispered.

"An insanity defense?" the detective asked.

Alma shook her head. "This is Walter's idea . . . to get the Fullers to forgive him. In court, it'll sound as flawless as a player piano. If the victim's parents can find forgiveness, then so can a jury."

"It'll save him from the death penalty," the detective said.

Mrs. Fuller didn't turn and follow the guard out but instead stepped forward and looked deeply into Kevin's eyes. "I know if we pray together, God will show us the way."

"Can't wait," Kevin said and fell to his knees.

Alma looked down at him and was disgusted. "I think we have all we need here," she said. "Gentlemen, could we speak outside?"

As the detective, Ian, and Walter passed Danielle Fuller she nodded to each one of them and they offered their sympathies for her loss. Her red-rimmed eyes and cracked lips made her seem to be in another world. The guard backed Kevin away from the bars, then set up a chair for Mrs. Fuller outside the cell. Alma paused, letting the men get ahead of her. She dipped her head to Danielle and asked, "Why are you putting yourself through this?"

Mrs. Fuller made an attempt at a serene smile but only managed to look all the more forlorn. "Absolution helps me cope," she said stoically and pulled herself up straight as if that would make her stronger. "If I can forgive my daughter's murderer, then I will have done my duty and lived by the creed I created for myself." She turned toward the cell.

Alma walked through the door and looked back at Mrs. Fuller sitting in the chair, hands folded, speaking in a whisper to Kevin—praying, she supposed. He sat on the end of his bunk, feet swinging and leaning so that his elbows were propped on his knees and his chin in his hands. Alma couldn't help but admire this woman's ability to forgive. Had it been her, she didn't think it possible to extend mercy under such circumstances.

Outside Walter launched his attack. "You have no evidence. You either charge him or you let him go, or I'll be in court this afternoon."

Alma knew he was right, but she had one card she'd yet to play. "I can hold him one more day."

"On what grounds?"

"The FBI wants to talk to him."

"The FBI?" Ian repeated.

"They can't get here until tomorrow," she said. "They're investigating a series of murders along the route that your group followed. Motorcycle tracks were found at some of the crime scenes." She tried not to look at Ian. She knew their investigation would cover him as well. He didn't know it, but all the students had been held in Memphis and questioned.

"Are we the only people in America riding motorcycles?" Ian asked, frustration edging into his voice.

"They didn't tell me anything," Alma said, feigning lack of knowledge and halfway wishing she didn't know as much as she did. "Only that the murders have similarities— so you'll have to wait one more day."

She nearly ran from the group before Walter could think of another reason to engage her. Once away from the jail she hurried to her office. The FBI had given her one more day. And in that day, she was under extreme pressure to find something. Danny had better start coming up with some answers.

38

Alma had intended to stop at her office only long enough to check messages, but Val waved an urgent fax from the state attorney general asking that she call him immediately. "He's also left two phone messages this morning. I hate to think what's on your home machine."

The information went through her like a spear. The recall petitions and that damn letter, she thought. This was the last thing she needed to deal with right now. She looked at her watch. If she waited five minutes it would be past noon and he'd be at lunch. "Thank you for coming in today," she said to Val.

"With all that's going on how could I sit at home." Val held open the door and made an odd gesture toward inside. "Besides I got all of last week's typing done."

Alma entered her offices and found Chief Coyle standing in front of the door. "If I'd left it unlocked," she said with a hint of sarcasm, "no doubt you'd be at my desk with your feet up."

"There ain't nothing in there I don't know about," he replied.

She opened her door but stood on the threshold and didn't invite him in. "Yeah?" she asked up into his face.

"I sure wish things could have been different between me and you." He held his cowboy hat in his hands and shifted back and forth as if he were a nervous high-schooler about to ask for a date. Behind his back Val put a finger in her mouth to mimic gagging. "At least professional."

"Can't imagine what you mean," Alma said. "It's very professional between us."

"Okay," he said, tossing the hat on Val's desk and fixing his hands on his hips. "Your brother ain't been seen since yesterday morning. Any idea where's he's stashing his boots?"

"He has a very thick little black book," Alma said innocently as Val picked up the hat and threw it on a chair. "Have you tried any of those numbers? You probably have some of them, too."

"I think he's with Danny Sloat and you're hiding him."

"Unless my brother has broken some law, I don't understand why you're talking to me about him."

"Your brother's on probation. Hiding that boy could get him in trouble. If you know where they are, I could charge you with obstructing justice."

"You . . ." Alma put her hand to her upper chest and feigned a misunderstood look. "You, you would charge me?" she asked with a false sweetness. "Last time I checked, my name was on this door."

Coyle laughed and shifted his weight to his left leg. "Well, maybe you ought to return your phone calls to the attorney general. All that could change."

Alma shut the door in his face and listened to make sure he'd left. When she heard Val clicking away on her keyboard, she pulled out her cell phone and booted up her computer at the same time. She dialed a number and Vernon responded with a disguised "Yep?"

"I can't get to you," she said. "Meet me at the funeral home in an hour."

"Got it." He hung up.

The computer flashed a message from Grady Forester. DID YOU HEAR THE ONE ABOUT THE LAWYER AND THE BRASS RAT? THAT COP JOKE WAS HITTING BELOW THE BELT. YOU KNOW HOW COPS ARE ABOUT THEIR BATONS. SEE YA LATER. GRADY.

"Val," Alma said into the intercom. "I thought I told you to get rid of Grady Forester."

Her assistant cracked the door open and peered inside so just half of her face appeared. She tentatively stepped inside, her eyes wide and her mouth hanging open. "I didn't expect you in so early. I didn't want to hurt his feelings."

"Do it today. His messages are weird, and what's this 'see you later' stuff?"

"Yes ma'am," she said, dejection filling her voice. "I'll handle it."

"Val, I don't want to be disturbed for the next few hours, by anyone." Alma got up and locked the door as her assistant exited. After waiting a few minutes, she changed into the pair of blue jeans and a T-shirt she kept in the closet then looked out the window. The courtyard was clear except for a half dozen people going to their destinations and an old man feeding some blackbirds. He casually looked up at her window several times while she paced to and fro, ensuring that he saw her. A little past noon she returned the call to the attorney general. As expected, he was out to lunch so she left a message.

In her private bathroom she opened the window leading to the fire escape on the side of the building and climbed out. At the bottom, she jumped and landed on the bank of Moccasin Creek then slid farther down on rubbery grass almost to the water's edge. She followed the canal to the end of the town's retail section, crawled up to the street, and entered the funeral parlor through the rear entrance.

Miss Millie looked up at her, surprised. "Why, Alma,"

she said, "you nearly scared the bejesus out of me." Miss Millie had been doing the hair and makeup of the deceased for nearly forty years. Her own coppery mane hadn't changed in style or color in the same amount of time.

"Miss Millie, I don't have a lot of time." Alma panted from her run up the embankment. "I need to go to Kitty's viewing room."

"Your Momma and Sue have already been here," she said, leading the way down a hall. "I tried to talk them into having the funeral tomorrow but—" Miss Millie did an up-and-down at Alma's clothing but withheld comment. "There's only so long we can wait." As she led Alma through a corridor of small rooms, only one had an open coffin. Alma paused to look in at a very old man laid out in a black suit that made his skin seem whiter than alabaster. They passed no other visitors to the funeral home. When they reached Kitty's viewing room, Alma felt relieved that the coffin was closed. Two people sat in the front row of seats—Vernon and Danny.

"I'll sit here," Miss Millie said, indicating a chair just outside the door, "in case you need me."

Alma thanked her and went to sit on the other side of Danny. He stared at the coffin. She touched his shoulder and shared a concerned gaze with Vernon.

"Can we get some batteries for my tape player while I'm in town?" Danny asked. "There's not a fricking thing to do out there." He stared steadily at the drapery hanging underneath his mother's coffin. Alma recognized the boy's way of trying to avoid feeling his grief. "Maybe I could come back to town now. I got friends I can stay with." He glanced up at her once and then back to the drapery.

"Danny," she said softly. "I need you to tell me about Cassidy." His eyes narrowed suddenly. Alma held her breath. If the boy was connected to the death, better she be prepared for it now. "You said the two of you were to meet at Jesus Falls."

"I can't say what happened to Cassidy." Danny twisted away from Alma.

"Do you mean you don't know, or you can't say?"

He rose and stepped halfway toward the coffin, seeming to be drawn to it and avoiding it at the same time. The reality of death must have worked its way into him because he reached out and touched the coffin lid. "I want to see my mom," he said and turned to Alma. His eyes were watery. He fought back tears and sniffed down congestion. "I want to see my mother!"

Miss Millie entered the room and hurried to Alma's side.

"Open it. I want to see her." Danny put his hand back on top of the coffin.

Alma looked at Miss Millie, both of them concerned. "In this case," Miss Millie whispered, "we recommend a closed coffin." She pulled Alma aside and whispered, "All those cuts, Alma. I had to use so much mortician's wax—your momma agreed with me to leave the casket closed."

"Danny, it's probably not a good idea to open it," Vernon said.

"I don't care," he said.

Miss Millie stepped toward him and spoke as softly as she could. "Honey, your momma was cut some . . . We did the best we could, but you don't want to see her that way."

"Danny," Vernon said, "your momma would want you to remember her walking in the mountains or throwing a snowball at you, not like this."

"In two days, you're gonna put my momma in the ground forever, and I'll never see her again in my life." He looked back and forth from Vernon to Alma. "I'm all that's left of her."

Alma felt a lump in her throat, not sure she was doing the right thing. "Miss Millie, go ahead. He knows what to expect."

"Well," she said, "we did the best we could."

She unhooked the hinges of the coffin then lifted back the lid. Danny stepped forward in slow awkward steps. Alma could see Kitty's profile and was grateful that the neck wound was fully covered. Her face had been puttied but her features were distorted and her skin appeared waxy, like a mannequin's. Danny looked down at his mother and breathed heavily several times. He spun around, his face at once questioning and angry. "Why'd you cut her hair? She loved her long hair. Why'd you cut it?"

"Why—why . . . I didn't," Miss Millie stammered. She seemed taken aback by the boy's hostility, even though she'd had years of dealing with bereaved relatives.

Vernon took hold of Danny's shoulders and nearly forced him to a seat. Alma quickly moved to close the coffin, but even she couldn't help but look upon her cousin's face one last time. She flashed on the pictures she'd seen of Kitty in her house, smiling face, sparkling eyes, and hair so long she might have been Rapunzel. Alma had assumed she'd gotten it cut, but if she hadn't, what had happened to it?

"It's okay," she assured Miss Millie. Alma walked her to the doorway. "We were fairly sure he'd be real upset and thought it best to get this out of the way before the funeral." Miss Millie nodded that she understood. "I'd appreciate your not mentioning this to anyone."

Miss Millie touched her hand. "Of course, dear. Nobody around here for me to tell anyway."

When Alma returned to Danny, Vernon had calmed him down. She sat on the other side of him and tried to look into his eyes though he averted them. "Danny, if you're in trouble or you did something wrong . . . something maybe you didn't mean to do, I'll help you." She wished she could break through to him. "But you've got to trust me and tell me what happened." She waited. The boy wiped his nose and stared from the coffin to the floor. "Why can't you say what happened to Cassidy?"

"Because nobody would believe me."

Alma leaned back in her chair. She hated admitting it, but even she was having doubts as to whether he might be involved in the girl's death. With the state he was in, an interrogation by Coyle would make him look so guilty he'd be tried as an adult. Obstructing justice or not, there was no way she was turning him over right now. She debated whether to tell him that Cassidy had been found, then looking over at Vernon and seeing his worried expression, she decided to keep the information from the boy.

"Do I have to go back to that hiding place?" Danny asked.

"For now," Alma answered. "For your safety."

"No electricity," he said without inflection, as if he really didn't care but needed to object. Danny pointed at the purple irises at the side of the coffin. "Did you bring them?" he asked.

"My mother did," Alma answered.

Cassidy liked purple irises," he said. "Maybe I could send some of those to her funeral."

Alma closed her eyes. She stood up without thinking and then looked at Vernon. His face mirrored her own distressed thoughts. Danny knew Cassidy was dead. He already knew. Did that mean he had killed her?

39

Another trip to the morgue was the last thing Alma had time for, but she didn't want to risk getting only half the information again as had happened when she learned that Kitty was pregnant. Nathan motioned her into the autopsy room. She swallowed hard and followed him.

In the center of the room she could see Cassidy's long blond hair hanging down from the table. It reached halfway to the floor and had dried to the golden color of ripe wheat.

"She did drown," Nathan said.

"Accidental?" Alma asked quickly, half hoping.

"The dead have their own way of speaking." Nathan pulled a blue sheet down past the girl's collarbone. "Neck trauma and bruises on her shoulders indicate she was held underwater." He raised one finger. "Here's our lucky break." Bringing up a frosty-colored white hand, he indicated the fingernails. "She scratched the hell out of whoever held her down, and we got a lot of skin material from underneath her nails."

"Isn't that typically washed away?"

"Yep," he said. "But she balled her fist, covering the tips of her fingers within her hand. The muscles stayed contracted and it protected the substance." He gently lay her hand back on the table and covered it with the sheet.

"You don't always get this lucky. I wish we'd had a little more luck with your cousin."

Alma patted his shoulder and they stood quietly for several seconds, mourning the child's final moments on earth. "I know you did your best." She looked down at a bluish-gray face that in life had been so troubled. "About Kitty," she said. "Did it seem to you that her hair was unevenly cut, maybe chopped?"

Nathan thought for a moment and looked confused. "I'm a coroner not a hairdresser. With today's styles it's hard to say. I'd ask Miss Millie, she'd know."

"One other question. What is the probability of Kitty and Cassidy being killed by the same person?"

Nathan shook his head and lowered himself into a chair, resting his arms on the desk. "I tell you what bothers me." He crossed his legs and cupped his chin between a thumb and forefinger. "This girl was cared for, almost prepared. Her hair was braided, her clothes neat, socks folded down properly, even a little bowtie underneath her collar. Your cousin—well, you know how they left her." He paused, his eyes darting back and forth as if checking on thoughts he wanted to be sure of. "I know it's improbable that two murderers live in Contrary, but no, Alma, I'd have to say the person who killed your cousin is not Cassidy's killer." He looked away from her and down at the floor. "You know, just about everybody in town is going to disagree with me."

"I'll be lynched if I suggest yet again that the Fullers take lie detector tests."

"Remember, Alma," he said gently, "you're after the truth here."

She knew his words were meant to encourage her to think beyond the obvious, and she knew that meant

Danny. "Maybe the killer didn't have time to do to Cassidy what he did to Kitty," she argued. She also needed to believe there was only one person in their midst capable of such deeds. "Your report did say Kitty's mutilation took place after she was dead. Maybe somebody interrupted him. Maybe he got scared off before he had a chance."

"Maybe," Nathan said. "But I never seen a body brought in here yet where the killer took time to tie a double tie in the victim's shoes." He pulled out a picture that had been taken at Jesus Falls and pointed to the girl's feet, which were clad in hightop black shoes with clog-type heels. "They had been taken off for some reason and were put back on the wrong feet. They're not easy shoes to wear. You have to untie them and retie them to get them on." He lay the picture on the desk. "I can almost see someone inviting her to wade into the water. She did so willingly, holding up her dress. After she was dead, the killer didn't want to leave the shoes or risk disposing of them in a way that might lead back to him, so he put them back on her feet. This person was in a hurry but took the extra time to care for her."

"You're thinking something," she said. "Tell me what it is."

"A stranger who kills a stranger doesn't care how they leave the body, and they certainly don't care where the shoes end up. Someone who cleans and dresses the victim—in effect takes care of them—loves that person despite having killed them. It's like they wanted her to have the shoes on so she wouldn't get cold. Whoever did this . . ." He wet his lips quickly, then hesitated. "Whoever did this knew her, and knew her well."

Alma thoughts filled with fears for Danny—the one person who had arranged to meet her there.

*   *   *

"Alma, that was the worst haircut I've ever seen," Miss Millie said. "It was chopped so uneven I was afraid I'd have to pixie it to make it lie right."

"I see," she said. Alma could have kicked herself for not getting more involved with the investigation earlier. She'd been so shocked by the murder she'd let Coyle foul it up royally.

"I'm so sorry the boy was upset, but I did the best I could."

"No, no, Miss Millie," she said quickly. "It's fine. I'm not asking because of him but for the legal investigation."

Alma's cell phone rang and she excused herself to answer it. The whole idea of Kitty's hair was getting confused with the lock she'd found that had led her to Danny's connection with Cassidy. Had Kitty's hair been hacked off by someone as a statement, as a form of punishment? But why and what would it mean?

"Alma, you got to get home right now." Her aunt Joyce's voice trembled with fear. "The boys are missing and—"

"Slow down, Aunt Joyce," she said. "Have you called the police?"

"No!" she yelled. "We can't call the police!"

"Why not? If they wandered off . . ."

"They're gone, Alma!" Aunt Joyce said hysterically. "Somebody's taken Larry Joe and Eddie!"

40

Alma hurried up the cracked concrete sidewalk, past the fern-green mailbox that had her sister's name painted in red underneath the names of her husband and sons. She saw Aunt Joyce looking out the front window, her face a stone cast of her worry. Her aunt swung open the door, letting out a misty smoke that colored the inside air. As Alma stepped in she smelled the odor of burned food.

"This note says for you to await instructions," Aunt Joyce said, her voice shaking. She was not a woman prone to hysterics, but the disappearance of the boys had her in near shock.

"Me?" Alma asked incredulously, taking the note and dropping her purse on the kitchen table.

"Yes, you." Aunt Joyce hiccuped a little cry, trying hard to maintain her composure. "They were in the backyard on the swings. Sue went out to check on them—and . . . Oh, Alma, she just feels like it's all her fault." Uncle George and Uncle Ames stood at a kitchen counter, oiling guns and reassembling them. "It keeps them occupied," Joyce said, as if sure Alma was about to say something disapproving.

"In this case," she assured her aunt, "it may be a good precaution."

Joyce looked relieved and nodded even though the

warning indicated that their situation was as bad as she feared.

"Where are Sue and Jack?" Alma asked, carefully opening the multifolded note by its edges.

"Jack's on his way to Johnson City to that construction job. We haven't been able to reach him." Joyce wrung her hands to keep them from trembling. "Your momma and Mamaw are with Sue." Joyce pointed down the hallway toward the closed bedroom door.

"Your nephews are in my custody," she read aloud. "Contact the authorities and they will be killed. The children are safe only if you follow directions. Wait for a phone call." Alma put the note in a plastic bag she found in a kitchen drawer, although she realized that by now the whole family had handled it and fingerprinting would be impossible. Dropping it into her purse, she started toward the bedroom.

As she passed the boys' room, she saw Vernon sitting on Eddie's bottom bunk. He bounced a ball on the floor between his knees. She entered the room and caught the ball on the upward bounce. The worried expression on his face was tense. "Could Coyle be behind this?" she whispered and knelt down on the floor beside him. "Or his drug-dealing brother-in-law?"

Vernon shrugged to show he was as much at a loss as she was. "Alma, if anything happens to those boys . . ."

She put a finger to his lips. "Don't even think it." She rose to go to Sue's bedroom, then needed to reassure herself. "We need to protect Danny. Is there any chance Blackburn can find him?"

He shook his head. "Not a chance. I left a cell phone there. Derek'll call if he sees anything."

She continued to the end of the hall. The whine of the bedroom door as it opened felt like a painful rip. Sue lay on the bed propped up by pillows. She held a telephone against her chest, a well-worn Kleenex in one hand and her other on a stuffed beanbag monkey that Eddie often carried around. Mamaw sat on the foot of the bed and Merl at a vanity. None of them spoke when they looked up at Alma. Sue gasped a small cry and wiped her eyes with the back of her hand. Alma couldn't help feeling blamed—the note was addressed to her, so the boys' disappearance did have something to do with her.

Alma sat on the bed beside Sue. She took the phone out of her sister's hand, but Sue grabbed it back and clutched it as if it were a lifeline to her sons. "We'll get them back," was all Alma could think to say, knowing that her words sounded empty.

"You haven't told anyone?" Sue asked through gasps of breath.

"No," Alma answered, "but we've got to tell the FBI."

"Don't tell anyone!" Sue screamed and sat up, dropping the phone off her lap. "The note said not to tell anyone!"

"Okay, okay." Alma put her arms around Sue and gently pushed her back on the pillows. She looked over her shoulder and saw that Merl had moved to the end of the bed beside Mamaw. The two women's faces were so grief-stricken that she feared they might break down any second.

"Promise me," Sue said. "Promise me you won't do anything!"

"Sue, honey," Merl said. "Calm down."

"Get her another one of your pills," Mamaw said.

"I don't want a pill," Sue cried. "I just want my boys back! I want my boys!"

The light ring of the phone squelched the hysteria. Alma looked at the base where a red light signaled another ring seconds before the sound. She punched the speaker-phone button. The silence in the room was deafening as thunder. "Yes," she said. "This is Alma Bashears."

"Thank God I found you," Val said.

"Val, I have to keep this line clear—"

"Alma, the FBI are here. They want to talk to you before interviewing Kevin Corey."

She tensed with frustration. Her sister covered her mouth to stifle sobs and Alma quickly picked up the receiver. "Val, I can't come now, I just can't."

"Alma, it's the FBI."

She looked around at her family. Vernon, Uncle George, Aunt Joyce, and Uncle Ames had all entered the room at the sound of the ring and now circled her, staring as if expecting some announcement. "Hold on." She moved the receiver away from her mouth. "If I don't go down there, it's going to seem very suspicious."

"For godsake, Alma," Val said. "I find your door locked from the inside, the state attorney general has called three more times, the FBI is here, and you're telling me you won't come in. I'm only a secretary!" Her voice took on an edge of hysteria tinged with anger. "What do you expect me to do?"

Alma looked again at the worried, almost hopeful faces of her family. She knew they all had expectations of her, but she wasn't sure she could live up to their belief in her. "I'll be right there, Val," she said and hung up the phone. Looking at them, guilt filled her. "If I don't go down there, they'll send someone here."

"You're going to tell them, aren't you?" Sue said between heaving breaths. "I know you, Miss Law-and-Order. You're going to do the right thing, and my sons will be dead."

"No, Sue," Alma pleaded, taking her sister's face between her hands. "You have to trust me. You have to trust me now." She hugged her and Sue dissolved into sobs. "I won't do anything to endanger the boys. I promise you. I promise you."

"Alma, you just can't leave now," her mother said. "What are we supposed to do when they call?"

"This phone has a memo button." She pointed to a side bar. "Vernon can program it not to beep. When they call, push the button and it'll record them. As soon as you know what they want, call me on my cell phone." She started to hurry away but stopped, knowing she needed to say something reassuring. The sight of the three women huddled like terrified kittens in the cold touched her as much as it frightened her. Her uncles, Aunt Joyce, and Vernon were backed against the walls as if they might hold out the dangers of the world. "This will be over soon," Alma promised.

Her grandmother held on to a bedpost. She looked up at Alma standing at the door. A single tear slid down her cheek. The sadness on her face seemed as permanent as in a portrait. Slowly, she parted her lips, and said, "Maybe I did make a mistake in having you come back here—as much for you as for us."

Alma put a hand on her chest, the pain of the words winding through her like hot liquid. Merl put her arms around Mamaw and the old woman cried into her daughter-in-law's shoulder. Alma started to return to them, but her mother waved her away. She mouthed the words, "She don't mean it." Alma walked down the hallway, her heart aching, feeling like it might burst.

41

"Each time the face had been cut and pulled away from the skin." FBI agent Steve Gilman lay three snapshots of murder victims in front of Alma. "This mutilation has been a characteristic of only the last few deaths."

"Like a step up?" she asked.

"Knowing how this gargoyle thinks is key to predicting his behavior."

"What could he do that is any worse?" Craig Carr asked.

"Torture," Gilman answered. "So far, what's been inflicted on the victims occurred after they were dead. If my man continues, he'll start conducting biology class on a live specimen." He looked around at the two agents who'd accompanied him. "We're focusing on men with medical training, maybe someone who's had a few years of medical school."

"That rather limits your profile," Alma said, expecting they would interpret her comment as an insult. The silence that followed was interrupted only by a humph and a cough that told her that the FBI wanted her information but weren't particularly interested in giving up their own.

"Why isn't the city police chief here?" Agent Gilman asked instead, his voice filled with a touch of condescension.

"No idea," Alma said. "I work for the state. He doesn't

report to me." She had a hard time looking at the photos, the image of Kitty's sliced face churning her memory.

Craig came up behind her and looked over her shoulder. "And there are eight victims?" he asked. "Starting at the tip of the eastern seaboard?"

"That includes missing women in Maine and New Jersey," Agent Gilman said, "but we haven't found the bodies yet."

"So my cousin was murdered by a madman with a fetish for killing a person in every state." Alma handed the grisly photos back to the younger agent who'd taken them from a file and turned toward the window.

"We class him a thrill-killer and a sexual sadist. His victims are ones of opportunity, but don't be surprised if he has a girlfriend or wife," said the younger agent. "If she's not totally under his control, she'll at least be susceptible to his manipulation."

Alma thought of Julie, the woman traveling with Kevin.

"He may revisit the crime scene," the agent continued, "if not through pictures or a souvenir from the victim, then perhaps by trying to insert himself in the investigation. Pay attention to anyone showing an unusual interest in the case."

"I don't get it," Craig said. "Why would he take the chance of drawing attention to himself?"

"Mental orgasm," Gilman said.

"That's why Kitty wasn't sexually assaulted," Alma said. "The fetish is in the death, in the killing, in the painful aftermath. I wonder what he learns from pulling off their faces?"

"Joe's our profiler," Gilman said, pointing to a silver-haired agent who looked to be about fifty. "The code is in how they leave the crime scene, which is why we don't think Cassidy Fuller is one of his victims."

"Because that would make two in Kentucky," Alma said. The implication made her uncomfortable. If Kevin hadn't killed Cassidy, then that left Danny as the main suspect. "When the Fullers discovered their daughter had been kidnapped—"

"Kidnapped?" the profiler interrupted. "They used the word 'kidnapped'?" He looked down then asked, "Did they also say they thought she might have been murdered?"

"It was their fear. I don't remember their exact words." Alma flared up at the interruption. "As I was saying . . . I have Kevin Corey in the area the morning of Cassidy Fuller's disappearance but can't prove he was anywhere near Silver Lake. If anything, his lawyer has a pretty airtight alibi for him that, pending substantiation, includes his signature on a sales receipt for a motorcycle." Her harsh mood infused the room with tension and the agents shifted around as if to distract her. She was sure they weren't telling her everything. "It could be that Kevin was interrupted and didn't have a chance to do to Cassidy what he did to the others. He was close enough to the state line that he may have thought he was in Tennessee—that would follow his pattern of one murder per state."

Joe Shamley, the profiler, stared at the braided bracelet on Alma's wrist. "Except for the peeled face," he said, "I can't guarantee that your cousin was our killer's victim. The Contrary police treated the crime scene like they were janitors at a picnic." He crossed one arm over his chest and stroked his chin with his forefinger. "There's not enough evidence to define where this case fits. Mutilation is common in fury killings among people who know each other—husband-wife, boyfriend-girlfriend. When it's with a stranger, the killer is visualizing someone he knows in the person of the victim. I think this act of peeling back the skin is the killer's way of seeing what a woman is composed of, what's beneath the surface, what she's made of."

"That presumes an initial confusion about women in general," Alma said. "I don't sense that in Kevin Corey. He thinks about women only one way."

"We have a saying among profilers: 'If you want to understand the artist, study the painting; if you want to understand the killer, study the crime scene.' There's always one element that's usually the best clue to his psyche." Shamley again stared down at her bracelet, a quizzical expression on his face. "Your initial interviews with Mr. Corey, as well as the way the evidence was collected, were slipshod," he said flatly.

"Just a minute!" Craig erupted. "We asked for FBI help, and you didn't have the time to drive down." He set his coffee mug on Alma's desk with a thud. "And now you walk in here second-guessing us because it might help your investigation?"

"I don't have an investigation," Gilman shot back. "I'm here just to advise." He smirked as if to say he knew the whole mess was their problem. "Until I talk to Corey, he could just be another tourist passing through town—from what I can tell based on your detective work."

"Then enlighten us," Alma said. "You've spoken in generalities long enough." She stood up and walked around her desk. "You want to treat Contrary's police chief like a hillbilly, go ahead. He might learn something, but don't be surprised if you end up with four flat tires and no rental agencies that will take your credit card." She leaned back against her desk between the younger agent and Gilman. "But if you want to come into *this* office and throw hardballs, you better be wearing a breastplate when we throw back. Corey is in our custody. Remember that as you decide what you're about to say next." She waited.

From Gilman's know-it-all attitude, she was fairly sure he had been playing big shot with the police forces in the other states. He evidently planned to continue the ruse with her.

Gilman exchanged a brief glance with Joe Shamley. He walked over to the window and opened it, allowing a warm breeze to enter the room. "In every case," he said slowly, "the killer has a signature." Agent Gilman looked down at the floor. "A clue, shall we say, that's peculiar to him. In Pennsylvania, he staked her through the heart with a steel rod. In Michigan, he replaced her guts with a carburetor. New York's victim had the Statue of Liberty carved in her chest, and Vermont's was fitted with a maple syrup spigot inserted into one of her temples. Nothing of this sort was done to your cousin or found by your detectives."

"He cut her hair," Alma said, one hand involuntarily covering her mouth. She slowly removed it, realizing that the suddenly quiet agents were focused on her intently. "She had waist-length hair and the killer cut it off."

"Has it been found?'' Gilman asked.

"No. We had criminalists from the State Police go over the area. If it was there, they would have discovered it."

"He might have thrown it into the lake," Craig offered. "Of course then we might never find it."

"Is there enough evidence to prove Kevin Corey's involvement in these other murders?" Alma asked directly. "If he can't be brought down for Kitty's death, at least tell me one of the others will take him off the street."

"It's a long shot," the young agent said. "The motorcycle group was both close enough to the crime areas for possible involvement and far enough away to provide alibis." He took out a small map and pointed to the red Xs in the states where bodies had been found. "In our questioning of the group in Memphis, we found that many times people would pair off and take side trips. We have a long way to go before we can connect the Corey brothers to any of this. It could just as easily be a truck driver meandering the same route or a sociopath on summer vacation."

"Brothers?" Alma asked, picking up on the word. "Is there any reason to think Ian Corey might be involved?" She held her breath as she waited for the answer.

"In the case of Kitty Sloat, there are certain similarities to their mother's death," Gilman said, "but proving it is another story . . . as I'm sure you know."

"What similarities? I read the Scotland Yard file. Their mother's death was ruled a suicide."

The two older agents looked at each other. The younger pulled out another file, but a look from Gilman caused him to put it away.

"Gentlemen," she said firmly. "You must understand that unless you can give me a reason for holding Kevin, I have no choice but to release him after your interview."

"I can't guarantee you anything," Agent Gilman said.

"Then fill in what you're not telling me." She pointed to the file.

Gilman did not follow her gaze. He kept a straight face. "I'll snare the man who committed these crimes," he said with a determination that was personal. "Unfortunately, it may take me a few more bodies to do so." He picked up his suit coat and draped it over his arm. The other agents followed his lead and prepared to leave. "You see, the state of Virginia is next and that's where we're headed after this party. Norfolk police are holding two men for us to interview. Both fit the profile and," he added with a bite to his tone, "they have medical school backgrounds."

Alma knew she'd come up against a brick wall. They were only going to tell her what they wanted her to know. She would have given anything to look at that file.

Obviously it held a telling secret. "Mr. Carr will accompany you," she said. "If I can be of further help, let me know."

"Likewise," Agent Gilman said.

As they walked out the door, Alma played her trump card. "I do have a question," she said. The men turned toward her with guarded expressions and a hint of impatience. "Does the name Jimmy Blackburn make anybody's blood pressure rise?"

The two older agents once again shared a knowing look. "Not in connection with this case," Shamley said.

"Of course," she said, letting her voice take on an edge of flippancy. "I've come into possession of certain information, and I'm wondering if the FBI would be interested in it?"

Gilman closed the door, shutting out Craig Carr and the younger agent. "Why don't you tell me?" he asked.

"Show me that file." She indicated the door and reached for the knob.

Agent Shamley let out a slight laugh and clasped a hand over hers. "I worked on Blackburn's profile for the Justice Department," he said, leading her back into the office. "You don't want to go after this man alone."

"He's small-time," Alma baited them. "I can get him for running drugs any time I want."

"He'd wipe up the floor with you," Gilman said.

"Shut up," Shamley told him. He chuckled again, looking admirably at Alma. "You should consider working for us if you ever get tired of small towns." He motioned for Gilman to wait outside.

When the agent followed his instructions, Alma realized that the profiler had the true power in the group. He'd deliberately held back to observe—a tactic she admired.

"Okay, maybe you deserve a break," he said, "but it'll

have to come in our time, in our way." He hesitated. "And maybe sooner than you think." He turned to leave and Alma caught his hand.

"Is Blackburn capable of hurting . . . a child?"

Shamley nodded once and studied her carefully, his eyes continually looking down at her braided bracelet as if it was a detail that he couldn't let go of. "Now, you tell me one thing," he said. "Why do you think that the medical training aspect limits the profile?"

Alma smiled and looked aside. "Because it's not that hard to skin a rabbit." His puzzled expression intensified. She explained, "Many people in this area of the country still hunt, not for sport but for food. Skinning an animal isn't that difficult. There's no medical procedure performed on any of these victims, only the skin peeled back—as you say, to see what is underneath. Anyone who's lived off the land would know how to skin an animal. Translating that skill to a human being wouldn't require medical education. It perhaps eliminates people from a city, but not anyone who's lived in the mountains, and the Appalachians span from upstate New York to just south of here."

Shamley nodded, looked at the floor, and then at the wall. "Okay, you've earned some icing for your cake," he said. "Here it is—our profilers have learned through many years of experience that parents whose children are missing go into a kind of denial. They seldom use the word 'kidnapped' or 'murdered.' It's too much horror for their minds to accept." He opened the door and stepped out.

"And there are parents who do use those words?" Alma asked.

"Yes, some do," he said. "I'm sure you'll figure out why."

After he left, Alma stared at the mess of coffee cups

scattered around the room. "Well, they're about as condescending as city boys can get," she said and pushed a cup into the trash can. Shamley's tone of voice about Blackburn worried her. Quickly she called Sue's house. Vernon told her still no phone call. It had to be Blackburn who took the boys, she thought. He wanted Danny and that would be the ransom demand. She gulped down several deep breaths. She knew Agent Gilman had not warned her in order to defend his own territory. He was saying this was as dangerous a man as there was. But Alma had no choice. She had to go see Jimmy Blackburn.

She grabbed her cell phone and headed toward the door. Val ran down the hall after her. "This fax just came," she said.

Alma looked at the dozen or so pages. They had been sent from a place called Bramshill in England. She folded them as she hurried down the hall. Inside her car she reopened the pages and read the handwritten note on the first page. *Mr. S. says to tell you that you're a sophisticated woman—that braided bracelet doesn't go with your pulled-together image.* Alma laughed and repeated the agent's words, "It'll have to come in our time, in our way." Shamley had come through. Well, she thought, I can tolerate his dislike of my jewelry if he gives me the answers I need. She hid the papers underneath her car seat then sped as fast as she could toward Quinntown. As eager as she was to study the entire file, her nephews came first.

42

Jimmy Blackburn had the muddiest brown eyes Alma had ever seen. The color was the dead shade of mud pies she used to make as a child, and staring into them put as bad a taste in her mouth. Quinntown's drug lord had let her be ushered right to his office, which took up the top floor of a midsize commercial building in the middle of the retail district. Blackburn was on the phone, both elbows on an oversize chrome desk. He pressed the receiver to the side of his head and held the other hand cupped over his ear. A balding, heavyset man whose paunchy gut hung over his belt when he leaned back in his chair and whose gold-capped teeth showed when he talked, he was the slick character she'd expected. What surprised her was to find Chief Coyle in Blackburn's office.

Alma sat in a chair across from the desk, Coyle already in the other. She noted that the chairs were short-legged, making Blackburn appear imposing and several inches taller than any friend or foe who might be occupying the seats opposite him.

She glanced over at the chief. He had a shiner on the side of his head that looked as if it would close the eye in a couple of hours. "Everyone's been looking for you," she said out of the side of her mouth.

"I been busy," he answered and slumped down in the seat.

"We could see our way to an understanding," Jimmy Blackburn said into the phone with a brief glance at Alma. He was dressed in a black casual suit with the sleeves rolled up and showing thick, hairy arms. The office was decorated in tourist-trap furniture, the ornate kind purchased at city liquidation stores. Several generic oil paintings lined the wall, a box of Cuban cigars sat on the table, and a full suit of armor stood in the corner, complete with a sharpened sword. A variety of stone, marble, and jade lion statues covered the desk, floor, and shelves, and a zodiac drawing of the constellation of Leo hung behind his head.

Blackburn's speech was not educated. Alma listened to him drop his *g*s and turn his *k*s into *t*s. But according to photographs of himself and his wife that lined a back table, he was well traveled. She saw photos of them in front of the Eiffel Tower, the pyramids, and the Taj Mahal. Alma realized he was no modern-day moonshiner—he was closer to Mafioso—and she was all too aware of the danger she was in.

He hung up the phone, turned toward her, folded his hands, and smiled as he spoke. "I bet you're here because of your little roughneck cousin."

"Danny isn't a threat to you," she said softly.

"I've watched you since you became commonwealth attorney," he said. "I'd sincerely hoped our paths would never cross." When she did not respond, he opened his hands and added, "But here we are."

"Frankly, I didn't even know your name until a few days ago."

Blackburn nodded and stood up, walking around the desk and leaning on the front of it. "My brother-in-law here . . . " He tapped Chief Coyle on the top of the head. "My very stupid brother-in-law here must have tipped you off to my activities."

Alma uncrossed her legs and avoided looking at Coyle. She wanted to appear as passive as possible. The thought of her nephews in this man's control terrified her. She sensed a lack of conscience in him. He thought of only one thing—himself. "I want my nephews back," she said, a wave of tears threatening to consume her. She swallowed and steadied her voice. "And I want them back unharmed."

"I got her nephews?" he asked Coyle.

"The price is not going to be my cousin's son," Alma said. "There'll be no trade, so don't even bring up the issue." She exhaled and the heat of her insides rose to the surface, bringing with it a slight sweat.

"Maybe Big Chief here is up to some no-good that I don't know about." Blackburn looked squarely at Coyle. "Well?" His tone deepened, edged with anger.

"I don't have those boys," Coyle said defensively. "I'd tell you before I did something like that." He twisted around in the chair and stared angrily at Alma. "Jimmy," he said, standing and pointing down at her, "this ain't like you. Taking her part against kin. Teach this bitch a lesson."

Alma leaned forward, looking directly into Jimmy Blackburn's eyes. "If you want to kill me, go ahead. Do it now. Do it in this office."

"Sit down," he told Coyle. The chief continued to stand rigidly for a few seconds, then with a single hand Blackburn shoved him into the chair. Blackburn bit the side of his bottom lip and chuckled. "You ain't no scaredy-cat," he said to Alma, "that's for sure." He circled around her and poked a finger on her shoulder, letting it travel the length of her back, and continued to his brother-in-law's chair. "I knock off a commonwealth attorney and I might as well invite the entire Justice Department for supper."

Blackburn stopped behind Coyle. "That's why it's stupid to beat up a public official unless they're on your payroll." He slapped the chief on the shoulder. "Only when you pay 'em do you have the right to hit 'em."

"I didn't hit her!" Coyle's expression twisted in panic.

"You think I don't have people watching you?" He clamped his hands on to Coyle's shoulders, squeezing them with the deliberateness of wringing a rag. "And now you lie to me," he whispered at the level of Coyle's ear. Stepping back, Blackburn smacked him hard on the side of the head.

"I only roughed her up," the chief whined. "It was to warn her."

Blackburn returned to his desk. "I offer my apologies to you, Miss Bashears. Hurting women ain't in my—hymnbook, you might say." He sat down slowly, adding almost to himself, "Unless they irritate me."

"They're only little boys," Alma said. "They have nothing to do with whatever happened between your organization and Danny."

"Let me be clear, Miss Bashears." Blackburn clasped his hands. "This business with your cousin is over and done with."

"What do you mean?" She held her breath, unsure she wanted to hear an answer.

"I said it's been handled," he said with the tone of the subject being closed. Blackburn leaned back in the over-sized swivel chair until his knees came to rest against the underside of the desktop. "Your nephews . . . I don't know nothing about them, but if you tell me they're missing, then you got my sympathies, and my assistance." He paused, leaning his head to one side. "You want my help?" He waited with a closed look that suggested it was now her move.

Alma stood up. He didn't have her nephews.

Blackburn matched her movements. "I'm sure we could come to an arrangement where you might help me out some day."

"I'll contact you if I have to," she said and turned to leave. As the door closed behind her she heard his loud voice cursing Chief Coyle. She prayed that she'd never have to call for that favor.

43

As she drove back toward Contrary a million thoughts sped through her mind. None of them made any sense. Jimmy Blackburn was the only person she could think of with a motive to take her nephews. Could Coyle have hidden them away? That might explain Blackburn's slap to the side of the chief's head—punishment. Her worst fears fed on each other in her mind: the children would never be found or they were already dead . . .

Alma jammed on the brakes, pulled over to the side of the road, and called Vernon on the car phone.

"Still no word," he said, his voice filled with the panic of waiting. "Alma, why are they taking so long?"

"They're waiting to see what will happen," she said. "And something has happened, or is going to happen." She couldn't help wondering what Blackburn had meant when he said that the matter of Danny was over and done. "We'll hear soon," she said, trying to reassure him.

"Alma, I don't know how much more Sue can take. Poor Mamaw is about to break down, too. If something happens to them boys, I don't think she'll live through it."

Alma struggled with ragged emotions as she disconnected the phone. She rested her forehead against the steering wheel and cried. This was all her fault. If she hadn't been who she was, if she didn't do the job she did, none of this would have happened. She should have left Contrary after her brother's trial. She should have stayed away forever because all she'd brought her family were tears and pain. What little she'd given them would never make up for this. "Larry Joe, Eddie," she said through hiccups of air. "I just wish I could hold you one more time."

She looked down and noticed that the fax Val had given her earlier had slid from under the car seat. To get ahold of herself and concentrate on something other than her nephews, she picked up the papers. Bramshill seemed to be an English equivalent of the FBI's training center at Quantico. This wasn't the same report she'd read from Scotland Yard. These pages told a very different story. She found a horrific picture of a woman's mutilated face so terrible that she had to put it down for an instant. It was several seconds before she could look again.

The skin had been stripped down to the chin, leaving the bloody muscle and misshapen eyelids hanging in place, exactly like Kitty. The woman's neck was gashed on one side as if the killer had been attempting to sever the head. Alma turned the page and read. The report was marked "classified" and some sentences had been blacked out— most notably the name of the highly placed member of Parliament who had been Eunice Corey's married lover.

So, Alma thought, Ian and Kevin's mother's death hadn't been a simple case of suicide. This much more gruesome death and dangerous involvement with a leading politician made Alma wonder how much the woman's sons knew, and how much had been concealed, even from them.

Alma repacked the papers and began to drive. She came to the road to Silver Lake and turned, curiosity prompting her in that direction. The winding dirt road was overhung by heavy white oak branches that gave the appearance of a tunnel, and at times visibility was so dim she had to switch on her parking lights. As she drove, her thoughts put together the only story that was possible from the information she'd read. Mrs. Corey's death was classified a suicide in order to protect someone. No law enforcement agency would purposely ignore the law. The order had to have come from someone very important, maybe even a foreign dignitary. "He might be suspected of the murder," Alma said aloud. "Perhaps someone who had diplomatic immunity."

Whatever the story, she realized, the death had been hushed up and sold as a suicide to protect reputations. Could Kevin have had something to do with it, she wondered? If so, then the FBI profile made sense. Did Ian know that his mother had been murdered? Some part of him must sense what kind of man his brother was.

The reflection of the lake was blinding. Alma held a hand up to shield her eyes even though she was wearing sunglasses. She walked around the area where Kitty had been killed. At one time, she'd been so sure that Harlan Fuller was the murderer. Now it looked like Kevin was guilty. She was sickened to realize that there was no way to prove it. The papers from Bramshill would be totally rejected by any government official either in the United States or in England. That she was in possession of classified information would make her allegations more suspect. Shamley had known what he was doing when he'd arranged for it to be faxed from a foreign country with no return number. He knew the facts would be useless except to answer her questions and put her mind at peace. Yes, they knew Kevin had killed her cousin and they would catch him, but as Agent Gilman had said, "It might take a few more bodies" before they could do so.

She walked into the shade of the willow tree and wished

with all her heart for one piece of evidence that would allow her to keep Kevin in jail. Holding a branch of the willow, she breathed in the grassy smell of the leaves, letting her fingers stroke down their length to the tips as if they were a child's long hair. "Witness Tree," she said to the leaves, "if you've really witnessed the sorrows of the world, why can't you tell me what happened here?" Her fingers caught in the twist of two vines and she unraveled them with some trouble.

She stepped back and looked at the leafy branch. Her gaze traveled upward. She gasped at what she saw. Just above her reach, the slender willowy branches were carefully braided together with long blond tresses of Kitty's hair. The silvery reflection of the leaves and color of the hair were so alike they were hard to distinguish. Alma reached up but could only touch the very end curl of her cousin's hair. And in the same instant, she saw that the intricate braid matched the braided bracelet on her wrist.

She ran as fast as she could to her car and ground it to a start. Racing down the road, she dialed the state police and told them to send a criminalist back to the crime scene to get the hair, then she called Craig Carr. "Keep him in jail," she said.

"It's too late, Alma," he said. "Kevin Corey was released about twenty minutes ago."

"It's not Kevin," she nearly screamed into the phone. "It's Ian. Ian's the killer." Her heart beat so fast she could barely talk. "Inform the state police and get those FBI guys back. Tell whoever's in charge of the station to set up roadblocks and . . ." Alma looked to the side as she turned onto the main route back to Contrary. The road curved around a wide U-shaped gulf that dropped off into a deep precipice. A thick forest grew down the slope. Through the treetops she caught the flash of a blue Ford. "I see them," she shouted.

"Alma," Craig asked. "Alma, where are you?"

"Fonde Mountain. Two miles east on the Quinntown road. I'm going to block it and stop them." She maneuvered her car so that it stretched across both lanes. The cliff dropped off on one side, and the rising mountain on the other made it impossible to go around.

"Get out of there!" Craig yelled. "These men are killers!"

"Send the police over here fast," she said, disconnecting the phone and getting out of her car.

Below her the blue car turned the last curve before entering her side of the mountain. She wasn't sure what she'd say to keep them from leaving, but she had to delay them long enough for the police to arrive. The two men saw her immediately. Ian was driving and Kevin, his hand moving animatedly, pointed at her.

The Ford stopped about twenty feet from where she stood. Her eyes connected with Ian's. Even at this distance the piercing quality of his eyes aimed at her, and for the first time Alma saw how sinister they were. Her heart pounded. Where are the police? she thought frantically. She stood in the center of the road.

He stared at her, his lips slightly parted as if he might smile. The faint sound of the siren grew in the distance. If he heard it, she thought, it might spook him. Alma held up her hand and figured that surely they wouldn't run her down. He looked behind him, then back at her. Ian's hands rubbed over the top of the steering wheel while his head tilted downward. The Ford's engine revved. The blue car's wheels screeched and sped toward her at top speed.

"No!" she yelled. Alma jumped sideways, tumbled over the cliff, and grabbed on to thick patches of weeds on the top bank. Gasping and dizzy, she dangled and prayed that the roots would hold her. The impact of Ian's car against hers sounded like a crash of thunder, punctuated by the screech of metal and heavy thuds. Her car sailed through the air in an eerie silence which was not long-lived. Trees snapped and a cloud of dust erupted into the air as the vehicle descended down the cliff.

Alma dug her nails into the dirt. The grassy embankment held and she pulled herself up onto the road. She looked down at her car wedged between two trees at the bottom of the cliff. Sirens in the distance grew louder and within minutes several police cars raced past her. The last one slowed and stopped to pick her up.

After she had assured the officer she was all right, he drove her back toward Contrary. He seemed surprised that she didn't want to continue after the Corey brothers, but her reasons for getting back to Contrary had more to do with her nephews than with Ian and Kevin. She had to get to a phone and call Vernon. Without her cell phone she didn't know what was happening at Sue's house. It might mean life or death for the children.

Over the police radio she listened to the officers' exchange. A roadblock had been set up at the crest of Fonde Mountain.

"You men hold firm," Coyle ordered, his voice fading with static. "Yonder they come."

The minutes that passed seemed to last forever.

"Out of the way! Out of the way!" Coyle yelled.

"What's happening?" Alma asked, staring at the radio as if it would answer her.

"Whhoooooa!" a policeman's voice said.

"Pancakes! Pancakes!" another said. "That car's mashed flatter than my wife's pancakes."

Then she heard Coyle's voice, full of excitement and

laughter. "Guess they learned you can't fly from mountain range to mountain range."

Alma covered her mouth with a hand, feeling both sick and grateful that she wasn't there to see it.

"Get the fire department out here," Coyle said. "I don't want the whole mountain burning up. We'll need a crane, too. That cliff they just sailed off must be two hundred feet down."

"Can we turn that off?" she asked and the officer flipped a switch. She leaned back into her seat, wishing she could sink into the upholstery and hide. Alma knew how steep the cliffs were on that part of the mountain. Ian and Kevin were dead. She crossed her arms over her chest, holding in the exploding sensations of hurt, anger, and senselessness. For several seconds the memory of Ian's touch, the lilt of his voice, and the quiet intensity of his eyes filled her with regret. But the dreams she'd harbored deep inside her burned up and died in the fiery crash.

For the moment, she was glad for the drive back. It would give her time to freeze any emotions she might want to feel. She had to push aside everything in order to focus on Larry Joe and Eddie.

44

As the police cruiser pulled into Contrary Alma got out at an office complex near the edge of town, taking time only to turn and wave a thank-you to the policeman who'd driven her back. She ran into the lobby of the building and up to the first pay phone she could find. Thankful that she had change in her pocket, she dropped in the coins and dialed. The phone rang three times. "Come on," she said, impatiently. Vernon answered.

"I don't have time to explain—"

"Where the hell have you been?" he demanded.

"The boys?" she asked frantically.

Vernon was silent as if struggling to gain control of his fears. "We got the call."

"What do they want?" Alma asked, holding her breath.

He hesitated. "They want you to release Kevin Corey."

The words left her too stunned to speak. She leaned against the phone and pressed the heel of her hand to her temple.

"Alma?" Vernon said. "Alma, are you there?"

"When did they call?"

"About twenty minutes ago."

"Twenty minutes?" she repeated incredulously. It had taken at least half an hour to drive back to Contrary.

"I told you I'd call the minute I heard. I've been trying

to find you since then." Vernon coughed and shifted around as if positioning himself so no one would hear him speak. "Alma, I know this violates every legal ethic you stand for, but you got to let that man go."

"Vernon—" she started.

"You got to," he nearly shouted at her. "Don't even argue with me about it."

"Vernon!" she said to stop his outburst then carefully looked around to make sure no one was listening. "Did you leave your cellular phone at Danny's hideout?"

"Alma, listen to me. They don't want Danny, they want Kevin Corey." Vernon huffed in agitated confusion. Finally, he said in an exasperated growl, "Yeah, it's there."

"Go get Danny," she said. "I'll call you with the instructions."

She hung up the phone and stared at the texture of the smooth marble wall. Almost no one yet knew of Kevin Corey's death. Surely the second he was released whoever was behind taking the boys would have known. Unless, she thought, it was someone who was not as much in the loop as he pretended. That definitely ruled out Jimmy Blackburn. He had no vested interest in Kevin—even to get at her. It ruled out Ian, who might have done it for his brother—but he couldn't have made that call twenty minutes ago. It had to be someone who needed Kevin released for their own reasons, but who? She stared at the wall, then turned in a circle, her gaze coming to rest on a bank of elevators. Walter Gentry exited one of them. This was his office building. He stopped at a water fountain and put down his briefcase to drink. Her thoughts gelled on the only possibility that made sense, but if she was right, she'd need a strong witness. What better witness than someone who hated and distrusted her as much as she did him?

"Mr. Gentry," she said, walking over to him. "I have a favor to ask you."

He spit some of the water into the basin as if her voice surprised him. "Favors between enemies has a Borgia ring to it."

"I'm currently without a car. If you'll drive me, I'll tell you what happened to—"

"I'm aware of the Corey brothers' fate," he said.

Alma nodded and looked around to ensure no one had heard. "You don't seem very upset," she noted.

"They paid their bill in advance." He started to walk away from her but she pulled on his arm. He sighed impatiently and shifted his weight to one leg. "I would think their deaths would satisfy that macabre sense of justice of yours. Now, will you leave me alone?" Once again he strode off.

"I need you," she said forcefully enough that he stopped, but he did not turn toward her. "I need a witness, a very impartial witness. The lives of two children are at stake."

Slowly moving around to face her, his eyes were narrowed with all the distrust that their shared past had infused into him. "If this is a criminal matter, call the police."

"There's no time. I can't get a search warrant today and I don't have any firm proof, much less probable cause."

"That's quite an acknowledgment coming from you." He took one step toward her. "And to admit it to me is extremely brave." Yet his demeanor was amused and condescending, not admiring. He stepped closer. "Obviously, if you're mistaken, I will use it to my advantage." His eyes narrowed even more and he tilted his head with a look of suspicion. "Why me?"

"You're the only son of a bitch I know who's enough of a bastard to stand back and witness my downfall."

"Why, thank you," he said. "From you I consider that a compliment."

45

Alma hid behind a hawthorn tree in the woods at the rear of the Mirror of Our Soul mansion. The triple whistle of a whippoorwill told her that everyone was in place. She ran to an open window on the back side of the house, pulled a trash can underneath it, and popped out the screen. Hoisting herself up, she fell into the darkness of a balmy room with the slight smell of bleach. The dark gave her exactly what she needed for the element of surprise.

Curling up on her knees, she waited for her eyes to adjust. A thin sliver of light on the floor showed her the location of the door. She crawled toward it until a hissing rattle locked her in her tracks. Snakes, she thought. Oh, God. I've landed in the room where they keep the snakes.

She judged the rattling sound to be far enough to her right to avoid a first strike. She prayed they were in cages and slid her hand along the floor toward the door. She tried thinking of what Danny had told her—that the snakes had been handled so much they were as tame as pets. It didn't relieve her revulsion. Trying to make herself as small as possible, she scooted her hands and knees along the floor to avoid directly landing on one. She reached for a door handle and grasped it just as something dropped on her back.

The undulating movement was like a coiled spring unwinding on her muscles. She held as still as she could. Her hand sweated on the metal doorknob. Up her spine and on the side of her neck the long form slid with rhythmic movement. The flicker of its tongue against her ear almost made her collapse. She closed her eyes and waited. The snake slithered down her arm and across her hand. When the last of its tail fluttered across her skin, Alma turned the doorknob and jumped for the hallway. She quickly closed the door, getting only a glimpse of a dozen serpents draped in every part of the room. She'd never fainted in her life, and only the thought of her nephews kept her from doing so now.

As she hurried through the house, she checked all the rooms. Offices, meeting rooms, nursery, and finally a set of bedrooms—all were empty. She sneaked around toward the front of the house, intending to check upstairs, then heard voices and stopped to listen.

"I want to thank you for your understanding," Walter Gentry said. "It is an unfortunate part of the business of being a lawyer that we defend people we don't always like."

"I've always believed justice finds a way," Harlan Fuller replied in a conciliatory tone.

Alma pulled her hair in a frustrated gesture. Damn, she thought, Gentry was supposed to distract Mrs. Fuller, not the reverend. She peered around the corner and saw them standing in the main foyer.

"It pleases me to no end," Fuller continued, "that you've found an interest in our work."

"This tour of your facility has been most enlightening," Walter oozed. "And it's so kind of you to take the time, considering your loss."

Alma came up behind them but stayed out of Fuller's view. Walter caught sight of her over the reverend's shoulder. He quickly glanced at the upstairs staircase and shook his head slightly to indicate that the upper portion of the house was empty.

"Keeping busy is the only thing that . . . " Fuller paused and looked at his feet. He inhaled deeply, sniffed, and wiped the side of his left eye. "That keeps me from going crazy." He squeezed his lips between forefinger and thumb, then patted Walter's shoulder as if to open a masculine camaraderie. "You recently lost your mother and probably understand more than anyone that it's our mission in life to be strong for others."

"Yes," Walter said slowly, his inflection indicating a true understanding. "Perhaps I've been wrong about you, Mr. Fuller. Perhaps many people have."

Alma gritted her teeth. She motioned Walter toward the Living Room. It was the only place that hadn't been checked. Gentry glanced quickly over his shoulder at the door then shifted uncomfortably as he cleared his throat. He obviously believed she had been mistaken and wanted to extricate himself from the situation. She waved her arms frantically, pointing toward the room.

"What's in there?" Walter finally asked, his tone agitated.

"Our main meeting hall." Fuller walked around Gentry and turned the handles on the double door. They were locked. He stepped back, somewhat surprised. "I would show you, but . . . " He stared down at the door grips. "This is very odd."

Alma stepped closer to the two men. "Why don't you use the secret passage?" she asked. Fuller spun around. The surprise on his face equaled Walter's disquieted expression.

"Miss Bashears," the reverend said. "I don't know what you mean."

"You know exactly what I mean." Alma moved closer to him. "You heard me that day I was here—behind the wall, behind the one-way mirror. All you have to know is where the secret door is in your front living area."

"Harlan?" A voice came from the other side of the door. "Is that you out there?"

Alma recognized it as Danielle Fuller's. "Tell her to open it," she whispered.

The confusion in Fuller's expression seemed genuine, but he didn't move toward the door.

"Seems like a good idea to me," Walter said. "After all, I'm here as a witness to Miss Bashears's folly." He allowed himself a slight smirk. "Couldn't have worked out better. I love it when a hunter trips on her own trap."

"I can't imagine what you hope to prove by this," Fuller told Alma then hesitantly tapped on the door. "Open up," he instructed his wife.

The door cracked open and Mrs. Fuller peeked out. She closed the door a bit when she saw Walter. "I'm waxing the floor," she said. "I can't let you in right now."

Alma stepped into her view. "You have my nephews in there and I want them."

Danielle's expression turned to stone and her alarm widened the pupils of her eyes. She started to close the door, but Walter put a hand onto its center and said, "Just a minute. Miss Bashears has just made an outrageous allegation, and I, for one, would love to see her proven a fool."

Danielle gently pushed against Walter's force. "I'm sorry. After all I've been through, not today."

Harlan clasped a hand to his chest with a grimace of pain. "I don't understand why you'd do this to me." He looked at Alma as if she'd just stabbed him.

"Open it!" she said sternly. Danielle pushed harder against Walter's hand. "NOW!" she screamed as loud as she could. With all the force of a fullback, Alma charged the door, knocked Danielle backward, and fell into the room.

The glass of the one-way mirror shattered and two little screams rose into the air. Alma saw Larry Joe and Eddie in front of the fireplace, playing with a basket of stuffed animals. Startled by all the noise, the boys had grabbed on to each other.

"You bitch!" Alma said as both women struggled to their feet. They sprinted simultaneously toward the children—Alma reached Larry Joe first and pulled him to her.

Danielle picked up Eddie and the Yellow Jacket Stinger he clutched to his chest. "Stay away," she said, moving behind a chair to keep a distance between them.

"Aunt Alma, look," Eddie cooed. "Buzzzzzzzz." He held out the toy.

The barrel of a rifle broke out the remaining glass of the one-way mirror. Vernon and Danny pushed themselves through the opening. They'd had no problem following Alma's directions to the hidden passageway.

"Give me the child," Alma said, focusing all her attention on Danielle while at the same time holding tightly to Larry Joe. Suddenly he seemed to realize the seriousness of the predicament and his little body began to tremble.

"Eddie," he cried and held out his arms to his brother.

Eddie looked up uncertainly at the woman holding him and then at Larry Joe. "I want Aunt Alma," he said. "Uncle Vernon!"

Vernon started to move toward Danielle and the boy, but Alma motioned him to wait.

"We—we—we have a day-care center," Harlan Fuller stammered. "I'm sure all this can be explained."

"Oh, yes," Alma said. "It can all be explained, and now it makes so much sense to me." She gently pushed Larry Joe behind her and circled in front of the fireplace as Danielle matched her movements in the opposite direction. "What was it you said? 'Christian to Christian,' but

Kevin Corey answered you 'killer to killer.' " She shook her head at the irony. "That was the more truthful description, wasn't it, Mrs. Fuller? You were two killers making a deal."

"You're cruel," Danielle said, stepping back. "I've lost my daughter. I found these children wandering through the woods and brought them here. I saved their lives. And you come here and attack me like this. You . . . you've been after my husband this entire time and everybody knows it!"

"I can guess what happened." Alma inched her way closer to Danielle. "You gave the Coreys an alibi, didn't you? You have a satellite office in Corbin, don't you? Will I find that one of your members runs the motorcycle dealership? Will I be surprised to discover it's the same one Kevin claims he and Ian were at when Kitty was killed?"

"Stop this at once," Harlan Fuller said. "You heard it from Kevin Corey's lips! Danny Sloat killed Cassidy. He must have killed Kitty, too."

"No," Alma said. "What we all heard was 'Danny did it'—but that was a warning to you." She stepped toward Danielle. "What he said was 'Dani did it.' " Alma spelled the name slowly. "D-A-N-I."

Harlan Fuller gasped and lowered himself to one of his thronelike chairs. "No," he said. "It's not possible."

"You had no way of knowing we were holding Kevin an extra day for the FBI," Alma continued. "You must have been shocked to find out he wasn't released. That must have scared the hell out of you. If he thought the alibi you provided wasn't holding up, he might conclude you weren't living up to your end of the bargain. Then he might have to tell what he saw at Jesus Falls." Alma's gaze slowly traveled down Danielle's legs. "That's why you took my nephews. Insurance—just in case you had to force me to release Kevin Corey." There was a bandage over the top part of Danielle's foot. "Cassidy scratched the person who held her under the water and we have the forensics." She pointed to the bottom of Danielle's black skirt that hung even with her ankles. The edge of a bandage could be seen across the left limb. "Kevin saw you. You gave him an alibi for the Silver Lake murder and he kept his mouth shut about what he saw at Jesus Falls."

"We had no reason to help that monster," Harlan Fuller said.

"But Danielle did," Alma said loudly, looking back at him then at his wife. "I wasn't sure at first which of you did it, but Kevin wasn't the only person watching you that day, Mrs. Fuller. Now I can see that you really do have just plain bad luck."

Danny stepped forward, his face twisted in anger and disgust. The memory filled his expression. Slowly, he raised an arm and pointed at Danielle Fuller. His posture was so stark and accusing that everyone in the room fell breathlessly silent.

"Dani, tell me what you've done," Harlan said softly.

She faced her husband, eyes narrowing into pure hatred. "You want to know my crime? My crime is running your church, caring for your congregation, keeping it clean, the grounds impeccable, the pictures straight on the wall, the people happy, taking care of all *your* problems, and still it's not perfect enough for you! My crime is being fat and ugly and smart, and mostly my crime is loving you."

"I can't believe these words." Even as he spoke he turned to Alma. "I had nothing to do with this."

"You had everything to do with it," Alma hissed at him. "With your slight touch on a woman's shoulder, the flirtatious wink, the lingering, knowing gaze . . . for every female except your wife. Do you really believe you didn't help make this woman what she is?"

Danielle's lower lip trembled. She kept a firm grip on Eddie and slowly moved toward the door that opened onto the side yard. Alma matched her movements. Vernon raised his rifle but Alma motioned him away, afraid for Eddie.

Danielle looked up at her husband, her eyes full of tears and her mouth a frown.

"Dani," Fuller said, stepping forward, "hand me the child."

She stopped in front of the door. "Stop," she said coldly. "Don't come any closer." She swung Eddie lower on her hip for a better grip and glared at all of them. One of her hands encircled his throat. "Or I'll break his neck."

46

"I'll drive," Alma screamed at Walter as they ran toward his Porsche.

"No, I'll drive," he yelled back.

The sight of Danielle's car speeding out of the parking lot was like watching a burning house. "She's getting away!"

"I know how to handle my car!"

"You're wasting time!" Alma insisted. "Give me the keys!"

He opened the passenger side and shoved her onto the seat, slamming the door after her. She howled in frustration and shouted, "Hurry!" as she jammed the seat belt in place. Having left Vernon with Danny, and Larry Joe to call the police, she knew Danielle was so desperate that Eddie's life was in more danger now than ever.

Walter started the car and sped after the burgundy Buick. "She can't outrun this," he assured Alma.

"Well, don't make her try," Alma snapped, the thought of Ian's wrecked car still fresh in her mind. "Just keep her in sight until the police can set up a roadblock."

"The police." Walter laughed, gunning the gas. "You've never been one to trust them."

"I know." She slammed a hand onto the dashboard as if the gesture could take away some of her frustration.

The burgundy car was a speck in front of them as it maneuvered a series of U-shaped turns. Alma's adrenaline shot up every time the vehicle disappeared. Walter drove fast, keeping the Buick in sight. Then, it was gone.

Walter slowed to a near stop in the road. "She's turned off," Alma said.

He backed up and swung around. "We've passed at least six roads. It could be any of them." They drove slowly, looking down every lane, but each one led to nothing.

"Oh, God," Alma cried, near despair. She rocked back and forth in the seat, unable to hold still. "Wait," she cried, seeing a haze of dust hanging in the air on a dirt road that led up a mountain. "There, that's where she went."

Walter glanced over at her and his expression turned to fear.

"Well, go," she said frantically.

"That's the back way to Jesus Falls."

He and Alma had eye contact for only a second before both of them stared forward. "Go," she said, her voice hoarse from yelling.

The car spit gravel as they plowed up the mountainside. The ground was so rough she couldn't tell if they were on a road or a horse trail. What if I am wrong? she worried.

"Why would Danielle go there?" Walter asked.

"It's where she killed her child." Alma picked up his car phone to call the police. "Mental orgasm."

As Walter approached the top of the mountain, he slammed on the brakes and nearly rear-ended the parked Buick. Both of them jumped from the car.

Neither Danielle nor Eddie were in sight. The clear, calm creek that fed Jesus Falls was ankle-deep and the gurgle was as soft and pleasant as the song of a choir. The ground was evenly shaped with several large boulders fashioned into sitting areas. From this height, the depth of the jewel-green valley spread before Alma and Walter. "Let's split up," he said, his discomfort obvious.

"No, wait," she said. "Listen." She turned toward a wooded area just at the top of the waterfall. The trees blocked the roar of the falls beyond it but a voice came toward them, faded and increased again. They headed toward the sound.

When Alma and Walter emerged on the other side, the two enemies reached out to steady each other at the sight of Danielle Fuller walking around in a circle on a flat slate rock that extended out over Jesus Falls.

"What am I doing?" Danielle asked herself. "What am I doing? What am I doing? What am I doing?" She repeated the words until they were a meaningless babble. Eddie lay motionless against her shoulder, still clutching his Yellow Jacket Stinger. She stared up into the sky, spinning in a slow circle and stepping precariously close to the edge.

Alma turned toward Walter. In her fear, her movements felt like she was treading through a deep swamp. "I'll try to talk her down. You go through the trees and get behind her." She looked up into Walter's eyes and he nodded. As they parted, she realized that she was gripping his hand tightly and had to let go with some effort.

She approached Danielle on the side of the stream that fed the falls. This gave Walter a wide berth to come up behind the woman unseen. Danielle looked down, her mascara making dark streaks under her eyes. When she stared up at Alma there was something of a wild animal in her expression. "I want to help you," Alma said slowly.

Danielle coughed out a harsh laugh, causing Eddie to stir and look up at her. "Let me go," he cried. "Aunt Alma."

His words tore at her heart. "Dani," she said, trying to show the familiarity that the distraught woman needed.

"No one hates you. Things sometimes get out of control. I understand that." Danielle looked away and Alma stepped closer. She saw Walter at the edge of the cluster of trees, inching up behind Danielle. "Cassidy was a handful, I'm sure," Alma said in an attempt to sound sympathetic.

"She wouldn't obey me," Danielle hissed. "I was her mother."

"You're a good mother," Alma said, gently, hoping to calm her. "A mother always knows what's best for her child."

"You said it yourself." Danielle wailed and started to fall to her knees but caught herself as if a power beyond her gave her strength. "Sometimes a mother is forced to weed out her litter." She pointed down at the baptismal pool and looked over the edge of the waterfall. "I didn't mean to do it," she sobbed. "I only meant to baptize her, baptize both of us, so we could be mother and daughter again. Our family needed healing! I just thought—and then it was too late."

Eddie began crying and he looked up, holding his arms out for Alma to take him. It only made Danielle hold him tighter. "It's a mother's right to choose." Eddie struggled against her. "If Cassidy had only done the things I told her to do." She gasped breaths, tears streaming down her face as she became more and more hysterical.

"She wasn't a very good girl," Alma agreed, using the boy's distraction to move closer, as did Walter. "She wanted—"

"She wanted to be me!" Danielle spun around, her face suddenly a twisted mask of pain. "She's in front greeting members and I'm in the damn garden digging holes! I'm not so presentable anymore! I tried so hard to keep everything perfect! It wasn't good enough! It was never good enough! If it had just stayed all the same."

"Children grow up," Alma said softly, trying to calm her. "Danielle, you can't control everything. It's okay to let go of all that control."

"I didn't mean to do it. Oh, God, I didn't mean to do it." She saw Walter and growled, "Keep away!" She stepped backward toward the waterfall. Less than half a foot separated her from the water. Danielle looked up at the sky and raised one of her heels to step backward again.

"Eddie," Alma said, knowing what was about to happen. "Close your eyes."

Danielle began to tip, losing balance with the boy in her arms, and both Alma and Walter pounced on her. Alma tore at Eddie. Walter fought with Danielle, who held on to the boy's midsection then let herself fall as if she'd given up her entire world. Alma tightened her grip on Eddie although it forced her over the edge.

Falling. The *whoosh* of air loud as a roller-coaster ride. Danielle, Eddie, Walter, and Alma tumbled over each other, their bodies colliding and clutching each other until they slammed into the cold water.

Underneath the waterfall, Walter vocalized unsaid words in a burst of bubbles. Eddie's mouth opened and closed as he swallowed. The heavy force of the falls swirled them past each other, around, atop and down. Alma grabbed Eddie and held him to her. A shove on her back sent her shooting to the surface. She looked behind and saw Walter. Eddie coughed along with her, spitting water from his mouth and nose. He clung to Alma's neck as she swam toward the shore. Policemen dove into the water to help them. When she crawled ashore with Eddie and collapsed onto the ground, she turned to see officers helping Walter to his feet and pulling unconscious Danielle Fuller from the baptismal pool.

Eddie gripped Alma so tightly that she had to push him

away for the paramedics to examine him. She held the little boy's hand until they forced her onto a gurney as well. As it was loaded into an ambulance, she stared out the back door at Jesus Falls. Savage and untamed, the foaming water was as dangerous as a stalking mountain lion. For a brief moment the falls seemed to be a sinister deity who demanded sacrifice. She bowed her head and thanked God that they had survived.

From the corner of her eye, she saw Walter waving away attendants trying to examine him. A cut on his forehead bled profusely and two policemen forced him to sit down. He stared at Alma in the ambulance and watched as they closed the door. She tried to sit up but fell back weakly. Alma knew she should speak to him and yet the words were too deep inside of her. Right now, she was unsure when she'd be able to communicate again. She needed to go inside of herself and closed her eyes.

47

Alma shook off the sense of spirits watching her from the Rose Hill Cemetery. The rolling green hills, marked with tombstones and statues of cherubs and angels, were as peaceful and well tended as a state park picnic area. She held a deep breath when she got out of the limousine, then exhaled slowly and tried to relax her tense shoulder muscles. Twenty feet up the incline was a gray granite headstone engraved with BASHEARS. Lined in front of it were the final resting places of her grandfather and two uncles who'd died in World War II. An empty section beside Papaw Bashears awaited her grandmother. Alma had a hard time looking at it.

Down the hill and angled to the right was an open-air tent covering a spread of floral arrangements. Chairs were set up opposite the flowers, blocking her view of the grave. Alma stood beside Danny and watched as funeral home assistants carried his mother's coffin to the grave site. He'd been strong through the service, not shedding a tear until the pastor had said that Kitty might have been "alone in the world, but now she was forever with God." Then his tears came slowly, one after another, until they ceased as silently as they had started.

They were walking up the hill when Jefferson Bingham approached them. "Thank you for coming," Alma said, but his preoccupied expression told her he had much more on his mind than attending a funeral out of politeness.

"Would both of you join me in the black limousine for just a few minutes?"

Alma looked down the road. It would be several minutes before the rest of the family arrived. Danny seemed perplexed but not annoyed. "Okay," she agreed and they followed Jefferson.

Inside the car Jefferson sat down opposite Mayor Hudson. He directed Danny to sit beside the politician, who was dressed in a black suit that contrasted with his bloodshot eyes. Alma shot Jefferson a look of surprise and he glanced away as if embarrassed by the situation. "What's this all about?" she asked.

Jefferson exhaled a deep breath and said to Danny, "A long time ago, your mother and . . . your father—"

"My father?" Danny asked.

"They made arrangements for you," Jefferson said, ignoring the interruption. "As hard as it is to hear, your father couldn't claim you. It was never the case that he didn't want to."

Danny leaned back in the chair. "I don't believe you. My daddy didn't want me, and if you're about to say this old man is him . . . " Danny pointed to the mayor. "Then Momma pulled off the scam of the century."

"He is your father," Jefferson said. Danny pursed his lips and made a cynical hiss.

Alma looked out the car window at the deep green grass tinged with yellow from the heat of the June sun. Whether what Jefferson said was true or not, all of his actions for the last week now made sense. Every time she was close to finding Danny, Jefferson was there. "Listen to him, Danny," she said and reached out to touch the boy's knee.

"My old man was a drifter," he said. "Mom told me plenty

of times. She threatened . . . " His voice broke. " . . . to turn me over to him."

The quiet of his breakdown stilled the atmosphere inside the car and Alma handed him a tissue. "Jefferson, Mayor," she said, "I know you mean well, but if this is only an assumption, it's far too painful to get into now."

"It's not," Mayor Hudson said and turned his body toward the boy. "I had tests done when you were born and again last year, when you went to the hospital for that dislocated shoulder."

"I wondered why they took blood," Danny said, shaking his head.

"The DNA test confirmed that you're my son." Hudson touched Danny's shoulder. The boy looked up at him and pushed his hand away, his face a mask of anger and confusion. "You know," Hudson said, "I have a wife and four children who are nearly grown now. As adults it's easier to deal with the failings of one's past . . . "

"You don't owe me nothing," Danny said, defiance entering his tone. "Nothing's changed—"

"I want you to be part of my family."

"Yeah, right." He turned away. The mayor looked up at Alma as if pleading for help then leaned closer to the boy and spoke with the fervor of a father intent on getting his point across. "My brother has a ranch in Montana. I go out there every August. Just me. It'd be a new start for you, boy. We'll get to know each other, and then we'll plan what you're going to do for the rest of your life. I want to help you go to college, make something of yourself."

Alma looked into Danny's face and said softly, "Sometimes life isn't all we want it to be. We have to make choices. We can't read the future. I can't tell you what's best for you. I can tell you that if you want to stay with us, you'll be accepted into the Bashears family as one of our

own. We'll also expect you to act as a responsible member
of that family. One thing you don't have a choice about is
that you'll have to overcome your past. No one in my
family or the mayor's is going to sit still while you continue down that path. You can do it here, in Contrary—or
maybe your father's offer will be an easier way for now."

Danny bit his lower lip and stared at the carpet on the
floor of the limousine. "What makes you all think I'll do
either of these? I can make it on my own."

"You're sixteen, that's two years from walking away
from us." Alma leaned back. She could tell from his tone
that he was on the edge of a decision. "Do you want the
embarrassment of Vernon hunting you down and hog-
tying you again?"

Danny looked out the car window and half smirked.
"Do they have horses on the ranch?"

"Yep," the mayor said, giving in to a slight smile. "And
my brother, your uncle, is a real rodeo clown—a hard
worker, but he likes a good time."

"I don't know," Danny said and again bit his lower lip.

"His wife's a great cook. I've talked to them about
you," the mayor said. "They'd love to have you. They got
no kids, so it'd be fun for them, too."

"Is there a place to ride my motorcycle?"

"More buttes than you'll know what to do with."

"Well," Danny said, looking sideways. "I guess I could
give it a try."

"Okay." The mayor smiled as his body relaxed in the
seat. The two of them looked at each other for several seconds, an uneasiness accompanying the bond wanting to be
born. "Let's go together to lay your mother to rest."

Alma watched as the mayor placed an arm around
Danny's shoulders and led him up the path to the grave
site. Danny had found his father. Would she ever find hers?

She thought of what a reunion with him might be like. If she found out that he was alive, could she overcome the past? Would it be as sweet? How could it, after all she'd learned? She looked over at Jefferson and shook her head.

"I'm sorry I couldn't tell you what was going on," he said.

"You don't have to explain client privilege." She held his hand and for the first time in a long time felt the depth of their friendship return. "I am worried about Jimmy Blackburn. He had people watching Kitty's trailer twenty-four hours looking for Danny."

"That's over." Jefferson waved his hand and pointed after the mayor. "He's a politician. Deals are struck."

Alma thought back to Blackburn's words: *The business with your cousin is over and done with*. She stared after the mayor. "That must have been a deal that cost him dearly," Alma said. "Whatever you do, Jefferson, don't tell me the terms."

After the funeral Alma stayed until the coffin was lowered into the ground. The family was having a dinner at Mamaw's house and she promised to join them soon. Two graveyard attendants booted their spades into the dirt with a crunch but the sound of the earth hitting the coffin didn't give her the finality she'd hoped for. Kitty, I'm so sorry this happened to you, she said to herself.

Alma stood up and walked to the edge of the grave. From her handbag she took a small cutting of the willow tree from Silver Lake and tossed it into the grave as her final witness.

When she turned to go to the car her family left for her, she was surprised to see Val coming toward her. She was followed by a tall, broad-shouldered man who could have been a double for Sean Connery. "Grady Forester?" she asked and reached out to shake his hand while shooting her assistant a questioning look.

"I'm so sorry to come out here at a time like this," Val said, "but Mr. Forester is on his way to Chattanooga for a job interview."

"I believe I signed the recommendation letter Val dictated," Alma said, holding back a strong feeling of irritation.

"He's found Allafair Adair," Val said.

For several seconds Alma couldn't speak. "Tell me," she managed to say. "Where is she?"

"Well," he said, his voice a deep, rich bass. "If the cemetery caretaker's instructions are correct, I believe we'll find her just over that hill."

The headstone was simple and made of pink granite. It rose up out of the ground in a graceful arch. "Allafair Adair," Alma read aloud, "born January 1955, died August 1997." Quickly she calculated that this woman would have been twenty years old when her father disappeared, and forty-two when she died.

"I'll never know," Alma said to no one. "I'll never know what happened." She bent down and balanced on her knees, one hand resting on the cold granite. "Damn that Charlotte Gentry," she said under her breath. "She knew the story, and she died with it," Alma said in a harsh, vindictive tone. "And she was right. Mrs. Gentry said I'd wish with everything that was in me that she was alive. And I do, because she is the only one who can tell me."

Grady knelt on the other side of the grave and stared at the stone. He cleared away some of the straw and dried-out grass from the bottom of the headstone. "Well, maybe not the only person," he said and pointed at another line of engraving.

Alma followed his gaze. "Beloved mother," she read aloud. A mixture of hope and dread filled her, and she leaned backward until she sat on the ground. "She had children." Could any of Allafair's children be her siblings? She looked up at Grady.

He offered her a hand and helped her steady herself on the bumpy ground. As they climbed back up the hill she thanked him for his help.

"Well, you wrote such interesting E-mail messages that I could hardly say no."

"Yes," Alma said and shot a look at Val.

She stared at Alma with a worried expression.

"Well," Alma said, a bit amused. "Val helps me with all that."

They paused at the crest of the hill in the shadow of a huge marble angel that towered into the sky. Alma stepped back when she read the name Gentry. She stood at the foot of the graves of Walter, Sr., and his wife. Charlotte had been buried at the very peak of the hill, as if placing herself at the head of the table. "Very Charlotte-like," Alma said. A row of dead dandelions lined the front of her tombstone. Alma picked one and blew the white tufts into the wind. They scattered down the hill over grave markers of Contrary's founding citizens.

The imposing angel had one hand pointing toward the ground and another to the sky. An inscription across the bottom read: AS ABOVE, SO BELOW. COME WALK WITH ME ON STREETS OF GOLD. The angel's face was tilted. Alma studied it, taken by the oddity of the tilt, not upward toward the heavens as one would assume, but down the hill. She turned her own head to assume the angel's perspective. Her eyes came to rest on Allafair's grave.

"It's going to be a difficult search," Grady said, coming up beside her.

"Yes," Alma agreed. "But I'll find them. I'll find Allafair's children if it takes the rest of my life."

48

It was dark when Alma finally arrived home. The answering machine showed three messages, but she left them and instead filled the bathtub with steaming hot water then lit several fragrant candles and placed them around the room. As she dropped her clothes, she stepped back and leaned against the doorframe. The golden glow of the room made such a peaceful image she couldn't help but acknowledge the happiness the simple pleasure invoked inside her. "Tender graces," she said.

Well, she thought as she stepped into the tub, if these are to be the tender graces in my life, then I guess I'll have to learn to be satisfied.

She lowered herself into the lavender-scented water and moaned as her muscles loosened and relaxed. Closing her eyes, she dreamt of beaches and sunsets that sheltered her from the rest of the world.

Bam! She shot up in the water. *Bam!* Both sounds came from the same direction outside the house. She reached for a terrycloth robe and cautiously peeked out a window.

The ceiling lamp in the kitchen cast enough light for her to see a fair distance into the yard. There was no movement. Two antique stone statues of hares sat ghostlike in the darkness. *Bam!* The sound was rhythmic, she decided, like . . . "A door," she said, laughing at her own fear as she caught sight of wooden slats on the toolshed swinging back and forth.

She leaned against the window frame, looking down at the puddle of water dripping from her legs. "Well," she said aloud, "I'm not going to enjoy my bath with that—" *Bam!* Hastily she slipped on a sweatsuit and tennis shoes and went out to close the door.

When she found the lock hatch on the ground, she examined the hinges. One was slightly misaligned. She propped a wheelbarrow against the door to hold it shut then looked around the yard and up into the dark mountain—so dark she couldn't make out the terrain. She remained still and listened. A solitary train whistle from the other side of the mountain blared in the distance, and the lights from the town offered a yellowish glow. The night was silent. Too silent. Where were the crickets? The croak of frogs from the gully? Usually at night she could hear a few howling dogs out on the hunt. Then she scolded herself, said, "Your imagination," and started back toward the house. "The lock fell off. That's all."

She glanced up at the amber glow from the bathroom window and her body felt a sudden yearning to return. The thought of the steamy water beckoned but she froze in her tracks when a sliver of a shadow passed over the same window. She watched, hoping it was only a flicker of the candles, perhaps a movement of the curtain. She saw no pattern in the wavering shadows and exhaled her nervousness. "Really, Alma," she admonished herself. "You keep this up and you'll have to move closer to civilization."

Once inside the house she paused and listened. No sound. She secured the front door. "Now to that bath." She took the time to pour some sauvignon blanc and sipped the fruity flavor as she headed upstairs. *Brrrring!*

Alma dropped the goblet and it shattered on the step. "Damn!" she said. *Brrrring!* The phone rang again. She pushed the broken glass to one side and went back downstairs to answer it. "Yes?" she asked with an edge to her voice.

"I've been trying to get you all day," Nathan Deever said. "Haven't you gotten any of my messages?"

"Nathan." Alma exhaled his name. "I've been with my family. Today was the funeral."

He paused as if processing her answer. "I'm still out at the wreck site. We're just now getting the car up on the main road."

She shuddered, imagining the block of twisted burning metal at the bottom of the rugged cliff. "Sounds like you're ahead of schedule," she remarked, struggling to maintain a professional tone. "It was a deep drop."

"Alma," Nathan said kindly, "the first rescue workers down there could see only one body in the car. We thought the other might be . . . " He hesitated as if trying to find a delicate way to describe it. " . . . crushed in the wreckage."

"What are you saying, Nathan?"

"There's only one body. At first light, we're going to start scouring the trees and cliffs. Maybe at impact, or during the descent, one of the men was thrown from the car."

A creak from above startled Alma. She looked up, her eyes focused on the ceiling as if she could stare through it. "Nathan," she said, her voice softened by an edge of fear, "could you tell which body?"

His long silence seemed to suggest that he knew how deeply bothered she would be hearing this information. "I'm sorry," he said. "It was very badly burned."

The creak sounded again and Alma gasped. "Hold on. I think someone's in my house." She lay down the phone. At the foot of the staircase she looked up and listened hard. The clear wine pooled on the stairs and dribbled down to the main floor. She picked up the stem of the broken glass, then hurried back to the phone and said, "I'm going to drive down to my uncle's house. Send the police."

The line disconnected.

Alma grabbed her car keys and backed toward the door, keeping her eyes on the staircase. A swishing sound came from upstairs and she held still. She opened the door slowly and stepped outside. As she jumped from the porch into the side yard, she realized the swishing sound was a window opening. She whirled around and looked at the roof just as a dark figure descended on top of her.

She and the attacker sprawled to the ground. Alma lost her keys but held tightly to the broken wineglass stem, which she jabbed into the torso on top of her. The man cried out and grabbed at his ribs. His face was hidden behind a black hood. Alma twisted sideways and ran. He circled around the car, blocking her path to the road. She dodged away from him but now there was only one direction she could go. Up into the mountains.

49

Panting. Out of breath. She managed to stay ahead of him only through her knowledge of the landscape, which she traversed in the dark more by instinct than logic. She held on to the side of a birch tree to catch her breath and balance herself on the uneven terrain. Some moss stuck to her cheek and she flicked it away, at the same time tearing loose twigs from her hair. As she peered down the mountain, she saw the dim beam of a flashlight and realized he'd taken it from her toolshed. He had no idea where to find her, but at least she could keep him in sight. She prayed that Nathan had heard her plea to send the police.

She stared toward the light that cut an uneven path through the forest. Was it Ian or Kevin? Everything the FBI had told her now ricocheted in her mind like errant thoughts. It was Ian they were after. Kevin was too loud, too coarse, too much the center of attention to be the killer. Ian's personality fit the profile. Alma clawed her way up the mountain toward her secret hiding place and prayed that he'd never be able to locate the cave in the dark.

Higher up, she fell into the rocky opening and leaned against the cold wall, inhaling heavily to catch her breath. Her heart burned from exertion. The trek up the mountain had left her panting and covered with sweat. Peering outside she saw only darkness. She had to wait until daylight, or for the police. She held her breath and listened. Silence. Maybe he'd gone away, decided it wasn't worth it, couldn't find her.

A rustle of leaves startled her and she backed into the cave another few feet. It could be a dog, she thought, or a rabbit, squirrel, snake. Deliberately she imagined an animal, was comforted, and hesitantly stepped toward the entrance.

A shape like a bear broke through the vines, crashing into her. His unfixed grip tore her sleeve as she shoved him hard into the cave wall. The man grunted and she ran blindly. The obsidian darkness surrounded her like thick curtains. Using her hands as a shield, she plunged toward a cold, gravelly wall. The wet, sandy grit scraped off on her hands. In the struggle she had gotten so turned around she was unsure if she was headed toward the front of the cave or the back.

Behind her a voice whispered lightly, "Alllmma."

Her name sent a shot of terror up her spine. She stopped when she heard the dripping of water into the pond. Oh, God, she thought. I'm at the back of the cave.

With one hand in front of her, she felt her way to the pile of rocks where the Springfield rifle was lodged. It might not fire, but at least she could use it as a club to fend off an attack.

"Alma," the voice said quickly.

Then all fell deadly silent. Almost five minutes passed with no sound. Terrible minutes, as each second ticked off in time to an awful heartbeat. She sat as motionless as possible, unsure if he was still there. The blackness in front of her was as dense as a wall. It seemed that any second a hand would reach out and grab her. She tried blocking the image from her mind, but with every moment she expected the touch of death.

She listened, holding her breath. Was it breathing she heard or only the whistle of wind in the cave? Finally, she could stand it no longer. "Are you there?" she asked.

"You know I'm here," he whispered.

Alma felt tears fall from her eyes. If she didn't emerge from the cave alive, no one would ever find her. "Why are you doing this?" she asked.

"I'm not crazy," he said louder, in an accent she knew so well.

"Ian," she said, her chin falling to her chest. "I had hoped it wouldn't be you."

"It wasn't me," he said, his voice softening to a gentle drone. "I had to come back and convince you."

"So you broke into my house?"

"Would you have opened the door for me? No, you'd have called the police and had me arrested for murders I didn't commit."

"Sometimes you have to trust," she said softly, standing to speak and then crouching low so he wouldn't get a good fix on her. Her hands reached out and felt the smoothness of the rifle. She lifted it from its perch and brought it down into her lap. The weight of it made her feel safer even though the reality of her position was precarious.

"Trust." He laughed "My mother taught me how to trust."

"She was a very important woman in Scotland," Alma said, playing for time as she struggled to get the bolt on the old rifle to close without making any noise.

"She loved life," Ian said. "I love women who love life. I love hearing how they want to live."

"Is that why you kill them." She said it more as a statement than a question.

The silence that followed was only made more frightening by the empty tone of his voice when he finally spoke. "They want to live so much. If you could just feel how much they want to live. Listen to them crying to their mothers and begging for their fathers as their lives drain away, feel the resistance of their muscles as the blade tears into their flesh." He breathed heavily, almost sexually, and his voice floated in a pacing motion. "They have so much to live for . . . My mother might have been minor royalty."

"Oh, God, Ian," she groaned. "Don't tell me."

"The bitch just had two too many bastard sons, and that didn't play well in sovereign circles."

"Ian, stop," she insisted. "This is something you'll need to tell a lawyer or doctor, not me."

He laughed out loud. "She tried to kill me!" His voice reverberated in the cave and the last two words echoed. As they faded, he sniffed and a tiny cry infiltrated his voice. "Why?" he asked. "Why would she do that? I had to know why. I had to know what was behind that beautiful face of hers. My brother helped me."

"Ian," she said. "No one knows. There are things in life that people do and we never know why." She paused. "I'll get you help. Someone more knowledgeable than either of us will have to explain it." She waited. "Okay?" she asked. "Will you come down the mountain with me?"

The musical drops of the water played like a symphony. "I need to see your face," he said finally. The scratchy sound of a match burst into flame and both of them shielded their eyes for a second. He turned and lit a candle left from their previous visit.

Alma saw that his forehead was cut and several rips in his clothing were bloodied. "I'll get you to a doctor," she said, standing from her perch on the stones.

He stepped toward her but stared at the sandy floor. "I need to see your face," he said.

Alma tried to look into his eyes, but he continued to stare down. She studied the width of his shoulders and peered down the length of his arm to catch a glint of the hunting knife in his hand. The alarm that shot through her spread to her muscles, and she felt her legs buckling.

He stared at the rifle and his lips curled into an eerie smile that faded with his next step toward her. Slowly he tilted up his head and his gaze locked into hers. "I need to see your face," he said. "What's behind that beautiful face?"

She swung the rifle around to strike him. Her finger pulled the trigger and the muzzle flashed like a firecracker. The kick knocked her backward as the blast exploded in her ears, ringing long after it was over. When she sat up, Ian was on the ground, his legs spread before him, his back against a rock, his eyes staring at her and his mouth drooped open. Blood spilling from his wound bubbled down his chest.

Alma dropped the rifle and fell to her knees. "Oh, my God." She slid across the sandy ground and knocked the knife away from his hand. "I'll go get help." She started to rise.

He caught hold of her wrist, gripping it so tightly that her previous terror returned. "Don't leave," he said then let go of her hand.

A tremble in her chest rose into a sob and she pressed her hands against the wound. Blood gushed over her fingers.

"It'll be easier next time," he said.

"Easier?" She sucked in hiccups of air.

"You've had your first kill, Alma." He coughed, blood spilling over his bottom lip. "It won't be your last." His head fell forward then hung limply while his auburn-colored eyes stared at her, vacant and detached.

Alma tried to stand, but her legs collapsed beneath her. "I'm sorry," she said. "I'm so sorry."

50

The Fourth of July was upon the Bashears family sooner than anyone expected, and with it came a softening of the grief they'd all suffered in June. Near dusk the family gathered at Alma's mountaintop house to barbecue and watch fireworks in the valley below. Another visitor she hadn't expected also found his way to the gathering—Grady Forester.

Fresh from his second job interview in Chattanooga, he made the excuse of being hungry as his reason to stop by. "Tales of your family's cookouts are known all the way to the hinterlands of Detroit," he said.

"You're such a good liar," Alma teased as she showed him around the top part of the mountain that formed her backyard.

"It's not against the law unless I'm under oath." He raised one hand and held the other out as if it were placed on a Bible.

She noticed the square shape of his hands and the long tapered fingers that shot off from strong, well-formed palms. "You can tell any lie you want," she said. "Right now, there is no police chief to arrest you."

"A job opening?" Grady's eyes widened and he faked a smile of malicious interest.

"Chief Coyle actually left a sign on his door that said 'Gone Fishin'.'"

Grady threw his head back and laughed, then spread out a blanket and turned on a small transistor radio to a local country music station.

"He called his family from Florida," Alma said, smoothing out the blanket over the uneven ground. "He met a woman down there, liked the weather, and decided to stay."

"Heat got too bad up here, huh?"

"I think he knew that in the coming years he'd have to face some decisions he didn't want to make." Alma didn't elaborate but thought of Jimmy Blackburn and the threat he posed to the future of Appalachia. "He was a conflicted man—loyal to his family yet some part of him would occasionally struggle to do the right thing. His methods were not always the wisest choices."

Grady gave her a sideways glance. "So there really is another job I could apply for."

"Now why would you want to be police chief of Contrary? Besides a full-blown strike for which the National Guard has been called out twice, we have murderers, stalkers, and kidnappers all sitting around the campfire at night plotting what they'll do next." Alma opened her arms wide on the entirety of the valley. "And on a serious side, we have a drug kingpin who's going to have to be dealt with in the next few years."

"Sounds like fun. Besides, this little hamlet is as beautiful as any I've driven through."

They settled in, high on the hillside above the fracas of Vernon, Danny, and even ungainly Mayor Hudson passing a football. Alma felt happy for Danny, and envious of him. A question about his past had been answered for him. He'd found his father, and she was still looking for hers. Larry Joe and Eddie vied for Uncle Ames to light their sparklers, with Sue following after them like a mother hen, a pail of water in hand in case of an accident. Merl snoozed in a lawn chair with a hat over her face, while Uncle George and Aunt Joyce attended to the barbecue. Mamaw had set herself on the ground and played with a pack of puppies that Vernon had brought out to allow everyone to pick the one they wanted before giving the rest to friends.

"Alma, you have a call," Aunt Joyce yelled up the hill and sent Larry Joe running up with the cell phone. Grady turned down the radio he'd propped on a rock.

"Hello," Alma said.

A woman's voice responded, "Please hold for the attorney general."

Alma swallowed. She'd managed to avoid this phone call until she thought Howard Burton had forgotten about her.

"Alma," he said, a healthy vigor in his voice. "Sorry to call you on a holiday, but I'm leaving for the month and knew I'd put this off too long."

"I know we have a lot to talk about," Alma said, hoping her voice didn't reveal too much dread.

"You have some strong support in your county," Burton said, "so these petitions are on their way to the circular file."

"I'm glad to hear that," she said, relief spreading through her chest.

"Especially from Jefferson Bingham and Walter Gentry."

"Walter Gentry?" she asked, unable to hide the surprise is her voice.

"Well, Mr. Gentry said you didn't do anything he wouldn't have done, so that's enough for me. You have a good July Fourth."

As she disconnected the phone, Grady turned up the

volume of the radio. "Did you just say the name Walter Gentry?" he asked.

She nodded, still processing the attorney general's comments.

"He's about to make a speech," Grady said, pointing at the radio. "Friend of yours?"

"Not exactly." Alma moved to the other side of the radio so she could hear clearly.

While they waited, he asked about the different kinds of trees that grew on the mountainside. "I can name skyscrapers in ten major cities," he remarked. "I guess if I move down here, I'll have to start learning the names of the trees."

Alma pointed out white oak and hawthorn, maple and dogwood. "In the fall they turn every shade of gold, green, and red."

"I can't wait to see it," Grady said almost subconsciously, and he seemed a bit surprised at his own words. He pointed to a twig held up by a strong piece of iron stuck into the ground. "What's the name of that tree?"

"That one . . . " Alma paused and inhaled a warm breeze. "A willow cutting I just planted. Its name is . . . the Witness Tree."

"Sounds interesting. I'd like to hear the story."

"I was told that its limbs draped to the earth like tears because the tree witnessed the sorrow of the world." Alma paused and reflected for a moment. "But the Witness Tree doesn't absorb all the sorrow of the world, only what we cannot bear. It leaves us just enough to make us better people. What is sadder than those drooping limbs is that some of us hold on to our pain until it warps us, destroys every dream we ever had for ourselves." She couldn't help thinking of the Fullers. Harlan had left town, no one knew where. Danielle sat in the city jail, under suicide watch. Their grand house was deserted.

"Ladies and gentlemen," the radio announcer said. "The following broadcast has been paid for by Walter S. Gentry."

A brief burp of static was followed by Walter's voice. "It was my pleasure to serve this county as commonwealth attorney for twelve years. Because I no longer hold that office does not mean that I have abandoned my best intentions for this community. The tragic events that befell us this early summer touched each and every one of our citizens. That is why in the interest of our town I am making a request of the city council to shut down Jesus Falls Park, the park my family created. Many of us have happy memories of times we've spent there, but too many of us . . . " He paused. "Even if one of us is hurt by the sight of this place, then all of us should endeavor to heal that hurt. I have asked that the park be closed and left to grow wild. Let the memories seep into the earth, and let nature take her course to grow free and wild, the way it was intended, and let her heal all of our scars. As we all go to dust, this land outlives us. It goes on and on and sees our histories as a minor intrusion upon her crust. Let the earth return to what it is, not what we impose on it."

Alma turned down the sound and stared in the direction of Jesus Falls.

"You know," Grady said, realizing that Walter's words had affected her deeply, "I've always heard that when people bear witness it cleanses their souls. Maybe that's what this Gentry is doing."

"Maybe," she said, fighting her desire to empathize with Walter's viewpoint. "I would have to admit that in the time I've been here, he's become a better person. A slightly better person," she corrected herself.

Grady watched her then remarked thoughtfully, "I guess he's got his very own Witness Tree."

Something inside Alma acknowledged Walter's act as more than a gesture of kindness. In some ways she knew that it was his atonement—paid in the only way he knew how.

"Hey, Alma," Vernon yelled, running up the hill with a brown-and-black pup in his hands. "This one's for you. I named him Sir William." He lay the tiny beagle at her feet and it began to lick her toes. "Willie, for short."

"Oh, Vernon," she said, "I don't have the lifestyle to take care of a dog."

"Too many dates?" he asked and winked at Grady.

"Too much work," she retorted with sisterly challenge.

"Well, Alma," he replied, "if you stop courting serial killers, you might get along better in life." He rolled backward and pounded on his belly in a deep laugh. Alma gave him a shove with one foot and Vernon rolled down the hill, still laughing like a hyena.

She leaned over and touched Grady's shoulder. He smiled and his hand reached up and petted hers. The quiet comfort of sitting together somehow felt so familiar that both of them knew not to break the spell.

A loud boom announced the beginning of the fireworks. She glanced up at Grady and felt herself smiling both inside and out. She had a feeling that if he applied for the job of Contrary's police chief, he would get it.

"So," she said to him, leaning a bit so that her head rested on his shoulder, "why don't you tell me about yourself?"

As he turned to her, a giant burst of fireworks lit the sky. The two boys twirled their sparklers. The rest of the family lined up along the edge of the mountain to watch the colorful spectacle. Grady and Alma stood, her eyes rising above the fireworks to the heavens—full of celestial bodies that had watched her grow up in these mountains. She looked up at a star she'd wished on when she was a little girl, but she couldn't remember her childhood requests. Was it for money? Career? Was it love? Now she couldn't think of a single circumstance for which to wish. At this moment, she knew the value of tender graces, not the ones we settle for, but the ones that simply exist and are God given. All else, including unanswered questions, she would leave to faith.

A CONVERSATION
WITH TESS COLLINS

Q. Tess, we know you grew up in a small coal-mining community in the Appalachian Mountains of Kentucky. Would you tell us more about your formative years?
A. While there were times I resented not having the advantages that a larger city might have given me, the mountains are a very magical kind of place to be a child. Our house was at the top of a hill with a small mountain behind it where my brothers and I knew every path, every hiding place, every stream. We invented kingdoms and mythologies all our own. We defended our side of the mountain from werewolves and invented life from a glutinous gel in our monster laboratory (they were actually tadpoles, but we didn't know). The view was a 360-degree mountain range that looked like a deep robe of green in the summer and a muted rainbow in the fall. To this day, I don't think I've ever seen a more beautiful place.

A little to the south is Cumberland Gap in Tennessee and at the top of Pinnacle Mountain there are huge rock formations that look out over the tri-state area. There's one that's shaped like a perching falcon, and I've used it often in fiction, making it its own special place called Falcon Rock.

Q. From your childhood to the themes and plots of your novels—can you trace any specific links or influences?
Definitely there is the influence of the small-town society. Everyone knows everyone else's history whether you're personally acquainted with the person or not. And what you don't know, you can find out by asking around. When ficitonalizing this kind of thing, it can go both ways. In one sense the isolation caused by the geography of the surrounding mountains creates a cauldron where people have to deal with each other whether they like it or not. In a city, you can move across town and probably not run into your enemy the rest of your life. When

there's no place to go, you can hate for a lifetime. In a city, you lose people and even parts of your history. You can become whomever you want to be. In a small town, you always run into your ex-husband, lover, in-laws. There's no getting away from who you are in this society. Fictionally, it opens up all kinds of possibilities—people who want to change and can't; people who leave and still can't escape who they are; people who must engage each other even though they'd rather not.

Q. Do people you knew growing up appear as characters in your books?
A. I don't base characters on any particular person. Sometimes I'll give a character certain characteristics of someone I've known. An example of that is Merl Bashears. (I've assured my mother and stepmother that Merl was not based on either of them.) There was this woman in my hometown who had a knack of saying the wrong thing at the wrong time or doing something so completely rude that your mouth would drop open. She could build you up and then humiliate you to the point that you couldn't quite believe what she'd just said. Perhaps she was less calculating than I'm assuming, but the last time I saw her—which was when I was in college—she stood in front of me and said, "My, you're so beautiful." Then she grabbed my arm, pinching it hard enough to bruise, twisted me sideways, inspected my butt to see if it was bigger than hers, then, let out a "humph" and walked away without a word. I never knew the meaning of the "humph" and as embarrassing as it was then, it's pretty funny to think back on it from the perspective of an adult. As a young girl, I was certainly no match for a woman like that. When developing the character of Merl, I gave her an uncensored personality in speech and action which was somewhat like this woman's. I try to use Merl's unpredictability for humor rather than outright meanness.

Q. Upon graduation from the University of Kentucky (where you studied journalism), did you pursue a career in journalism?
A. I completed college in three years and oddly, haven't worked a day in my life as a journalist, but I never stopped writing. Even in the journalism school I was more drawn to

feature writing than hard news, and in a sense, features are a kind of storytelling. While I always had a deeply ingrained sense of being a writer, it took me a number of years to realize that I was meant to be a storyteller. In my early twenties, I wrote when I could, but during those years I was starting a career and struggling for economic survival. When I was more financially secure I began taking writing classes again, and even with that, it took a while to find the right teacher. Once I found James N. Frey's writing classes, I was like a sponge. I couldn't get enough of what this man had to teach. This was one of those life-changing experiences. I learned to take my stories and apply craft to them. My talent didn't change, or increase, or mutate, but I changed—I became a crafter of tales.

Q. We know that The Law of Revenge *was your first published novel; but was there any (unpublished) fiction before that?*
A. I have two unpublished novels. Like my mystery novels, they're set in Appalachia, but they have a more epic quality about them. Sometimes my characters simply have this way of wanting two round out their stories to more mythic conclusions. This was definitely the case with these two stories, and I'm certain there's a third novel that I'll write someday to finish it off as a trilogy. Even though they're unpublished at this time, they hang on my internal list of things-to-do, and will irritate me until I complete them.

Q. When you decided to emigrate from Kentucky—why San Francisco?
A. That's an interesting story. I waited in San Francisco, hoping to unite with a boyfriend who'd indicated an interest in relocating there, but he never showed up, and I ended up staying. In the long run that was probably the best thing he ever did for me. After finishing college in 1978, I wasn't sure what I wanted to do. My best friend, Tashery Shannon, had entered the creative writing program at the University of Oregon. I told her I'd drive her cross-country—always planning to circle down and (if San Francisco didn't work out), then drive back to Kentucky. Tashery and I had our version of Jack Kerouac's *On the Road*—two girls, two unhappy Siamese cats, and a

1968 Buick Electra that my father gave me for graduation. At least in that car no one got in our way.

Lexington, Kentucky, was still a college town when I left, so San Francisco was quite a change. The first few months I was there the mayor was assassinated, Jim Jones's San Francisco–based church had staged a mass murder/suicide in Guyana, and the Moonies invited me to dinner. Looking back at it, I was a country-hick Alice in a weird urban Wonderland.

Q. And what led to your long-going stint as manager of the city's highly regarded Curran Theatre?
A. The theatre was probably my salvation in San Francisco. Working in theatre is a lifestyle, not a job. You work a tremendous number of hours and the people you're with become your family. I was only twenty years old when I arrived in town and I grew up in this company. My distinction from most baby boomers is having worked for this one organization my entire career. My colleagues and I saw each other through our wild twenties, our searching thirties, and now, we discuss our IRAs and pension plans.

Q. Tell us about the origins of Alma Bashears. How similar are you and your protagonist? Or are you poles apart?
A. Generally, I think Alma is more wordly, quicker on the comeback, and more of a people person. Writers tend toward the introverted; even in my career at the Curran, I've become more of a behind-the-scenes player. Alma, like any protagonist, must be more out there and ready for action. I suppose we're alike in the sense that when something is bugging us, we just won't let it go until we ferret out the truth of the matter. We're both Cassandras like that, a little ahead of our time and knowing things that, if spoken, everyone would ignore or choose not to believe. We both have a good sense of when people are lying to us, but Alma's more likely to hold somone's head out the window until they tell the truth. I'm more likely to let them continue the ruse until they hang themselves.

We both have defining moments in our past which changed the rest of our lives. She was raped as a teenager, and my parents' marriage split up when I was ten. While one is a violent act and the other an emotional event—which didn't involve me directly—they were both circumstances which caused us to have to restructure, if not reinvent, the rest of our lives. From that point on, nothing about life is normal and most every important decision you make is unconsiously affected by the past.

Q. Your villians are very complex characters, often with a sympathic side. Why do you draw them this way?
A. If there is any mission I have as a writer it is to attack the Appalachian stereotype. Whether it is the victimized hillbilly or the evil sheriff in the black hat, we've all seen them on TV or encountered them in books too many times. The villians, in particular, are important because utlimately they drive the story. If the villians are simply evil, then they are interesting for about twenty minutes and the reader figures them out fairly quickly. Villians who struggle with their own actions are ones that interest me. Internal conflict makes villians far more untrustworthy than simple evilness. I don't know what decisions they're going to make. Certainly they'll always protect their own best interests whereas a protagonist might be a little more self-sacrificing, but just how far a villain will go is one of the reasons to continue reading the book. Having a complex antagonist also adds a dimension of conflict for the protagonist as well. Justice and retribution have a different meaning in fiction and it is the main character who has to dish it out. It's easy to send a villian to jail, but far more interesting to read about a comeuppance that strikes the character to their very core.

I believe I was most influenced by this from *Paradise Lost* and *Dracula*. In high school English class I was the only student who felt sorry for the Devil—bringing an nervous giggle from the teacher. And in college Gothic literature class, I made the argument that Dracula was simply trying to survive and Van Helsing's gang were the tormentors. If a writer can make every single character, including villians, struggle with all the passion of a devil or demon then we've come a step closer to creating beings who are shades of humanity rather than rewriting another spaghetti western where it's the white hats vs. the black hats and we all know the ending.